Francis Henry Hill Guillemard

The Life of Ferdinand Magellan and the First Circumnavigation of the Globe

From 1480 to 1521

Francis Henry Hill Guillemard

The Life of Ferdinand Magellan and the First Circumnavigation of the Globe
From 1480 to 1521

ISBN/EAN: 9783337415211

Printed in Europe, USA, Canada, Australia, Japan

Cover: Foto ©Raphael Reischuk / pixelio.de

More available books at **www.hansebooks.com**

THE LIFE OF

FERDINAND MAGELLAN

AND THE

FIRST CIRCUMNAVIGATION OF THE GLOBE.

1480—1521.

BY

F. H. H. GUILLEMARD, M.A., M.D., CANTAB.

LATE LECTURER IN GEOGRAPHY AT THE UNIVERSITY
OF CAMBRIDGE.

LONDON:

GEORGE PHILIP & SON, 32 FLEET STREET;

LIVERPOOL: 45 TO 51 SOUTH CASTLE STREET.

1890.

PREFACE.

IT is a curious circumstance that, while the world is year by year presented with biographies of persons who cannot lay claim to a tithe of the renown so justly accorded to Magellan, no life of the great circumnavigator has yet been written in English, or indeed—if we make one exception—in any other language. The exception is Snr. Diego de Barros Arana's *Vida y Viages de Hernando de Magallanes*, which in 1881 was translated into Portuguese by Snr. F. de Magalhães Villas-Boas, with the addition of an original appendix. This work, although accurate, does not aim at detail, and Magellan's early life in India under Almeida and Albuquerque is dismissed in five pages. Students desirous of a further knowledge are forced to gather it as best they can from the pages of Navarrete, or to tread the thorny paths of the old chronicles and the documents of the Torre do Tombo and Simancas.

Under these circumstances I have been led to depart somewhat from the plan upon which this series was instituted. While striving to offer the present volume in such guise as may not be unacceptable to the general reader, I have thought it advisable to treat my subject as thoroughly as it deserves, or, more accurately, as thoroughly as space permits me. I have, therefore, sacrificed some of the trivial details of the voyage as related by Pigafetta and others, which are accessible to the English reader in Lord Stanley of Alderley's "First Voyage round the World," and endeavoured not only to render the account of Magellan's earlier life as complete as possible, but to leave no detail of the more important questions and difficulties unconsidered. The solution of the latter has not always been an easy task, and has necessitated the perusal of a much larger mass of material than, from the size of the present volume, might be inferred. In the ensuing pages I have given my authorities—wherever it seemed necessary—together with the discussion of all points of a technical nature, in the footnotes. In consulting the old Spanish documents relating to the subject, I have come across much of interest which want of space has prevented me from using. I can only trust that I may not be considered to have made a wrong selection.

F. H. H. G.

CAMBRIDGE, *September* 1890.

CONTENTS

LIST OF ILLUSTRATIONS.

[1] For this illustration the Publishers are indebted to the kindness of the South American Missionary Society.

LIST OF MAPS.

LIFE OF MAGELLAN.

CHAPTER I.

INTRODUCTORY.

ERE we begin the story of Magellan's life, we must consider for a moment the condition of geographical knowledge at the time when he first appeared upon the world's stage as an explorer. Himself destined to immortality, a chapter-writer in the history of the world, the First Circumnavigator, he witnessed in his lifetime the three most distinguished deeds of geographical discovery—the rounding of the Cape by Bartholomew Diaz, the first voyage to India by Vasco da Gama, and the discovery of America by Columbus. It is remarkable that all these, together with his own great voyage, should have occurred within the limits of so short a period, but that they were the natural outcome of preceding work is evident enough if we glance at the history of the Peninsula during the fifteenth century.

As in most sciences, so in geography, a great discovery is rarely sudden. It is foreshadowed and led up to by a train of minor facts which are for the most part lost sight of in the *éclat* of the greater. Had we to assign a definite date to the commencement of the

Renascence in geography, it should, perhaps, be placed at the period when Prince Henry the Navigator, removing from the court, gave himself heart and soul to the adding of new lands to the crown of Portugal. But even before his time some part of the African seaboard had been coasted — the end of the clue grasped which, when followed up, was to lead those who held it to India, the Moluccas, and Cathay.

If we turn to the map and consider the geographical position of the Peninsula, and to the pages of history and make ourselves acquainted with the events preceding the culmination period just mentioned, we realise how inevitable was it that the deeds of exploration and conquest which made Spain and Portugal the greatest countries in the world should have been undertaken and carried out by them. Hardly less easy, too, would have been the prediction of their rapid effeteness and downfall, but with this we have nothing to do. In the present volume we are concerned only with their rise, and though this was brought about by the coincidence of many factors, it is probable that the most permanent of them, namely geographical position, was the strongest determinant of the result. With the Portuguese this was especially the case. Hemmed in on the landward side by a power with whom it was useless at that time to cross swords, the sea was manifestly their *metier*. Their long coast-line, their good harbours, and the broad Atlantic, made them perforce a race of sailors. Yet they had no Mediterranean, as had the Spaniards, to set natural bounds and limits to their voyages. Almost within sight, and, as it were, in their own waters, lay the shoulder of the vast continent of Africa, tempting them onwards with its unbroken coast-line. It was a period, moreover, when expansion and commercial activity were inevitable. The centuries of Moorish oppression had ended. Not only had the Portuguese driven their former masters from the country, but they were pushing them hard in Morocco itself. The desire of conquest had been aroused in them, and the advent of Prince Henry was the final term in a series of events which led them, a few years later, to become so great a maritime nation that no one can read their history without wonder and admiration.

Prince Henry, then, was the true mainspring of Portuguese activity at the time of which we speak. His whole life was given up to the encouragement of discovery and navigation. Renouncing the pleasures of court, he remained in almost complete retirement at Cape St. Vincent, in the constant companionship of those learned in cosmography and kindred sciences. At this date the Canaries had long been known. Bethencourt had conquered them, and Spain and Portugal had squabbled over them, as indeed was their wont upon the occasion of each fresh discovery. Their trade was making itself felt at Seville, and Prince Henry doubtless had it in mind when he fitted out his first expedition. Cape Non—"the impassable"—had at length been passed. Cape Bojador, however, though scarcely beyond the Canaries, was the furthest southern point then reached by European ships, and it was with the intention of doubling it that the Prince, in the year 1418, despatched Zargo and Tristão Vaz in a single ship with orders to carry their explorations as far southwards as was possible. They met with the happiest of failures. Driven out of their course by a gale, they sighted an unexpected island in mid-Atlantic, and from Porto

Santo—thus named from the welcome shelter it afforded them—Madeira revealed itself as a matter of course. The settlement and administration of the latter turned attention for some time from the west coast of Africa, and it was not until 1432 that Gil Yanez finally succeeded in passing Cape Bojador.

Year by year, little by little, the coast thus became known and charted. Hitherto, as each promontory was rounded, some other beyond it was deemed to be impassable. Now, as they approached the equator, the old fables of the impossibility of existence beneath its heats were retold, and this difficulty appeared more formidable than any previously encountered. Nevertheless, the navigators pressed onwards. Expeditions left Portugal nearly every year, and the leader of each was able to add his quota of discovery to the work of his predecessor. In 1446 Diniz Fernandez reached Cape Verde, and in the following year Nuno Tristão passed it and met his death at the hands of the natives beyond the Gambia. Despite the early Spanish settlement of the Canaries, and certain occasional voyages of the Dieppe caravels, the Portuguese so thoroughly identified themselves with the work of exploration on the African coast that their claims were recognised by the Pope, and a grant was made to the crown of Portugal of all lands then and at any future time to be discovered which lay between Cape Non and India.

Hard as he had worked in the cause, Prince Henry was destined to see no world-renowned exploit or substantial benefit result from his efforts. At his death, indeed, no one had yet reached the equator, and ten years or more elapsed before it was actually crossed. With him perished, for the moment, the interest in geographical exploration which he had aroused. But it was only for the moment, for João II. proved well-nigh as ardent an advocate and supporter of the cause as Henry, and under his rule the Portuguese passed through the comparative stage of their fame as navigators and discoverers, to reach its culminating term in the reign of his successor, Dom Manoel.

João, although not fated to witness the conquest of India and the mastery of the spice trade, saw two of the four great geographical events of history, and was himself the instigator of one of them. The third, and greatest, lay within his grasp, but he failed to seize the opportunity. When Columbus expounded his views before the king's *junta* of geographers they were laughed at as impossible, and he was called a boasting Italian. But it must be remembered that João sneered in good company—for Henry VII., to whom Columbus also applied, held the same opinion—and even if he were not gifted enough to foresee the discovery of America, he was at least thoroughly alive to the importance of following up the work already begun upon the coast of Africa. To this he turned his whole attention. Moreover, as we shall see, he had a definite plan in so doing.

The progress made was rapid enough. In 1484 Diogo Cão discovered the mouth of the Congo, and pushed on till he reached a river in the neighbourhood of the Tropic of Capricorn. Settlements were established upon the Guinea Coast, and trade encouraged in many places, but these were not the limits of João's aims. His commercial horizon lay beyond the ivory and palm-oil of the West Coast, and held within its boundaries the spices of the Indies. The procuring of information concerning these far distant countries and their products was at

that time no easy matter.   To obtain it João despatched
two trusty envoys, Pedro de Covilhão and Affonso de
Payva, to the kingdom of Prester John.

On the extended wanderings of these two travellers
we need not dwell.   There being no Prester John, and
therefore, demonstrably, no kingdom belonging to him,
it is needless to say that they never attained their destination.   But they got to Abyssinia—in those days
accounted much the same thing — and Covilhão was
sufficiently fortunate and adventurous to reach Goa and
Calicut.   Payva died in Cairo, and Covilhão remained a
prisoner in the hands of the Abyssinians, but he was
able on more than one occasion to send letters to his
sovereign.   They contained accounts of the cities he had
visited in India and of their trade, together with important
information concerning the route thither.   The southern
promontory of Africa, he wrote, could be rounded without fear, and, once at Sofala, the course across the
Indian Ocean to the shores of Hindostan was easy.   All
this information, however, came too late.   By the time
it reached Portugal the task had already been accomplished.

It would serve no purpose to discuss here the authen-
ticity of the doubling of the Cape of Good Hope by the
ancients.   It is sufficient to say that there is a probability of such a feat having been really accomplished,
but the evidence is so brief, and the date of its supposed
occurrence so far distant, that the credit attaching to
Bartholomew Diaz as the first person to perform the
exploit in modern times is in no way touched by it.
Diogo Cão's discovery of the Congo and Angola led him
far down the coast.   Indeed, as we have seen, he penetrated so far south as nearly to pass beyond the Tropic.

Thence to the Cape is no great distance, and two years later Dom João sent Diaz on the expedition which brought it to the actual knowledge of the Portuguese, and rendered its discoverer's name imperishable. The voyage was performed with extraordinary rapidity; but having once rounded the Cape, Diaz preferred to bring home the intelligence of his success with all speed rather than press his explorations further. The furthest point reached by him was that now known as Algoa Bay. From the violent gales experienced Diaz named his discovery the Cape of Storms (Cabo Tormentoso), but Dom João refused, for obvious reasons, to adopt his nomenclature. As the finger-post of the route to India it was worthy of a more auspicious title, and at his order it became the Cape of Good Hope.

It is difficult to explain why, after this success, no further action should have been taken for so long a period. Possibly the discovery of Columbus had not a little to do with it, for the effect of his news was to direct all eyes westward. João's reign, moreover, was drawing to a close. Whatever may have been the cause, ten years passed ere the Cape was again sighted by European ships. This time the Portuguese pushed far beyond it, and in May, 1498, Gama anchored his ships in Indian waters.

The Cape once rounded, the attaining of India was found an easy matter, as Covilhão had written; and Vasco da Gama secured immortality upon terms as easy, perhaps, as any ever granted, either before or since. Guided by the pilot who had accompanied Bartholomew Diaz, he reached and named Natal on Christmas Day, 1497. Keeping northwards along the coast he arrived at Melinda. From this place—and indeed from many others on the east coast of Africa—a long-established trade existed across the Indian Ocean to the Malabar coast, and Gama found no difficulty in obtaining an Arab pilot experienced in the navigation of those seas to bring him to Calicut. At the cost of little danger and less trouble he found himself famous. When Camoens sang his deeds his fame became immortal.

The reign of Dom Manoel, in which the "discovery period" of history, as we may term it, reached its height, was well inaugurated by Vasco da Gama's exploit. The results of the voyage became almost immediately apparent. Gama found the trade of the East entirely in the hands of the Arabs. The produce of Malaysia and the China seas found its way, as it does now, through the Straits of Malacca. Upon this city all western-directed lines of trade converged, and there the Arabs met, ordered, and controlled it. On both sides of the Indian Ocean alike they, and they alone, were the merchants through whose hands the exports of the different countries passed. Finally, everything, whether ivory from Africa, silks from India and Cathay, or the yet more coveted spices of the Malay Islands, entered Europe by way of the Red Sea and Egypt, or—though to a very much less degree—by the Persian Gulf. It was evident from the very moment of Gama's success that a great struggle was impending—the struggle between the Portuguese and Arabs for supremacy in the East.

We must here leave our sketch of the gradual advance of the Portuguese upon the Eastern gate of the Pacific. How they reached and passed it we shall presently see. In the ensuing chapters the story of the establishment of Lusitanian rule in the Indies is dwelt upon more fully, for Magellan served for seven years under the two great Viceroys, Almeida and Albuquerque, and the history of his life at this period is but the history of the period itself. But before we commence it we will pass for a moment to the other side of the Pacific.

Five years before Vasco da Gama's exploit, Columbus sailed upon his first great voyage, and returned as the discoverer of the West Indies. We know with what enthusiasm the exploration of the New World was carried out, and how expedition after expedition sailed in search of its riches. The track followed, however, was in almost every case influenced by that of the great admiral himself, and it was Central, not South America, which became earliest known. Nevertheless, in those days, when men were possessed with a hunger for exploration—or for the results of it—so fierce and insatiable that to our cool nineteenth-century eyes they appear hardly other than madmen, Brazil at least was not likely to remain long undiscovered. Nor did it. Vicente Yañez Pinzon, one of the captains of Columbus in his first voyage, led the van, and in 1499 carried out an extended *reconnaissance* of the northern shores of South America, and viewed the coast as far south as lat. 8°, where Pernambuco now stands. Hardly three months later mere chance led the Portuguese to nearly the same spot. Cabral, in command of the outward-bound Indian fleet, who had kept a more westerly course than usual in his passage down the Atlantic, was driven still further towards America by stress of weather, and woke on the morning of the 22nd February, 1500, to find a vast, and to him unknown, continent under his lee. The work he had in hand did not permit him properly to explore it, and he was forced to leave his discovery to be followed up by others.

If we compare the time occupied in the tracing of the coast-line of the two opposite shores of Africa and South America the difference is astonishing. While the Portuguese took innumerable expeditions and a hundred years to double the Cape, the neighbourhood of the Strait of Magellan was reached in less than a decade by the work of a bare half-dozen of explorers. We need not enter into the consideration of Vespucci's voyages on this coast, concerning which much controversial ink has been shed, but will confine ourselves to surer ground. With the advent of the sixteenth century the knowledge of this part of the world advanced by leaps and bounds. Almost contemporaneously with Cabral's accidental visit, Diego de Lepe was taking up Pinzon's work, and pushing still further to the south. But the name of the latter, together with that of Juan de Solis, must ever remain most linked with the history of South American discovery. In 1508 these two navigators visited the Rio Negro in lat. 41° S., working beyond the Rio de la Plata, which was yet unvisited. Indeed, a great peculiarity in the mapping out of this coast was the fact that its most distant parts became earlier known than those nearer home. We shall have, later, to consider the voyages of Gonzalo Coelho and Christovao Jaques. It is sufficient here to say that they were undertaken in 1501 and 1503, and that they made known to Europeans the coast of Patagonia, if not to the Strait of Magellan itself, at least to some point at no very great distance from it.

So much for the approaches of the Pacific. The existence of that ocean itself, or rather the existence of a sea of some description upon the other side of Central America, was known to Columbus in 1503 from the accounts of the natives of that region, but, as we all know, he never reached its shores. It was the happy fate of Vasco Nuñez de Balboa first to view it, and, sword in hand, to march into its waters and claim them and the unknown lands they laved for the crown of Castile. Ten years, however, had meanwhile intervened, and discovery had marched with such giant strides that the question of ownership of the new countries, of their boundary lines, and other kindred matters, which for a long time past had been exercising the minds of monarchs and cosmographers alike, became yet more complicated. For a period of nearly fifty years the two great maritime nations of the world were engaged not only in finding out new lands but in squabbling over them when found.

The Hispano-Portuguese difficulty, as we may term it, was so intimately connected with Magellan's work that an account of his life would be incomplete without some reference to its leading features. It was historically expressed by four great facts : the Bull of Pope Alexander VI. in 1493; the Tordesillas Agreement of the following year ; the Badajoz Junta of 1524; and the Cession of the Moluccas in 1529. A lengthy consideration of these would be. impossible here, but to comprehend the action of Magellan and others at this period a rough outline of the political results of the wonderful discoveries which electrified Europe at the beginning of the sixteenth century is necessary.

The first differences between the two countries arose in 1471 concerning the right of ownership of the gold mines on the coast of Guinea, but they soon passed over. The discoveries of Columbus, however, immediately renewed them. It was at once realised that vast possibilities lay open to the European world—countries of unknown extent and riches, and of easy access, having the additional advantage of being peopled by mild and well-disposed natives. It was not likely that the Portuguese would submit without protest to the annexation of these by the sister power. The Pacific was unknown, or at least only considered as a part of Ptolemy's Sinus Magnus, and they regarded, or pretended to regard, the Spaniards as poaching in their waters. It fell to the spiritual head to settle matters. At that time Alexander VI., the father of Cesar and Lucrezia Borgia, and a native of Valencia, was Pope, and his sympathies were of course in favour of Spain. Portugal, as the greatest maritime power of the Roman Catholic world, was nevertheless not to be ignored. Accordingly, on the 4th May, 1493, a Bull was promulgated which divided the world into two halves—giving to Spain the Western Hemisphere, and to Portugal the Eastern. The line of demarcation was drawn from pole to pole, passing 100 leagues to the west of the Azores and Cape Verde Islands.[1]

So far as Spain and Portugal were concerned this arrangement was an equitable one. Roughly speaking, the line thus·drawn passed north and south through mid-Atlantic, and gave to each Power the countries they had been concerned in discovering. Had it remained unaltered, the whole of America would have fallen to Spain, and Malaysia, Papua, and even Australia to Portugal. But it did not, for from the moment of its

---

[1] "Quæ linea distet a *qualibet* insularum quæ vulgariter nuncupantur de los Azores et Cabo Verde centum leucas versus Occidentem." This lack of exactness concerning its position was one of the chief sources of dispute at the Badajoz Junta in 1524.

publication the latter Power remonstrated, fearing—although at the time nothing was of course known—that no share of the riches of the New World would fall to her. Dom João II. appealed to have the line shifted 300 leagues further to the west, and his appeal was partially heard. On the 7th June, 1494, was granted the Tordesillas Capitulacion, by which the *raya*, as it was termed, was fixed 370 leagues west of the Cape Verdes—30 leagues short of the claim of the Portuguese monarch.

Brazil was at that time undiscovered. After Pinzon and others had brought it to the knowledge of Europeans the *raya* was considered to fall through the western mouth of the Amazon in the north, while in the south its position was supposed to be beyond the Rio de la Plata. If we turn to the map we see that in the former case it would be in long. 50° W., in the latter in 60° or thereabouts—a difference of ten degrees or more. Such uncertainty was only to be expected at that period, when no proper means for estimating longitude existed. The very *point de départ* of their reckoning was vague to a degree. The Azores and Cape Verde Islands were presumed to be in the same meridian! By the words of the Papal Bull, moreover, any island might be chosen from which to measure, so that the position of the line —even had accurate instruments been available—could by no possibility have been fixed within several hundreds of miles.

Up to this time it had only been the settlement of the home line of demarcation which had presented any features of interest to the contending parties. But with Magellan's voyage matters assumed quite a different complexion. The Moluccas, not the New World, now became the prize at which each aimed. But if the fixing of the Atlantic line had been a matter of dispute, it may be imagined that that of the Antipodes presented ten times greater difficulties. When the safe arrival of the *Victoria* with her cargo of cloves roused Charles V. at once to set about the despatch of another armada to the "Spicery," Dom Manoel protested. The Portuguese not only claimed the islands by right of discovery, for Francisco Serrão had resided there since the fall of. Malacca, but also asserted that they fell within their boundary—as, indeed, we now know to be the case. The Spaniards were no less confident of the justice of their claim. This time it was agreed that the matter should be settled without the intervention of Papal authority, and eventually, in the spring of 1524, the celebrated Badajoz Junta commenced its sittings.

Each country was represented by its Jueces de Posesion, Jueces de Propriedad, Advocates, Fiscals, and Secretaries, and several of the most renowned pilots and cartographers of the day. Juan Sebastian del Cano was in attendance, and Ferdinand Columbus, son of the admiral—both being Jueces de Propriedad. Sebastian Cabot, Estevão Gomes, who had so basely deserted in the *S. Antonio*, Nuño Garcia, who constructed the charts for Magellan's armada, and Diego Ribero, the great cosmographer, were also present. The meetings were held alternately on either side of the frontier, one day in Badajoz, and the next in Elvas, and thus they remained for several weeks of daily wrangling—*porfiando terribilisimamente*, as Gomara tells us.

We need not follow these arid discussions at length. After two months of squabbling the Junta was dissolved. While in 1494 the aim of the Portuguese had been to get the dividing-line placed as much as possible to the west lest they should be shut out from the prospective benefits of the New World, it was now their object to insure their inclusion of the Moluccas. Unwilling to give up the slice of Brazil that had fallen to them, they were at the same time afraid that their 180 degrees would hardly bring them far enough eastward, and that the spice-trade would come into the hands of their opponents. Their policy, therefore, was that of obstruction, and their object that no conclusion should be arrived at. In this they were partially successful. At the dissolution of the Junta the Spanish Jueces de Propriedad, taking the best globe, drew a line 370 leagues from San Antonio, the most western island of the Cape Verdes, and pronounced their decision upon the bridge of Caya. The Portuguese could not, of course, hinder them from doing this, but they refused to consent to the adjudication, alleging that the facts were not sufficiently established to admit of it, and departed, threatening with death any Spaniard whom they should find in the Moluccas.

In this state of uncertainty matters remained until the year 1529, when an arrangement was made between the two sovereigns. It was facilitated by the family connection then subsisting. Charles V. had married Doña Isabel, sister of Dom João, while the latter in his turn had married the emperor's sister, Doña Catalina. Anxious, therefore, to get rid of all sources of dispute between the two nations, Charles agreed to cede what he considered his rights for the sum of 350,000 gold ducats, and the Moluccas accordingly passed into Portuguese hands. It had been originally intended to grant a lease only, but from some unexplained cause, no exact period

was fixed, and the matter was tacitly regarded as settled.
In 1548 the Procuradores de Cortes besought the emperor
to recall the lease, but he refused. " At this some marvelled and others grieved," says an old historian, " but
all held their peace."

CHAPTER II.

EARLY LIFE AND INDIAN SERVICE.

OF the deeds of the great adventurers and explorers who
drew their swords for Spain and Portugal at the period
of the Renascence, the archives of those countries have a
tolerably ample record.   The Castle of Simancas contains
a collection of documents so enormous as to be well-nigh
beyond the possibility of order; the archives of Seville are
almost equally rich; and beneath the dust of the shelves
of the famous Torre do Tombo in Lisbon there still
exists, despite the great earthquake, a mass of historical papers of almost equal importance with anything that
Spain can show.   Until the end of the last century these
treasures remained almost unknown.   Now, although
much of the greatest interest is doubtless still inedited,
a number of them have been given to the world; for it
was into this Augean stable of literature that the historian Muñoz adventured himself in search of material
for his *Historia del Nuevo Mundo*—a work hardly begun
ere ended by his death.   His mantle fell upon Don Martin
Fernandez de Navarrete, and in 1837 was published the
Coleccion de los Viages, a rich fund of historical material
from which the student of Spanish conquest and exploration draws his chief information.

In this work there is much concerning Magellan of
which earlier historians had left us in ignorance; many

documents, given *in extenso*, which provide us with the fullest information on certain periods of the expedition which has stamped him as the greatest of the world's explorers. But they relate almost exclusively to the last three years of his existence. Over the earlier part of his career the iniquity of oblivion blindly scattereth her poppy. We know the name of the youngest cabin-boy who sailed with him, of the humblest sailor before the mast. We know how many dozen of darts were taken upon the voyage, and the exact number of fish-hooks provided. But, interesting as are even these minutiæ, how gladly would we give our knowledge of them, and how much more beside, for a fuller knowledge of the man himself—some further scrap of information, however trivial, of his youth or childhood! Of this period the irony of history has left us in comparative ignorance. The lapse of four centuries has bequeathed to us a singularly unequal portrait of his life,—the foreground startling in the clearness of its outline—the distance so dim and blurred as to be almost indistinguishable.

Fernão de Magalhães was born about the year 1480—we do not know the precise date—at Sabrosa, near Chaves, in the province of Traz-os-Montes, one of the wildest districts of Portugal. Separated from the tamer seaboard province of Entre Douro e Minho by the bold Serra de Marão, the country presents few features of attraction to the ordinary traveller. Its inaccessibility, the roughness of the accommodation, and the lack of anything of interest save a certain gloomy grandeur in its scenery, do not invite a visit. Nor has its climate anything to offer. There is even a proverb anent it, to which, despite the general untrustworthiness of such dicta, a certain amount of truth must be allowed, " Nove mezes de inverno, e tres de inferno."   Situation and climate have been not without their effect upon the people, who present the characteristics that a natural law teaches us to look for from the co-existence of two such factors as mountain and isolation.   Obstinate, gloomy, and as superstitious as Scandinavians, they are also, like the Scandinavians, honest and faithful to a degree, and possessed of all their determination and power of physical endurance.   The waves of innovation that sweep over and change the face of a Pays-bas but lap the feet of a country such as this.   The inhabitant of the Traz-os-Montes of to-day can differ little, if at all, from his ancestor of four hundred years ago.

It could not be but that Magellan should inherit some of these qualities so characteristic of the land of his birth. It is true that he left it in his youth, and that we hear nothing of his return ; that his short life seems, after a brief period of attendance at court, to have been spent in a swift succession of intoxicating successes with sword and compass—a ceaseless medley of fighting and exploration, which can have left little time for home-thoughts, and none for the strengthening of home-ties and friendships.   But the influence of his childhood's surroundings was there.   As we follow his life step by step, we are not left long in doubt as to the character of the man. Its leading feature is what his enemies would term an overweening confidence in his own powers—an obstinacy without an equal.   Others would name it differently. His faults, if faults they were, were those of strength. If men have been termed men of iron, Magellan may fairly be said to have been of steel.   For him difficulties were made only to be disregarded, dangers only to be despised.   Through the barriers of an impossibility he passed confident and unmoved.   With almost every one against him, the India House, the ambassador of the King of Portugal, and his own friend, he started upon his voyage.   With a mutiny but half repressed and starvation imminent, he pressed southward till he found his long-hoped-for straits.   With his captains' advice to the contrary ringing in his ears, he went to his death. The story of his life is full of such traits, and it is hard not to ascribe them in some measure to the influence of the country in which his boyhood was passed.

Other reasons, it may be, lay in his birth ; for Magellan was of noble family—" of the oldest in the kingdom," as he himself tells us.[1]   There were at that period five grades of nobility in Portugal, to the fourth of which the family of Magalhães belonged—the " fidalgos de cota de armas e geração que tem insignias de nobreza "[2] —a rank to which we have in England no equivalent.[3] Of those who bore it before the great navigator we have no such clear account.   Various names have been given by Antonio de Lima and other genealogists as those of his father and grandfather, but as they do not agree, we are forced to reject them and to fall back upon surer evidence.   Of this there is something, though unfortunately far less than we desire.   In a receipt for

---

[1] In his will Magellan leaves his property to his brother-in-law: "com a obrigação que o dito meu cunhado ha de juntar ao brasão das suas armas o de Magalhães, que é do meus avós, *e por ser muito distincto, e dos melhores e mais antigos do reino.*"

[2] De Barros Arana, *Vida e Viagens de F. de Magalhães,* cap. i. p. 11.

[3] This coat-of-arms we know.   On a field argent three bars checky, gules and argent ; the crest an eagle, wings displayed.

COAT-OF-ARMS AND AUTOGRAPH OF MAGELLAN.

his salary as "moço fidalgo" in the king's service,[1] dated June 12, 1512, Magellan describes himself as "filho de Pedro de Magalhães;" but this appears to be the sum total of our certain knowledge of his forbears. Even of his own family we know little. He seems to have had but one brother. We learn incidentally, from the mention of their names in his wills, of the existence of two sisters, Isabel and Thereza, who married a certain João da Silva Telles, of whom we shall hear more presently. A shadowy Ginebra figures as a third sister, but her existence, at all events in that relationship, is doubtful. His own two children dying as infants, the family of Magalhães became extinct in his father's line.[2] The name, however, appears frequently in the old chroniclers at the early part of the sixteenth century. A certain Martin de Magalhães accompanied the navigator in his great voyage, and the deeds of two brothers, Antonio and Pero Barreto de Magalhães, who were doubtless members of his family, are many times recorded. Both served under the first Viceroy of India, Don Francisco d'Almeida, and both fell in battle—the former in the noble defeat of Don Lourenzo by the Turks under Mír Hoseyn and Malik Jaz at Chaoul, the latter by the side of the Viceroy himself, when he and sixty-five of his men perished in a skirmish with the Kafirs of Saldanha Bay.[3] Of yet another, Christovão de Magalhães, we hear as accompanying Alfonso d'Albuquerque in his expedition to Ormuz; but beyond the fact

---

[1] *Liv. de Moradias da Casa Real*, vi. fol. 47, v; Navarreto, *Coleccion de los Viages*, iv. p. lxxiii.

[2] For the genealogy of the family of Magalhães see Appendix I., p. 315.

[3] Damião de Goes, *Chronica de Dom Manoel*, 2da parte, fols. 14, 44, and 75.

that, together with many other of the Viceroy's captains, he was badly wounded in an engagement with the Persians at Lara, we know nothing.[1]

Magellan lost his father and succeeded to the estates when still comparatively young, for in his first will, made at Belem before sailing for India under Almeida, we find him bequeathing the Sabrosa property, in which parish he owned the Quinta de Souta. He makes no mention of the Casa da Pereira, which, from a most curious and interesting document not long since brought to light, we know to have also belonged to him.[2] In this—which is the will of Magellan's great nephew, Francisco da Silva Telles—the testator inveighs in the most vehement terms against his ancestor, ordering that thenceforward over his house in Sabrosa (the Casa da Pereira) no heir or descendant soever should restore the coat-of-arms of the family, "since I desire that it should for ever remain obliterated, as was done by order of my lord the king, as a punishment for the crime of Ferdinand Magellan, in that he entered the service of Castile to the injury of this kingdom, and went to discover new lands, where he died in the disgrace of our king."

To understand this, it is necessary to anticipate. Magellan, unable to obtain a recognition of his services at the hands of his sovereign, Dom Manoel, did what a triad of great navigators—Columbus, Cabot, and Vespucci—had already done before him, and what was at that period by no means unusual: he left his country and offered his sword to Charles V. These others have

---

[1] Gaspar Correa, *Lendas da India.* Ed. da Acad. Real das Sciencias, tom. i. pt. ii. p. 883.

[2] This document is in the possession of Dr. A. M. Alvares Pereira de Aragão, of Villa Flor, the present representative of the family of Magalhães.

escaped with hardly a word of blame, but, owing to a combination of circumstances which will have presently to be considered, a quadruple obloquy appears to have fallen upon Magellan. The result we have partly seen. The King of Portugal, furious at the rise of Spanish influence in the Moluccas, commanded that the arms of Magellan should be erased from the gateway of his house. The effect of an order such as this in a remote village like Sabrosa may be imagined, and we can understand, even though we may not be able to forgive, the animus of Magellan's heir. We know that no man is a prophet in his own country. His fellow-townsmen forgot his years of faithful service in the East; forgot the coldness of his king; forgot that the glorious exploit in which he met his death made him one of the world's greatest men, and remembered him only as a renegade, whose heirs and their belongings were to be treated as they would have treated him. Every sort of insult was offered to Francisco da Silva; his name was execrated, and stones were thrown at him in the streets. Ultimately he was compelled to leave the country, and it was in the far-off province of Maranham, in Brazil, that he dictated the will to which allusion has just been made.

The house, deserted by its owners, fell eventually to ruin. The family remained for long expatriated. It was not until much later—towards the end of the seventeenth century, in fact—that any of its members resumed the name. About that time Don Pedro II. gave the title of Visconde de Fonte Arcada to a certain Pedro Jaques de Magalhães. But the family appear never to have returned to Sabrosa. The old house, or rather its ruins, passed into other hands. A modern building has taken its place, constructed in part from the stones of the older mansion.   One of these was that bearing the coat-of-arms "*rasadas por ordem de El Rey.*"   Torn from its place over the doorway, it now occupies an ignoble position at the corner of the house.

Of Sabrosa and its belongings little more need be said.   Upon Magellan's actual life there history is silent.   "We can picture him amid his native moun‑tains, riding the horses for which the district is still so famous, and hunting the game with which its woods abound.   We feel that in some such way his youth must have been spent, in active and vigorous exercises such as these, for, as we shall see, action and vigour were the two most marked features of his temperament. But however probable the assumption, it will never pass within the domain of proof, for even Correa—most diffuse and garrulous of historians—treats us to no details of this period of his life.

Neither student nor courtier by nature, it was never-theless Magellan's fate to become both in the course of his career.   From the wilds of the Traz-os-Montes he was early transplanted to the capital.   As in other courts, so in that of Portugal it was the custom at that period for the heirs of noble families to receive their education under the eye of their sovereign, their studies directed by him, and their successes rewarded by his approval.   "Criose Magallanes en seruicio de la Reyna doña Leonor," Argensola briefly tells us;[1] and from the *Anales de Aragon* of Çurita we learn that he was brought up as one of the pages of this queen, the widow of D. João II., " the Perfect."

He did not long retain the post.   In 1495 the King Dom Manoel, first of the House of Vizeu, came to the

---

[1] Argensola, *Conquista de las Molucas*, liv. i. p. 6.

throne, and young Ferdinand Magellan passed into his service. In the whole course of the history of Portugal, no one—alone excepting Prince Henry the Navigator—had more to do with the foundation of her maritime power and the extension of her dominion than this king. His *idée mère* was to establish Portuguese influence in the East. In the half century immediately preceding, the aim and object of Prince Henry's work had to some extent been lost sight of. Exploration had indeed been going on, but in a more desultory manner. Bartholomew Diaz, it is true, had doubled the Cape of Good Hope, but eight long years had already elapsed when Dom Manoel came to the throne, and no action had as yet followed upon that event. Dom João II., a great geographer, a prince of the widest views upon the foreign policy of Portugal, and one of the most intellectual of her rulers, was, however, less a man of action than Dom Manoel. With the advent of the latter the half-awakened energies of the Portuguese leapt suddenly into life, and within the short space of two decades the nation had reached the zenith of its glory, and had become the greatest maritime power of Europe.

Even at the present day, habituated as we are to the rapid march of events, and with the remembrance of the presto-like unfolding of the secrets of an almost unknown continent fresh in our memory, we find it hard to grasp the suddenness of this development of the Portuguese dominion; still harder, perhaps, to realise the boundless enthusiasm which it must have created. Let us turn for a moment to the consideration of actual facts—to a list of the expeditions despatched about this period from the shores of the mother country. Vasco da Gama, passing the Cape ten years after Bartholomew Diaz, had brought India from the shadowy regions of romance into those of vivid reality, and the Peninsula was ringing with his fame. Cabral, sailing for India in 1500, had discovered Brazil, and Gaspar Cortereal, almost at the same time, was coasting Labrador. In the following year the fleet of João da Nova discovered St. Helena, and in 1502 the second expedition of Vasco da Gama left the Tagus for India, combined with the fleet of Vicente Sodre. Two months later a second Indian expedition was despatched under Estevão da Gama, and when the season was sufficiently advanced, ships were sent to the "Terra de Bacalhaos" and Labrador to carry on the work of exploration, and to search for the missing Cortereals. In 1503 Alfonso and Francisco d'Albuquerque captained another armada for the East, and Gonzalo Coelho ventured far southwards along the unknown coasts of South America. From year to year this activity increased rather than diminished, and in 1504 no less than three great expeditions were despatched; an armada of thirteen ships proceeded to India under Lopo Soarez d'Alvarenga; Don João de Meneses headed an expedition against the Moors of Larache; and Antonio de Saldanha left the kingdom a few weeks later with another Indian fleet.

Such, in a few words, is the bare list of expeditions which must have been fitted out and despatched under the very eyes of Magellan at the most impressionable period of his life. Of their coming and going, of their many victories and rare defeats, of their successful venture or disastrous loss, how much he must have heard! The whole country was seething with excitement. The new worlds, alike of the East and of the West, held out a brilliant picture of infinite possibilities to the humblest

in rank. The dockyards rang with the sound of axe
and hammer, and the ships were barely launched ere
they sailed for the lands that were to bring riches and
distinction to every one—to every one, at least, who lived.
One had but to be equipped with youth, and health, and
ambition. Men left their country in shoals, careless
of danger, heedless of death-rates, mindful only of the
possible glory that awaited them. We can imagine the
effect that experiences such as these must have had upon
one so adventurous as Magellan. At such a time, when
all around him were up and doing, it was impossible
that he should remain a mere spectator. He did not
hesitate for long. Applying to his sovereign for leave
of absence, he bade adieu to court life, and at the end of
1504 enlisted as a volunteer in the great armada of Dom
Francisco d'Almeida, at that time preparing to sail for
India.

Almeida's fleet was the largest that had hitherto set
out for that promised land. Successful as other expeditions had been upon the whole, they had from time to
time met with such difficulties and opposition as had
served to warn Dom Manoel that a stronger hand would
be advisable, and that the time had come for the appointment of a resident official who should hold the reins of
government. The distance of the mother country from
her Eastern possessions was indeed so great and the
latter so scattered, that this had become an imperative necessity. The King's choice fell upon Francisco
d'Almeida,[1] son of the first Conde d'Abrantes, and it would

---

[1] Dom Manoel had at first selected Tristan da Cunha for the post,
but owing to his having become suddenly afflicted with complete blind-
ness, he was unable to accept it. Castanheda, *Historia do Descobri-
mento e Conquista da India pelos Portugueses*, liv. ii. chap. i. ; and
Correa, *op. cit.*, tom. i. pt. ii. cap. i.

have been hardly possible to make a better selection. To him, as first Viceroy of India, fell the task—Herculean in difficulty—of organising and ruling countries and peoples as yet almost unknown to their conquerors, and nobly he fulfilled it. His name—extinguished by the greater glory claimed for his successor, Albuquerque—is unfamiliar to many of us, but few, if any, have left the East with cleaner hands and a record more unsullied than Almeida. "Much did they love him," says Correa, "as being one blameless in his actions . . . a man without a shadow of deceit."[1] Such a man naturally attracted to him persons of like qualities, and his ships were not long in being manned. From all parts of the kingdom there flocked to him "many fidalgos and cavaliers, and people of distinction," says Correa—"many gallant men and cavaliers experienced in war," another writer tells us. Magellan could not well have begun his Indian experiences under better auspices or with better comrades.

The preparations made for Dom Francisco's fleet in the way of stores and outfit were in keeping with the importance of the expedition. Never before had things been done upon a larger scale. Of the exact number of ships of which the armada itself consisted, the historians

---

[1] "Muyto amauão o Visorey, por ser homem muy perfeito en suas cousas, e de muy nobre condição, e muyto inclinado a grandezas, homem sem nenhum engano, e que muyto estimaua e louvaua os seruiços dos homens ; homem manso, prudente, e muyto sezudo, e de bom saber con que governaua a India."—*Correa, op. cit.*, vol. i. p. 790. Nor is Pedro de Mariz less laudatory : "Era D. Francisco homem de graue & honrada presensa, bom caualleyro, & muyto prudente & sagaz, em quanto andou na India, onde ha materia de muytos vicios, foy castissima, nunqua lhe ninguem sentio cobiça, senao de honra."—*Pedro de Mariz, Dialogos de varia Historia*, dial. iv. chap. xxv.

of the period have left us in doubt.[1] There were, however, at least twenty. Correa speaks of them as eight
large ships (*naos*) for cargo, six of smaller size (*nauetas*),
and six caravels; and in addition wood was carried—
already shaped into the necessary planks and beams—
for two galleys and a " bargantym," which were to be
constructed on the arrival of the fleet in India. They
bore fifteen hundred men-at-arms, two hundred bombardiers, and four hundred seamen as supernumeraries
for Indian commissions. Artisans of almost every kind
were taken, and among them many carpenters, rope-
makers, and blacksmiths. The artillery and ammunition were " em muyta abastanza "—in great plenty—as
indeed might be expected, for Vasco da Gama, in virtue
of his new appointment as Admiral of India, gave to
them his especial supervision. The daily presence of
the King stimulated the labours of his subjects. The
preparations advanced with great rapidity, and almost
before the winter was over the ships were ready for
sea.

In those days the departure upon an expedition such
as this was looked upon as a serious matter. The most
limited acquaintance with the historians of that date
leaves no cause for wonder upon the subject. Sword and
fever on land, and scurvy and shipwreck at sea thinned
the ranks in a manner that was positively appalling. It
would be interesting to know the usual percentage of
survivors in these armadas. In some cases we do know
it—in the final voyage of Magellan, for example, when

---

1 " A armada que foy de quinze naos e seis carauelas."—*Castanheda*,
liv. ii. cap. i. " Dezaseis naos, & seis carauellas."—Damião de Goes,
Chronica de Dom Manoel, 2da parte, fol. i. Osorius is silent upon
the subject, and Correa gives twenty as the number.

we find that for every man who returned, six, or nearly
six, perished.   And so we scarcely wonder at the solem-
nities which custom demanded of those who took part in
them—at the special confession and mass, at which
attendance was enjoined.   On this present occasion the
ceremony was invested with a more than ordinary interest, for the standard of the Viceroy of India, after
having been blessed by the bishop, was to be formally
presented to Almeida by the King.   Correa relates the
function at some length, in words quaint and bald enough
even for the days in which he wrote, but quite as power-
fully descriptive, perhaps, as those from some more florid
pen.   We have little difficulty in realising the scene :—
the cathedral, filled almost to the doors with the members of the expedition alone ; the king-at-arms " clad in
his rich habit," holding above Dom Manoel the " royal
flag of white damask with Christ's cross in crimson satin
bordered with gold ; " Almeida kneeling at the King's
feet and receiving it into his solemn care and keeping ;
his silent prayer before the high altar with the standard
in his hand ; and finally, the loud-voiced proclamation
by the herald, " Dom Francisco d'Almeida, Governor,
Viceroy of India for our lord the King." [1]   Upon a mind
like that of Magellan, in which religion had taken deep
root, the scene must have made a strong impression, not
less from the fact that it was the last day he was destined
to spend upon his native soil for some time to come—
for seven long years it actually proved.

Things temporal were nevertheless not entirely ex-
cluded from Magellan's mind by the pomp and ceremonial of religion, and before leaving Portugal he
executed the will to which allusion has already been

[1] Correa, *op. cit.*, vol. i. pt. ii. p. 532 *et seq.*

made.   In it he makes his sister, Doña Thereza, wife of João da Silva Telles, his sole heir, with instructions for the saying of twelve masses yearly at his altar of Our Lord Jesus in the Church of Santo Salvador at Sabrosa.   He speaks of the "pouquidade dos bens que tenho"—of the smallness of his property—but there is little else of interest in the document save at the beginning, where he desires that his funeral "shall be conducted as that of an ordinary sailor, giving to the chaplain of the ship my clothes and arms to say three requiem masses."[1]

The blessing of the flag over, the fleet dropped down the river to Belem, and anchored off the church for which it was then, as now, so famous—a building inseparably connected with the memories of the great Portuguese explorers.   Here, in the days of Prince Henry the Navigator, and erected by him, stood a little chapel, much favoured by sailors, in which—only eight years before—Vasco da Gama had prayed for his success ere starting on his memorable voyage.   Now the pile of florid Gothic, built in gratitude therefor, had usurped its place, white and new from the builder's hands, the last monument upon which the sailor's eye would rest on leaving his native land.   Within it the bones of Gama, of Camoens who sang his successes, and of Dom Manoel who inspired them, were destined ultimately to rest. It was an ideal spot for the start of such an expedition. Next day—the 25th March 1505—the final departure took place.   The King came down in state from the city and went on board the Viceroy's ship; anchors were then weighed and the whole fleet proceeded slowly towards the bar, the King accompanying them, "going

<hr>

[1] See Appendix I.

THE TOWER OF BELEM.

from ship to ship and speaking to the captains, taking leave of them and wishing them a prosperous voyage."[1]

Clearing the mouth of the Tagus, the fleet proceeded southwards and touched at Port Dale on the Guinea Coast, where they took water and lay at anchor nine days. Here the Viceroy, finding that some of the ships were much more speedy than the others, divided the fleet into two squadrons. They crossed the line the 29th April,[2] and continuing their voyage, passed the Cape as far south as lat. 40° S., where they encountered severe weather and underwent great hardships.[3] On the 20th June, Almeida, estimating that they had cleared the meridian of the Cape, shaped his course northward.[4] They had already met with one misfortune, for the ship of Pero Ferreira had foundered in the equatorial calms, and now, on reaching the Indian Ocean, Lopo Sanchez

---

[1] Castanheda, *op. cit.*, lib. ii. cap. 1, relates an amusing incident that took place at the moment of departure, which is at the same time interesting as possibly marking the date of the introduction of the words larboard (*bombordo*) and starboard (*estribordo*) into the Portuguese navy. It appears that on weighing anchor, and on the pilots giving their orders larboard or starboard to the helmsmen, the latter were "greatly embarrassed in their minds, as not being as yet learned in such expressions," and in consequence got into difficulties owing to the number of craft around them. Upon which João Homem, captain of one of the caravels, "ordered the pilot that he should speak to the sailors in a language that they could understand, and that when he wished to steer starboard, he should say 'garlic,' and when to larboard, 'onions,' and on either side (of the helm) he ordered a string of these things to be hung."

[2] Damião de Goes, *op. cit.*, 2da parte, cap. ii. fol. 3; but Castanheda gives the 20th of April as the date.

[3] Osorius, *De Rebus Emmanuelis Gestis*, lib. iv. fol. 116 v.: "Faciebat densa caligo, et imbres immodici, et niues immensæ, quæ nostris intolerandis frigoribus grauissimam molestiam exhibebant."

[4] In the account given by Castanheda the fleet are said to have gone to lat. 44° S ("passando alamar cĕto & setenta & cinco legoas"), and to have passed the meridian of the Cape on the 26th June. Lib. ii. cap. i. p. 5.

C

was forced to run his vessel ashore, after having in vain tried to overcome a leak.   The survivors, although many perished on the way, eventually reached Mozambique in safety, where they were picked up by their countrymen.

Before leaving Portugal, the fullest instructions had been given as to the disposal and action of the fleet; instructions which show how gigantic was the scale upon which the subjugation of India and Eastern Africa had been planned.   Arriving at Sofala, a fortress was to be erected and garrisoned; and this done, the fleet was to sail for Quiloa without loss of time.   Here the same steps were to be taken, but, in addition, two ships—a caravel and a " bargantym "—were to remain, in order to patrol the coast north and south of the port.   Proceeding then to the farther shores of the Indian Ocean, the Viceroy was instructed to build a strong fortress upon the island of Anchediva.   The two galleys—the timbers of which had been brought in the fleet—were to be put together here, and two caravels were appointed to patrol the coast around the station, which was regarded as of great importance.   Hence they were to pass southwards along the coast to Cochim, seeking for ships of the King of Calicut, " with whom the King for ever waged bitter war; " and visiting Coulão, were by every means in their power to obtain leave to make a fortified settlement in that city.   Finally, after the despatch of the annual homeward-bound fleet, an expedition was to be sent to the kingdom of Ormuz and the mouth of the Red Sea, to seek a site for a fortress which should act in some degree as a check upon the stream of Arab trade, which at that time bore not only the gold and silks of Hindostan but the spices of the Farther East to Mecca and the " Sultan of Babylonia."

Such were the orders under which Almeida sailed.
If we reflect that less than six years previously India
was a *terra incognita*, and the Cape only known by the
fierceness of its storms, they appear marvellous in their
comprehensiveness.   We see, too, how wise was the
policy that dictated them.   Short as was Dom Manoel's
acquaintance with the new world into which he adventured himself so boldly, it would seem that he had made
himself master of the situation almost at a glance.   The
traffic of the East was to pour into Europe through the
gates of the Lisbon *Alfandega*, and in order that this
object might be attained, it was necessary that the first
blow should be struck at Arab influence.   Gama, in
the course of his memorable voyage, had found these
" Mouros " in every city, and had not noted their riches
and the extent of their influence in vain.   The more
important of the native monarchs, therefore, were to be
conciliated with the special view of obtaining leave to
build strong fortresses, which, connected by cruising
bargantyms and caravels, should form a chain of nuclei
of Portuguese influence.   The " Mouros," when too
strong, were to be temporised with ; but, for the most
part, the " *ôte-toi, que je m'y mette* " policy was that
adopted.   From the very beginning Dom Manoel recognised the enormous importance of mastering the entrance and the exits of the Indian Ocean.   It was reserved
for Albuquerque to conquer Malacca, but Almeida was
charged to reduce Ormuz and gain possession of the
strongholds round the Straits of Bab-el-Mandeb without
loss of time.   It was the outgoing streams of traffic that
first demanded attention.

Upon the deeds of the Viceroy and his captains at
this period we can only touch lightly.   So rapid was the

succession of events, and so packed with incident the history of his administration, that volumes, not pages, would be necessary to record them. It is not often that we hear of Magellan. Amid so large a company of distinguished men, of "fidalgos e cavalleiros experimentados na guerra," of whom many had already served under Gama, it could hardly be otherwise. His post could only have been a subordinate one, and we do not even know in which ship he sailed. But that he made the best use of his opportunities is evident from the fact that he eventually became a most expert navigator.[1] Later, when his name appears more frequently in the pages of the historians of that epoch, it is generally mentioned in connection with some distinguished act of bravery.

On the 22nd July the ships arrived off the bar of Quiloa. They were received badly, and the king declining to meet the Viceroy, the latter landed his forces and stormed the city, which was taken without the loss of a single Portuguese. No time was wasted, and the construction of the fort was begun upon the following day, the Viceroy himself personally aiding. On the 8th August,[2] a large garrison having been left to complete the work, and the rightful king, Mohammed Anconi, restored to his throne, the fleet started for Mombaza.

The city of Mombaza was one of the most important on the coast of Africa; it carried on a large trade with the interior, and was strongly fortified. Such a nut was no easy one to crack. The excuse for the attempt,

---

[1] "Tinha muyto saber n'arte de nauegação, e espirito que se lançou a ysso."—*Correa*, ii. pt. i. p. 28.

[2] Manoel de Faria y Sousa, *Asia Portugueza*, vol. i. pt. i. cap. 8. Correa, vol. i. pt. ii. cap. 2, tells us that the fleet left on the 13th.

however, was not long wanting, for the ships were fired
upon as they arrived.   Two days later the city was
stormed, and the Moors, although numbering ten thousand men, were overpowered by the superior skill and
courage of their enemics.   The fighting was severe, and
the Portuguese had a very large number of wounded.
Dom Lourenço, the only son of the Viceroy, first made
himself famous at the assault.   His great strength and
extraordinary courage combined to make him almost
worshipped by the men he led.   Short as was his career,
for he died in battle only two years later, his name
became even more renowned throughout the East than
did, later, that of Albuquerque ; and there is little doubt
that the Portuguese owed their success in many cases to
his personal influence and to their enemies' belief in his
invincibility.   After the fall of the city the king formally
tendered his submission, agreeing to pay a yearly tribute
of 10,000 serafins, and a column of white marble was
erected by the Viceroy to commemorate the event.[1]
Victors and vanquished became firm friends, and the
king, "for the great love he bore Dom Lourenço," presented him with a valuable sword and a collar of pearls,
worth 30,000 cruzados, upon his departure.

It was the Viceroy's wish to visit both Melinde and
Magadoxo, but the season being now so far advanced,

---

[1] The custom of setting up a cross or a column in the countries
visited or conquered was early adopted by the Portuguese.   "Porque
mandou El Rey ao Visorey que em todas as terras que conquistasse, e
metesse a sua obediencia, pusesse huma columa pera lembrança o
sinal que erão de sua conquista."—Correa, *op. cit.*, vol. i. pt. ii. p. 559.
They had always been of wood, but in the early part of his reign
Dom João II. gave orders that they should be constructed of stone,
and the first was erected at the mouth of the Congo in the year 1484.
Faria y Sousa, *Asia Portugueza*, vol. i. pt. i. cap. 3.

the pilots were strongly opposed to such a step. The plan was accordingly relinquished, and the fleet shaped its course across the Indian Ocean to the island of Anchediva, whither they arrived on the 13th September. The fame of their successes had preceded them, and the Viceroy found letters from the King of Cananor informing him that there were 20,000 quintals of spice in his port ready for the homeward-bound ships, and that three rich Mecca galleons were daily expected in Calicut. Almeida began work, as usual, without the loss of a moment's time. The very next day after his arrival, the construction of the fortress was commenced ; ships were sent off to cruise in search of the Mecca squadron ; the keels of a galleon and two " bargantyms " were laid down, and letters were sent to Cananor, Cochim, and Coulāo to make known the Viceroy's advent. In twenty days the fortress was completed. The loot taken at Mombaza was sold by public auction, and the money handed to the treasurer of the fleet.

The King of Onor, a province lying about thirty miles to the south, had already made a treaty of peace with the Viceroy. Its duration was, however, of no great length, for being unwise enough to send an insolent message in reply to a request made to him by the Viceroy, the latter at once brought his fleet against him, and entering the river on the 16th October, burnt his ships and took the town with a readiness which soon brought the monarch to his senses. Dom Lourenço took his wonted place at the head of the storming party, but he had little opportunity of displaying his prowess, for the enemy yielded almost without striking a blow, and the Portuguese lost only one man in the assault. The king, whose sin had been that of cupidity rather than

an open defiance of the Viceroy, made a most ample
submission, and the latter behaved so generously to his
adversary, that all former differences were forgotten in
the friendship thus begun.

The rapidity of Almeida's movements, although characteristic of the man himself, owned at the same time
another cause. The winter was fast approaching, and
with it the north-east monsoon, whose favouring gales
were to waft the home-returning fleet upon their voyage.
But as yet the Viceroy had not reached Cananor, still
less Cochim, where he was to assume the reins of government. There was, therefore, no time for delay at Onor,
and leaving this port as soon as possible, the fleet proceeded southwards to Cananor and came to anchor off
the town on the 22nd October. The Portuguese had been
upon the most friendly terms with the king of this
country since the time of Gama's first visit, and the
Viceroy's arrival was welcomed with the greatest enthusiasm. The armada entered " gay with flags and standards, discharging salvos of artillery, the larger vessels
remaining outside, but those of lesser draught anchoring
in the bay, the galleys and the bargantym rowing—a
sight that many people came to see, for in India they
had not as yet seen galleys, the which are rowed with a
great precision in the stroke." [1]

The usual visits of ceremony having been paid, Almeida,
who had hitherto called himself Governor, assumed the
full rank and title of Viceroy. Next day he received an
embassy from the powerful King of Narsinga, who was
desirous of making a treaty with him. Learning from
the resident Portuguese factor that nothing could be
done in Cananor without a fortress — for the Arab

---

[1] Correa, _op. cit._, i. pt. 2, cap. vi. p. 580.

merchants of the city had become greatly incensed with the growing influence of the new-comers, and had already plotted to kill the king—he sought leave to construct one. It was at once granted to him, and in five days, with the assistance of the natives, the erection of its walls, together with bastions to carry cannon, were completed. A day or two later it received its name—the Fort Saint Angelo—and Lourenço de Brito, with a garrison of 150 men, entered into possession.[1]

Delaying a bare five days at Cananor—where two caravels were left to guard the coast—the fleet of Almeida, now much reduced in numbers, at length arrived at Cochim. Of the meeting between King Nambeadora and the Viceroy Correa gives us a long account :—the " king on his elephant with its trappings, and much people, the which the Viceroy left the fort to receive, accompanied by all his men, and before him his guard with trumpets and kettledrums, his captains dressed very gaily, the Viceroy himself clad in a coat of red satin, with a narrow black sash worked with gold, black buskins, a round cap, and an open black damask cassock, which formed a train, as was then the custom."[2] Almeida next day publicly crowned the king with the greatest display of ceremonial that lay within his power. With the neighbouring states in a condition of hostility, overt or covert, it was of the utmost importance to lose no chance of strengthening the bonds of alliance with so powerful a prince. Almost at this moment, indeed, news arrived of the rising of the Moors at Coulão—a

[1] Damião de Goes, *op. cit.*, 2da parte, cap. vii. fol. 12 v. ; but Correa gives a very different account, stating that only a ditch and palisade were made, and this almost surreptitiously, " isto fisesse deuagar por milhor dissimulação."

[2] Correa, *op. cit.*, i. pt. ii. cap. 10, p. 606.

port some sixty miles farther south—and the murder of
the Portuguese garrison, an act which the Viceroy was
not the man to leave long unpunished. The duty devolved upon Dom Lourenço, and he performed it with
his usual quickness and success. In two or three days
he returned to Cochim, having burnt twenty-seven ships
and killed numbers of the enemy without the loss of a
single man.

Meanwhile the Viceroy was busy with the despatch
of the homeward-bound squadron under Fernão Soarez.
Having loaded all the pepper and spices in the Cochim
factories, the ships proceeded to Cananor, and took the
remainder of their cargo from that port, which they
left on the 2nd January, 1506, taking with them only
sufficient men for the navigation of the vessels ; for, with
the daily losses by fighting and disease, and the scattered disposition of their forces, every sword was of
importance. The voyage was noteworthy from the fact
that the eastern coast of Madagascar was discovered for
the first time. "They arrived," says Goes, "off a land
which not one of the pilots had ever seen before, . . .
and having sailed in sight of it for seventeen days, they
cleared it on the 18th February—the which, although at
that time it was not known, they found afterwards to be
an island which the old cosmographers call Madagascar,
and the Moors the Island of the Moon."[1] The ships
arrived safely in Lisbon on the 23rd May, 1506.

With the departure of the homeward-bound fleet, and
the reduction of Coulão, the Viceroy doubtless looked
forward to a more peaceful period in which to consider
the many political questions that presented themselves
for solution. He was not destined to enjoy it either

---

[1] Damião de Goes, *op. cit.*, 2da parte, fols. 13 v, 14.

then or indeed at any future time, for at the very
moment when he least expected it, a danger greater than
any hitherto encountered menaced the Portuguese power
in India.   The advent of the Viceroy's fleet, the uniform
success that had attended him in Africa, and the almost
superhuman strength and courage with which Dom
Lourenço was credited, had filled both the Moors and
the Zamorim of Calicut with consternation.   It was
felt that if action was to be taken at all, it should be
taken then.   The homeward fleet had started, the Portuguese were considerably reduced in numbers, and no
reinforcements were possible before the onset of the
south-west monsoon.   If a decisive blow could only be
struck, if the fleet of the hated infidels could once be fairly
annihilated, it might put an end for ever to their power
in India.   It was at all events worth trying.   The Arabs
saw ruin staring them in the face, and neither their
creed nor their feelings inclined them to tame submission.

The Zamorim of Calicut accordingly summoned a
meeting of all the leading Moors.   Opinion was divided
as to the course to be pursued.   Some, recognising the
formidable strength of the enemy, and mindful of the
almost uninterrupted series of successes they had obtained, counselled alliance with the King of Portugal.
They were overruled.   It was felt that the time for this
had passed, and that no alternative now lay before them
but to cross swords.   It was resolved, therefore, that a
great armada should be equipped, which should attempt
the conquest of Cochim itself, the very stronghold and
seat of government of their enemies.   Measures were
accordingly taken to inform the Moors at every port of
the plot and to request their aid.   The vessels thus
raised were to collect in Calicut.

Such a design could not long remain concealed. Dom Lourenço, being in Cananor, was visited by a man in the habit of a Moor, who, on being granted a private interview, revealed himself as an Italian, one Ludovico Vartema, a great traveller—"qui studio orbis terrarum cognoscendi multas regiones peragravit," as Osorius tells us.[1] This man had escaped from Calicut, and hastened to bring the news of the preparation of the armada. Unexpected and harassing as it was, Dom Lourenço did not lose heart. Despatching Vartema without loss of time to the Viceroy, who was then at Cochim, he set about the organisation of his own forces. The orders sent back by the Viceroy were not other than he had expected; that he was to fight "for the Catholic faith and for his honour, and bear himself as a Christian and his son."

The battle that ensued was one of the most celebrated of the many fought by the Portuguese in India. The armada, which was composed of 209 vessels—84 being

---

[1] Osorius, *op. cit.*, lib. iv. fol. 130 v. Luigi di Vartema (Luis Vuartman or Barthema, or Luis Patricio, as he is variously called) was a Roman who left Europe in 1502 to wander for many years in the East. His travels were published in 1510 in Italian, and were afterwards given to the world by Ramusio in his *Navigationi et Viaggi*. In them he speaks at some length of the incidents here narrated (edit. of Venice, 1613, fol. 170 *et seq.*). Both the traveller and his narrative, however, are interesting on other grounds. It is to him that we owe the first description of Borneo, and he also visited the Moluccas. There is every probability that the Portuguese at this time obtained from him the information which led Albuquerque five years later to despatch Abreu's expedition—in which Magellan is supposed to have sailed—to these islands. Vartema was knighted by Almeida after the fight at Calicut, and returned to Portugal in the fleet of Tristão da Cunha. He arrived at Lisbon in July, 1508, and receiving confirmation of his knighthood from Dom Manoel, returned to Rome. Damião de Goes, *op. cit.*, 2da parte, cap. xxiv. fol. 41 v. Ramusio, *Navigationi*, fol. 174.

ships and the rest large praus—encountered Dom Lourenço's valiant little fleet on the 16th March, 1506, a short distance to the north of Cananor. "It seemed," says Vartema, "like some huge forest, from the great masts of the ships." But so little did Dom Lourenço fear the result, that he permitted his adversaries to pass until they were off Cananor—"per mostrarli quanto era l'animo de' Christiani." It was not until they were within a bombard-shot of the town that he commenced the engagement.

Against such an overwhelming force the Portuguese could bring only eleven ships.[1] They were manned, however, by men as brave as they were experienced,—"all distinguished men, educated at the King's court—very noble men," Correa tells us. And very nobly indeed did they bear themselves. "For really, to say the truth, I have been in many a fight in my day, and seen many a fierce encounter," says Vartema, "but never have I seen braver men than these Portuguese."[2] They had need of their courage, for they were but eight hundred fighting men against some thousands. The great ship of Rodrigo Rebello, in which sailed Dom Lourenço and the flower of his men, led the van, and turning neither to the right nor left, made straight for the enemy's flag-ship. Three times did she grapple with her, and three times were her grappling-irons cast off. At length their attempts were successful, and the Portuguese sprang on

---

[1] Catsanheda, Osorius, De Goos, and Vartema (who was himself present at the engagement) all state that the number of D. Lourenço's force was only eleven ships, but Correa gives it as twenty-oight. The accounts of the affair are in other ways differently given by the old historians; but that of Vartema, as being an eye-witness, has been chiefly followed in the present narrative.

[2] *Itinerario di Ludovico Barthema*, lib. vi. cap. xxxvii.

board, headed by their beloved chief, who "fought with his little halberd." The result was for the moment doubtful, for they found themselves engaged with six hundred of the enemy. It was not for long. Lourenço's valour bore everything before it, and ere many minutes had elapsed, every man of the six hundred had been killed or driven into the sea.

Meanwhile the others had not been idle. João Serrão, brother to the Francisco Serrão who afterwards became the great friend of Magellan, was fighting as he never fought before, his ship attacked by more than fifty praus, from which he eventually shook himself free, though at the price of having almost all his men wounded. Simon Martins, the most daring of the Viceroy's captains, was in an even more desperate case, his low sloop being surrounded by four much larger vessels, who poured in a galling fire, until the Portuguese—their men all dead or wounded, and all their powder expended—were compelled to take refuge below deck. The Moors boarded, thinking she had struck, but they were quickly undeceived, for the captain, making a sally at the head of the survivors, cut down seven of them with his own hand, and the remainder were quickly driven overboard.

While these two desperate struggles were continuing, Dom Lourenço had laid his ship alongside a second antagonist. She proved to be a heavier craft than his first prize, and carried over fifteen hundred men. Their very number was probably against them, and Nuño Vaz Pereira boarding at the same time on the other side of the ship, the Moors found themselves between two fires, and were very soon overpowered. The enemy perceiving their two largest vessels taken, and many others either disabled or sunk, resolved on flight. The delight of the

Portuguese was unbounded, for the victory, however much anticipated, was by no means safely within their grasp. "God be praised," exclaimed Dom Lourenço; "let us follow up our victory over these dogs;" and the order was at once given. A scene of the most frightful slaughter ensued. Quarter was neither given nor asked. The sea was dyed with blood, and the bodies washed ashore next day "formed as it were a hedge" upon the beach. More than 3600 of them were counted.

Upon the Portuguese side between seventy and eighty fell, and over two hundred were wounded. Among the latter was Magellan, who, indeed, appears to have been habitually unfortunate in this respect, to judge from the expression used by Gaspar Correa—"and at the affair with the Turks, and always in the armadas, and in Calicut, was he much wounded."[1] He was cared for, no doubt, at the hospital at Cananor, whither, we are told, all the wounded were brought. The dead were buried at sea, in order that the Moors might not discover the extent of their antagonists' losses.

A victory so decisive was not without its effect, not only upon the Moors, but upon the native rulers, and matters now appearing more settled, Dom Lourenço was despatched at the head of a small squadron to the Maldives. Owing to bad navigation, they missed their destination, but sighting Cape Comorin, eventually came to anchor off Point de Galle, and for the first time relations were established between Portugal and Ceylon. Magellan, meanwhile, was sent to Sofala under Nuño Vaz Pereira.[2] As has already been stated, Dom Manoel's

---

[1] "E foy no feito dos Rumes, e sempre nas armadas, e em Calicut, muyto ferido."—*Correa*, ii. cap. iv. p. 28.

[2] Faria y Sousa, *Asia Portugueza*, tom. i. pt. i, cap. x. § 6.

orders on the Viceroy's departure were that a fortress should be constructed in this city, but it will be remembered that the first port the latter entered in Eastern Africa was Quiloa. This was through no disobedience on the Viceroy's part, but the ship of Pero d'Anhaia, who accompanied Almeida as the future captain of Sofala, having gone ashore at the very moment of the sailing of the Viceroy's fleet, her officers and crew were forced to defer their voyage. Ultimately Sofala was reached and the fortress built, but Pero d'Anhaia's administration was a short one, for he was killed in the following year by the Moors.

Nuño Vaz sailed with instructions to take over the command. His orders, however, were that he should first visit Quiloa. In that port the greatest disorder prevailed, owing to a dispute as to the succession to the throne, and on his arrival he had to decide upon the merits of the two claimants. Sailing thence for Sofala, he established himself as captain of the settlement, but his term of office was even shorter than that of his predecessor. On the 8th September, 1507, the fleet of Vasco Gomez d'Abreu arrived from Lisbon, and he had to resign his post. A few days later he left for Mozambique in the ship of Rui Gonçalvez de Valadares. The pestilential climate of the coast had told terribly upon his men, and he landed with a great number of sick. So numerous were they, indeed, that his first care was to build an hospital. The captains themselves took turns in attendance upon the patients. Correa naively describes the treatment adopted : " Much did they occupy themselves," he tells us,[1] " with the care and healing of the sick, to whom they gave many marmalades and conserves, in

---

[1] Correa, *op. cit.*, i. pt. ii. 1507, cap. i. p 785.

the eating of which they were greatly benefited." The season being now far advanced, and the north-east monsoon established, Nuño Vaz Pereira and his comrades, unable to return to India, were forced to prolong their stay in Mozambique. They occupied themselves in building a church, and, it is needless to say, a fortress. Upon the change of the monsoon they sailed for Cochim, leaving a mere handful of men in charge under a *feitor*.[1]

Upon their arrival in India, Magellan and his comrades found the aspect of affairs much altered. They had left the country soon after a defeat of the most crushing kind had been inflicted upon their enemies. The power of Portugal seemed by it to have been fairly established in the East, and some of the lesser potentates, whose action appeared at one time doubtful, had formally acknowledged the Viceroy. Now all was changed. The fortress of Anchediva, which had cost them so much anxiety and so many lives, had been given up and razed to the ground. The King of Cananor, who had been most friendly, had been replaced by a successor whose sympathies were with the Zamorim of Calicut, and the Portuguese had undergone a siege of many months in their fortress, and suffered unusual hardships. But a far more serious danger confronted them. Hitherto the Moors had been the only foemen worthy of their steel. Now they were suddenly brought face to face with other enemies, who, at the very first rencontre, had put to flight their ships and slain their beloved leader, Dom Lourenço.

---

[1] From this fact it is evident that Magellan could not have been present at the defeat of Dom Lourenço by Mír Hoseyn and Malik Jaz at Chaul in the spring of 1508. The expression already alluded to, that he was wounded "*no feito dos Rumes,*" "in the affair with the Turks," must therefore refer to the great battle off Diu, in which D. Francisco d'Almeida avenged the death of his beloved son.

Their new foe was the Sultan of Egypt, or rather his admiral, Mír Hoseyn. The Moors, finding themselves powerless to cope unaided with their adversaries, sought help from Cairo. It was readily afforded them. Not only were the Sultan's revenues affected by the check in the stream of traffic that poured into the Mediterranean through his dominions, but the enemy was at his very gates, and action of some kind had become an imperative necessity. Unprovided, however, with a fleet in the Red Sea, and without wood wherewith to build it, he was forced to cut the latter in Asia Minor, and transport it on camels from Alexandria to Suez. Despite these difficulties, a fleet of ten ships was constructed at this port; it was placed under the command of the Emir Hoseyn, and at the end of December, 1507, it came to anchor off the great city of Diu, at the mouth of the Gulf of Cambay. Here the Emir joined forces with Malik Jaz, the governor of Diu, and a few weeks later the armada sailed for Chaul, in which river the Portuguese fleet under Dom Lourenço was at that time lying. The action that ensued, albeit a defeat for the Portuguese, was one of which they might justly be proud. Dom Lourenço, cut off from the rest of his fleet, and with his leg shattered by a cannon-ball, fought his sinking ship until her decks were nearly level with the water, and perished with the flower of his men, his end a fitting termination to a life brilliant in its untarnished honour, and conspicuous for deeds of the coolest daring.

Against these reverses the Portuguese would have found it hard to make headway, had it not been that upon the northern shores of the Indian Ocean the name of Affonso d'Albuquerque had already become a terror to the Mussulmans. Albuquerque had left Portugal with the understanding that he was eventually to supersede Almeida as Viceroy, and having finished his cruise upon the coasts of Arabia, turned southwards to India to deliver his papers. The two great captains met at Cananor on the 5th December, 1508, but Almeida refused to hand over his seal of office until he should have taken his revenge on Hoseyn and Malik Jaz—with which end in view he was then sailing for Diu—and Albuquerque had no alternative but to give way.

Nuño Vaz Pereira—and with him, no doubt, Magellan—had meanwhile returned safely from Mozambique to India in the summer, and had been almost immediately despatched to Ceylon. Whether Magellan went thither with him or not we do not learn from the records of contemporary historians, but it is more than probable that he accompanied his old commander, who got back from Ceylon just in time to join Almeida's avenging fleet. On the 12th December the armada sailed. It consisted of nineteen ships,[1] which carried thirteen hundred Portuguese and four hundred Malabaris. On his way, the Viceroy, after touching at Baticala and Onor, made a descent upon Dabul, and so completely destroyed the city, that the action passed into a proverb, "May the vengeance of the Franks overtake you, as it overtook Dabul."

Arriving off Diu on the 2nd February, 1509, the Viceroy found both Mír Hoseyn and Malik Jaz awaiting him. The former, thinking that the open sea offered the best chances of success, crossed the bar to meet the enemy. An engagement followed which advantaged neither party, and on the approach of night Mír Hoseyn

---

[1] De Goes, *op. cit.*, 2nda parte, fol. 63; but Correa, vol. i. pt. ii. p. 924, says, "partio . . . . com vinte e uma velas armadas."

retired to the harbour, resolving there to await the renewal of the Viceroy's attack. Next day the Portuguese boldly entered the river and the two fleets engaged. Almeida found opposed to him a force numbering over a hundred sail, which bore eight hundred Mamelukes, and many Christian soldiers, Venetian and Sclav, all of whom were clad in chain-armour. A large number of Malabaris from Calicut and the formidable contingent of Malik Jaz crowded the smaller vessels. The Viceroy wished personally to engage the ship of Mír Hoseyn, but, at the earnest entreaty of his officers, allowed himself to be dissuaded, and deputed the task to his beloved captain Nuño Vaz Pereira. With him, there is little doubt, went Magellan, in company with many of the most distinguished of the Viceroy's lieutenants. Thus manned, the *Holy Ghost* led the van, and fought her way to the great galleon of Mír Hoseyn. Desperate as was the struggle that ensued, the issue was not for long doubtful. The Egyptian admiral, boarded on both sides, was soon forced to yield, and the loss of the flag-ship so disheartened the captains of his other vessels, that the battle was from that moment practically decided. The ship of Malik Jaz, owing to her unusual strength, for a long time bade defiance to the Portuguese, but she was at length sunk by a broadside from the large bombards. The slaughter was even greater than on the occasion of the defeat of the Zamorim of Calicut. Between three and four thousand men were killed, and of the eight hundred Mamelukes but twenty-two survived. The victory was decisive; Malik Jaz submitted, and Diu was entered in triumph by Almeida. But it was not without its cost. Nuño Vaz Pereira fell, shot in the throat, and other brave souls with him. Great numbers, too, were wounded, and among them, Correa tells us, was Magellan. The engagement over, and a treaty of peace having been signed with Malik Jaz, the Viceroy returned with the fleet to Cochim. The power of the Portuguese in India was now fairly and indisputably established.

CHAPTER III.

SERVICE WITH ALBUQUERQUE AND IN MOROCCO —DENATURALISATION.

ALMEIDA, who had not yet delivered the seal of office to Albuquerque, returned to Cochim on the 8th March, 1509, and found his successor awaiting him. After his years of loyal service, after having at length brought security and success almost within measurable distance, he was called upon to resign his post. He had borne the burden and heat of the day, and now another was to reap the benefit of his toil. The trial was a most bitter one for him, and the differences in which he soon found himself involved with Albuquerque were not without excuse. Instead of resigning, he placed Albuquerque under arrest, and sent him to Cananor.

Whether Magellan joined with others in openly expressing disapproval of this action we do not know, but there is some reason to believe that he did so. On the 21st April there arrived at Cochim from Lisbon an armada destined for the reconnaissance of Malacca, under the command of Diogo Lopes de Sequeira. Almeida affected to think that this force was insufficient, and added another vessel, with a crew of seventy men, under the command of Garcia de Sousa, with whom he was not upon the best of terms. Some of the officers are mentioned by Barros and De Goes; among them Nuño Vaz de Castellobranco, who was sent " on account of the differences between him and the Viceroy;" and we learn that Magellan and Francisco Serrão, who later became his bosom friend, also sailed in the same vessel.[1]

The little fleet, consisting of four ships of about 150 tons, and a "*taforea*,"—a sort of barge—sailed from Cochim on the 19th August,[2] and sighting Ceylon upon the 21st, made for Sumatra. Sequeira was now in unknown seas—seas, at least, which had never before been navigated by European vessels. His first port was Pedir, at the northern extremity of Sumatra, and having made a treaty of peace with the king both of this place and of the neighbouring city of Pacem, he proceeded without loss of time to Malacca, and anchored in the port on the 11th September, 1509.

Malacca had been for years a familiar name to the Portuguese as the great mart for all the merchandise of the far East. Now that they had at last reached it, they found that it in no way fell short of their expectations. Hither, Barros tells us, had gathered Arabs, Persians, Gujaratis, Bengalis, Burmese, Liu-kiuans, Javanese, Chinese, and natives of the Philippines; and

---

[1] De Barros Arana, *op. cit.*, p. 14, speaking of Magellan, says, " Em principios de 1508 estava elle de volta em Portugal," and tells us that he sailed *from Lisbon* with Sequeira ; but Barros (*Decadas da Asia,* Dec. ii. liv. iv. cap. iii.) concurs with De Goes, who writes : " Por lhe pareçer que leuaua pouca gête pera hum tamanho negoçio, lhe deu hũa taforea com sessẽta homẽs, capitão Garcia de Sousa, com que iha Fernão de Magalhães & Frãçisco Serrão." Barros uses nearly the same words. If Magellan accompanied Nuño Vaz Pereira to the East African coast in October 1506, and went with him the following year to Mozambique, and if he was " no feito dos Rumes " in the beginning of 1509, as we gather from Faria y Sousa (*Asia Port.*, vol. i. pt. i. cap. x.) and Correa (ii. cap. iv. p. 28), he certainly could not have returned to Portugal at the date mentioned by Arana.

[2] " Partido Diogo Lopes de Cochij a oito de Setembro," says Barros, Dec. ii. bk. iv. cap. iii., thus differing from Castanheda and De Goes.

the city, although not of any great depth, extended along the coast for a vast distance. The port was crowded with shipping, and the enormous trade carried on with all parts of the world was evinced by the busy scenes upon its quays. The advent of the Europeans, whose deeds in India were not unknown, was productive of a temporary panic. Confidence was soon restored, and on the third day the king formally received the envoys of Dom Manoel, and appeared desirous of showing them the greatest kindness and respect. His attitude was nevertheless intended to conceal his real designs, which were to seize Sequeira's fleet at the first opportunity, and inflict such a decisive blow upon the Portuguese as should effectually check their threatened move upon the gates of the Pacific.

Sequeira, it must be confessed, did his best to further them. No one ever adventured himself more confidingly into a nest of hornets. Warned that the Malays were not to be trusted by some friendly Chinese captains and again by a Persian woman, of whom one of the Portuguese was the lover, he persisted in ignoring the advice, and his men visited the city and the natives Sequeira's ships " as though they had been at anchor off the city of Lisbon." The king's first. plot was to invite the Captain-general and a large number of his people to a banquet, and, their forces thus weakened, simultaneously to attack his guests and the ships. Even Sequeira, however, declined to fall into so transparent a trap, and another ruse had to be adopted.

The Portuguese had expressed their desire of leaving as soon as they could get their cargo of spices, in order that they might not miss the monsoon for their homeward voyage. Taking advantage of this, the king informed Sequeira that he had got together a large quantity of pepper and other goods, which he would deliver to him if he would send all his boats ashore on the following day, together with plenty of men to load them. The Captain-general gladly acceded. Francisco Serrão in command of a large party, and with all the boats except that of the "*taforea*," proceeded ashore, and the strength of the fleet being thus reduced, the natives crowded to the ships with the ostensible purpose of trading, and awaited the signal for a general onslaught, which was to be given from the citadel.

Garcia de Sousa, more quick-witted than his commander, was not long in realising the impending danger. Without the loss of a moment's time, he drove the Malays out of his ship, and sent Ferdinand Magellan in the only remaining boat to the flag-ship to put Sequeira on his guard. Magellan found the Captain-general playing at chess, surrounded by eight Malays, even then unwilling to believe that any treachery was contemplated. Hardly taking his eyes from the board, Sequeira merely ordered one of the sailors into the main-top to see if all were well with the shore party, and Magellan at the same moment left the ship. While aloft, the sailor chanced to look down, and saw a Malay standing behind Sequeira with his kris half drawn, while a comrade in front motioned to him not to strike, as the signal had not then been given. At the same moment Francisco Serrão and two or three others were seen running for their lives to the beach, and the puff of white smoke—the signal for the massacre—floated from the summit of the citadel. The sailor's warning cry of "Treachery! treachery!" came not an instant too soon. Sequeira bounded from his seat, and escaping

the blow from the kris of his would-be murderer, ran
to arms.   The Malays, seeing themselves outnumbered,
jumped overboard.   Serrão meanwhile, in a small skiff
and almost unarmed, was making desperate efforts to
shake himself clear of a number of boats by which he
was hard pressed.   Already one of his men had been
severely wounded, and the enemy had boarded their craft,
when Magellan and Nuño Vaz de Castelbranco came to
their rescue.   Although a bare handful of men, they
fought so desperately that the Malays were driven overboard, and the Portuguese reached their ship in safety.
It is not too much to believe that the courage and
presence of mind of Magellan on this occasion greatly
strengthened the bond of friendship between him and
Serrão, and to this friendship, as we shall see later, the
great voyage of the greatest of navigators was more or
less due.

The situation of the Portuguese at this moment was
critical.   Not only had the greater number of those on
shore been captured or murdered, but a second party,
who had landed upon a little island hard by, had also
been cut off.   Sequeira had hardly realised his position,
when a large fleet of armed praus was seen rounding a
corner and making for the vessels of the Portuguese.
However great his folly, the Captain-general was no
coward.   Instant action was necessary, and he took it.
Slipping his cables, he at once bore down upon the
enemy, and so well were his guns served that the Malays
were soon only too glad to retire, many of their ships
being sunk and others hopelessly crippled.

Sequeira waited a day or two in the hope of ransom-
ing some of his men.   Sixty were missing, and although
many were known to have been killed, he had reason to

suspect that as many as thirty were prisoners. His efforts were fruitless, and accordingly, putting ashore two of his captives with an arrow through their brains and a message affixed to their bodies that " thus the King of Portugal avenged the treason of his enemies," he sailed for India.[1]

The homeward voyage of the fleet was signalised by the capture of several junks. In one of these actions Magellan again distinguished himself in the same manner as at Malacca; for the Portuguese of Nuño Godin's ship being almost overpowered, Castelbranco and himself, with only four sailors, went to their assistance in the small boat of the "*taforea*," and brought the fight to a successful issue.[2] In January, 1510, the fleet arrived at Travancore, reduced to three vessels—one having gone ashore in the Straits, and one having been purposely burnt. In this port they learned the news of Almeida's departure from India,[3] where-upon Sequeira, who had sided with him in his quarrel with Albuquerque, thought it better to sail direct for Portugal. Teixera's ship and the "*taforea*," bearing Magellan and his friend Serrão, proceeded on their course, and anchored a few days later in the harbour of Cochim.

---

[1] Correa's account of the Malacca difficulties differs *in toto* from the above, which, with the exception of a few unimportant details, is that given by all the other old historians. In the *Lendas da India* the Portuguese are attacked by night in a small fortress which they had previously obtained permission to erect.

[2] Castanheda, *op. cit.*, liv. ii. cap. cxvi.

[3] Almeida, "the enemy of avarice," a great man in the best sense of the term, was destined never to reach home. Landing a small party in Saldanha Bay in search of water and provisions, a fracas occurred with the Kafirs, and in an attempt to revenge themselves next day (March 1, 1510), the Portuguese lost sixty-five men, among whom were eleven captains and their beloved chief.

Magellan and his comrades must have reached that capital almost simultaneously with Albuquerque. However great a failure Sequeira's expedition had been, that of the Viceroy to Calicut, whence he was now returning, had been even greater. Upon the 2nd January he had arrived off the city with a large armada. A few days later he left it, himself badly wounded, seventy-eight of his best men killed, and over three hundred *hors de combat*, with no advantage, save the slaughter of a large number of Moors, accruing to his side. Neither his wounds nor his defeat, however, prevented Albuquerque from busying himself in the execution of his projects: He at once ordered an armada to be got ready to proceed against the cities at the entrance of the Red Sea, and despatched the rest of the homeward-bound fleet—the first part of which had already sailed—to Portugal *viâ* Mozambique.

The three vessels of which this second division of the fleet was composed left Cochim about the middle of January.[1] One ship, commanded by Gomes Freire, sailing a little before her companions, had a prosperous

[1] The chronology of this period of Magellan's history is a little obscure. After the fight at Calicut, Albuquerque is mentioned by Correa (vol. ii. pt. i. cap. iii. p. 25) as sending Rebello thence to Cananor on the 10th January, and the historian adds, "O gouernador esteue no porto de Calecut dous dias, despachando as cousas como já disse, e se partio pera Cochym." It is probable, therefore, that he arrived at the latter city about the 14th. But De Goes (3ra parte, cap. iii. fol. 5 v.) tells us that "partio Afonso dalbuquerque de Cochim na fim de Janeiro"—a not impossible date, since we know that he occupied Goa February 17th. If Magellan was with the Viceroy in his first descent upon Goa, as Arana (*op. cit.*, p. 17) states, there is little enough of intervening time left for the preparation and despatch of the homeward fleet, the wreck upon the Padua Bank, the reaching of the mainland in the boats, the sending of the caravel to succour the shipwrecked party, and their return to Cananor. Most probably Magellan was not present at the first occupation of Goa.

voyage, reaching Mozambique in safety, but the others
—in one of which Magellan sailed—ran at night upon
a shoal of the Great Padua Bank,[1] and remained. The
weather was good, and though the ships filled, they
did not break up, and the captains, Sebastian de Sousa
and Francisco de Sá, were able to save not only sufficient provisions, but a good deal of the cargo also. The
crews landed with their belongings upon a small island
which was close at hand, and at daybreak a discussion
took place as to the course to be pursued. It was
resolved to make for the coast of India—distant about
a hundred miles—in the boats, but owing to the want
of room "there was much contention among them concerning which of them should go first. The captains,
fidalgos, and persons of position desired so to do, but
the sailors said that they should not unless they went
also."[2] In this state of affairs Magellan came to the
rescue, promising, with the ready coolness which, as we
learn later, was so characteristic of him, that he would
remain with the crews if they would swear to him that
assistance should be sent immediately on the arrival of
the boats in India. This was done, and the boats departed, reaching Cananor in eight days. Sebastian de
Sousa kept his word, and sent Antonio Pacheco to their

---

[1] The Padua Bank or Pedro Reef has now twenty-one fathoms as its
minimum depth of water, and it would naturally be concluded that the
ships went ashore at some other place in the Lakadivhs ; more especially from the fact that, according to one writer, the crew landed on
an island or rock close at hand. But it appears that the banks off
this part of the coast are gradually sinking. On the Elicapeni Bank,
in lat. 11° 12′ N., long. 73° 58′ E., there is now from 8–15 fathoms,
while in 1835 Captain Byrom found only 3¾–9 fathoms. Such a rapid
alteration renders it quite possible for the wreck to have occurred on
the " Bassas de Pedro."

[2] Herrera, Dec. ii. lib. ii. cap. xix.

relief in a caravel without loss of time. Crew and cargo were safely got on board, and eventually the coast was reached with little more loss than that of the two vessels.

From Barros we learn one possible reason for Magellan's action on this occasion—that there was a friend whom, "since he was a person of no great importance," the captain was about to leave behind. We are not told his name, but there is little doubt that it was Francisco Serrão, and that it was his loyalty to him as a friend that prevented Magellan from considering his own safety.[1] Whatever may have been the case, however, the deed was that of a cool, unselfish man, and it is recognised as such even by historians so adverse to him as Barros and Castanheda.[2]

At the moment of the rescue of Magellan and his comrades, Albuquerque was bound northwards with an armada of twenty-three ships for Ormuz, touching at Cananor and other neighbouring ports on his voyage. Whether the shipwrecked crews were incorporated with

---

[1] This incident is related by Herrera (Dec. ii. lib. ii. cap. xix.), Barros (Dec. iii. lib. iv. cap. i.), Castanheda (lib. iii. cap. v.), and Damião de Goes (2da parte, cap. xliii. fol. 73), but the latter does not mention Magellan. Correa (vol. ii. pt. i. cap. iv. p. 27) gives an account which differs in many particulars from that of the other historians, stating (a far from probable occurrence) that the crew remained in the vessels, which they shored up by means of the yards ; that all this was arranged and ordered by Magellan ; and that Gonzalo de Crasto—not Pacheco—returned with the caravel. See also Lord Stanley's *Magellan*, Hakluyt Soc., p. xvii.

[2] It is worthy of remark that, in Herrera's laudatory comments upon Magellan's action on this occasion, we learn one of the few facts concerning his personal aspect to which history has treated us :—"Albeit his appearance was not greatly in his favour, since he was of small stature" (äunque no le ayudaua mucho la persona, porque era de cuerpo pequeño").

this fleet or not is uncertain, but it is by no means impossible that such was the case.[1] The Viceroy altered his plans *en route*, and leaving the siege of Ormuz for a future occasion, made a descent upon Goa, which yielded to him on the 17th February, 1510, almost without striking a blow. He was not at that time, however, in a position to hold the city against a large force, and three months later—May 30th—was compelled to evacuate it. It was only for a time. During his short tenure of the place Albuquerque had realised its importance, and the next occasion on which Magellan appears upon the scene is at a council held by the Viceroy on the 10th October, 1510, upon questions connected with a second siege he had then resolved on.[2]

The council was held at Cochim, and was composed of "all the captains of the King," to which rank it may be concluded that Magellan had by this time attained. The question for decision was whether the merchant ships—then loading in Cochim—should assist at the intended siege of Goa or not. Magellan, called upon to speak, gave a very decided opinion on the subject, saying that they "ought not to take the ships of burden to Goa, inasmuch as, if they went thither, they could not pass this year to Portugal, . . . and that there would not remain time for them to lay out their money, nor to do anything of what was necessary for the voyage." Albuquerque was of a different opinion, and said that "he

---

[1] Correa says that they returned to Cochim, while Castanheda implies that they went to Cananor. Barros, however, distinctly states that Pacheco returned with the rescued crew to Goa, and that they there found Alfonso d'Albuquerque.

[2] The document recording this council is preserved in the Torre do Tombo at Lisbon (*Corp. Chron.*, pt. 2a, maç. 23, doc. 190), and a translation appears in Lord Stanley's *Magellan*, p. xxi.

AFFONSO D'ALBUQUERQUE.

would sail with as many ships and men as he could get together, and would go and take Goa, as he trusted in our Saviour's Passion that He would aid him;" but he added that he would not take any one away with him against his will. The captains, Correa tells us, paid little attention to this, being occupied with the profits resulting from the sale and embarkation of the goods which they had to convey to Portugal.[1]

Magellan, we know, did not belong either actually or in spirit to such men as these, and although we do not find him mentioned by name in Correa's list of the "valentes cauallèiros" who accompanied Albuquerque in this expedition, he may well have come under the head of the "outros caualleiros honrados" who were present. The Viceroy arrived off Goa on the 24th November. The fleet consisted of thirty-four sail, which carried fifteen hundred Portuguese troops and three hundred Malabaris. On the following day the assault took place —a splendidly fought action, which resulted in the fall of the city and its occupation for the second time by Albuquerque. Under his administration order and prosperity were rapidly restored. Money was coined; the ambassadors of the kings of Narsinga and Cambay arrived to establish relations with the Viceroy; the native women, embracing the Christian religion, became

---

[1] Lord Stanley, *op. cit.*, p. xxiv., suggests that the adverse opinion given by Magellan on this occasion was the cause of the subsequent coldness and ill-will of his sovereign, and hence also of the great navigator's desertion of his country for Spain; but this is hardly probable. None of the contemporaneous historians make any adverse comment upon the subject. An incident so trivial, unaccompanied by quarrel of any kind, would have passed almost unnoticed in such stirring times. The explanation of the King's attitude is more probably to be found a few years later in Magellan's return from Africa without leave.

the wives of the conquerors, and trade was once more resumed.

Affairs once satisfactorily settled in Goa, Albuquerque, who in energy and ambition was no whit inferior to Almeida, determined on fitting out an armada "a buscar hos Rumes." Not only were the ships of the Caliph—the bitter enemy of Lusitanian influence in the East—to be sought for and destroyed, but a fort was to be built at Aden, and another upon the Kamaran Islands in the Red Sea. The fleet left Goa at the end of March, 1511, but in doubling the Padua reefs they encountered such continued bad weather that they were forced to return, and it was ultimately settled that they should proceed to Malacca instead. In August, therefore—just two years subsequent to the sailing of Sequeira's expedition—an armada of nineteen vessels left Cochim for that city, bent on taking a full though tardy revenge for the treacherous slaughter of Serrão's comrades. During their voyage they captured no less than five ships from Cambay, and having lost the galley of Simon Martins in a storm, they touched, as before, at Pedir in Atjeh, and confirmed their treaties with the king. At Paçem (Passir) they were again well received. Farther south they encountered two junks and a caravel, all of which they captured. Unwittingly they had begun their revenge, for upon the latter ship, after she had struck, they found the body of Nahodabegnea, the organiser of the plot against Sequeira.[1]

---

[1] De Goes relates a fable concerning this occurrence, embodying a belief which is not uncommon in many parts of the world. They find the body hacked to pieces, but no blood flows. On his wrist is a bracelet in which is set the "bone of a species of large cattle found in Siam, called 'Cabis.'" On pulling this off, the blood gushes out, and Nahodabeguea dies instantly.

On the 1st July, 1511, the fleet arrived off Malacca.[1] It was not until six weeks later that the city fell. Although unprovided with fortifications, the number of cannon it mounted and of fighting men by whom it was garrisoned made its reduction no easy matter. In the history of Portuguese India the taking of Malacca by Albuquerque is perhaps the most striking event, not less from its political import than from the difficulty of the task and the richness of the booty.[2]   Upon the pro-

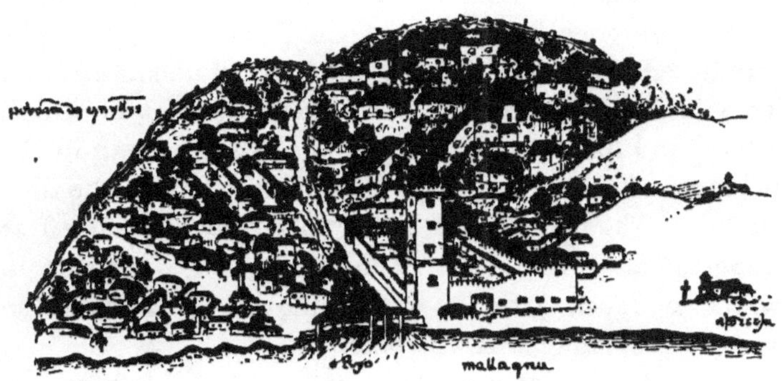

MALACCA (*from Correa*).

tracted struggle which ended so fortunately for the Viceroy's forces it is unnecessary to dwell. Even at this period Magellan had not yet fought himself into the first half-dozen or so of distinguished captains whose names and individual deeds were thought worthy of mention by the chroniclers of that date. For the present, he remained for the most part hidden in the obscurity

[1] Correa states that the fleet arrived in mid-June (vol. ii. pt. i. p. 219).

[2] "Se tomou despojo de grão valor, o mór que nunqua se tomou n'estas partes, nem outro tal tomará."—Correa, *Lendas da India*, vol. ii. pt. i. p. 248.   See also *Comentarios do grande Afonso d'Albuquerque*, cap. xxviii.

of the " outros caualleiros valentes " whose presence in the engagements is only rarely otherwise recorded. One writer,[1] however, speaks of him as " giving a very good account of himself " on this occasion. It is only what might have been expected from him, or indeed from any one of the courageous band who effected the downfall of the most important city of the East. Against the twenty thousand fighting men, with three thousand pieces of artillery, whose workmanship, as we learn from the Commentaries of Albuquerque, could not be excelled even in Portugal, the Viceroy could bring a bare eight hundred Portuguese and six hundred Malabar archers. They had indeed need to give a good account of themselves, and for a protracted period the issue hung in the balance. " Assuredly," says Castanheda, " from the time we began the conquest of India until now was no affair undertaken so arduous as this battle, . . . nor one in which so much artillery was employed, or in which so many were engaged in the defence."

The fall of Malacca was of greater political importance than that of Goa. Not only was the city the key to the Eastern gate of the Indian Ocean—the gate through which the whole commerce of the Moluccas, the Philippines, Japan, and " far Cathay " passed on its road to the Mediterranean—but it was at the same time one of the largest marts in Asia. In its harbour rode the ships of countless nations and peoples, from " Cipangu " to Timor. It is little surprising, therefore, that the news of Albuquerque's success spread far and wide throughout the Eastern world, and that the sovereigns of the neighbouring countries were anxious to solicit his

[1] Herrera, *op. cit.*, Dec. ii. liv. ii. cap. xix. p. 66: " Dando de si muy buenas muestras."

protection.   The alliances concluded with them tempted
—if not to fresh conquests—at least to further explorations.   The Spice Islands—an Eldorado even more
glittering than the New World—had by this time
passed from the cloud of uncertainty that hung around
them, to become a reality almost within grasp.   The
Viceroy and his comrades had doubtless talked over
their riches a hundred times, had met their ships and
men, and had made themselves acquainted with such
details as were possible of their navigation.   But it
must have been from Luigi Varthema, the Italian—the
first European who had ever sailed into these waters
—the traveller who had seen with his own eyes the
hitherto unknown wonders of the Moluccas—that they
derived their most trustworthy information.   His
accounts of "Maluch" and its cloves; of Banda—the
"isola molto brutta & trista"—and its nutmegs, must
have been fresh in their memories.   Little wonder,
then, that we find Albuquerque fitting out and despatching an expedition to these long-sought-for lands without
a moment's delay.   The streets of Malacca were hardly
cleared of the *débris* of the assault, the conquerors hardly
rested from their labours, ere Antonio d'Abreu weighed
anchor with his three galleons, and sailed in quest of
the unknown islands whose perfumed products were
even more coveted than the gold of America.

The captains of the other ships were Francisco Serrão
and—according to Argensola—Ferdinand Magellan.[1]
The Portuguese forces had been so weakened by battle
and disease that it was impossible further to reduce

---

[1] According to De Goes and Correa, the third vessel was commanded
by Simão Afonso Bisagudo (*Chronica de D. Manoel,* 3ra parte, cap.
xxv. fol. 51).

them to any considerable extent, and barely a hundred
European soldiers sailed. The ships, however, bore
numerous Malabaris and other mercenaries upon their
roll, in addition to their ordinary complement of seamen. Leaving Malacca at the end of December, 1511,[1]
the fleet followed a southern track, skirting the north
coast of Java.[2] They passed between that island and
Madura, and holding an easterly course, left Celebes on
their port-hand and entered the Banda Sea. The instructions given by Albuquerque were most explicit.
No prizes were to be taken, no vessel was to be chased
or boarded, and at every port the greatest respect was to
be shown for the authorities and customs of the country.
Further to secure their good reception, a junk preceded
them, having on board a certain Nakoda Ismael, well
versed in the navigation of these seas and in the commerce of their islands. Passing to the north of the

[1] "Em nonembro d'este ano de 1511" (*Correa*, vol. ii. pt. i. p. 265),
perhaps a more probable date, as Albuquerque left Malacca for India
December 1.

[2] With regard to this first voyage of the Portuguese to the Moluccas
the greatest discrepancies exist, in spite of the diffuseness of its narra-
tion by some of the contemporaneous historians, and the extreme importance of the enterprise. The question is whether Magellan really
did sail with D'Abreu upon this occasion or not. Barros does not
mention his presence, nor does the almost equally prolix Castanheda,
and Correa, De Goes, and Galvão are also silent upon the subject.
Again, from a document found in the Lisbon archives, it is known
that Magellan was in that city in June, 1512. If the expedition left
Malacca for the Spice Islands in December, 1511, or even in the middle
of November, a very limited space of time is left for the completion
of its work and the return of Magellan to Portugal. On the other
hand, Argensola tells us very plainly that Magellan went as captain of
the third ship, and a few pages farther on says, " Auiendo Magallanes
passado seyscientas leguas adelante házia Malaca, se hallaua en unas
islas desde donde se correspondia cõ Serrano " (*op. cit.*, lib. i. p. 15).
Oviedo also, referring to Magellan, calls him " diestro en las cosas de

volcanic islet of Gunong Api, they touched at Bouru, and finally reached Amboina in safety.

The distance between Amboina and Banda is such as, with a fair wind, might be easily accomplished in one day, even by the clumsily-built galleons of that period. Abreu chose, therefore, to visit this group, the home of the nutmeg, before proceeding northward to Ternate. Serrão's command—a Cambay ship taken at the siege of Goa—had, however, become so unseaworthy that it was found necessary to abandon her. Officers and crew were taken on board the *Santa Catalina* to Banda, where a junk was purchased to take her place. So abundant was the supply of spice in that port, that they were able fully to lade their ships, and Antonio d'Abreu resolved to return to Malacca without visiting Ternate, not only because he was unable to take more cargo, but also on account of the weather.[1]   On the return voyage Serrão

la mar, y que *por vista de ojos* tenia mucha noticia de la India oriental, y de las Islas del Maluco y Espeçieria" (Oviedo y Valdes, *Hist. General de las Indias*, lib. xx. cap. i.). A still stronger argument, perhaps, exists in Magellan's own letter to Charles V. in September 1519 (Leg. 1 of Molucca documents, Seville archives; Navarrete, vol. iv. p. 188), in which he speaks authoritatively of the geographical position of the different islands of the Moluccas.

These arguments in their turn are open to objection. Argensola is the least accurate of all the historians, and an obvious anachronism occurs in the same sentence with the passage quoted. Magellan's knowledge of the Moluccas, too, may very well have been obtained through his friend Francisco Serrão, who at that time had been resident in Ternate for nearly eight years. The question, having regard to probabilities, must be answered in the negative, but it is of great interest. For, if Magellan did reach Banda, it may be justly claimed for him that at the period of his death in the Philippines he had in his own person completed the circumnavigation of the globe—an honour that is in general assigned to his successor, Sebastian del Cano.

1 "Por culpa dos tempos lhe torçarã mal," says Castanheda. Perhaps the strongest argument against Magellan having sailed on this expedition with d'Abreu is afforded us by a consideration of the

was destined again to meet with misfortune, or at least with what appeared at the time to be such. Getting separated from the rest of the fleet in heavy weather, his vessel struck on the reefs of the Schildpad Islands,[1] and became a total wreck.

Of Serrão's future history, romantic and interesting as it is, it is impossible here to give a detailed account, though, from its connection with that of his friend Magellan, a glance at it is perhaps necessary. Thrown upon a deserted island, famous as the resort of pirates and wreckers who reaped the harvest of its formidable reefs, they feared that "if they met not their death from thirst and hunger, they might expect it from these corsairs." The very thing they most dreaded proved their salvation, and Serrão extricated himself from his dangerous position by a ruse as clever as it was laughable. Some pirates, having sighted the wreck, landed to hunt down the survivors. Serrão, meanwhile, had hidden his men close to the beach, and waiting until the new-comers had disembarked, quietly emerged from his place of concealment and took possession of their ship. His antagonists, with the prospect of being left without food or water, begged for mercy, which was granted upon condition that they should repair the wrecked junk. All reached Amboina in safety, and were well treated by the natives. The kings of Ternate and Tidor

prevailing winds of those seas. Even had the fleet sailed in November, and reached Amboina in a fortnight, it is extremely unlikely that an attempt would have been made to beat back against the west monsoon. The east monsoon is fairly established in July, and it may be said, with a confidence approaching certainty, that such of the fleet as returned to Malacca arranged their departure so that they might take advantage of it.

[1] The Schildpad Islands lie in lat. 5° 30′ S., long. 127° 40′ E., and about 140 miles W.S.W. of the Banda group.

were at that time engaged in a dispute about their
boundaries, and not unwilling to obtain an aid of which
both were wise enough to perceive the advantages, made
overtures to the powerful foreigners, whose fame had by
this time spread to the farthest boundaries of Malaysia.
Serrão cast in his lot with that of the ruler of Ternate,
and for the remainder of his life established himself in
the Moluccas.   From Ternate he wrote many letters to
his friends, and especially to Magellan, "giving him to
understand that he had discovered yet another new
world, larger and richer than that found by Vasco da
Gama." These letters, joined possibly with a personal
knowledge of those regions, formed, it may safely be
conjectured, no slight inducement to the undertaking
of the voyage which ended our hero's life and made his
name immortal.[1]

Whether, then, Magellan did or did not see with his

---

[1] "Das quaes cartas começou este Fernão de Magalhães tomar huns
novos conceitos que lhe causáram a morte, e metteo este Reyno em
algum desgosto, como logo veremos " (*Barros*, Dec. iii. liv. v. cap. vi.).
"Este Francisco Serrão foy o que mandou enformação de Maluco à
Fernão de Magalhães, que fez despois treyção aa casa real de Portugal,
querendolhe tirar estas ilhas da sua conquista & dalas a coroa de
Castela " (*Castanheda*, lib. iii. cap. lxxxvi.).   The letters written by
Magellan to Serrão were found among the papers left at the latter's
death.   In them he promises "that he will be with him soon, if not by
way of Portugal, by way of Spain, for to that issue his affairs seemed
to be leading" (*Navarrete*, vol. iv. note v. p. lxxiv. ; *Barros*, Dec. iii.
lib. v. cap. viii.).   A certain mystery enwraps the prolonged stay of
Serrão in the Moluccas.   It is quite possible—nay, almost certain—that
it was contrary to orders, but that on the next visit of the Portuguese
he was a person of such influence that they found it advisable to leave
him alone.   This is borne out by a document found by Muñoz in the
Seville archives, which says, "Francisco Serrano, grande hombre de
navegacion, y muy amigo de Magallanes . . . el qual con temor y
desagrado del Rey de Portugal y de sus gentes huyó de Malaca en un
junco de los que solian ir a comerciar en Maluco" (*see* Navarrete,
iv. p. 371).

own eyes this promised land,[1] one thing at least is certain, that the two friends never met again. In what ship or by what fleet he returned to Portugal we do not know, but that he did return about the period is conclusively proved, not only from the fact that the historians give the length of his Indian service as seven years,[2] but from the evidence of certain documents of the Casa Real de Portugal, brought to light by the historian Muñoz. It was the custom in those days that all who belonged to the king's household—the "criação de El Rey"—should receive a stipend which, though merely nominal in value, corresponded to their rank.[3] This stipend was known as the *moradia*. Magellan, borne on the books as "moço fidalgo," received a monthly pension of a milreis,[4] and an *alqueire* of barley daily, and on the 12th June, 1512, we find him signing a receipt in Lisbon acknowledging the fact.[5] It is probable that this receipt was signed not long after his arrival in

[1] Upon the Molucca expedition see *De Goes*, 3ra parte, caps. xxv. and xxviii. ; *Argensola*, lib. i. pp. 6 and 15 ; *Barros*, Dec. ii. liv. vi. cap. vii., and Dec. iii. liv. v. cap. vi. ; *Castanheda*, bk. iii. caps. lxxv. and lxxxvi. ; *Correa*, bk. ii. pt. i. pp. 265, 267, and 280 ; Galvão, *Descobrimentos*, Hakluyt Soc., p. 115.

[2] Gomara, *Hist. General de las Indias*, cap. xci.

[3] Osorio, *De Rebus Emmanuelis*, lib. xi. p. 327 (ed. Col. Agrip. MDLXXVI.), tells us the origin of this stipend. "Olim erat apud Lusitanos in more positum, ut in Regia, qui Regi serviebant ipsius Regis sumptibus alerentur. Cùm verò multitudo domesticorum tanta fuisset, difficillimum videbatur cibos tantæ multitudini præparare. Quocirca fuit à Portugaliæ Regibus statutum, ut sumptum, quem quilibet erat in Regia facturus, ipse sibi ex regia pocunia faceret. Sic autem factum est, ut cuilibet certa pecuniæ summa, singulis mensibus assignaretur."

[4] The milreis or dollar, although at that period of considerably greater value, is now worth about 4s. 5d. of our English money. The *alqueire* is as nearly as possible 28 lbs.

[5] Bk. vi. of Moradias da Casa Real, fol. 47 v.

Portugal, as from a similar document, dated one month later (July 14, 1512), we learn of his promotion to the rank of "fidalgo escudeiro," which he presumably obtained for his services in the East. The increase in his pension was, comparatively speaking, considerable (850 reis), but of far more importance was the improvement in his position at court; for, as we learn from Osorio, "each person was esteemed the more noble according to the amount of salary that he received."

Returned once more to his native land, Magellan remained there for nearly a year. Whether he retired to his estate at Sabrosa or breathed the more stirring air of the court at Lisbon, we are not informed. But to one of his temperament—one who for seven long years had led a vivid life of adventure by sea and land, a life of siege and shipwreck, of endless war and wandering—a country existence must have become impossible. To be with his fellows, with men who had tasted of the sweets and bitters of the wider life, to be within reach of news from India, to watch the preparations for further and perhaps greater expeditions—this must have been to him as the breath of his life, and we cannot doubt that he remained in Lisbon. It is wonderful that he should have remained so long. That he was not the man to sink into inaction either of mind or body we may be quite sure, and we can picture him perfecting himself in the art of navigation[1] or planning fresh explorations

---

[1] Magellan's ability as a trained navigator is constantly referred to by writers of the period. It is not actually stated that he was a pupil of Martin Behaim, but he may quite well have been so. That cosmographer, after completing his globe in 1492, left Nuremberg for the Azores *viâ* Portugal, but returned to the latter country shortly afterwards. He died in Lisbon in 1506. Between these two dates— with the exception of a mission to Flanders—he is believed to have

or conquests in the vast island-scattered seas through which—well-nigh spent with hunger and scurvy—he was afterwards destined to wander for so many weary weeks. It was to India, doubtless, that Magellan looked as the scene of his future success—to the Farther India of which Serrão had written to him, and of which he himself later said that he would find his way thither, "if not by way of Portugal, then by way of Spain." It was not, however, in India that he was next to serve. In the summer of 1513 difficulties arose with the Moors of Azamor in Morocco. In the time of Dom João II. a treaty had been concluded with them. Portuguese subjects resided in the city, their ships entered the harbour free of dues, and their goods passed the customs without charge. The peace remained unbroken until, tired of paying tribute, Muley Zeyam rebelled. Dom Manoel was not the monarch to leave an insult long unavenged. An armada was fitted out in Lisbon such as neither before nor since weighed anchor from the shores of Portugal.[1]

Why so large a fleet was despatched is not clear. It consisted, all told, of more than four hundred ships, which bore no less than eighteen thousand men-at-arms in addition to the cavalry and sailors. The command was given by Dom Manoel to his nephew Jayme, Duke of Bragança. Leaving Belem on the 13th August, 1513, the force arrived off Azamor on the 28th. A pretence of fighting was gone through, but the Moors were wise enough to realise that they had not sufficient strength

resided partly in Fayal and partly in Lisbon. Magellan, as we know, passed these years at the Portuguese capital. That the two never met is in the highest degree improbable.

[1] Çurita, *Anales de Aragon*, lib. x. cap. lxxix. fol. 374 v. Goes, *op. cit.* 3ra parte, cap. xlvi.

to cope with so formidable an enemy, and the city opened its gates without further bloodshed.

Among the many distinguished captains who entered them, we look in vain through the chronicler's list of names [1] for that of Magellan, although we know, from his being mentioned in the pages of Barros very shortly after, that he must have been present. The Duke of Bragança returned in November to Portugal, and left Dom João de Meneses in command, a general noted for valour and energy, of whom it was said that " he ceased not for a moment from making cruel war against the Moors." [2] The city was scarcely settled ere a series of " *entradas* " or armed reconnaissances was instituted, which, making their descent where least expected, greatly harassed the Moors and kept the country in a perpetual state of terror. In one of these, under the leadership of João Soarez, Magellan was wounded in the leg by a lance, which appears to have injured some tendon behind the knee in such a manner that he remained slightly lame for the rest of his life. [3]

Towards the end of March, 1514, the Portuguese received information that the kings of Fez and Mequinez were preparing a large army for the recapture of Azamor. On the 12th April the patrols sent out from that city gave notice of the approach of the advance-guard, and Dom João de Meneses led his troops at once against them. Although the Moors were completely routed, leaving over two thousand of their men upon the field,

[1] Faria y Sousa, *Africa Portugueza*, cap. vii. ; De Goes, *op. cit.*, 3ra parte, fol. 87.

[2] Pedro de Mariz, *Dialogos de varia Historia*, dial. iv. cap. xviii. fol. 286 v.

[3] " Parece que lhe tocou em algum nerva da juntura da curva, con que depois manquejava hum poco."—*Barros*, Dec. iii. liv. v. cap. viii.

the Portuguese also suffered considerable loss, and the advance of the enemy was unchecked. On Easter Eve they arrived at the river of Azamor. So great were their numbers, that seven days were occupied in the crossing, while behind them " everything was consumed, laid waste, and destroyed." The very size of the army was, however, the cause of its ruin. Already *au bout de ses forces*, it arrived in the neighbourhood of the city only to find the wells destroyed and the country devastated. The Portuguese had an easy task. With the aid of their native allies the invading host was soon put to flight. The booty was large. Over eight hundred horses alone were captured and a thousand Moors made prisoners.

Either on this occasion or very shortly after an incident occurred which, if we may believe the historians, was indirectly the cause of the differences between Magellan and his sovereign. Owing partly to his lameness and partly to his friendship with João Soarez, our hero was selected, in company with another captain, Alvaro Monteiro, as *quadrileiro mór* in charge of the booty. Whether he had refused to wink at irregularities, and had hence become unpopular and open to unfounded accusations, or whether he was really guilty, it is impossible with certainty to discover; but the fact remains, that, together with his comrade, he was accused by certain people of selling the cattle to the Moors, and permitting them to be carried off at night with his full knowledge and connivance. It is probable that under his old commander, Dom João de Meneses, he would have had little difficulty in clearing himself, but the sudden death of the latter and the succession of Pedro de Sousa to the command of Azamor placed matters on a different footing.   Magellan, desirous perhaps of personally explaining the affair, left Africa and returned to Lisbon.

Dom João de Meneses had died on the 15th May, 1514. It must have been, therefore, at some date not far removed from this that Magellan presented himself before his sovereign. It is probable that he thought little or nothing of the charge that had been brought against him and that his conscience was clear, for we are told that he took the opportunity of preferring his claims for promotion on account of his long service in the East, and petitioning for an increase of *moradia*. It was perhaps not the wisest of actions. Dom Manoel was by no means disposed lightly to regard the matter, the more so from the fact that he had received a letter from Pedro de Sousa informing him that Magellan had left Africa without his permission. It was in vain that the supposed culprit tried to justify himself. The King refused to listen to him, and ordered him at once to return to Azamor to answer the charges of which he stood accused.

Magellan had no alternative but to go, but on his arrival the authorities declined to proceed against him. No greater argument in favour of his innocence could be adduced, and he returned without loss of time to Portugal, bearing the documents which, he confidently expected, would restore him to his sovereign's favour. Doubtless he looked forward with certainty to the coveted rise in the *moradia*—that minute increase which, paltry though it was in actual value, meant so much to those who were of the King's household.[1]

---

[1] The increase of stipend for which Magellan petitioned was a half-cruzado per month, about equivalent to 13d. of our money. " Subir

Foremost in his mind, however, must have been the hope of a command—of a return to India. He was doomed to disappointment. "Sempre lhe ElRey teve hum entejo"—"the King always loathed him," Barros tells us.[1] His reception was not more gracious than it had been on the occasion of their last meeting. Dom Manoel turned a deaf ear to his entreaties, and Magellan, cruelly hurt at the ingratitude shown him after his years of honourable service, was left to realise that, so far as his king and country were concerned, his career was over.

The lapse of nearly four hundred years renders it difficult, perhaps, for us to judge between the two, but there is no doubt that such evidence as we have is in favour of subject rather than king. Mariz, in his *Dialogos de varia Historia*,[2] has treated us to a eulogy of the stereotyped kind upon the latter—a florid tribute which has little genuineness in its tone. If we turn to facts, however, the story reads differently. Vasco da Gama, to whom must at least be conceded the honour of discovering India, whatever may be said with regard to his cruelties, was left in obscurity by his royal master for eighteen years, and his services only properly acknowledged on

cinco reales en dinero, es subir muchos grados en calidad," however, as Faria y Sousa tells us (*Asia Portugueza*, vol. i. pt. iii. cap. v.). That the refusal of one king to raise the pay of an old and faithful servant thirteen shillings per annum led to endless disagreements with another, to a great loss of profit to the first power of Europe, and to a still greater loss of glory, is a reflection not devoid of interest. " Que mysterios de estreitezas fazem os Reys muytas vezes em cousas que pouco importão, sendo prodigios de prodigalidades em outras!" remarks a Portuguese historian.—Fr. Luiz de Sousa, *Annaes de ElRei Dom João III.*, lib. i. cap. x. p. 41.

[1] *Decadas*, Dec. iii. liv. v. cap. viii.

[2] Pedro de Mariz, *op. cit.*, dial. iv. cap. xix. fol. 305 v. *et seq.*

the accession of the next monarch, Dom João III.   Lord
Stanley[1] describes Dom Manoel as " of a most niggardly
disposition, suspicious of his servants, and very jealous
of directing personally all the details of government."
That the former attribute was true there can be no
doubt, and no better instance could be given than that
on the occasion of the great defeat inflicted upon the
Calicut armada, when the Viceroy doubled the pay of
the men who had been wounded in the engagement, the
King " did not approve of his action in this matter."[2]
Osorius would have us believe that Magellan's applica-
tion was refused on principle by the King;[3] but we
gather from Barros and others that while he himself
was denied, he was exposed to the double mortification
of seeing others promoted whose success "was due to
intrigue and patronage rather than to any merit of their
own."   The bitterness with which he felt the injustice
of his treatment was in no way mitigated by the insinua-
tion that his lameness was feigned in order to support
his claims.

Of Magellan's movements subsequent to this affair we
are unfortunately left for some time without any detailed
account; but even without the general statement of the
historian João de Barros that he "was always busied
with pilots, charts, and the question of longitudes," we
should have had little difficulty in guessing his occupation.   He was unemployed, and was likely always to
remain so, so long as Dom Manoel was on the throne;
but it is probable that this fact disturbed him very little,

---

[1] *Vasco da Gama* (Hakl. Soc., 1869), p. xvii.

[2] Correa, vol. i. pt. ii. cap. ix. p. 604.

[3] " Rex, ne aditum ambitiosis aperiret, id negavit."—Osorius, *De
Rebus Emmanuelis*, lib. xi. fol. 327 v.

and that he had long decided what action he would take. It is not by any means certain, indeed, that he had not an alternative in his mind on the memorable occasion of his interview with the King—a question to which we shall have presently to return. Be that as it may, however, his future action was probably not a little influenced at this period by his becoming strongly united, if not by the bonds of friendship, at least by those of common interests, to a fellow-countryman, Ruy Faleiro.

Of Faleiro's antecedents we know little or nothing. Of what happened to him after the paths of the two lives diverged, we know almost less. But for two years or more their histories were so closely linked together that it is impossible not to feel an interest in him. Like Magellan, though not a native of the wild Traz-os-Montes, he too was from the highlands of Portugal,[1] and like him he was in disfavour with his king. Both had as mistress the science of cosmography. But while Magellan—the soldier who had served under Dom Lourenço, the sailor who was the first to navigate to Malacca —was essentially the man of action, Faleiro was of a very different stamp. Student and dreamer, a lover of books and theories, he was little fitted for the practical life. His reputation as an astronomer and cosmographer was nevertheless undoubted, although his enemies declared it to be the work of a familiar spirit.[2] His knowledge

---

[1] In an *obligacion* made by Magellan and Faleiro with Aranda, dated February 23, 1518, and now in the archives of Simancas, the place of residence of Faleiro is given as Cunilla. It should have been Cubilla, as Navarreto (iv. p. 110) has spelt it, which is a mere transcript of the Portuguese Covilhã.

[2] " Ruy Falero, que mostraua ser gran Astrologo y Cosmographo ; del qual afirmauan los Portugueses que tenia vn demonio familiar, y que de Astrologia no sabia nada."—*Herrera*, Dec. ii. lib. ii. cap. xix.

of the principles of navigation was probably as extensive as that possessed by anybody at that period; and his treatise upon the means of calculating longitude was given to Magellan on his departure, to serve as guide and text-book throughout the voyage.　Each man doubtless found in the other much to be admired; but, while Magellan benefited greatly from his companion's acquaintance with the sciences, the fact that the latter did not accompany him upon his memorable voyage is not much to be regretted.　Of uncertain temper, gloomy, and jealous of Magellan's influence and position, his presence would have served but to add one more difficulty to the many with which the indomitable navigator had to contend.

At what exact period this friendship, or rather acquaintanceship, originated does not appear.　It is said by a contemporary historian [1] that the two men had previously arranged to denaturalise themselves and offer their services to Spain, and it is therefore more than probable that they were known to each other at the time when Magellan's humiliation at his sovereign's hands was still fresh in his memory.　That that incident did not consist in the mere refusal of *moradia* there is every reason to believe, even had Barros not strongly implied the contrary.[2]　But he tells us that it was shortly after his interview with the King that Magellan wrote to Serrão in the Moluccas, to tell him that he would be with him soon—"if not by Portugal, then by way of Spain."　There can be little or no doubt that for a long time—perhaps for years, possibly ever since his Malaccan

---

[1] *Barros*, iii. lib. v. cap. viii.; *vide* Navarrete, *op. cit.*, vol. iv. p. xxxiii.

[2] *Decadas*, Dec. iii. lib. v. cap. viii. p. 627 (edit. 1777).

F

experiences had put him in relation with the farthest East—the project of reaching the Spice Islands by the western route had been the *idée mère* of the great navigator's restless brain. That it was this project that he laid before Dom Manoel is almost certain. Whether, like Columbus, he was laughed at as a visionary and a fool,[1] we do not know. All we know is, that his plans met with a cold refusal. At seven-and-thirty, a born leader of men, of varied Eastern experience, a master of the art of navigation, his mind filled with an all-absorbing project, Magellan found himself condemned to a life of obscurity and inaction. The former might perhaps have been possible to him—inaction was not. Still more intolerable must have been the thought that, with his hands thus fettered, another might come and grasp the prize which he was now the only one to see. Already Christovão Jacques had led his ships far south along the coast of Patagonia, and Vasco Nunez de Balboa had seen the vast Pacific lying at his feet from the summit of the Darien sierra. To a man of Magellan's character and training but one course lay open, and that course he took. Bidding adieu for ever to Portugal, he publicly denaturalised himself, and passing into Spain, entered the service of the Emperor Charles V.[2]

This action of Magellan drew down a perfect storm of abuse and invective, not only from Portuguese writers

---

[1] "Teniendo a Colon por ytaliano burlador."—Garibay, *Comp. Hist. de las Chron.*

[2] From Correa we learn something of the final severance of relations between Magellan and his sovereign. The former "demanded permission to go and live with some one who would reward his services. . . . The King said he might do what he pleased. Upon this Magellan desired to kiss his hand at parting, but the King would not offer it to him."—*ii. Anno de* 1521, cap. xiv.

of that date, but from others to whom a more enlight-
ened age and absence of the *odium patrium* should have
taught broader views and a calmer judgment. With
these violent outpourings whole pages might be filled.
We have seen something of them in the will of Francisco
da Silva Telles,[1] and Osorius is perhaps even more
unmeasured in his language.[2] André Thevet, borrowing
from the latter, reviles the offender as one who " imagina
en son esprit vn tel mes-contentement qu'oubliant toute
foy, pieté, et religion il ne cessa iusques à ce que (entant
qu'en luy estoit) il eut trahy le Roy, qui l'avoit esleué,
le pays de sa naissance, et hazardant sa vie à de merueil-
leux dangers, eut mis l'estat en extrème danger." [3] But
all these are put into the shade by a later writer of
Portuguese history. " The two monsters Magellan and
Faleiro," he says, " traitors to the King whom it was
their duty to serve, barbarians towards the country for
which it was their duty to die, conspired to bring about
a fatal war between two neighbouring and friendly
powers." [4] Manoel Faria y Sousa, and later Barbosa,

---

[1] *Vide* p. 23.

[2] " Abiura fidem quantum voles ; perfidiam tuam publicis literis
contestare ; insignem memoriam sceleris infandi posteritati relinque ;
nullis tamen testimoniis numinis offensionem et dedecoris sempiterni
maculam vitare poteris."—Osorius, *op. cit.*, lib. xi. fol. 328.

[3] Thevet, *Les Vrais Povrtraits et Vies des Hommes Illustres*, p. 528.

[4] D. Antonio de Lemos Faria e Castro, *Historia Geral de Portugal*,
liv. xli. cap. vii. tom. xi. p. 193. The continuation of this passage is
still stronger, and possesses also the merit of being amusing. " Agora
porem, nas primeiras conferencias, os dous Portugueses—trahidores
pelas suas dimensões geographicas e astronomicas respectivas às Indias
Orientaes e Occidentaes, a que o odio e a paixão lançava as linhas e
formava os triangulos e angulos que (as leis da Historia me darão
licença para dizer) tinhão mais de agudos que de rectos—elles persua-
dirão ao Rei Carlos e ao Cardeal Ximenes que as Molucas pertencião
à Castella."

are among the few who refused to join in this cuckoo-cry of traitor. "The renderer of many a service to his country," says the latter, "the owner of a name whose glory he had made imperishable, he returned to Portugal, where he besought from the King some increase in his *moradia*. . . . The King, to the lasting injury of his country, refused this most just request, and Magellan, deeply hurt at his refusal, left a country so unworthy of such a well-deserving son."[1]

It is hardly necessary at the present day to offer an apology for Magellan's act of denaturalisation, although, were it so, the elaborate arguments of Lord Stanley of Alderley[2] should prove more than sufficient. A great discoverer, whether in the realms of science or cosmography, belongs to no country, and, moreover, has no right to permit any false ideas of patriotism to check the advance of knowledge. That they were false ideas, and that Magellan in no way injured Portugal, is evident. By the Tordesillas capitulation of 1494 the world had been divided into two halves, of which Spain was to have one, and Portugal the other. The western line of division had been agreed upon, but where the eastern fell geographical knowledge was not then sufficiently far advanced to discover. Upon which side of it the Moluccas were situated was unknown. But his countrymen appear to have forgotten that no action of Magellan could affect the question. Either the islands belonged to Spain or they did not, and the great explorer, with all his geographical knowledge, was unable to shift their longitude one hair's-breadth. Nor, even with the most critical eye, can we discover any ground for the anger of the historians save

1 Barbosa, *Bibliotheca Lusitana*, vol. ii. p. 31.
2 *First Voyage Round the World by Magellan* (Hakl. Soc.), p. ii.

the extreme jealousy then existing between the two
nations. The custom of denaturalisation was fully recognised; it was not regarded as blameworthy, and it
was at that period a common occurrence. Among navigators especially the taking service under a foreign power
was almost as much a rule as an exception. Columbus, Cabot, and Vespucci are only three of many instances. But even with this, Magellan was careful not
to offend in the slightest degree against the country
which, after his long services, had treated him so cava-
lierly. "Before consulting his own interests," says
Faria, "he first did everything that honour demanded of
him."[1] By a clause in his agreement with the Emperor
of Spain he pledged himself to make no discoveries within
the boundaries of the King of Portugal, and to do nothing prejudicial to his interests. He did not sail upon
his great voyage until two years after he had signed the
act of denaturalisation. Finally, it should be remembered that there was a sort of tacit understanding that
the Spanish were to prosecute their discoveries to the
west and the Portuguese to the east.[2] Magellan's long-
planned expedition was to lead him into occidental
waters, and it is probable that this fact was not without
its effect upon his action. "Yet this," says Faria, "is
the man whose honour has been so fiercely assailed by
the great writers."[3]

[1] Manoel Faria y Sousa, *Comentarios a la Lusiada de Camões*, canto
x. 140.

[2] "Hinc factum est, ut Castellani per meridiem in occidentem
semper nauigauerint. . . . Portugallenses uero per meridionem et
littora Hesperidum, et æquatorem, et tropicum Capricorni præter-
euntes in Orientem nauigauerunt."—Munster, *Cosmographia Univers.*,
p. 1103.

[3] *Europa Portuguesa*, vol. ii. pte. iv. cap. i.

But whether Magellan was justified in his action, or whether he was not, matters little as far as regards the result.　The fact remains, that, for the second time, Portugal threw away the chance that fate had offered her. Hardly a quarter of a century before, King John II. had ridiculed the ideas of Columbus, and regarded him as a boasting adventurer.　Now Magellan learnt from his successor that "he might do as he pleased."　The discovery of the New World and the circumnavigation of the globe are the two greatest deeds of geographical history, but Portugal, who had both within her grasp, cannot claim the credit of either of them.

CHAPTER IV.

MAGELLAN'S PROJECT AND ITS ADOPTION BY CHARLES V.

IT was for Seville, the centre of the West Indian trade
and the busiest city of Spain, that Magellan set out
upon leaving Portugal, taking with him other navigators
"suffering from a like disorder"[1]—the neglect or enmity
of their king. Faleiro, as we have seen, came under
this head, but he was unable to travel with his friend.
On the 20th October, 1517, Magellan arrived at his destination.   He found himself immediately among com-
patriots and men whose interests were of the same nature
as his own. Foremost among them was one Diogo Barbosa, also a Portuguese, a commendador of the Order
of Santiago, alcaide of the arsenal, and a person of considerable importance in Seville. At his hands Magellan
received the greatest kindness and assistance. From
his personal knowledge of the East this help was of
double value. Nor did he limit it to advice and counsel.
He persuaded Magellan to be his guest, and it appears
that the latter resided at his house until his departure,
three months later, for the Spanish court at Valladolid.

Diogo Barbosa, although he had held his post under
the Spanish flag for nearly fourteen years,[2] and had

---

[1] "Levando alguns pilotos tambem doentes desta sua enfermidade."
—*Barros*, Dec. iii. lib. v. cap. viii.

[2] We learn from an *auto fiscal* of the 3rd June, 1529, executed

" served much and well in Granada and Navarre," had also drawn his sword for Dom Manoel and Portugal in the far East. In 1501 he captained a ship of the fleet of João da Nova, and sailed for India.[1] Although this armada returned almost immediately, the voyage was conspicuous for the discovery of the two islands, Ascension and St. Helena.[2] His son, Duarte Barbosa, was even more distinguished. At what exact period he had sailed from, and in what fleet he returned to his native land is unknown, but he had navigated the Indian seas for years, making notes of all he saw and heard. These notes—*O Livro de Duarte Barbosa*—a description of all the ports then visited in the Indian Ocean, and even beyond—he finished in the year 1516, a few months before Ferdinand Magellan came to live beneath his father's roof.[3]   Father and son were sailor-adven-

by a son, Jaime Barbosa, and now in the Archivo das Indias (1-2-3/3), that Diogo was made " Alcaide en los Alcázares " in 1503, and continued to hold that post until his death in 1525. *Vide* Medina, *Coleccion de Documentos inéditos para la Historia de Chile*, 1888, vol. ii. p. 308.

[1] According to Correa, he was only an *escrivão* or clerk, and was borne on the flag-ship.   Vol. i. p. 235.

[2] The former was discovered on the outward voyage, the latter on their return home in 1502.

[3] This work of Duarte Barbosa was first published, in an abbreviated form, by Ramusio in his *Navigationi et Viaggi*.   In 1813 the full text was given in the *Collecção de Noticias para a Historia e Geographica das Nações Ultramarinas*, published by the Acad. Real das Sciencias, vol. ii. No. vii.   Some time ago a MS. was discovered in Madrid with the following title :—"Descripcion de los reinos, costas, puertos e islas que hay en el mar de la India Oriental desde el Capo de Buena Esperanza hasta la China, de los usos y costumbres de sus naturales; su gobierno, religion, comercio, y navegacion; y de los frutos y efectos que producen aquellas vastas regiones, con otras noticias muy curiosas ; *compuesto por Fernando Magallanes*, piloto portugues que lo vio y anduvo todo ;" but it has been conclusively proved by Varnhagon and others to be only a copy of Barbosa's work.

turers born and bred, and even if no family connection existed between them and Magellan,[1] the bond uniting them must have been of no ordinary strength.   It was, moreover, of no disadvantage to the new-comers that the Alçaide-mór or chief of the arsenal was also a Portuguese, and a person of great distinction—Don Alvaro of Portugal.   A brother of the celebrated Duke of Bragança, who was executed by João II.; he was only one of many such refugees; and, all things considered, Magellan could scarcely have met with kinder or more influential protectors than those who welcomed him on his arrival in the country of his adoption.

Close as was the friendship between host and guest, the two were destined before very long to be still more nearly connected.   The life of Magellan had been, and was yet to be, one of the most vivid interest.   Full of vigour and incident, kaleidoscopic in its change of scene, never resting, it ended in a grand success and a great disaster.   Romantic in many ways it doubtless was, but of romance in the present acceptation of the word little or none has been handed down by the historians to interest or amuse us.   In the drama of life Magellan was not one to be cast for the part of lover, although we feel that his character, from its vigour and undaunted tenacity of purpose, must have strongly appealed to women's admiration.   Such a rôle, however, it fell to his lot at this period to play.   He made the part as short as possible.   Before the year 1517 had elapsed, within two months of his arrival in Seville, he married

---

[1] Such a connection, apart from that of his marriage, is suggested by De Barros Arana (trad. de F. de M. Villas-Boas, p. 26), though upon what grounds is not stated.   Herrera (Dec. iii. lib. i. cap. ix.) speaks of Duarte Barbosa as *primo* or cousin of Magellan, but the term was sometimes used merely in the sense of relation.

Beatriz Barbosa, the daughter of his friend and host.[1]

We may finish the history of Magellan's married life here, so short is it, and so limited our information anent it. A year and a half later he sailed on the voyage from which he was destined never to return. A son, Rodrigo, had meantime been born to him, who, at the time of his departure, was about six months old. Neither mother nor child were fated to live much longer than the father. In September 1521, five months after the death of the latter in the Philippines, Rodrigo died. In March of the following year—" having lived in great sorrow from the news which she had received of the death of her husband "—Beatriz died also.[2] Around the story we are left to throw what halo of romance we please, but it

[1] Although the date of Magellan's marriage is given as 1518, there is little doubt that it is incorrect. In his will of August 24, 1519, he speaks of his son being at that time six months old. This would fix the date of the marriage at some time previous to May 1518. But we know that from January 20th until August of that year Magellan was with the court at Valladolid and elsewhere. The probability is,. therefore, that Beatriz was married in order to accompany her husband thither. This is made nearly certain by the evidence of her brother, Jaime Barbosa, on the 3rd June, 1520, "y se casó y veló con la dicha doña Beatriz Barbosa en esta ciudad de Sevilla en un dia del dicho año" (1517). Vide *Autos Fiscales de Jaime Barbosa, q. cit. ; Archivo de Indias*, Medina, *op. cit.*, vol. ii. pp. 306–307. Gomara falls into the mistake of making Beatriz a daughter of "*Duardo*" Barbosa (cap. xci. p. 83). For an attempt at the genealogy of the Barbosa family see Appendix I., p. 315.

[2] "Porque (yo, Guiomar de Silvera) la vido viva é con mucha pena por la nueva que le habia venido de la muerte del dicho su marido." This, the evidence of a witness in support of Jaime Barbosa's claim to Magellan's estate (*vide* Medina, *op. cit.*. vol. ii. p. 322), is extremely interesting, as showing that the news of the arrival of the *Victoria* and *Trinidad* in the Moluccas must in some manner have reached home *via* the Portuguese Indies before March 1522. The *Victoria* did not arrive in Spain until September 6th of that year.

seems more than probable that the loss of her husband, child, and brother within so short a period may have had some connection with her own untimely death.

Magellan's courtship, it is to be presumed, had little or no effect upon his plans. These had been carefully pre-arranged, and he lost no time in furthering them to the best of his ability. His agreement with Faleiro before leaving Portugal had been most explicit. Both were to be equal; to stand on precisely the same footing. If anything should occur to either touching the project they had in hand, he was bound to communicate with his comrade within six hours, and if either desired to renounce the arrangement and return to Portugal, he could do so on fulfilling the same conditions. Their project—the attempt to reach the Moluccas by way of America—was to be revealed to no third party until the arrival of Faleiro at Seville. However much its broad outline might be surmised, the details and the actual route were to remain a secret.

We have already considered the gradual development of the Hispano-Portuguese difficulty.[1] The line of division fixed by the Bull of Pope Alexander VI. on the 4th May, 1493, fell, it may be remembered, a hundred leagues west of the Azores and Cape Verde Islands. The protests of Dom João II. of Portugal caused it, a year later, to be placed about 21° further to the west, and Brazil—as yet undiscovered—fell to his country's share. As the knowledge of the South American coast-line gradually progressed, the continent was found to trend westward until it was once more crossed by the dividing line, and again became Spanish. It was to this part, as yet dimly known from the explorations of Gonçalo

---

[1] *Vide ante,* p. 11.

Coelho and Christovão Jacques, and possibly from other sources, that Magellan and his friend Faleiro proposed to direct their course. Columbus, as we know, considered his new world only as a portion of the old. Nor did his later discoveries undeceive him. It was only when, on the one hand, the work of Gama and Albuquerque had begun to give a definite outline to the Indies, and, on the other, when each western-sailing navigator found land at whatever latitude he might choose to cross the Atlantic, that the European world realised the existence of a new continent, and realised it as a vast, interminable barrier which stretched apparently from pole to pole. Then came the search for some strait by which to pass it. The inward trend of the land at the Isthmus of Darien led later explorers to seek it there. Others, however, had tried before them. Columbus had attempted, upon leaving Cuba on his fourth voyage, to navigate westward with the idea of returning to Spain by sea. Far to the north, too, efforts had been made, and made in vain, although Sebastian Cabot wrote to Ramusio that he believed the whole of North America to be divided up into islands.[1] But the isthmus and the north alike proved impenetrable, and Magellan felt, even at that date, that it was not through the ice of a north-west passage that he was likely to reach the Moluccas. His route lay by the far south. Whether he actually knew of the existence of the strait that bears his name is a question we shall have presently to consider. One thing we do know; that he went for the special purpose of seeking a passage from the Atlantic to the already known Mar del Sur, or

<hr>

[1] Ramusio, *op. cit.*, vol. iii. preface, p. 6.

South Sea,[1] and that for the discovery of that passage he was prepared to push on to 70° S.

Magellan, we have seen, allowed nothing to delay the execution of his plans. Although bound not to reveal them in detail by his promise to Faleiro, he was equally engaged to bring them before the notice of those who had to do with Indian affairs. He offered, then, firstly to show Spain the shortest route to the Spice Islands, and, secondly, to prove that they lay within her legal boundaries.[2] With his introductions he had no difficulty in gaining access to the authorities. It was to the Casa de Contratacion that he first applied.

On the history of this body—the India Office of Spain, and of all corporate bodies the most important at that time—it is unnecessary here to dwell. It had, among other rights and duties, the power of granting letters of

---

[1] Vasco Nunez de Balboa—the man who "knew not what it was to be deterred" ("hombre que no sabia estar parado ")—was the first European to sight the Pacific from the West. Taking with him a picked band of 190 Spaniards, he sailed from Darien for Carreto. Leaving some of his men in charge of the ship, he took Indian guides and started for the Sierras. At Quarequa he was opposed by the chief Torecha, and in the engagement which followed the latter perished with 600 of his men. Leaving the sick and wounded, Vasco Nunez continued his march with the sixty-seven soldiers remaining to him, and reached the summit of the chain on the 25th September, 1513, where he knelt and gave thanks to God and besought help "a conquistar esta tierra i nueva mar que descubrimos." Descending, the little band of Spaniards reached the sea at the Gulf of San Miguel, and it is recorded that Alonso Martin de San Benito was the first European to adventure himself upon its surface. (Peter Martyr, *De Orbe Novo*, Dec. iii. cap. i. p. 182 ; Gomara, *op. cit.*, cap. lxii. ; Herrera, *op. cit.*, Dec. i. lib. x. cap. i.) Balboa's reasons for calling it the South Sea are very evident if the sharp westward turn of the isthmus be taken into consideration. The Pacific must have appeared as a vast ocean lying directly to the south.

[2] Fr. Luiz de Sousa, *Annaes de ElRei Dom João III.*, bk. i. cap. x. p. 41.

marque, of giving instruction in navigation, of collecting information upon newly-discovered lands, and of settling all legal difficulties that might arise in connection with these and kindred matters.[1] Whether the Casa was at that time too much taken up with other affairs—for it was just then the most eventful period of the history of the New World—whether it really considered Magellan's project as that of a visionary and a faddist, or whether it felt it unwise to adventure upon thin ice and court misunderstandings with the sister kingdom, we do not know. The result, however, was that the scheme, if not actually rejected, was shelved, and but for a chance circumstance might never have been carried out.

It happened that one of the three chief officials[2]—a certain Juan de Aranda—was very much more astute than his fellows. Possibly he saw his way to a share in the future glory of the expedition, and, as we shall see, in its pecuniary benefits; possibly he had no interest beyond the advancement of his country. It is not necessary, at this distance of time, to impute motives. The fact has merely to be recorded that he took the earliest opportunity of questioning Magellan more closely. Whether from his adroitness, or from the latter's feeling that he could be trusted, does not appear, but it was not long before he had persuaded the navigator to acquaint him with every detail. They were such as to commend the plan still more strongly to his favour. But he was cautious. Before taking further steps he wrote privately to certain friends in Lisbon for

---

[1] For the first ordinances of the Casa de Contratacion (January 20, 1503), *vide* Navarrete, vol. ii. p. 285, and Hakluyt, *Divers Voyages*, Hakl. Soc., p. 14.

[2] These, we learn from the Ordinances, were a *tesorero*, a *factor*, and an *escribano*.

information about the two men.[1]　What he learnt was
in their favour, and from that moment he threw himself
heart and soul into the affair.　He wrote instantly to
the Chancellor of Castile, warmly counselling the despatch of an expedition, and recommending Magellan
as "one who might do a great service to his Highness."

Meanwhile, at the beginning of December, Faleiro
arrived in Seville.　Aranda had as yet said nothing of
the letters, but he now told the two friends of the steps
he had taken.　Magellan was merely vexed at his want
of straightforwardness, but Faleiro was furious, and his
anger was especially directed against Magellan, whom
he upbraided for his "*ligereza*" and failure in the fulfilment of his promises.　It was in vain that the latter
pleaded that he had only acted, as he thought, for the
best.　Faleiro's temper, as ready to take offence as it
was slow to forgive, caused a rupture between the two,
which, though temporarily healed, was destined to break
out afresh at no very distant date.　Magellan's partner-
ship with such a firebrand as Faleiro rendered his

---

[1] "Habia escrito á Cobarrubias mercader é á Diego de Haro mercader que residian en Lisboa."—*Archiro de Indias*.　*Vide* Medina,
op. cit., vol. i. p. 27.　Our only source of information concerning this
period of Magellan's life is this long *procès-verbal*, in which Aranda
was arraigned for having, while an official of the Casa de Contratacion,
illegally contracted with Faleiro and Magellan to receive a certain
percentage of the profits arising from the expedition.　The evidence
of the three parties in the case is given at length, followed by nine
letters from Aranda to the King, bringing forward his services, how he
had spent 1500 ducats over his two protégés, and had succeeded in
preventing their return to Portugal, and finally how he had worked
to get people to join the fleet.　At a meeting of the Consejo de las
Indias in Barcelona, June 25, 1519, under the presidency of the Bishop
of Burgos, he was severely censured, and again on the 2nd July by
the King's fiscal, but it seems that the affair was subsequently allowed
to drop.　The greater part of the very lengthy evidence tends to
exonerate Aranda from blame.

position most difficult, and such it remained almost up to the moment of the departure of the expedition.

It was perhaps not the best of times to choose for the initiation of plans such as these. Affairs in Spain were at this period in a condition which, at best, could not be regarded as other than uncertain. Charles V., who had at last made up his mind to visit his kingdom, had set out from Flanders, and landed in Villaviciosa, on the north coast of Spain, on the 13th September, 1517. Proceeding with the army to Santander, he marched thence to San Vicente de la Barquera, and by Burgos and Palencia to Tordesillas, where his unhappy mother Joanna—for years hopelessly insane—still resided. On the 18th November he entered Valladolid. Ten days previously the Regent of Castile—Cardinal Ximenes de Cisneiros—wisest and most capable of rulers, had ended his long life while on his way to meet and welcome his sovereign, and with his loss the affairs of the kingdom became yet more complicated. The King was surrounded by Flemings, anxious only to get what pecuniary benefit they could from their position. Himself hardly able to speak the language of his people, he looked upon the country merely as a means of affording supplies to aid him in his designs in Middle Europe. Mistrustful of their sovereign and bitterly jealous of his Flemish courtiers, the Cortes was summoned to Valladolid. It was into this mixture of nationalities and interests, this hotbed of *brigue*, that Magellan and Faleiro proposed to adventure themselves in order to expound their views upon an obscure point in geography, concerning which it was more than probable that no single one of their auditors would be interested.

On the 20th January, 1518, the two men started

together to ride from Seville to Valladolid.[1] Aranda had arranged to go also. They joined the party of Doña Beatriz de Pacheco, Duchess de Arcos, and went by the Toledo road. Faleiro, still unforgiving, refused to travel in company with Aranda, and the latter, though he left at the same time, took another route.[2] He had begged them to await the arrival of the answer to the letter he had written to the Chancellor, but in vain. On his journey he met it, and finding that its tenor was in every way favourable to his protégés, he sent it on to them, together with a letter to say that he would wait for them at Medina del Campo, a town some thirty miles from Valladolid. The messenger met them as they were crossing the Sierra de Guadarrama, at Puerto de Herradon, and Faleiro's resentment had sufficiently cooled to permit of his acceding to Aranda's proposal. They met at the town indicated, and went to the same *posada*, and in a short time good relations were once more established between the trio.

They were now within easy distance of the court, but as yet Aranda had not found an opportunity of bringing forward a proposal he had doubtless long had in view. It was hardly to be supposed that such kindness as he had shown them—strangers, it must be remembered, who had no claim whatever upon him—should be entirely disinterested. Unaided and alone, it was in the highest degree unlikely that they would obtain the King's ear when business of much greater moment remained untouched ; but to Aranda, the most important official

---

[1] Francisco Faleiro, brother of Ruy Faleiro, went with them, and most probably Beatriz, Magellan's wife.

[2] The "Camino de la Plaza" (? the Estremadura road). *Vide* Magellan's evidence in Aranda's action already alluded to.

of the India House, much was possible. To ensure the success of their scheme, he had undertaken a long and wearisome journey, had exposed himself to frequent rudeness at Faleiro's hands, and was now about to spend still more time and pains in introducing them at court. His kindness, however, did not end here. At Seville he had offered them his purse, and he again renewed his offer before arriving in Valladolid. Faleiro, Magellan tells us, had actually taken advantage of it. And so, as the little party crossed the Duero, a few miles only from their destination, Aranda asked them if they would give him a share of the profits in the event of the King deciding to despatch an armada.

The request was not an unfair one, and Magellan's frank and generous character was ready to grant it at once. But it was different with Faleiro. Suspicion held in his mind the place that gratitude should have occupied. A careless half-assent given by his comrade again aroused his anger. Precisely what occurred it is not easy to make out from the conflicting accounts of the three interested parties. It seems that Aranda suggested that he should receive one-fifth of the profits as his share, but only upon condition that the armada was commissioned at the expense of the King. If the cost of it had to be borne by the two navigators and their friends, he neither asked for nor expected any return. Faleiro at first would not hear of anything being promised, and his brother was of the same opinion. Magellan, wiser and less mean, proposed that Aranda should have one-tenth. The ill-temper of Faleiro, however, was such as quickly to cause a rupture. Aranda took it with his usual good-humour. "If they did not wish to give him anything, he did not want anything, and whether they gave it him or not, he would still advance their cause to the best of his ability, since by so doing he did a service to his sovereign." With this he rode on alone to Valladolid, while Magellan and his comrade stopped at Simancas to talk the matter over.[1]

The result of their discussion was a resolve to offer Aranda an eighth share. Three days later they rode into Valladolid. Aranda came out to meet them, and took them to his inn, where they lay that night as his guests. Next day, anxious to be independent, they sought another *posada*. Aranda lost no time. He took them first to Sauvage, the Lord High Chancellor, who had succeeded to that post on the death of Ximenes, and then introduced them to the Cardinal Adrian of Utrecht and to the Bishop of Burgos. Finally, he procured them a personal interview with Charles V. himself. All this, we gather, was done upon the day following their arrival, or if not, within a very short period after it. Aranda had gone a long way towards proving his title as a man of business. He went still further by having a document ready for the two navigators to sign, in which they legally bound themselves to fulfil the oral promises of the day before. This agreement was executed on the 23rd February, 1518.[2] In it it is worthy

---

[1] Navarrete, vol. iv. p. xxxv. ; Medina, *op. cit.*, vol. i. p. 21 *et seq.*

[2] "Otorgamos é conoscemos," the text runs, "que todo el provecho é interese que hobieremos del descubrimiento de las tierras é islas que placiendo á Dios hemos de descubrir ó de hallar en las tierras é límites é demarcaciones del Rey nuestro Señor Don Carlos, que vos hayais la octava parte, é que vos daremos de todo el interese é provecho que dello nos suceda en dinero, ó en partimiento, ó en renta, ó en oficio, ó en otra cualquier cosa que sea." (Navarrete, vol. iv. p. 110; Medina, *op. cit.*, vol. i. p. 2.) The whole affair is instructive. Whatever their motives, interested or disinterested, those who aided the armadas in those days were apt to find their claims entirely ignored. The result

of note that Magellan has become Spanish even to his signature. Fernão de Magalhães has ceased to exist, and we make acquaintance for the first time with Fernando Magallanes.

Everything, so far, had gone well with the plans of the two friends, and Magellan might have been excused in feeling that success was within his grasp. Had he known more of those with whom he had to deal, he would not have been too sanguine. Three out of the four were Flemings, and the fourth—Fonseca, Bishop of Burgos—had made himself conspicuous for his bitter enmity to Columbus and other explorers of the New World. The Flemings were men of very unequal merit. Far superior to the others in ability and force of character was Charles's minister and guardian, Guillaume de Croy, Seigneur de Chièvres. A man of the court rather than of the schools, he nevertheless encouraged Charles in the study of history and the art of government, and, from his early appointment as his tutor, had contrived to gain extraordinary power over him. He exercised it in keeping his charge as much as possible away from Spanish influence, and, knowing and caring little for foreign affairs other than European, was not likely to interest himself much in projects of exploration. His avarice, which was boundless, was perhaps the only channel by which he might be approached. In this he was equalled, if not excelled, by Sauvage, the newly appointed successor to Ximenes, of whose character little more is known.[1]

of this venture of Aranda was a lengthy lawsuit, a loss of all the money he had advanced, and, as already mentioned, a public censure by the Consejo de las Indias.

[1] Of the corruption of Charles V.'s court at this time history has given us a full account. "Everything was venal and disposed of to

The third—Cardinal Adrian of Utrecht, afterwards Pope Adrian VI., who was made Charles's preceptor under De Croy—was a person of no real ability. Of low extraction, a theologian of a conventional type, and a person of weak character, his advancement must always be regarded with wonder. Nominally he had acted in conjunction with Ximenes as Regent of Castile, but the latter, though on the best of terms with his coadjutor, had never even pretended to consult him. His opinion upon an affair of this kind was of little importance. That of Fonseca, Bishop of Burgos, on the other hand—the last of the four—was of very different weight. As President of the India House, he took an assured position as an authority upon colonial matters. Less a prelate than a man of business, Las Casas tells us he was well suited for such work as the fitting out of armadas. His character, nevertheless, was a despicable one. His hatred of Columbus has already been referred to.[1] He thwarted Las Casas upon every point in his struggle to ameliorate the condition of the Indians.[2] Cortez he declared a traitor and a rebel, and it is more than probable that he instigated a plot to assassinate him.[3] To Balboa he was equally opposed. The most sanguine of project-mongers would have gone to him with something more than diffidence.

These were the men, together with a boy-sovereign of eighteen, on whom Magellan's future depended. It

the highest bidder." (Robertson, *Charles V.*, vol. ii. p. 58.) Peter Martyr, who, from his position, had special means of information, wrote that in ten months 1,100,000 ducats were remitted from Spain into the Low Countries. (Pet. Mart., *Opus Epist.*, Ep. 608.)

[1] Irving, *Columbus*, Appendix, No. 34.

[2] Herrera, *op. cit.*, Dec. ii. lib. ii. cap. iii.

[3] Herrera, *op. cit.*, Dec. iii. lib. iv. cap. iii.

might be imagined that support from the Flemings was an accidental possibility, but that none could be expected from Fonseca. Nothing is more certain, however, than the unforeseen. Whether the Bishop, venal and avaricious like his fellows, looked to the possibilities of future profit, or whether, having lost prestige from his opposition to the projects of Columbus, he was anxious to win it back over an expedition whose probable success he was wise enough to foresee, we do not know, but from the beginning he took up the cause of the two petitioners. From that moment its success was ensured.

Magellan came well prepared with arguments, animate and inanimate, to support his project. At the first formal meeting of the King's ministers he showed the letters from his friend Francisco Serrão, in which he told him that if he desired to get rich he should come to the Moluccas. He produced Vartema's account of his voyage to those islands; how they lay beneath the Equator, and far distant from Malacca. He showed a slave whom he had bought in the latter city, and who was a native of the Spice Islands, and a slave-girl from Sumatra, "who understood the tongues of many islands." "Other bids for credence did he make," we are told by Gomara,[1] "conjecturing that the land (*i.e.*, South America) turned westward, in the same manner as did that of Good Hope toward the east, since Juan de Solis had coasted it up to 40° S., with his course always more or less westerly. And since on the track thus taken no passage existed, he would coast the whole continent till he came to the cape which corresponds to the Cape of Good Hope, and would discover many new lands, and the way to the Spice Islands, as

---

[1] *Op. cit.*, cap. xci. p. 83.

he promised." Such an expedition, Gomara goes on to say, "would be long, difficult, and costly, and many did not understand it, and others did not believe in it; however, the generality of people had faith in him (Magellan) as a man who had been seven years in India and in the spice trade, and because, being Portuguese, he declared that Sumatra, Malacca, and other Eastern lands where spices could be found belonged to Castile." The arguments and projects of the two navigators were illustrated by means of a globe that Magellan had brought with him from Portugal.[1] Upon it were shown the continent, as he conceived it to exist, and his intended route. But, according to Herrera, the strait which it was his purpose to seek was intentionally omitted, in order that no one might anticipate him.[2] Finally, when his companion had finished his demonstrations, Faleiro took up the argument and proved to his audience that the coveted islands lay within the line of demarcation arranged by the Tordesillas *capitulacion* of 1494.

It was not to be expected that the project should meet with entire and instant approval. Some of the ministers pooh-poohed it; others took no interest in it. But upon further discussion the advice of Fonseca prevailed, and it was finally agreed to recommend the enterprise to the favourable consideration of the young King.

---

[1] A *planisphere* according to Argensola (*Conq. de las Molucas*, bk. i. p. 16).—"Vn planisferio dibuxado por Pedro Reynel."

[2] "Trahia Magellanes un globo bien pintado adonde se mostrana bien toda la tierra, y en el señaló el camino que pensava lleuar; y de industria dexó el estrecho en blanco, porque no se lo pudiessen saltear" (Herrera, Dec. ii. lib. ii. cap. xix.). *Dexar en blanco* should, of course, be rendered "to omit," but it is amusing to note that— probably from the presumed antithesis of the *bien pintado*—it has been literally translated by one author!

We can understand the delight with which the news of this resolution—tantamount to an actual order for the preparation of their armada—must have been received by Magellan and Faleiro. It only remained for them now to lay their proposals in due form before the King. Two ways—both commonly adopted at that time —were open to them. They could either fit out the expedition at their own cost, giving a certain percentage of the profits to the Crown, or, leaving the expenses to be borne by the King, sail as the captains of the ships, investing a certain fixed amount in articles of barter, and looking to their sovereign, upon their return, to confer upon them what benefits he thought fit.

Neither of the applicants was in the position to purchase and equip ships at his own expense. Faleiro was a poor student. Magellan, though a noble and a landowner, had profited no whit by his seven years' residence in the East. Most of those who survived the glorious uncertainties of that life made money. But Magellan was not as other men, and whatever sin might be laid to his charge, that of greed was not one. In the East, we are told, " perdeu a sua pobrêza "—he lost the little that he had. But there were plenty of rich and influential friends to assist him. His father-in-law, Diogo Barbosa, was a man of position, and Aranda was willing enough to place himself, purse and voice, at his disposal. Just at that moment, moreover, he had made an acquaintance which effectually banished all anxieties on the score of money. His acquaintance, who afterwards became his friend, was the great merchant Christopher de Haro.

The Haros were an Antwerp firm of traders—the Rothschilds of that day—who carried on an enormous

and most profitable business with both the East and
West Indies.   In the various towns of these countries
they had agents and clerks, who kept them informed
upon every point of interest in trade, politics, and geography.   Christopher de Haro resided in Lisbon, and
had an agreement with Portugal concerning the Guinea
trade.   For some reason which does not appear, he had
seven of his vessels sunk by the King's ships while on
the coast.   He sought indemnification, but his claim was
ignored, and feeling that it would be wiser to quit a
country where so little justice could be had, returned to
Spain, his native land.[1]   He had but recently arrived.
Magellan's project was the one above all others to commend itself to his favour.   It gave him an opportunity
of indirectly revenging himself upon Portugal, and at
the same time of making a very profitable speculation.
His ships had traded to the farthest East, had even
reached China,[2] and he knew what a monopoly of the
spice trade would mean.   He did not hesitate to offer all
the aid that lay in his power.

Fortified with such strong support, the two Portuguese
addressed their proposals formally to the King.[3]   They
fell under two heads—those made with the understanding that the King should charge himself with the entire

[1] It appears from the letter of Maximilian Transylvanus that Haro
(who, it may be remarked, was his father-in-law's brother) corrobo-
rated Magellan's evidence before the Council as to the position of the
Moluccas.   "Cæsari ostenderent (M. et Haro) . . . sinum magnum et
Sinarum populos ad Castellanorum nauigationem pertinere.   Hoc
item haberi longe certissimum, insulas quas Moluccas uocant . . . in
occidente Castellanorum contineri."

[2] "Et tandem Sinarum populis mercaturam fecerat."—*Letter of
Max. Transylvanus.*

[3] Arch. de Sevilla, Leg. 1º, pap. d. Maluco, 1519-47 ; *Medina*, vol. i.
p. 5 ; *Navarrete*, vol. iv. p. 113.

cost of the armada, and those suggested in the case of the expenses being borne by themselves.

In the first case they sought the concession of the following privileges :—That no other exploring expeditions should be sent out to the Spice Islands for a period of ten years, but that, if this could not be granted, they should have the right to a twentieth share of the resulting profits; that of all the lands and islands discovered by them a twentieth share of the annual profit should be theirs ; that in this and every other succeeding expedition they should be permitted to send goods to the value of a thousand ducats for trading purposes ; that in the event of the discovery of more than six islands, the *Señorio* of two should be conferred upon them ; that of this first expedition, they should have one-fifth of the net profits : and finally, that the title of Almirante should be conferred upon them.

In the case of the armada being commissioned and despatched at their own expense, they besought the King to grant them the trade and ownership (*señorio*) of all the lands discovered by them, and the privilege of the sole right of exploration and discovery for ten years. In return, one-fifth of the profits were to be handed to the Crown.

The document was returned, with comments under each section, to Magellan, leaving the matter still undecided ; but a few days later, on the 22nd March, 1518, a *capitulacion* was granted by Charles V. which definitely settled the terms under which the two explorers were to sail.[1]

They were as follows :—First, the King engaged with-

---

1 Seville Archives, Leg. 4°. See Navarreto, vol. iv. p. 116 ; Medina, vol. i. p. 8.

out delay to fit out an armada of five ships, provisioned for two years, and bearing a complement of 234 officers and crew. Under certain restrictions and reservations, he conceded the demand that no other explorers should be sent out for ten years.[1] He stipulated that no exploration should be prosecuted within the territories of his "dear and well-beloved uncle and brother the King of Portugal." Of all the profit arising from their discoveries, Magellan and Faleiro should receive the twentieth part. Henceforward they might be permitted to send goods to the value of a thousand ducats for trading purposes in every armada, but for this voyage they were to content themselves with one-fifth of the proceeds. If more than six islands should be discovered, they might choose two, from which they would be permitted to receive one-fifteenth of the profits. Of the lands discovered they were to have the title of governors or *adelantados*, which title was to be hereditary. Finally, it should rest with the King to appoint a factor, treasurer, *contador*, and clerks, who should be responsible for the accounts of the expedition.[2]

Accompanying this document was another, by which Magellan and his comrade were appointed Captains-general of the armada, entitled from that moment to

[1] Part of this passage is interesting :—"Pero entiendese que si Nos quiseriemos mandar descubrir ó dar licencia para ello á otras personas por la via del hueste, por las partes de las islas á tierra firme é á todas las otras partes que estan descubiertas hácia la parte que quisieremos *para buscar el estrecho de aquellos mares*, lo podamos mandar."

[2] By a *cedula* of 30th March of the following year (1519) Charles appointed Luis de Mendoza treasurer at a yearly salary of 60,000 maravedis, and Juan de Cartagena *Veedor-general* at 70,000 maravedis, and also captain of the third ship at 40,000 maravedis. On the 30th April Antonio de Coca was made *Contador* of the armada at 50,000 maravedis. Roughly speaking, 1000 maravedis were equivalent to 11s. 6d. of our money.

draw pay at the rate of 50,000 maravedis per annum from the Casa de Contratacion at Seville.

Charles, who in his bid for popularity had succeeded but ill with the Castilians, now resolved to visit Aragon. Summoning the Cortes of that country to meet him in Zaragoza, he marched thither in the beginning of April. Upon the way he stopped at Aranda de Duero, where his brother Ferdinand was then living, a prince so great a favourite with the Spaniards that the King's design—which was to send him out of the country—was no ill-advised step. But, in spite of the many intrigues and difficulties in which he found himself involved, and the barrier to external influences interposed by his Flemish courtiers, Charles found time to interest himself in the affairs of the future expedition. Magellan and Faleiro had followed the court, and being in constant communication with the King, were enabled to escape the delays which must otherwise inevitably have arisen. By certain *cedulas* issued by Charles at this time the pay of the two captains was raised to 146,000 maravedis, and they were granted a sum of 30,000 maravedis to defray initial expenses. The privilege of appointing a pilot was given to them, with the promise that, if approved by the Casa de Contratacion, he should have the title of "*piloto real*" conferred upon him. Not less welcome was a grant to the heirs of either navigator, in the event of his death, of all the privileges and profits to which the latter was entitled.[1]

Although charged to proceed to Seville in order that

---

[1] This *cedula*, dated from Aranda de Duero, April 17, 1518, was that upon which his relation, Lorenzo de Magalhães, afterwards (1567) founded his claim to Magellan's estate. *Vide* Medina, *op. cit.*, vol. ii. p. 356.

they might place themselves *en rapport* with the officials of the India House and forward the preparation of the armada, Magellan and Faleiro were led to defer their journey. Leaving Aranda de Duero, Charles proceeded by Calatayud to Zaragoza, into which city he made a formal entry on the 15th May. The two friends followed in his train, for a check had lately come upon the progress of their scheme. Against want of money and interest, against the apathy or opposition of those in power, they had fought for months, and fought successfully; but now they were confronted by an obstacle not less serious, though long foreseen—the silent intrigues and loudly-expressed remonstrances of the Court of Portugal.

CHAPTER V.

PREPARATIONS FOR THE VOYAGE.

It could hardly be otherwise than that the news of
Magellan's approaching voyage should reach Portugal.
The defection of two such well-known navigators, and the
fact that they took others with them "sick with a like
disorder," could not be passed unnoticed, and the subsequent movements of the Consejo de las Indias at Seville
were, no doubt, fully reported to Dom Manoel by the
Portuguese "factor" resident in that city. But it
happened that a special circumstance brought the matter
still more prominently forward—so prominently, in fact,
that, advanced as were the preparations, the expedition
was within an ace of being countermanded.

The question of the marriage of Dom Manoel to Doña
Leonor, sister of Charles V., was at that time under
consideration,[1] and Alvaro da Costa, the ambassador of
Portugal at the court of Spain,[2] was charged with the
arrangement of the alliance. The treaty was concluded
at Zaragoza on the 22nd May, 1518, and ratified at the
same place on the 16th July. It was the very period

---

[1] Eleanor became the third wife of Dom Manoel in November 1518,
although at that time only twenty years of age, and thirty years his
junior. After his death in 1521, she married Francis I. of France,
who also predeceased her.

[2] Alvaro da Costa was chamberlain and Guarda-rôupa Môr to Dom
Manoel.

when Charles was most taken up with the project of
Magellan, and Da Costa, naturally, was brought much
in contact both with the affair and the principals concerned.   They appear to have caused him far more
anxiety than the marriage.   From a letter to his sovereign, still existing in the Torre do Tombo, we get a
glimpse of the means he employed to frustrate them.
It was not the first time that the Portuguese, having
been led by their ignorance and folly wilfully to reject
one of the world's greatest chances, fought tooth and
nail to counteract its outcome.   When Columbus reached
the shelter of the Tagus upon his first return from the
New World, it was suggested by some of those at court
that much future trouble with Spain would be obviated
by his assassination.   Not that these methods were confined to Portugal.   The value of each discovery, owing
perhaps to the rapidity with which it followed upon a
previous one, was so little understood, that either of the
two countries was ready at a moment's notice to take up
an attitude of protestation, if not of something worse.

At first Da Costa confined himself to simple dissuasion.
In the course of various interviews with Magellan, he
told the latter that, if he persisted in his enterprise, not
only would he sin against God and his King, but would
for ever stain the honour of his name, and, moreover, that
he would be the cause of dissension between two kings
who would otherwise, by the approaching marriage, still
further strengthen the ties of friendship which already
existed between them.   Magellan's answer was that his
first duty was to his King; that he had pledged his word
to him, and that he too would sin against his honour and
his conscience should he break it.   To Da Costa's temp-
tation of reward if he went back to Portugal he turned

equally a deaf ear. Failing thus both in threats and persuasion, the Portuguese ambassador turned his attention to the King's ministers. The Cardinal, Adrian of Utrecht, weak and vacillating, half fearful of consequences and half mistrustful of the success of the expedition, played into his hands. "The Cardinal," writes Alvaro to his sovereign, "is the best thing here."[1] Chièvres, too, was hardly against him; but Fonseca's convictions were so strong and his influence so great, that it was impossible to ignore them. Again foiled, Alvaro wrote to Dom Manoel. The news was received with renewed irritation, and discussed in various juntas and conselhos. Some advised that Magellan should be bribed to return; others were against this, as affording a bad precedent. There were not wanting those who advised that he should be put out of the way. One of them was a bishop. Lafitau, in his *Conquêtes des Portugais*, hides, as a Jesuit, the name of this honourable counsellor;[2] Faria and De Goes give it to us for eternal obloquy—it was Ferdinand Vasconcellos, Bishop of Lamego, who afterwards became Archbishop of Lisbon.[3]

The news of his contemplated assassination reached Magellan while still in Zaragoza, but he paid but slight attention to it, and pursued his daily avocations, although exposing himself as little as possible, and " when night surprised them in the house of the Bishop of Burgos," Herrera tells us " the latter sent his servants to guard

---

[1] "Eu, senhor, o tynha ja bem praticado com o cardeal que he a milhor cousa que qua ha, e lhe nom parece bem este negocio."—*Letter of Da Costa*, Torre do Tombo, fav. 18, maç. 8, num. 38.

[2] Lafitau, *op. cit.*, vol. ii. liv. viii. p. 35.

[3] Faria y Sousa, *Europa Portugueza*, pt. iv. cap. i. tom. ii. p. 543. " O bispo dixe que seu parecer era que o mandasse el Rei chamar e lhe fezesse merces, ou o mandasse matar."—*Goes*, 4ta. pte. cap. xxxvii.

them home."[1] Of Faleiro they made little account.
His odd manner and uncertain temper led people to the
conclusion that he was not quite of sound mind.[2]

There were other reasons besides those of caution
which called for the departure of the two navigators from
Zaragoza. Their presence was needed in Seville. The
Casa de Contratacion, as a body, had never been very
favourable to their scheme. Some jealousy with Aranda
possibly stood in the way ; possibly the officials really did
not believe in its chances of success. But they opposed
it, if not actively, at least with a dead wall of difficulties
which rendered the future prospects of the expedition
none of the brightest. Charles, with a quiet but firm
hand, now put all these obstacles aside. In a letter
written on the 20th July, 1518, he informed the India
House that it was his intention to carry out the proposed expedition ; that certain moneys lately arrived
from the West Indies were to be used for the purpose of
defraying the expenses ; and, finally, that he desired the
armada should be fitted out in every way in conformity
with the ideas and wishes of Magellan and Faleiro.[3]
But at the same time that he wrote the letter, anxious
to hasten these preparations, he intimated his wish that
the two captains should depart for Seville without delay.

In order to mark still further his sense of the importance of the expedition and of his confidence in those

---

[1] Herrera, Dec. ii. lib. ii. cap. xxi.

[2] "Polo bacharel nom dou eu muito que anda cas fora de seu
syso."—*Letter of Alvaro.*

[3] " Y que de los 5000 pesos de oro que habian llegado para S. M.
de la Isla Fernandina gastasen hasta seis mil ducados ó lo que fuese
necesario conforme á dicho memorial, á vista, contentamiento, y
parecer de los mismos Magallanes y Falero."—*Arch. de Seville. Vide*
Navarrete, vol. iv. p. 123.

to whom he had intrusted its command, Charles signified his intention of conferring upon Magellan and his comrade the honour of the Order of Santiago. They were decorated with the cross of Comendador in the presence of the Council, and at the same time the conditions of the agreement concluded at Valladolid on the 22nd March were formally confirmed.[1] A few days later—at the end of July—the two Comendadores left the court for Seville.

In answer to the remonstrances expressed by Alvaro da Costa, Charles had written to Dom Manoel to explain the object of Magellan's voyage. In his letter he assured his future brother-in-law that nothing should be done in any way to the detriment of Portugal, and that if he had not complied with his wish, it was because the explorations proposed would not be carried beyond the limits of Spanish waters.[2] His reasoning was in vain. Alvaro renewed his complaints and remonstrances, and Chievres being ill, succeeded in obtaining a private interview with the King. The sum and substance of it he gives in the letter addressed to Dom Manoel, and dated from Zaragoza, September 28th, 1518, to which allusion has already been made.

✠

" SIRE,—Concerning Ferdinand Magellan's affair, how much I have done and how I have laboured, God knows, as I have written you at length ; and now, Chievres being ill, I have spoken upon the subject very strongly to the King, putting before him all the inconveniences that in this case may arise, and also representing to him what an ugly matter it was, and how unusual, for one king to receive the subjects of another king, his friend, contrary to his wish,—a thing unheard of among cavaliers,

---

¹ Horrera, Dec. ii. lib. iv. cap. ix.

² Argensola, *Anales de Aragon*, i. caps. lvii. and lxxix.

and accounted both ill-judged and ill-seeming. Yet I had just
put your Highness and your Highness's possessions at his service
in Valladolid at the moment that he was harbouring these persons against your will.   I begged him to consider that this was
not the time to offend your Highness, the more so in an affair
which was of such little importance and so uncertain ; and that
he would have plenty of subjects of his own and men to make
discoveries when the time came, without availing himself of
those malcontents of your Highness, whom your Highness could
not fail to believe likely to labour more for your dis-service than
for anything else ; also that his Highness had had until now so
much to do in discovering his own kingdoms and dominions, and
in settling them, that he ought not to turn his attention to these
new affairs, from which dissensions and other matters, which
may well be dispensed with, may result.   I also represented to
him the bad appearance that this would have on the year and
at the very moment of the marriage,—the ratification of friendship and affection.   And also that it seemed to me that your
Highness would much regret to learn that these men asked
leave of him to return,[1] and that he did not grant it, the which
are two faults—the receiving them contrary to your desire, and
the retaining them contrary to their own.   And I begged of him,
both for his own and for your Highness's sake, that he would do
one of two things—either permit them to go, or put off the affair
for this year, by which he would not lose much ; and means
might be taken whereby he might be obliged, and your Highness might not be offended, as you would be were this scheme
carried out.

"He was so surprised, sire, at what I told him, that I also was
surprised ; but he replied to me with the best words in the world,
saying that on no account did he wish to offend your Highness,
and many other good words ; and he suggested that I should
speak to the Cardinal, and confide the whole matter to him.

"I, sire, had already talked the matter over with the Cardinal,
who is the best thing here, and who does not approve of the
business, and he promised me to do what he could to get off the
affair.   He spoke to the King, and thereupon they summoned the
Bishop of Burgos, who is the chief supporter of the scheme.
And with that certain two men of the Council succeeded in

---

[1] This statement, there is every reason to believe, was a pure fiction
of Da Costa.

making the King believe that he did your Highness no wrong, since he only ordered exploration to be made within his own limits, and far from your Highness's possessions ; and that your Highness should not take it ill that he should make use of two of your subjects—men of no great importance—while your Highness himself employed many Spaniards. They adduced many other arguments, and at last the Cardinal told me that the Bishop and the others insisted so much upon the subject, that the King could not now alter his determination.

"While Chievres was well, I kept representing this business to him, as I have just said, and much more. He lays the blame upon those Spaniards who have pushed the King on. Withal he will speak to the King, but on former occasions I besought him much on this subject, and he never came to any determination, and thus, I think, he will act now. It seems to me, sire, that your Highness might get back Fernão de Magalhães, which would be a great blow to these people. As for the bachelor,[1] I do not count him for much, for he is half crazy.

.　　.　　.　　.　　.　　.　　.　　.　　.

"Do not let your Highness think that I went too far in what I said to the King, for beside the fact that all I said was true, these people do not perceive anything, nor has the King liberty up to now to do anything of himself, and on that account his actions may be less regarded (*por iso se deue de syntyr menos suas cousas*). May the Lord increase the life and dominions of your Highness to His holy service. From Saragoça, Tuesday night, the 28th day of September.

"I kiss the hands of your Highness.

"ALUARO DA COSTA."[2]

This letter was not the last of its kind, for though the protestations of the Portuguese ceased for the time being, they were again renewed upon the removal of the court to Barcelona. Nor did they end until Magellan

[1] Ruy Faleiro.

[2] Arch. da Torre do Tombo, Gav. 18, Maço 8, No. 38. The letter is given in the original Portuguese by De Barros Arana, p. 181, and also by Lord Stanley in his *First Voyage.* Navarrete (vol. iv. p. 123) gives an excerpt, and Medina (*op. cit.*, vol. i. p. 16) a translation into Spanish.

finally weighed anchor at S. Lucar de Barrameda, and started on his voyage.

We must return to Seville, whither the two newly-made knights had meanwhile arrived. Their presence was regarded by Fonseca as likely to smooth the difficulties made by the Casa de Contratacion. This body, although definitely instructed by the King's *cedula* in March, as we have seen, demurred somewhat to the arrangement therein contained, and wrote again asking for a confirmation of a despatch signed by the Chancellor of Burgundy,[1] expressing themselves, however, as ready to fulfil the King's orders " if we have at the time money of his Highness at our disposal." The reply was Charles's letter of July 20th already mentioned, charging them to fit out the fleet according to the ideas and wishes of its commanders. It is probable that they themselves carried this document and presented it in person.[2] But whatever may have been the way it reached its destination, its effect was magical. "We are greatly pleased," write the officials, "at the arrangement concluded; . . . it is a very honourable and advantageous undertaking, as we inform the Bishop of Burgos."[3] They add that a certain sum of money had arrived from India, and ask whether it should be used for the expenses. Everything seemed to be *couleur de rose.* But even at the hands of the Casa de Contratacion Magellan and his friend had yet to experience difficulties and unpleasantnesses, and to learn that the King of Spain—despite the lengthy titles heading his *cedulas*—was not all-powerful.

[1] This letter is dated May 31, 1518. *Vide* Lord Stanley's *First Voyage*, p. xxxiii.

[2] " Recibimos la de V.A. de 20 de julio *con el Comendador Magallanes.*" *Vide* Navarrete, vol. iv. p. lxxvi.

[3] Navarrete, *idem.*

The altered attitude of the India House, together with
the energy of Magellan, gave an impulse to the work of
preparation which must have gone far towards compen-
sating the great navigator for the months of disappointment and heart-burnings through which he had passed.
Now his way seemed clear before him, and he worked
with double vigour, writing letters to the King and the
Bishop of Burgos to inform them of the progress of
affairs. At the outset, good-natured and a hater of
quarrels, he had ceded to the fitful temper and morose
disposition of his comrade, and permitted him to take
the lead; but when it came to practical work—to the
fitting out of a fleet and to the choice of his men, then
the experience gained by years of service in the East
necessarily placed Magellan in a position of authority
which was beyond the power of Faleiro to question. So
long as they had to bow the knee in kings' houses,
petitioners and place-seekers, they were equals; but
upon the ship's deck in Seville, away from the flattery-
laden air of the court and almost within sound of the
sea, there was little doubt as to which meant to command. And so, little by little, it came about that
Faleiro, albeit nominally on the same footing—the "*conjunta persona*" with Magellan—fell insensibly into the
second place.

The preparations, then, were pushed on with all speed.
The King, in his letter of July 20th, 1518, had informed
the officials of the Casa de Contratacion that since so
many articles were to be obtained both better and cheaper
in Biscay, he had sent thither to purchase them. Other
materials were apparently brought from Flanders.[1] The

---

[1] Navarrete, iv. p. 123.

ships, as we learn from documents in the Seville archives,[1]
were all bought at Cadiz.   The duty of purchasing them
devolved upon Aranda, who was probably totally lacking
in the technical knowledge necessary for such a responsible task, for we learn from the Portuguese factor
Alvarez, then residing in Seville, that they were not in the
best condition. " They are very old and patched," he says,
" . . . and I would be sorry to sail even for the Canaries in them, for their ribs are as soft as butter."[2]   In
Charles's original *capitulacion* to the two captains he
had promised that two should be of 130 tons, two of 90,
and the fifth of 60.[3]   Those obtained for the expedition
were tolerably close to the promised tonnage, being in
the aggregate only twenty tons short.

The names and burden of the five vessels were as
follows :—*Santo Antonio*, 120 tons; *Trinidad*, 110 tons;
Concepcion, 90 tons; *Victoria*, 85 tons; *Santiago*, 75
tons.[4]   What they were, how rigged and masted, we do not
know.   From a few chance words of Herrera[5] we learn
that the poop and forecastle of each was provided with

---

[1] *Papeles del Maluco*, leg. i.   *Vide* Navarrete, iv. pp. 162, 3.

[2] " Sam muy velhos e Remēdados porque os vy em montu corregeer,
ha onze messes que se correjeram e está na agoa agora calefetam asy
nagoa eu entrey neles alguas vezes e certifico a vosa alteza que ṵa
canaria navegaria de maa vontade neles, porq' seus liames sam de
sebe."—*Letter of Alvarez to the King of Portugal.   Vide* Arana, p. 184
et seq.

[3] Navarrete, iv. p. 119.

[4] It is difficult to assign an exact value to these " toneles de porte."
They may perhaps be taken as roughly representing the ordinary tons
of the present day.   Navarrete (vol. iv. p. 3) says that *toneles* and
toneladas must not be confused.   "The Biscayans reckoned formerly
by *toneles* and the Sevillians of the Indian trade by *toneladas*, which
measures are in the relation of five to six—ten *toneles* making twelve
toneladas."   In Nuñez's Dictionary, however, the latter measure is
said to be equivalent to two *toneles*.

[5] *Herrera*, Dec. ii. lib. ix. cap. xi., and Dec. iii. lib. iv. cap. ii.

high *obras muertas*—with castles, in short—as was not unusual at that period. Such vessels are seen in the illustrations of De Bry, and indeed in Columbus's own sketch of the *Oceanica Classis*. It is, however, nearly certain that all the ships in Magellan's fleet were decked, while but one of the three which the discoverer of America took on his memorable voyage was thus advantaged.

The ships once obtained, Magellan occupied himself unremittingly in overhauling them and putting them in a seaworthy condition before starting upon his long and dangerous voyage. It was when engaged in this work, on the 22nd October, that an incident occurred which once more brought forcibly before him the fact that the emissaries of Portugal were still at work to thwart his plans. He had no longer Alvaro da Costa at hand to tell him that he was a renegade to his face, and to connive at his assassination in secret, but his place was taken by an individual even more unscrupulous—Sebastian Alvarez, the factor of the King of Portugal at Seville, and it was probably at his instigation that the incident arose.

On the day in question, Magellan had taken advantage of the tide to careen the *Trinidad* at an early hour. At daybreak he ordered four flags bearing his own arms to be placed upon the four capstans. In this position it was the custom always to carry the captain's flag, while the royal ensign and that of the vessel itself were flown at the mast-head. On this occasion these latter were not hoisted, having been sent to be painted, and Magellan, engaged with his work, had not noticed their absence.

As the work proceeded, a gradually increasing crowd of idlers watched its progress. It was maliciously suggested by some one that the capstan flags bore the arms

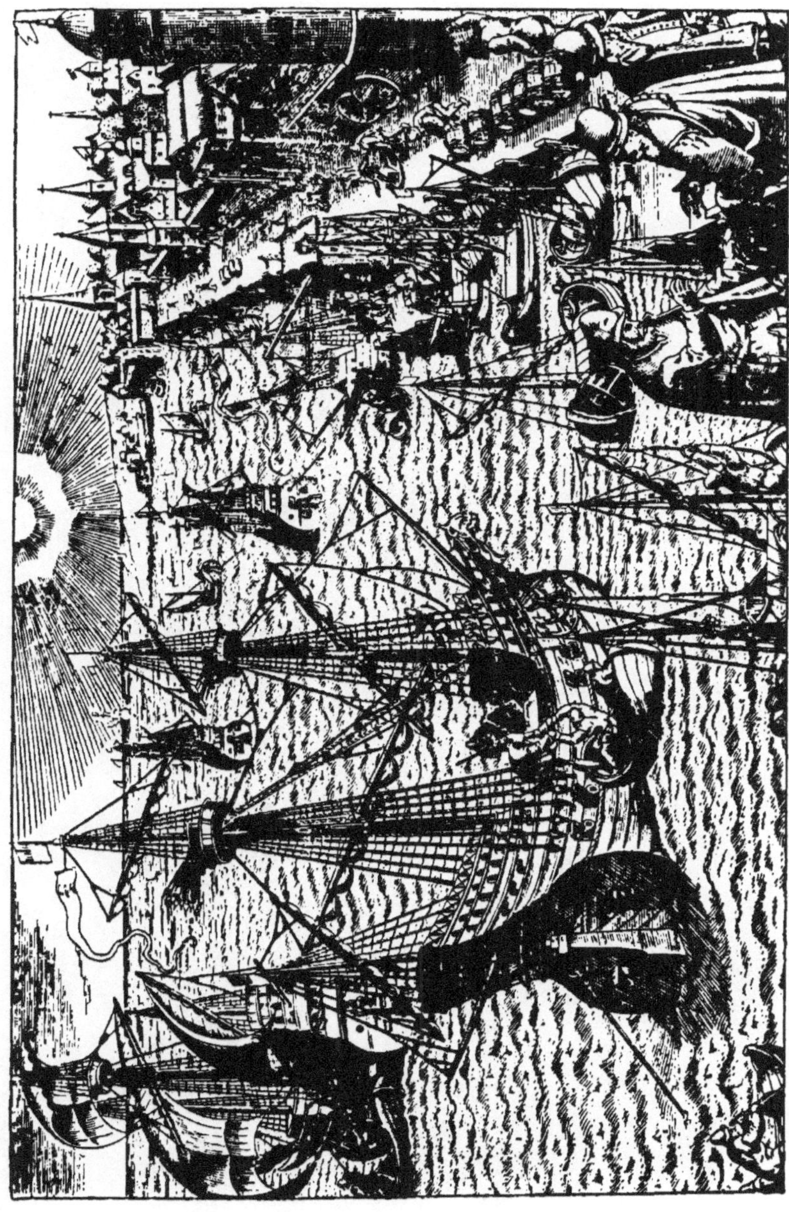

of the King of Portugal, and, in the midst of considerable disturbance and murmuring, an alcalde arrived upon the scene. Without consulting Magellan, he incited the bystanders to tear them down. The crew now summoned their captain, till then engaged below, who explained to the official that " the arms were not those of the King of Portugal; that they were his arms, and that he was a vassal of the King of Spain." Sailor and aristocrat, Magellan was not one to bandy words with an alcalde, and he returned to his work without further discussion. The alcalde was not so easily satisfied, and insisted upon the removal of the obnoxious flags, and Matienzo,[1] the chief official of the India House, who arrived at this juncture, advised Magellan to yield for the sake of calming the mob. He agreed, but the moment was a bitter one for him, for among the crowd he recognised an agent of the King of Portugal,[2] whom he felt to have been the instigator of the riot. Meanwhile the alcalde had gone in search of the port-captain (*teniente del almirante*), whose appearance was the signal for a renewal of the tumult. Arriving on the scene, he called upon his men to " arrest the Portuguese captain who flew the ensign of the King of Portugal," at the same time roughly demanding of the Comendador " where were the flags, and why were they hoisted upon the capstans ? " Magellan's answer was that he was not

---

[1] The learned doctor, Sancho Matienzo, a well-known person at that period, was a Canon of Seville and a personal friend of Magellan, who appointed him as his executor in his will of August 24th, 1519.

[2] " Puesto que me era afrenta hacerlo por estar alli presente un caballero del Rey de Portugal, que por su mandado vino á esta ciudad á contratar conmigo que me volviese á Portugal, ó á hacer otra cosa que no fuese mi provecho."—*Letter of Magellan to Charles V.*, 24th October, 1518 ; *vide* Navarrete, iv. p. 125. There is little doubt that the *caballero* in question was Sebastian Alvarez.

responsible to him for his actions. The port-captain instantly called upon the *alguaciles* to arrest him, but Matienzo cautioned the irate official that if he laid hands upon the King's captain he would have to answer for it to the King. His interference so enraged the *alguaciles* and companions of the *teniente*, that they rushed upon him with their drawn swords, threatening to kill him. Seeing the highest official of the India House thus treated, Magellan's people—or such of them, he naively remarks, as had been paid in advance—thought it best to decamp.

The ship was at the moment in a somewhat dangerous position. Magellan, ever ready of resource, saw in this fact a means of strengthening his hand. He threatened to leave it, and to make the officials responsible for any damage that might occur. Already conscious, perhaps, of having gone too far with Matienzo, the port-captain thought it best to alter his tactics, and he eventually left the ship, contenting himself with arresting some of the crew and disarming others. The *teniente del asistente*, to whom Magellan had appealed for support, refused to interfere.

Two days later Magellan wrote a full account of the affair to Charles V., begging him to order a searching inquiry to be made. The fearlessness and independence of the letter is characteristic of the man. He asks for full satisfaction, reminding Charles that " the insult was offered not to Ferdinand Magellan, but to one of your Highness's captains." He requests that the principal actors in the *émeute* may be punished, and that for the future he may be secured against the recurrence of such acts of violence.[1] We have not Charles's answer, but

---

[1] See Magellan's letter, already referred to. Herrera also gives a detailed account of the occurrence (Dec. ii. lib. iv. cap. ix.) ; and Argensola also refers to it in the *Anales de Aragon*, lib. i. cap. lxxix.

we have Herrera's account of it. The King expressed
his regret at the incident, and his approval of Matienzo's
action.   He censured the *teniente del asistente* and the
Sevillians for refusing to aid Magellan, and ordered the
officials who had taken the chief part in the disturbance
to be severely punished.   His prompt action and readiness
to support the two Portuguese on this occasion went far
towards smoothing their difficulties for some time to come.

In January, 1519, Charles V. left Zaragoza. He
arrived at Lerida in the beginning of February, and
entered Barcelona on the 15th of that month.   Fonseca,
the staunch friend and supporter of the explorers, accompanied him, and kept their undertaking and its many
needs constantly before his notice.   Fearing anticipation
by Portugal, he counselled the prompt despatch of the
fleet at all costs.   At Seville the two treasurers of the
armada, Alonso Gutierres and Cristobal de Haro—the
great East India merchant already mentioned—were
doing their best to forward the preparations.   Money
was greatly needed.   The coffers of the India House
were well-nigh exhausted, and Charles, who regarded
Spain as the milch-cow of the Netherlands, was not
likely, even if it lay within his power, to replenish them
from his own pocket.   At this juncture Haro offered
his purse, and we learn from the letter of Alvarez, by
which private information was given to the King of
Portugal of the affairs of the armada, that he advanced
four thousand ducats, the fifth part of the whole cost.[1]
Haro himself claims to have given 1,616,781 maravedis.[2]

---

[1] "A q'nta pte desta armaçã he de xpovã do haroo q nela meteo iiij.
ducados."—*Vide* Arana, *op. cit.*, p. 189.

[2] Medina, *op. cit.*, vol. ii. p. 235.   It was not a remunerative venture.   Haro met with the not uncommon fate attending those who at

IIis coadjutor, Gutierres, also aided, and, with permission of the Bishop of Burgos, other Seville merchants joined in the venture. In this manner the entire cost of the armada, 8,751,125 maravedis, or £5032, was finally defrayed.[1]

From the court in Barcelona the King's *cedulas* were now despatched in quick succession. Writing on the 10th March, 1519, he grants to the merchants who have advanced money the right of investing an equal sum in the three expeditions next succeeding.[2] On the 30th of the same month Luis de Mendoza was appointed trea-surer to the fleet, with a salary of 60,000 maravedis per annum during the voyage. At the same time Juan de Cartagena was gazetted captain of the third ship and *Veedor-general*, for which he was to receive pay at the rate of 110,000 maravedis. Gaspar de Quesada was nominated captain of the fourth or fifth ship on the 6th April, and a few days later Antonio de Coca was made *Contador* of the armada at 50,000 maravedis.

On the 18th April Charles orders that, ready or not ready, the fleet must sail before the end of May, and on

that period were unwise enough to put their trust in princes. After an interminable lawsuit with the Crown, he at length got back his money, with no interest or profit whatsoever, *after an eighteen years' delay*. He had also been unfortunate enough to invest a nearly equal sum in the succeeding expedition, which was also returned under the same conditions. *Vide* Medina, vol. ii. p. 292. Others who had lent money were not even so lucky as Haro. Twenty years after the expe-dition sailed the plaint of Antonio Fucar (Fugger) and Company was brought before the courts. They had advanced 10,000 ducats, and had not had a maravedi. But they were Germans, and the Consejo had no hesitation. It declared the Crown free and quit of all liability, "and from henceforth we decree that the said Antonio Fucar y Ca. shall for ever hold their peace!"—*Idem.* vol. ii. p. 324.

[1] *Herrera*, Dec. ii. lib. iv. cap. ix. p. 129.

[2] Navarrete, *op. cit.* iv. p. xlvii.

the following day issues a species of sailing orders, charging the officers and crew " to defer to the opinion and orders of Magellan, and to proceed straight to the ' spicery.' " [1] The despatch of a second armada by the same route appears to have been early contemplated, for in a *cedula* of the 30th April, Francisco, brother of Ruy Faleiro, is assigned a salary of 35,000 maravedis to reside in Seville and take in hand the affairs of the fleet " which was to be sent after that of which Magellan and his brother were in command."   A week later, May 5th, the King desires that the number of the crew of the squadron should be limited to two hundred and thirty-five men, and directs that, if possible, it may further be reduced.   It was left to Magellan, " por cuanto tiene mas experiencia," to choose his men. The captains were directed to declare in writing the course they meant to take, and the rules to be followed in making observations.   At the same date Charles granted certain *entretenimientos* to Magellan's wife, ordering that during the voyage her husband's pay should be received by her. He also offered to reward the pilots and masters according to their services upon their return to Spain ; but whether he yielded to the petition of the former to raise their pay to three thousand maravedis per mensem does not appear.

Such is the gist of some of the many *cedulas* that the labour of Muñoz disinterred from the mass of papers in the Seville archives.   The last, and most lengthy of all, was despatched from Barcelona on the 8th May, and

---

[1] " Pã q los del armada sigan el parecer y determynaciõ de Magallañs pã q ants y pᵐᵒ q a otra pt vayã a la especerya." This document appears to have fallen into the hands of the Portuguese in Ternate when Antonio de Brito seized the *Trinidad*. See Lord Stanley's *First Voyage*, p. xxxiii., and Appendix, p. xii.

contains the most minute instructions for the voyage. So minute and diffuse are they indeed, that a bare reference to the subjects touched upon can only be given here. The document is divided into seventy-four heads, and might with advantage have been furnished with an index. The captains are cautioned not to overload their ships, and to keep the orifice of their pumps well out of the water. They are to communicate every day if the weather permit, and to follow certain rules with regard to lights at night, while in the case of a ship getting lost full details are given as to the course to be pursued. There are instructions about landing in unknown countries, about making friends with the chiefs, about dealing with " Moros," about prizes, and about the distribution of prize-money. The last article is specially interesting as showing the comparative value of each rank in the service at that time. The captains are specially enjoined to treat their men *amorosamente*, to personally visit the wounded and the sick, and to prevent the surgeon from taking any fees. Stringent regulations are given with regard to the rations, which are to be issued every other day, and from time to time to be carefully inspected. A dozen or more of the seventy-four heads relate to trade and barter; others guide the morals of the crew, who are not to swear, and not to play games of chance, such as dice and cards, "for from such often arise evil, and scandal, and strife." Insult and violence offered to women were to be severely punished, but a tolerable amount of liberty appears to have been allowed to the crew, and every one was permitted to write home as he thought fit. There are wise regulations about guarding against fire, and still wiser anent building houses in the tropics, counselling their erection in good air, on the slopes of the mountains, and not on marshy ground or shut-in valleys. The document ends with a long list of the "*quintaladas*" permitted to the different members of the ship's company.[1] Finally, while the King orders that "under no condition whatsoever shall they touch at or explore land, or do anything within the boundaries of the most Serene King of Portugal," he nevertheless takes care to direct that, in the case of a Portuguese ship being found in Spanish waters, she should be called upon to quit the neighbourhood and to surrender her cargo.

Charles's strong support with regard to the *émeute* about the flags on the 22nd October had rendered inadvisable, for the time being, at all events, any interference on the part of the agents of the King of Portugal. It is possible that another reason existed. Gomara[2] tells us that at one time Dom Manoel was not greatly disturbed about Magellan's projected voyage, being persuaded in his own mind that there was no other route to the Spice Islands save and excepting that taken by his own ships. But as the months passed, and the armada approached completion, this faith became less secure, and before long another attempt was made to persuade Magellan to relinquish the expedition. The author was Sebastian Alvarez, the Portuguese factor at Seville, and the instigator of the disturbance just mentioned. A letter written by him to Dom Manoel on the 18th July, 1519, is still existing. It throws a flood of light upon the various plots surrounding the explorers.

---

[1] The *quintalada* was the free freight allowed to officers and crew. It was permitted to every one, from captain to cabin-boy, and varied from 8000 to 75 lbs. according to rank. It paid a duty of one-twenty-fourth to the Crown.

[2] Gomara, *op. cit.*, cap. xci. p. 83.

After acknowledging two letters from his royal
master, from which it may be concluded that he had
not failed to keep him well informed with regard to
Seville affairs, he goes on to acquaint him of the arrival
of Cristobal de Haro and Juan de Cartagena, bringing
instructions more or less at variance with those of
Magellan.   Upon this, he says, the officials of the Casa
de Contratacion summoned the latter, and demanded to
know, amongst other things, why he took so many Portuguese with him.   Magellan answered that, as captain
of the fleet, he should do as he chose, without rendering
an account to them.   High words passed.   The factors
of the India House ordered pay to be given to all
except the Portuguese, and, charged with the complaints
of both parties, a messenger was despatched at once to
Charles V. to obtain his decision.   Having put Dom
Manoel in possession of these details, Alvarez thus
proceeds :—

"And seeing the affair begun, and that it was a convenient
season for me to say what your Highness commanded,[1] I went to
Magellan's house, where I found him filling baskets and chests
with preserved victuals and other things.   I pressed him, pre-
tending that, as I found him thus engaged, it seemed to me that
his evil design was settled, and since this would be the last word
I should have with him, I desired to bring back to his memory
how many times, as a good Portuguese and his friend, I had
spoken to him, dissuading him from the great mistake he was
committing.   And after asking pardon of him, lest he should be
offended at what I was about to say, I reminded him how many
times I had spoken to him, and how well he had always replied
to me, and that from his replies I always hoped that in the end
he would not go, to the so great injury of your Highness.   And
what I always told him was, that the path he had chosen was
beset with as many dangers as the wheel of Saint Catherine, and

---

[1] Hence it appears certain that Alvarez acted under the King's
orders.

that he ought to leave it and take that which led to Coimbra, and return to his native land and to the favour of your Highness, at whose hands he would always receive benefits.   In our conversation I brought before him all the dangers I could think of, and the mistakes he was making.   He said to me that now, as an honourable man, he could only follow the path he had chosen. I replied that unduly to gain honour, and to gain it with infamy, was neither wisdom nor honour, but rather lack of wisdom and honour, for he might be sure that the chief Castilians of this city in speaking of him held him for a low person and of no breeding, since, to the dis-service of his true king and lord, he embarked in such an undertaking, and so much the more since it was set going, arranged, and petitioned for by him.   And he might be certain that he was considered as a traitor, engaging himself thus in opposition to your Highness's country.   Here he replied to me that he saw the mistake he made, but that he hoped to observe your Highness's service, and by his voyage to be of assistance to you.   I told him that whoever should praise him for such an expression of opinion did not understand it; for unless he touched your Highness's possessions how was he to discover what he said ?   Besides, it was a great injury to the revenues of your Highness, which would affect the whole kingdom and every class of people, and it was a far more virtuous thought that inspired him when he told me that if your Highness ordered him to return to Portugal that he would do it without further guarantee of reward, and that when you granted none to him, there was Serradossa, and seven yards of grey cloth, and some gall-nut beads open to him.[1]   So then it seemed to me that his heart was true as far as his honour and conscience were concerned.   Our conversation was so long of duration that I cannot write it.

"At this juncture, sire, he began to give me a sign, saying that I should tell him more ; that this did not come from me, and that, if your Highness commanded me, that I should tell him so, and also the reward that you would grant him.   I told him that I was not a person of such weight that your Highness would employ me for such a purpose, but that I said it to him as I had

---

[1] Magellan's irony is the more amusing from the fact that it is utterly lost upon Alvarez, who takes his alternative of a hermit's life *au pied de la lettre*.

on many other occasions. Here he wished to pay me a compliment, saying that if what I had begun with him was carried on without the interference of others, your Highness would be served, but that Nuño Ribeiro had told him one thing, which meant nothing (*q ño fora nada*), and João Mendez another, which bound him to nothing, and he told me the favours they offered him on the part of your Highness. He then bewailed himself greatly, and said he was much concerned about it all, but that he knew nothing which could justify his leaving a king who had shown him such favour. I told him that it would be a more certain matter, and attended with a truer honour, to do what he ought to do, and not to lose his reputation and the favours your Highness would grant him. And if he weighed his coming from Portugal (which was for a hundred reals more or less of *moradia* that your Highness did not grant him, in order not to break your laws), and that there had arrived two sets of orders at variance with his own, which he had at the hands of the King, Don Carlos, he would see whether this insult (*desprezo*) did not outbalance it—to go and do what it was his duty to do, rather than to remain here for that for which he came.

"He was greatly astonished at my knowing so much, and then he told me the truth, and how the messenger had left—all of which I already knew. And he told me that certainly there was no reason why he should abandon the undertaking, unless they failed to fulfil anything in the terms of the agreement; but that first he must see what your Highness would do. I said to him, what more did he desire to see than the orders?—and Ruy Faleiro, who said openly that he was not going to follow his lantern,[1] and that he would navigate to the south, or he would not sail with the fleet; and that he (Magellan) thought he was going as admiral, whereas I knew that others were being sent in opposition to him, of whom he would know nothing, except at a time when it would be too late to save his honour.[2] (And I told him) that he should pay no heed to the honey that the Bishop of Burgos put to his lips, and that now was the time for him to choose his path, and that he should give me a letter to

---

[1] The *capitana* or flag-ship always carried the *farol* or lantern.

[2] "Eu sabia que avia out^{os} mandados em cont^rairo, os quaes elle nõ saberia senã a tpo que nõ pudese Remedea^r sua onrra." From this the previous plotting of the mutiny is evident.

your Highness, and that I, out of affection for him, would go to your Highness and plead his cause, because I had no instruction from your Highness concerning such business, and only said what I thought I had often said before.[1] He told me that he would say nothing to me until he had seen the answer that the messenger brought, and with this our conversation finished. I will watch the interests of your Highness to the utmost of my power.

"... I spoke to Ruy Faleiro twice, but he replied nothing to me, save 'how could he do such a thing against the King, his lord, who conferred such benefits upon him;' and to all that I said to him he gave me no other answer. It seems to me that he is like a man affected in his reason, and that this his familiar has taken away whatever wisdom he possessed. I think that if Fernão de Magalhães were removed that Ruy Faleiro would follow what Magalhães did."

The rest of the letter of Alvarez, which is one of great length, need not be quoted. He gives the King of Portugal information about the ships and their armament, together with a list of the Portuguese who had at that time taken service in the fleet. A passage concerning the proposed route and the charts and instruments provided is, however, of interest :—

"The route which it is reported they are to take is direct to Cape Frio, leaving Brazil on the right, until they pass the boundary-line, and thence to sail W. and W.N.W. direct to Maluco, which land of Maluco I have seen laid down on the globe and chart which Fernando de Reynell made here, the which was not finished when his father came here for him, and his father finished the whole and marked these lands of Maluco, and on this pattern are constructed all the charts which Diogo Ribeiro makes. And he makes all the compasses, quadrants, and globes, but does not sail with the fleet; nor does he desire anything more than to gain his living by his skill.

"From this Cape Frio to the islands of Maluco by this route there are no lands laid down in the charts they take. May God

---

[1] That this was a direct untruth can be seen by a reference to the first sentence of the letter.

the Almighty grant that they make a voyage like that of the Cortereals,[1] and that your Highness may remain at rest, and ever be envied—as your Highness is—by all princes."

Such a letter as this gives us some idea of the difficulties with which Magellan had to contend. They were augmented by the relations existing between his colleague and himself. Always of uncertain temper, Faleiro had of late become still more difficult to deal with. What was his real condition it is impossible to say. Although the suggestion has been stoutly combated by some historians, the balance of evidence is in favour of the fact that he became insane. Both Acosta and Sebastian Alvarez in their letters to Dom Manoel already quoted speak of him as being half-crazy. From what we know of his previous history, the supposition is not an impossible one—is even probable, perhaps. The contemporary writers for the most part support it. Argensola tells us that having gone out of his mind, he was sent to the madhouse in Seville. Gomara says that he went mad from the fear that he would be unable to fulfil his promise, and Oviedo speaks of him as *muy loco*, having lost both his health and his reason. By others it is hinted that the madness may have been feigned with the idea of commanding the squadron which was to follow that of Magellan. Barros gives a still more ingenious story—that Ruy Faleiro, being an astrologer, cast his own horoscope, and finding that the voyage would be disastrous and end in his death, he feigned madness at the last moment to avoid sailing.[2] Herrera

---

[1] The Cortereals sailed in Cabot's track to find a north-west passage, and of either of them—Gaspar in 1501 and Miguel in the following year—no tidings were ever heard.

[2] Argensola, *Conq. de las Molucas*, lib. i. p. 16 ; Gomara, *op. cit.* cap. xci. p. 83 ; Oviedo y Valdes, *op. cit.* lib. xx. cap. i. ; Argens,

tells us that differences arose between the two commanders, and it seems that Alvarez was instrumental in
fomenting them.   But whatever may have been the
difficulty, the King had ultimately to dismiss Faleiro.
By a *cedula* dated from Barcelona on the 26th July, 1519,
he ordered that he should remain in Seville to superin-
tend the preparations of the second fleet,[1] and Magellan
from this date remained practically in sole command, in
spite of Juan de Cartagena—to whom Faleiro's ship was
given—being spoken of in some documents of the India
House as his "*conjunta persona.*"   His position was
further strengthened by an order from the King that
Luis de Mendoza, the captain of the *Victoria*, and
treasurer of the fleet, who had been insolent and inclined to question his authority, should render unhesi-
tating obedience.   We may be sure that with this
Mendoza's hatred of Magellan was in no way mitigated.
It culminated before long, as we shall see, in the mutiny
of Port St. Julian, where a swift and terrible punishment was the reward of his treason.   It would have

Anales de Aragon, lib. i. cap. lxxix. ; Barros, *op. cit.* Dec. iii. lib. v.
cap. viii. p. 631.

[1] "Mandó elRey que pues Ruy Fálero no se hallaua con entera
salud, se quedasse hasta otro viage."—*Herrera*, Dec. ii. lib. iv. cap.
ix.   Faleiro afterwards returned to Portugal, and was imprisoned
there.   From prison he wrote to the Cardinal Adrian, begging that he
would interest himself with the King to procure his release.   Possibly
this was done ; we know at least that he was in Seville on March 22,
1523, and that he wrote thence two letters to the King upon the
importance of retaining the spice trade, and begging that his pension
should be paid, as he had not received it, and was in want.   He also
sought permission to fit out a small armada, suggesting that with his
charts and instruments he would be of great service.   Both these
letters exist in the Seville archives, together with the letter to the
Cardinal, which is written in Latin.   *Vide* Medina's *Coleccion*, vol. i.
p. 313.   It is believed that Faleiro died in Seville in 1523.

been better for him had he been dismissed his ship, as were two mutinous Portuguese at this period. The plots of Alvarez had already begun to work, and disaffection was rife long ere the ships left the Guadalquivir.

One of the points upon which Charles V. had most strongly insisted was that the number of Portuguese borne upon the ship's books should be reduced to the smallest possible limits. In a letter written from Barcelona on the 17th June he gives orders that under no circumstances whatever are these to be more than five in number. Writing again on the 5th July to Ruy Faleiro, who had sought permission for his brother to accompany him, the permission is given, but only on condition that he should form one of these five. On the 26th July the same order is reiterated. Nevertheless, circumstances brought it about that many more ultimately sailed. It may well be imagined that there were not wanting people who ascribed the worst of motives to Magellan with regard to the matter. To clear himself he presented an *informacion* to the India House on the 9th August, drawn up in the then customary form of question and answer, and giving the evidence of five men of known position and character, among whom we find the name of Sebastian del Cano. From it we learn several facts of interest. It tells us how in the streets and squares and quays of Seville the public crier announced the departure of the fleet, and called for volunteers ; how the people said the pay was too small, and would not go ; how the officers were sent to Cadiz and Malaga and other ports, and still could not get their complement ; and how, finally, a number of foreigners—and among them several Portuguese—were enrolled, with whom

the captains were, nevertheless, quite satisfied. Of the
varied nationalities and tongues thus brought together
one reads with astonishment. Besides the Spaniards,
Portuguese, and Basques, there were Genoese, Sicilians,
French, Flemings, Germans, Greeks, Neapolitans, Corfiotes, Negros, and Malays. One Englishman there
was, and one only, a certain Master Andrew of Bristol,
master-gunner of the flag-ship.[1] Of Portuguese there
ultimately sailed no less than thirty-seven—probably
indeed even more, for our sources of information, though
wonderfully full, are not absolutely complete.[2]

Despite the difficulty in obtaining men, the preparations were by this time nearly finished. From a letter
of Magellan to the India House we learn that his chief
anxiety was to obtain possession of Ruy Faleiro's book
of the various methods of taking observations. He
desires to take Francisco Faleiro as captain in place of
his brother, but fears that even then the latter may not
see fit to put him in possession of the coveted book.
His fears, however, were groundless, for though Francisco Faleiro decided not to sail with him, but to await
the following expedition, the book upon which Magellan
so greatly depended for his observations was presented
to him by his former friend and comrade before sailing.[3]

Before starting upon an expedition of such magnitude

---

[1] We cannot claim him as one of the immortals—the little band of
survivors who shared among them the glory of being the first circumnavigators. He died on 9th March, 1521, just after the fleet had
reached the Ladrone Islands.

[2] See Appendix, No. III., for this and other information concerning
the *personnel* of the expedition.

[3] This book consisted of thirty chapters, and is referred to at some
length by Barros, in conjunction with the book of Andres de San
Martin, who practically filled his place upon the expedition. *Barros*,
Dec. iii. lib. v. cap. x.

as this, it was the custom, as we have already seen, to attend a solemn church service *en masse.* Upon this occasion the ceremony was one of more than usual interest. It must have been felt by all that the voyage before them was of no ordinary character. They were not bound for the now well-known West Indies, nor about to sail the trite waters of the Indian Ocean. Their very first experiences would be in almost unknown lands and seas. And so, when the Corregidor of Seville, Sancho Martinez de Leyva, solemnly entrusted Magellan with the royal standard in the church of Santa Maria de la Victoria, and received from him the oath that, as a good subject of the King, he would carry out his enterprise, there must have been few of the onlookers to whose minds the difficulties and dangers of their future path did not present themselves. To Magellan the captains and officials of the armada swore a like oath of allegiance, promising to follow the course ordered by him and to obey him in everything. Alas for man's sincerity and honour! Many of those who knelt before the altar were at that moment pledged to join in open mutiny against their leader directly the fitting opportunity should arrive.

The preparations were now sufficiently far advanced to permit the fleet to leave the quays of Seville. On Wednesday the 10th August, 1519, the vessels weighed and dropped down the river to the port of S. Lucar de Barrameda, at its mouth. Here they remained for more than a month. It was now evident that, so far as the actual start of the expedition was concerned, the efforts of the Portuguese had failed, and their predictions proved incorrect. To within a few months of his sailing, Magellan had been represented to Dom Manoel as "a boaster and a man of little worth, who would not carry out his promises."[1]   Now they formed a different opinion.   The plots and intrigues to let and hinder the expedition did not therefore cease even with its departure.   Dom Manoel sent ships to the Cape, and also to Santa Maria in the Rio de la Plata, with orders to intercept their passage, and these having failed in their object, Diogo Lopez de Sequeira was instructed to send six ships from Cochim to the Moluccas for the same purpose—an order he was unable to fulfil on account of there being no vessels available at the time.[2]

Unconscious of these added dangers, Magellan worked hard at the innumerable matters of business connected with his immediate departure.   Together with his captains, he went backwards and forwards between Seville and the ships, supplying the various omissions which at the last moment so frequently declare themselves.   One of his last acts was to address a memorial to Charles V., assigning the geographical position of various places more or less connected with the line of demarcation— among them the Moluccas [3]—giving as his reason "that the King of Portugal may assert that they lie within his limit, and that no one understands the matter as he (Magellan) understands it."

On the 24th August he made his will.   The document is still in existence in the Seville archives.   It bears evidence of strong religious influence, if not religious feeling.   In it he desired that one-tenth part of his

---

[1] "Dezian los Portuguesos que el Rey de Castilla perderia el gasto, porque Hernando de Magallanes era hombre hablador y de poca sustancia, y que no saldria con lo que prometia."—*Herrera.*

[2] *Pigafetta,* lib. iii. p. 141, Milan edit. of 1800.

[3] Seville Archives, leg. i. of Molucca documents. *Navarrete,* iv. p. 188.

share of the profits of the expedition (which share was
to be one-fifth of the whole) should be taken and divided
into three equal shares, one of which was bequeathed to
the Convento de los Minimos of Victoria de Triana, where
he was to be buried if he died in Seville. The other two
shares were to be equally distributed between the monastery of Monserrat in Barcelona, the convent of S. Francisco in Aranda de Duero, and S. Domingo de las Dueñas
in Oporto. Of the effects he might die possessed of in
the fleet and of his real and personal property in Seville,
he desired that a fifth share should be expended in saying
masses for his soul.

The rule and seignorial rights of the lands he might
discover he desired should pass in regular succession, first
to his son Rodrigo, or, to the child which might be born
to him—his wife being then pregnant—or, failing direct
descent, to his brother Diogo de Sousa, or to his sister
Isabel. If the property should pass to the side branch,
the holder of the *mayorazgo* should, in the event of the
survival of Doña Beatriz, his wife, pay to her annually
a fourth part of the revenue and a sum of two hundred
ducats.[2]

Of the 50,000 maravedis of pension conferred by the
Casa de Contratacion upon his life and that of his wife,

---

[1] Magellan's son Rodrigo died in 1521 ; his second child was still-
born ; his wife died in 1522 ; Duarte Barbosa was killed in the surprise of May 1, 1521, and the father, Diogo Barbosa, dying in 1525,
the Crown took possession of the estate, which was claimed by Jaime
Barbosa and other sons of Diogo. The case, after having remained
seven years unheard, was again brought forward on the 6th June,
1540. The claimants had spent all their money and were reduced to
want, and though Magellan had given his life in the service of Spain
nineteen years before, they had not received a maravedi. What was
the ultimate result we do not learn, but knowing what we do of
Spanish justice at that period, we can guess.

the latter was to pay annually to the said sister Isabel the sum of 5000 maravedis. His son or sons were left residuary legatees. His heirs were to take the name and arms of Magallanes, and to reside and marry in Spain.[1]

Magellan appointed as executors his father-in-law, Diogo Barbosa, and Don Sancho de Matienzo, the *canónigo* of Seville who had supported him on the occasion of the riot instigated by Alvarez. At the same time that he made his will he addressed a letter to the King, asking that the 12,500 maravedis presented to him on the occasion of his decoration with the Order of Santiago might be paid to the convent of Victoria de la Triana, he having already promised it to them.

All was now ready, and the Captain-general rejoined his ship and hoisted his pennant. Every day, Pigafetta tells us, officers and men had gone ashore to hear mass at the church of Nossa Señora de Barrameda, and now, on the eve of sailing, Magellan gave orders that all should confess, " in the which he himself showed the way to the others." Next day, Tuesday the 20th September, 1519, a favourable breeze having sprung up, he gave the order to weigh, and a little later the ships cleared the river and commenced the memorable voyage which, through almost unparalleled suffering and disaster, was to win an immortal name for its survivors as the first circumnavigators of the globe.

----

[1] See Appendix II.

CHAPTER VI

THE LAST VOYAGE—I. S.E. AMERICA AND THE MUTINY IN PORT ST. JULIAN.

BEFORE entering upon the narrative of Magellan's final expedition, the issue of which was to stamp him as the greatest of the world's discoverers, we must turn for a moment to consider the materials with which he was provided. To the ships themselves allusion has already been made. They were for the most part old, small, and in anything but good condition. The *Trinidad*, though not the largest, was the most seaworthy and most suitable for *capitana*, and at her mast-head Magellan accordingly flew his pennant. Juan de Cartagena captained the *S. Antonio*, the largest vessel of the fleet. The *Concepcion* was commanded by Gaspar Quesada, and the *Victoria* by the traitor Luis de Mendoza, treasurer of the armada, who had already been reprimanded by the King for insolence to the Captain-general. The little *Santiago* was given to João Serrão, whose long experience in the East and great knowledge of navigation rendered him one of the most important members of the expedition.

The command of the *Santiago* by Serrão was, as it happened, an affair of no little moment to Magellan. But for his old friend and comrade it is more than possible that the mutiny of Port St. Julian might have proved too much for him, and the great discovery of

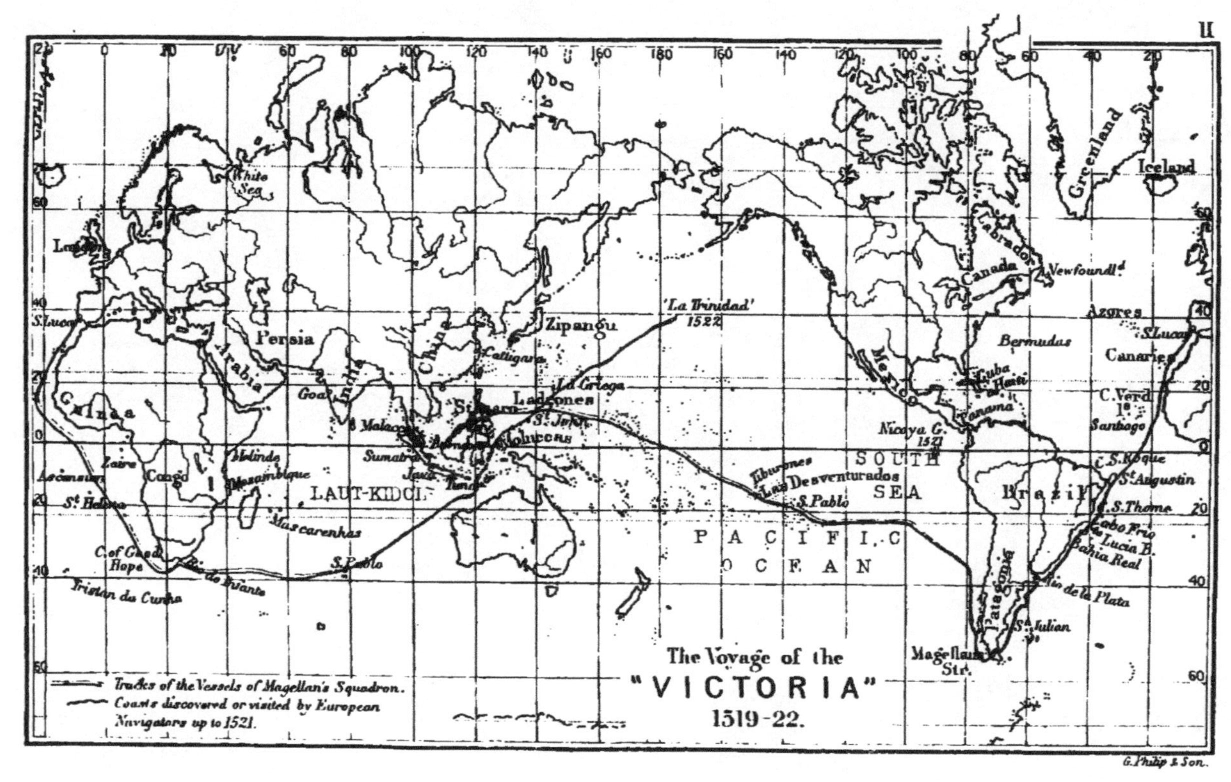

II
Iceland
Greenland
Canada
Labrador
Newfoundld
Azores
S. Lucar
Bermudas
Canaries
Cuba
Haiti
C. Verd
18
Santiago
Nicoya G. 1521
Panama
C. S. Roque
S. Augustin
Brazil
S. Thomé
Cabo Frio
Lucia B.
Bahia Real
Rio de la Plata
S. Julian
Patagonia
Magellan Str.
Mexico
SOUTH SEA
Eburones
Las Desventurados
S. Pablo
PACIFIC OCEAN
'La Trinidad' 1522
Zipangu
Catigara
La Griega
Ladrones
St. John
Moluccas
Sebu
Java
Timor
Sumatra
Malacca
Goa
India
China
Persia
Arabia
White Sea
Lisbon
S. Lucar
Guinea
Zaire
Lo Cinsura
Congo
Melinda
Mozambique
LAUT-KIDOL
Mascarenhas
S. Helena
C. of Good Hope
Rio de Puente
S. Pablo
Tristan da Cunha
The Voyage of the
"VICTORIA"
1519-22.
Tracks of the Vessels of Magellan's Squadron.
Coasts discovered or visited by European Navigators up to 1521.
G. Philip & Son.

Magellan's Straits might have been postponed to deck another brow with laurels. Upon the Portuguese in the fleet, despite his altered nationality, Magellan relied even more as friends than as navigators. By the time the squadron had crossed the bar, the originally-permitted number of five had greatly increased. Among the 280 men, more or less, who sailed, thirty-seven, as we have seen, were Portuguese, and of these many held most important posts. On the *Trinidad* were Estevão Gomez the pilot, Magellan's brother-in-law—Duarte Barbosa—Alvaro de la Mezquita, and eight others. The *S. Antonio* bore the cosmographer Andres de San Martin and João Rodriguez de Mafra. All the pilots of the fleet, indeed, were Portuguese, just as the gunners were foreigners; and João Lopez Carvalho and Vasco Gallego navigated respectively the *Concepcion* and the *Victoria*.

The armament of the fleet was on an extensive scale. The artillery comprised sixty-two culverins, ten falconets, and ten large bombards. Small firearms were not then greatly used, and only fifty arquebuses were carried. There were, however, a thousand lances, two hundred pikes, ten dozen javelins, ninety-five dozen darts, sixty crossbows, with 360 dozen arrows, and " sundry swords which the captain took." One hundred corselets, with gauntlets, shoulder-pieces, and casques, appear in the list, together with an equal number of cuirasses. Finally, we learn that as much as 5600 lbs. of powder were put on board.

The " *instrumentos* " with which the navigators were provided were of the simplest nature. Twenty-three parchment charts by Nuño Garcia, six pairs of compasses, twenty-one wooden quadrants, seven astrolabes, thirty-five compass-needles, and eighteen hour-glasses formed the entire list; and not all of these, we are told, were ultimately taken. The number of articles for barter was, however, very large. In the " Priuie Notes given by a Gentleman to the Marchants of the Muscouie Company," with which Hakluyt has made us acquainted, the importance of such expeditions being provided with "looking-glasses for women, great and fayre," is dwelt upon, and Magellan's squadron was amply supplied with these, together with 500 lbs. of " crystals, which are diamonds of all colours." Knives, fish-hooks, stuffs, and velvets, ivory, quicksilver (2240 lbs.), and brass bracelets all figure largely in the list; but it appears that bells were considered to be the most useful objects of barter. Of these no less than 20,000 were taken.

The cost of the fleet, with its stores and armament, was for those days considerable. From papers existing in the Seville archives, we know the exact amount to a maravedi. The entire expenditure was 8,751,125 maravedis, or £5032, 6s. 3d. But some of the stores having been left behind, the sum was reduced by 416,790 maravedis, or about £240. The ships, together with their artillery, powder, and small-arms, cost £2249; the victualling, £913; the articles of barter, £965, and the instruments and minor expenses, £238.[1] Of the whole sum, about one quarter was supplied by Cristobal de Haro and his friends, the rest was at the King's expense.

Our knowledge of the events of Magellan's great yet disastrous expedition is drawn from limited sources. Of those persons who actually took part in it, only four have left any description of its incidents. In Ramusio's

---

[1] For modern money the equivalent would be about five times these sums.

Navigationi et Viaggi occurs an exceedingly brief account by an unknown Portuguese, so brief, indeed, as to be almost valueless.   In the Seville archives there exists a *derrotero* or log-book, supposed to be written by Francisco Albo, the *contramaestre* of the *Trinidad*, but it is little more than a collection of nautical observations, which, though of the greatest interest in furnishing data for the actual course sailed by the vessels of the fleet, tell us little or nothing of the ordinary incidents of the voyage.   A third account is that of the so-called Genoese pilot.[1]   From the fact that the manuscript is in the Portuguese language, and, moreover, in remarkably pure Portuguese, it has been conjectured that the author was not a Genoese.   The narrative is tolerably full, but it bears no evidence of having been written by a pilot, and it is further worthy of remark that no Genoese sailed as pilot in the fleet.

The chief source of information we have, however, is neither of the foregoing.   When the despatch of the fleet was finally decided upon, a certain Italian gentleman—Antonio Pigafetta by name—a native of Vicenza, being in Barcelona, and "desirous of seeing the wonderful things of the ocean," obtained permission to accompany Magellan on his voyage.   Through the many adventurous months of wandering that fell to his lot, he kept his journal, finally publishing it upon his return. In it hearsay evidence is largely mixed with personal experience, but upon the whole it gives by far the best and fullest account of the expedition.   There are reasons for supposing that it was originally published in French——reasons too lengthy to discuss here.   It was dedicated

---

[1] Published in vol. iv. of the *Collcção de Noticias* of the Lisbon Academy.

to the celebrated Grand Master of Rhodes, Villiers de
l'Isle Adam—Pigafetta himself being a Knight of
Rhodes—and a copy was presented by him to the
Regent, Louise of Savoy, mother of Francis I.

The most careful account written by mere historians
of the event, who had taken no part in the voyage, is
that of Maximilian Transylvanus, an under-secretary
at the court of Charles V.   This person, who had
married Cristobal de Haro's niece, was a natural son of
the Archbishop of Salzburg, and a pupil of the celebrated Peter Martyr.[1]   Upon the arrival of the survivors of the expedition at Valladolid (whither they had
gone to present themselves to the Emperor), they were
carefully interrogated by both Peter Martyr and Maximilian.   The former, we are told, wrote a long account
of the affair.   "This viage," says Eden in his translation of the *Decades*,[2] "was written particularly by
Don Peter Martyr of Angleria, being one of the coun-
sayle of Themperours Indies, to whom also was com-
mytted the wrytynge of the hystorie and examination of
al suche as returned from thense into Spayne to the
citie of Siuile in the yeare MDXXII.   But sendynge it to
Rome to bee prynted in that miserable tyme when the
citie was sacked, it was lost, and not founde to this
day, or any memory remaynynge thereof, sauynge suche
as sum that redde the same haue borne in mynde."

---

[1] Peter Martyr of Angliora, so called from having been born in the
suburb of Milan in 1455, entered the service of Ferdinand and Isabella,
and was sent by them as ambassador to Venice and Egypt.   He lived
the greater part of his life in Castile, becoming secretary to Charles V.,
and dying in 1526.   As protonotary of the Consejo of the Indies,
he was brought· much. in contact with geographical matters, and
besides the well-known *Opus Epistolarum*, wrote the *De Navigatione
et Terris de Novo Repertis*.

[2] Rich. Eden, *The Decades of the Newe Worlde*, 1555, fol. 214.

Maximilian's account, however, remains. It was written on the 24th October, 1522, to his father, and reached him in Nuremberg in the following month. The description of such a voyage naturally attracted much attention, and the manuscript, which was in Latin, was printed in Cologne in January of the following year, thus probably preceding the *Nauigation et Descouurement* of Pigafetta.[1]

In addition to these sources, both Correa and Herrera give descriptions of the voyage which bear evidence in a greater or less degree of first-hand information; and among the mass of documents in the Seville archives are sundry *informaciones* and other papers throwing considerable light upon the mutiny and other salient incidents of the expedition.

We must return to the squadron, whose course on leaving Spain was shaped southward for the Canaries. Immediately on getting to sea, Magellan instituted a strict system of signalling at night by means of lights, and appointed the watches, as was even at that time customary. The admiral's ship led the van, bearing on the poop the *farol* or lantern, which it was the duty of his fleet to keep in sight. The night was divided into three watches—the first at the beginning of night; the second, called the *medora*, at midnight; and the third towards daybreak. The last was known as *la diane*, or

---

[1] The precise date of the publication of Pigafetta's narrative is not known. In August, 1524, he petitioned the Doge and Council of Venice for permission to print his book in that city, and to have the exclusive copyright for twenty years (*vide* Lord Stanley's *First Voyage*, Appendix, p. xiv.). The permission was granted. But it will be seen that ample time existed for the publication of a previous edition. The edition for the most part referred to and used in these pages is that of Amoretti, published in Milan in 1800.

the watch of the morning star.   Each night they were
changed; those who had kept the first watch kept the
second on the following day, the second the third, and
so on.   In accordance, too, with the customary rules laid
down by the India House, the crew of each vessel was
divided into three companies—the first belonging to the
captain or *contramaestre*, who took it in turns to command; the second to the pilot; and the third to the
maestre.   "The Captain-general, a discreet and virtuous
man, careful of his honour," says Pigafetta, "would not
commence his voyage without first making good and
wholesome ordinances."

On the 26th September the fleet arrived at Tenerife,[1]
and remaining three or four days to take in wood and
water, sailed for a port called Monte Rosso on the same
island,[2] where they again delayed two days to supply
themselves with pitch, or, according to Herrera, to await
a caravel which was to bring them fish.   It was while
they were in Tenerife that an incident occurred which
early brought home to the Captain-general the difficulties
which lay in his path.

Of the existence of disaffection among his crew Magellan must have been well aware.   Before starting, two of
his men had been dismissed for insubordination.   We have
seen how, in Sebastian Alvarez' letter to Dom Manoel,
he hints at a prearranged conspiracy.[3]   Pigafetta tells us
that the captains of the other ships hated their leader,[4]
and the fact must have been patent enough.   But though
he may have been fully conscious of the danger which

---

[1] The log-book of the " Genoese pilot " gives the 29th as the date.

[2] ? Punta Roxa, at the south end of Tenerife.

[3] " Eu sabia que avia out^{os} mandados em contrairo os quaces elle nõ
saberia senã a tpo que nõ pudese Remedear sua onrra."

[4] Pigafetta, *Primo Viaggio intorno al Globo*, Milan, 1800, p. 8.

threatened him, this danger had not as yet assumed definite shape.   Now, at the very beginning of his voyage, at the moment of adventuring himself into unknown seas, it was to do so.   A caravel arrived bearing a secret message from his father-in-law, Diogo Barbosa, warning him to " keep a good watch, since it had come to his knowledge that his captains had told their friends and relations that if they had any trouble with him they would kill him." [1]   Argensola gives us the same story— that " his captains had resolved not to obey him, particularly Juan de Cartagena." [2]   The news—which probably was no news to Magellan—did not dishearten him one whit.   He sent back answer to Barbosa that, were they good men or evil, he would do his work as a servant of the Emperor, and " to this end," he added, " he had offered his life."   His letter, Correa tells us, was shown by Barbosa to the Corregidores, " who greatly lauded the stout heart of Magellan."

Pigafetta, ere leaving the Canaries, duly chronicles the semi-fabulous story of the island of Hierro—old even in those days, for Pliny records it—how its single tree is perpetually enveloped in a cloud from which it distils an unfailing supply of water—a story founded upon fact, as we know now, for both in Madeira and the Canaries the laurel and other heavy-foliaged evergreens condense abundant water from the daily mists.   The fleet left Tenerife at midnight on the 3rd October,[3] running under foresails only until they cleared the land, when they closed and held a south-west course until noon on the following day, when the observations taken placed

---

[1] Correa, *Lendas da India*, vol. ii. p. 627.
[2] Argensola, *Conq. de las Mol.*, lib. i. p. 16.
[3] On the 2nd, according to Herrera's account.

them in 27° N. lat., having made a run of twelve leagues.

From here they followed in the wake of the admiral's ship, steering sometimes south, sometimes south by west, and early on the following morning the *S. Antonio*, running under the stern of the *Trinidad*, demanded the course. The pilot replied that it was south by west. It having been previously settled, Herrera tells us, that, until they reached the latitude of 24° N., the course was to be south-west, Juan de Cartagena demanded to know why it was changed. Magellan replied that " he was to follow him and not ask questions."[1] The captain of the *S. Antonio* retorted that he ought to have consulted the captains and pilots, and not to have acted thus arbitrarily, and added that it was an error of judgment to keep so near the African coast. Magellan's reply was to the same effect as his first answer—that the squadron must follow his flag by day and his lantern by night.

For fifteen days the fleet held good weather, passing between Cape Verde and its islands without sighting either, and running along the African coast. Between the cape and Sierra Leone they encountered calms and baffling winds for twenty days or more, during which time they advanced only three leagues upon their way. Provided with few or no data in physical geography, they had chosen what we now know to be a disadvantageous course. Following on the calms they had an entire month of head winds and very heavy storms. So heavy indeed were some of these squalls, that the vessels dipped their yardarms, and the captains were more than once on the point of ordering the masts to be

---

[1] " Que lo siguissen y no lo pidiessen mas cuenta."—*Herrera*, ii. iv. cap. x.

cut away. Striking all sail, they ran under bare poles at the mercy of the wind. Pigafetta, to whom the sea and its natural phenomena were novelties, gives us a vivid account of the terrors of this period. " In these tempests," he says, " the Corpo Santo or St. Elmo's fire often appeared, and in one which we experienced on a certain very dark night, it showed itself at the summit of the mainmast with such brightness that it seemed like a burning torch, remaining there for a space of more than two hours; the which was of such comfort to us that we wept for joy. And when it left us, it cast such a vivid light in our eyes that for near a quarter of an hour we remained as blind men, crying out for mercy, for we gave ourselves up for lost." [1]

For nearly sixty days they encountered rain while in the neighbourhood of the Line, " a thing very strange and unaccustomed to be seen," according to the ideas prevalent at that time. Sharks often came round their ships—"large fishes with terrible teeth "—and were caught by hooks; but the sailors do not seem to have appreciated the flesh, which they pronounced, in the case of the large ones, to be hardly fit to eat, while the smaller fish were little better. Notes of a like naive nature follow upon birds. [2] The men had fitted the well-known legend of the bird-of-Paradise—heard doubtless by the old hands in some far Eastern port—to some petrel or diver. " They make no nest," it ran, " because they have no feet, and the hen lays her eggs on the back of the cock, and there hatches them."

---

1 Pigafetta, *op. cit.*, p. 18.
2 " Vidimo varie specie d'uccelli strani : alcuni non hanno culo. .·. . Altri son detti Cagassela perché cibansi dello sterco d'altri uccelli."— *Pigafetta, op. cit.*, p. 14.

The slowness of their progress during this early part of the voyage caused some anxiety as to the sufficiency of provisions, and the crew were accordingly placed on diminished rations. Four pints of water only were allowed daily, a smaller measure of wine was given, and the weight of bread reduced to a pound and a half. The voyage was destined to be attended by unusual difficulties and disasters, even for those perilous times—disasters only equalled by the world-famed success of its issue— and foreshadowings of the miseries awaiting the navigators in the Pacific early darkened their path.

Their troubles with regard to the insufficiency of stores were, however, at that time of no. very great moment. They were forgotten before a more serious difficulty than any that had hitherto arisen. The dissensions which had already commenced between Juan de Cartagena and his chief had shown no sign of abatement as the voyage progressed. Before the Line was reached they culminated in open rupture. It was the custom, ordained by the King and embodied in his letter of instructions to Magellan,[1] that every evening, whenever the weather rendered it possible, the captains should communicate with the flagship, to salute the admiral and to take his orders. One day the quartermaster of the *S. Antonio,* hailing the *Trinidad,* gave as greeting, " Dios vos salve, señor capitan y maestre, ó buena compañia." Magellan, resenting the studied omission of his proper title of Captain-general, informed Juan de Cartagena that he expected to be rightly addressed in future. The latter

---

[1] " Dareis luego por ordenanza á los capitanes de las otras naos que cada dia á las tardes vos den sus salvas, segund se acostumbra hacer á los capitanes mayores de cualquier armada."—*Seville Archives, Pap. de Maluco,* leg. i. ; *Navarrete,* iv. p. 131.

replied that " he had sent the best man in the ship to salute him, and that another day, if he wished, he would salute him through one of the pages."   For three days, however, he failed altogether to comply with the rule.

Magellan, though not the man tamely to submit to insults from his subordinates, took no immediate action, but a day or two later, a court-martial being held upon a sailor of the *Victoria*, Cartagena was summoned with the other captains to the flag-ship.   The trial over, a discussion of the course to be steered followed.   Cartagena, emboldened by Magellan's quiescence and the success of his former insults, renewed them without more ado.   But he had mistaken his man.   The Captain-general, seizing him by the breast, exclaimed, " You are my prisoner."   Cartagena called in vain upon those present to aid him and to seize Magellan.   No one stirred, and he was led off in custody to the stocks, and entrusted to the keeping of Luis de Mendoza, captain of the *Victoria*.   The command of the *S. Antonio* was given to the *contador*, Antonio de Coca.   It was a pity for the offender that the prompt and resolute action of the admiral upon this occasion did not serve as a warning to deter him from future insubordination.

Steering a more westerly course, the fleet approached the New World, and arrived off Cape St. Augustin, near Pernambuco, on the 29th November.   They continued to hug the coast, and on December 8th were close to land, and in only ten fathoms.   Next day they found themselves in lat. 21° 31′ S., in sight of a very high mountain near Cape St. Thomas.   Rounding Cape Frio, they anchored in Rio harbour, which, since they entered it on the day of that saint, the 13th December, they called the Bay' of Santa Lucia.   Here they remained a fortnight, taking in wood and water and trading with the natives, "a good people and numerous," as Alvo records. Pigafetta has left a lengthy record of their stay here, and of the customs and peculiarities of the country and its people, partly from his own observation, partly from that of former voyagers, notably Vespucci. The pine-apples—"a very sweet fruit, more tasteful than any other"—sweet potatoes, fowls, and tapir were much appreciated by the sailors after their reduced rations. They were to be had in abundance and upon the easiest terms. For a knife or a fishhook five or six fowls might be obtained; for a comb or mirror enough fish for ten men, and for a little bell a large basket full of sweet potatoes. A still better bargain was made by Pigafetta himself, who exchanged the king from a pack of cards for six fowls. Besides articles of food, parrots and other birds were brought for sale by the natives, who were ready enough to barter away their children for an axe or a large knife. The admiral, however, forbade the purchase of any slaves, not only on account of the difficulty of feeding them, but in order that the Portuguese, within whose country the territory lay, should have no ground of complaint.

It is unnecessary to dwell on Pigafetta's evidently hearsay or borrowed account of the Indians and their customs. He speaks of their sleeping in "nets of cotton that they call *amache*," and of their boats called *canoe*. On the authority of João Carvalho, the pilot of the *Concepcion*, who had resided with them for four years,[1]

---

[1] Brazil, it must be remembered, had been discovered twenty years at the time of Magellan's voyage, and it is worthy of record that Carvalho took with him upon this voyage a son whom he had by a native wife during his former residence in Rio. We learn incidentally that

he describes their cannibal customs, and dilates upon the wonders of the country. His account of his personal experiences is more interesting. It had not rained for two months before the visit of the fleet, and the arrival of the strangers coinciding with the termination of the long drought, the people thought they had brought the rain with them, and were easily converted to Christianity. Mass was said twice on shore while the ships lay in the bay, and the natives assisted with the utmost devotion at it, " remaining on their knees with their hands joined in great reverence, so that it was a pleasure and a pity to see them." It is remarkable that none of the historians of the voyage mention the presence of Portuguese in Rio de Janeiro, although there is every probability that some may have been there at the time, since a trading station had been established in the bay some years before.

The fleet, well furnished with fresh provisions, resumed its voyage on the 26th December.[1] Before doing so, however, an attempt had been made by the cosmographer Andres de San Martin to fix the longitude of the bay. On the 17th December the altitude of the moon and Jupiter were observed, and from their position it was computed that the latter was in conjunction with the moon at the place of observation at 7h. 15m. after noon of the previous day. The tables of Regiomontanus were supposed to give the time of the conjunction at Seville. Herrera describes the observation at some length : it led to no definite conclusion, for the

another Brazilian of semi-European parentage was borne on the rolls. Carvalho's son never returned, having been made prisoner by Sri Pada, King of Borneo.

[1] On the 27th, " El dia de San Juan," *teste* Herrera, ii. iv. 10.

result obtained was evidently erroneous, and Andres ascribed the error to the almanac.

Sailing along the coast on a W.S.W. course, the vessels arrived off the Bahia de los Reyes [1] upon the last day of the year. No landing was effected, and they continued their route to the southward, still hugging the coast and constantly taking soundings. They were well acquainted, even in those days, with the art of arming the lead, and Herrera tells us on more than one occasion what bottom was found. On the 8th January, being in shoal water, they anchored for the night. On the 10th [2] they were passing very low land, with no landmarks save three hummocks, which appeared to be islands. These the pilot Carvalho declared to be Cape Santa Maria, saying that he recognised it from the account of João de Lisboa, who had been there. Losing the land here on their then course, they ran back northwards in search of shelter—having met with a terrific storm of thunder and lightning—and anchored. On the following day they weighed and proceeded W. $\frac{1}{4}$ N., but the water becoming very shallow, the *Santiago* was sent ahead. They were at the mouth of the great river where Juan de Solis lost his life at the hands of the cannibals—the Rio de la Plata of to-day.

Their exploration of the river was a careful one. The account given of it by Herrera differs somewhat from that of Alvo the pilot, but in general outline it is the same. For two days they followed up the stream. The pilots grumbled at the risk, for the greatest depth they found was three fathoms, and Magellan gave the order to anchor. They remained here six days, taking in water,

---

[1] Probably the Bay of Paranagua, in lat. 25° 28′ S.
[2] January 11, Herrera.

and catching great quantities of fish. Many natives
gathered in canoes, and, mindful of the fate of Juan
de Solis, the Captain-general ordered three boats to be
manned and armed, upon which the people fled ashore.
The Spaniards landed and tried to catch them, but in
vain. "They made such enormous strides," says Pigafetta, " that with all our running and jumping we could

EAST COAST OF PATAGONIA.

not overtake them." The country was found to be
beautiful, but without sign of habitation. At night an
Indian dressed in goat-skins came alone in a canoe and
visited the flag-ship without a sign of fear. The admiral
presented him with a cotton shirt and a jersey of coloured
cloth, at the same time showing him a silver plate, to
ascertain if he knew the metal. The native gave him
to understand that there was much of it among his

tribe, but Magellan's hopes of barter were doomed to disappointment, for the man went away next day and did not return.

By Alvo's log-book we learn that the vessel or vessels sent on in advance were absent fifteen days, and that two other ships were also sent southwards. Of these, the *S. Antonio* was one, and in her Magellan himself went, anxious to examine the coast with his own eyes.[1] Alvo's description of this incident, especially when read side by side with Pigafetta's account, is of great interest. Both the reconnaissances were made with the object of seeing if there might not by chance exist a strait leading into the Pacific.[2] Such a strait, according to the Italian, had been rumoured, or its possibility surmised. But twenty leagues to the south the Captain-general reached the opposite bank of the river, and fresh water still washed the sides of his ships. He had to do, then, with the mouth of a great river only, and with nothing more; and the *fine della terra*, which Cape Santa Maria had been supposed to form, was not yet.

Rejoining the other ships, and beating back against strong head-winds to "Monte Vidi," Magellan anchored with his squadron off the site of the present city. On the morning of February 3rd he weighed and resumed

---

[1] Herrera, *op. cit.* Dec. ii. bk. ix. cap. x.

[2] "Por ver si habia pasage," "á ver si habia pasage para pasar," are the two phrases used by Alvo. Lord Stanley of Alderley, in his *First Voyage* (p. 214), has rendered *pasage* as "roadstead"—"to see if there was a roadstead for staying at"!! Speaking of the Rio de la Plata and Capo Santa Maria, Pigafetta says, "Si era creduto una volta esser questo un canale che mettesse nel mar del Sur, cioé del mezzodi." The mere fact that Magellan sought for a strait here (or perhaps sought to disprove its existence) proves nothing with regard to the great question of what he knew concerning the straits that now bear his name.

his voyage to the south.   Next day a leak was discovered in the *S. Antonio*, but it was got under after a delay of two days, and on the 6th the course was once more resumed.   Keeping close to the coast off Cabo San Antonio, they rounded what is now known as Cape Corrientes, which, owing to its sandhills and shoals, they called Punta de las Arenas.   On the 12th February they encountered a very severe storm of thunder and lightning and rain, the worst of which being over, the "glorioso cuerpo" of S. Elmo appeared to them, "the which some call that of S. Pedro Gonzalez, others of Santa Clara, and others again of S. Nicholas."   Whichever it may have been, it afforded them much spiritual consolation, and "many who held the matter in derision," says Herrera, "not only saw it, but believed in it, and affirmed its truth."

On the 13th February they found themselves among shoals,[1] and the *Victoria* bumped several times, but fortunately did not remain.   They thought it best, however, to keep off shore, and a course was steered which took them out of sight of land for two or three days.   It does not appear whether Magellan thought that during this time he may have missed the possibility of a strait, or whether some other reason came into play, but either on the 22nd or the 23rd he decided partially to retrace his steps, and a W.N.W. course was set.   It brought them, February 24th, to the mouth of the Gulf of San Matias, which they entered "to see if there were not an outlet for the Moluccas."[2]   None appeared, and at the approach of night, finding no proper anchorage, they again stood out to sea.   The bay received its name from its discovery

---

[1] The "Bajos anegados" of Ribero's map.

[2] Genoese pilot.   "Viendo si habia alguna salida para el Maluco." See also Herrera, Dec. ii. bk. ix.

upon S. Matthias' Day. It was here that they appear to have first felt the effects of the oncoming winter. Herrera speaks of the great cold they experienced, and chronicles a succession of storms which separated the ships for three or four days.

Three days later, February 27th, they arrived at an inlet to which they gave the name of Bahia le los Patos,

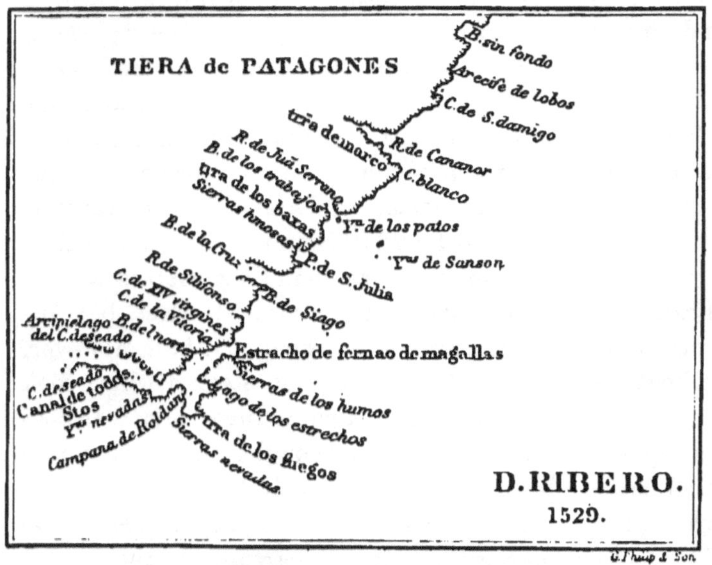

TIERA DE PATAGONES (*D. Ribero*, 1529).

or Duck Bay, from the number of penguins frequenting it. A boat with six men was sent to get wood and water, but, fearful of the natives, they went to a small island instead of visiting the mainland. Upon it they found so many "sea wolves" [1] and penguins that they were astounded. The whole fleet could have been laden

---

[1] These "sea-wolves" were probably some species of the Otariidæ or fur-seals.

with them. Unable to discover either wood or water, the sailors filled their boat with these creatures, but a storm springing up, they found themselves unable to return, and they were forced to spend the night upon the rock, fearing that they would either be devoured by the "wolves" or die from the cold. Next morning a number of men were sent to their rescue, who found their boat upon the rocks, and concluded that they had perished. On shouting out for their comrades, an enormous number of seals sprang out, of which they killed many ; and searching farther, they came upon the missing men buried beneath the seals they had killed, and half dead from cold and exposure. On their return to the fleet another storm came on, so heavy that the cables of the *Trinidad* parted, and only one held. Close to the rocks, and horribly afraid, they promised a pilgrimag to N.S. de la Victoria, and commended their souls to God. With morning the storm ceased, and there was not sufficient wind for them to get under way. But their troubles were not over, and they had yet to learn the meaning of autumn and winter on the shores of Patagonia. At midnight another storm burst upon them, lasting three days, and carrying away their forecastles and poops. Again they vowed pilgrimages in their distress, and again their prayers were heard. The three holy bodies, S. Anselmo, S. Nicholas, and S. Clara appeared at the mastheads, and the storm ceased.

Great as their anxiety and hardships had been, it seemed that they were destined to grow worse as the fleet advanced. A few days later they arrived at a bay with a narrow entrance, which appeared, since it was roomy inside, to be suitable for them to winter in. They entered it, and in six days encountered severer storms and ran greater danger than had yet fallen to their lot. A boat that went ashore to water upon their arrival was unable to return, and the crew subsisted as best they could upon shell-fish. " At last,"—Herrera tells us,—" at last it pleased God that they should leave that bay, and they named it the Bay of Toil."[1]   How long a time had been passed in it does not appear, but considerable delay must have occurred either in the bay itself or its immediate neighbourhood, for it was not until the 31st March, 1520, that the fleet anchored for the winter in Port St. Julian in lat. 49° 20′ S. The weather had become too severe for a farther advance, and, well sheltered and abounding in fish, the harbour seemed in every way a suitable one.   But it was destined to be no haven of rest to Magellan, for it was here that the mutiny, so long planned and so long foreseen, at length broke out.

Upon their arrival, one of the first steps taken by the Captain-general was to place officers and crew once more upon diminished rations. Bearing in mind the long winter they had before them, no wiser action could have been taken. But such actions, however wise or even necessary they may be, are rarely popular, and this was no exception to the rule. The sailors grumbled, as sailors will grumble, and, hating Magellan, and anxious only for the failure of his expedition, it is little probable that the Spanish captains showed much energy in checking them. Matters grew daily worse. The extreme cold they were beginning to experience, the frequent storms they encountered, their disbelief in the existence of a strait, combined to render them oblivious alike of potential honours and of duty. They openly demanded either that they should be put on full rations, or that the home-

[1] " Bahia de los trabajos "—possibly B. de los Desvelos, in lat. 48° 15′ S.

ward voyage should be at once commenced.　It was evident, they said, that the land stretched without a break to the Antarctic Pole, and that there was no hope of finding any strait; that the winter, from whose rigour some had already died, was upon them; and that to remain meant the loss of ships and men, which were of more importance than all the cloves and spices of the Moluccas.　They alleged that it was not the intention of the King that they should continue to seek the impossible, and that it was sufficient that they had arrived at a point whither no one hitherto had been bold enough to penetrate, adding that if they went farther south they would in all probability be wrecked upon some inhospitable coast, where every soul would perish. ②

Magellan's answer was such as we might expect from him.[1]　Although so many were against him, nothing was further from his intention than to yield.　The voyage, he said, was undertaken at the King's orders, and come what might, it was imperative to push on to the termination of the continent and to the strait, which they could not fail to find.　The winter, indeed, made their task impossible for the moment, but upon the advent of spring they could continue, if they pleased, to latitudes where the days were three months long.　He marvelled that Castilians should be guilty of such weakness; and as for the want of provisions, there was little cause for complaint, since in the bay in which they lay at anchor there was plenty of wood, good water, and an abundance of fish and birds.　Neither the bread nor wine had as yet run short, nor would they.　In fine, since he himself was determined to die rather than shamefully to turn

---

[1] "Magellan," says Herrera, describing the incident, was "hombre prompto, y acudia luego al remedio de qualquiera novedad."

② Conception : Vol 1 — p. 76 .

back, he felt sure that among such comrades as embarked on such an expedition there could be no lack of that spirit of valour which always animated the Spanish nation, and he asked them, therefore, to endure patiently until the winter should pass. The greater their labour and privation, the greater would be their sovereign's reward. They were to reveal to him, he concluded, an unknown world abounding in gold and spices, which would bring wealth to each and all concerned in its discovery.[1]

For a time, we learn, the crews were content, satisfied with the arguments he had advanced, but it was not for long. The treachery of his captains was at work, and the murmurings broke out afresh. The men began to talk to one another of the long-standing hatred between the Portuguese and Spaniards, and of Magellan being a Portuguese, saying that he could do no greater service to his country than to lose this fleet and all its sailors ; that it was incredible that he should wish to find the Moluccas even if he could, and that it would be enough if he could delude the Emperor for a year or two with false hopes. Even their course, they said, was not towards the Moluccas, but towards snow and ice and perpetual storms.[2] This time Magellan took other measures to repress the discontent. As a man of spirit and honour, Gomara tells us, he showed his teeth, and seized and

---

[1] The demands of the crew, and Magellan's speech in reply, are almost identical in Oviedo and Herrera. Both perhaps are borrowed from the letter of Maximilian Transylvanus, which they also resemble almost word for word. Faria y Sousa, in his *Asia Portuguesa*, puts an absurdly bombastic and most voluminous speech into Magellan's mouth, which, it is unnecessary to state, is purely imaginary. *Asia Portuguesa*, vol. i. pt. iii. cap. v.

[2] Letter of Max. Transylvanus.

punished the offenders.[1] His action was, however, too late to ward off the blow that was about to fall. An early warning of the coming storm was afforded not long after the arrival of the fleet in Port St. Julian. Magellan had given orders that upon Easter Day all should go ashore and attend mass, and that afterwards the captains of the ships should dine at his table. Some changes had been effected in the command. It will be remembered that, upon the degradation of Cartagena, Antonio de Coca had been appointed captain of the *S. Antonio*. We do not learn what action of his deprived him in his turn of his post, but deprived he was. Arana tells us[2] that Magellan mistrusted him. Whatever may have been the cause, his command was conferred upon Alvaro de Mesquita—a first cousin of the Captain-general. It is not improbable that the appointment of a Portuguese was obnoxious to the Spaniards. At any rate, both Gaspar Quesada and Luis de Mendoza refused to attend mass, and Mesquita alone dined with his kinsman on board the *Trinidad*. Magellan, we are told, looked upon the affair as of ill augury, and his suspicions proved only too well founded.

The blow fell the very same night. In the middle watch Gaspar Quesada, captain of the *Concepcion*, accompanied by Juan de Cartagena, Juan Sebastian del Cano, and some thirty armed men, boarded the *S. Antonio*, and entered the cabin of Alvaro de Mesquita with drawn swords. Resistance was useless. He was immediately put in irons, secured in the cabin of Geronimo Guerra, and a guard placed over him. The disturbance at once brought the *maestre*, Juan de Lorriaga,

---

[1] Gomara, *op. cit.*, ch. xcii. p. 84.
[2] *Op. cit.*, p. 66.

upon the scene, a faithful Basque, who had no thought of joining the rebels, even in face of such serious odds. He called upon Quesada instantly to leave the ship, and upon his refusal, ordered the *contramaestre*, Diego Hernandes, to summon the crew to arms. Quesada, exclaiming, " We cannot be foiled in our work by this fool," sprang at him and stabbed him repeatedly with a dagger, leaving him for dead.[1] The *contramaestre* had meanwhile been overpowered and made prisoner. So rapidly and unexpectedly had the affair taken place, that the crew, deprived of their officers, had no alternative but to submit. They were at once disarmed, and the arms placed in the cabin of Antonio de Coca, who had cast in his lot with the mutineers.

Measures were next taken to secure the ship against recapture. The command was given to Juan Sebastian del Cano, to whose name the stain of mutiny must ever attach, despite the honour so justly won by him at a later period. The artillery was mounted, and the decks cleared for action under his orders. Antonio Fernandes and Gonçalo Rodrigues, two Portuguese who had resisted Quesada's authority, were put in irons, together with a certain Diego Diaz, who had helped them. The stores were broken open, and the wine, bread, and other provisions freely distributed. In this and other matters Antonio de Coca, the former captain of the *S. Antonio*, was active in assisting Quesada, as was also Luis del Molino, the latter's body-servant. The chaplain of the ship, Pedro de Valderrama, though occupied in confessing the apparently dying *maestre*, observed them, and mentioned the fact in his evidence before Magellan. It obtained for Molino a sentence of death, but for lack of

---

[1] Lorriaga died from the effects of his wounds on 15th July.

an executioner his life was spared, upon the condition that he himself should execute his master.

The ship *Victoria*, whose captain, Luis de Mendoza, treasurer of the armada, had always been a bitter enemy of Magellan, had from the beginning given in its adherence to the mutineers, although a marked element of loyalty existed among the crew. The *sublevados* were therefore in a very strong position. They held the *Concepcion*, the *S. Antonio*, and the *Victoria*, and were headed by Quesada, Juan de Cartagena, Antonio de Coca, and Mendoza. Of the little *Santiago* we hear nothing. Her captain, Serrão, was the brother of Magellan's staunchest friend, and of her crew of thirty-two, one-half only were Spanish. It is unlikely that any attempt was made to interfere with her, either by force or persuasion. Quesada and his party felt strong enough to carry out their plans without her assistance.

Such was the state of affairs to which Magellan woke upon the morning of the 2nd April. The *S. Antonio* had been carried so rapidly and quietly that no suspicion of the truth had occurred to the officers of the flag-ship. It first dawned upon them, the chronicler Herrara tells us, on Magellan sending a boat to the *S. Antonio* to pick up some men for a watering-party. They were hailed and told to keep off, and informed that the ship was under the orders of Gaspar Quesada, and not Magellan. Hearing the news, and at once suspecting the serious nature of the affair with which he had to deal, the Captain-general ordered the boat to go round to the ships and ask for whom they declared. Quesada's reply was, "For the King and for myself," and like answers were given from all except the *Santiago*. Shortly afterwards a boat arrived with a letter from Quesada. He had seized the ships, he said, in order henceforward to do away with the possibility of a repetition of the bad treatment which officers and crew alike had received at the hands of the Captain-general, but if Magellan would agree to their demands, they were ready once more to acknowledge his authority. Magellan, in reply, said that he would meet them on his ship, and would hear what they had to say; but the mutineers, fearing that they would be seized if they ventured on board the *Trinidad*, declined to see him, excepting on the *S. Antonio*.

Magellan had before him a task of which the difficulty would have appeared to most men almost invincible. Unless he won the day, the theories and hopes of his lifetime were doomed to complete and final failure. With the *Santiago* only the continuation of the voyage was impossible. To return once more to the Seville quays, having achieved nothing after so great a flourish of trumpets at his departure, was, of course, to return to disgrace and oblivion. At any risk and cost, therefore, the mutiny must be suppressed, but how it should be suppressed was another matter. We have seen enough of Magellan's life and actions under Almeida to know that in cool daring few men were his superiors. But openly to attack the three revolted ships with no assistance other than the little *Santiago* would have been madness, and no one knew it better than he. If he was to succeed at all, it must be by *finesse*—by the exercise of that faculty which, Herrera tells us, supplied him with a way out of every new difficulty as it arose.

Magellan did succeed. *Periculosior quies quam temeritas* seemed to him an apt motto for the occasion. His first action was to seize the boat of the *S. Antonio* which brought him Quesada's message. Bearing in mind the large proportion of foreigners upon the *Victoria*, and the fact that he knew many of them to be loyal to him, he decided to address himself first to the capture of that vessel, hoping, if he were successful, to be more than a match for the others. The skiff, accordingly, carrying the alguacil Gonzalo Gomez de Espinosa and five men bearing concealed arms, was despatched with a letter to Mendoza, summoning him at once to the flag-ship. Mendoza smiled at its contents—as though he would say, "no me tomará allá"—"I am not to be caught thus." He did not calculate upon the instructions given by Magellan. As he shook his head in refusal Espinosa drew his dagger and stabbed him in the throat, and at the same instant he was cut down by another of Magellan's men. He fell dead upon the deck. The dangerous position of the alguacil and his handful of men had, of course, been foreseen. A boat with fifteen picked men of the *Trinidad*, captained by the trusty Duarte Barbosa, brother-in-law of Magellan, had been kept in readiness, and almost at the moment that Mendoza fell the *Victoria* was boarded with a rush. Hardly an effort at resistance was made. Either overawed at the death of their captain or loyal in reality to the leader of the armada, the crew surrendered at once. Barbosa hoisted Magellan's ensign, and, weighing anchor, placed the captured ship in close proximity to the *capitana* at the entrance of the port. The *Santiago* took up a similar position upon the other hand. The three ships together effectually guarded the harbour's mouth, preventing the escape of the others, and Magellan held the game in his own hands.

The mutineers were summoned to surrender, but refused, and it was conjectured that the two ships would attempt to escape under cover of darkness. Early in the day the *Trinidad* had been cleared for action. An order had been issued to " make a plentiful provision of much darts, lances, stones, and other weapons, both on deck and in the tops." The watch was now doubled; the men were allowed a good meal, and the strictest injunctions were given to guard against the escape of the vessels. A little after midnight the *S. Antonio* hove in sight. She was supposed to be bearing down upon the flag-ship, but was in reality dragging her anchors. Upon the quarter-deck was Gaspar Quesada, who, armed with lance and shield, called upon his men. No one stirred, and the *Trinidad*, opening fire with her large bombards, grappled her and poured her boarders over her side. At the same moment she was boarded on the starboard hand by the sailors of the *Victoria*. Their cry " Por quien estais? " met with the answer, " For the King and Magellan." Quesada and his fellow-mutineers were quickly seized, and the captain and pilot, Alvaro de Mesquita and Mafra, set at liberty. Not a man was killed; hardly a blow struck. Mafra alone had any narrow escape of death, a ball from the flagship passing between his legs as he sat imprisoned below deck.

The mutiny was now over. Juan de Cartagena, perceiving the loss of the *S. Antonio* and the surrender of Quesada, realised that nothing was to be gained by further resistance. When the boat from the *Trinidad* came alongside and called upon him to surrender, he obeyed the order at once. He was placed in irons and brought back to the flag-ship, there to await his sentence.

Next day the body of Mendoza was brought ashore.

He was publicly cried as a traitor, the body was drawn
and quartered, and the quarters spitted on poles. An
inquiry was then held upon the circumstances of the
mutiny, of which no details are given us. Forty men
were found guilty of treason and condemned to death;
but partly because they were necessary for the service of
the fleet, partly because he did not wish to make himself unpopular by too severe measures, Magellan par-
doned them. Such a clemency, however, could not be
extended to Quesada nor Cartagena, whose insubordination had been an affair of old date. Quesada, doubly
guilty by the brutal manner in which he had stabbed
the *maestre* of the *S. Antonio*, was sentenced to be
executed. On Saturday, the 7th April, he was taken on
shore and the sentence carried out, his head being struck
off by his servant, Luis del Molino, and his body quartered, as in the case of Mendoza. No more justifiable
punishment could have been inflicted.

A different fate was reserved for Juan de Cartagena.
Whether, since he had been directly appointed by Charles
V., Magellan did not wish to take his life, or whether
he considered that there were extenuating circumstances
connected with his case, we cannot tell. A violent death
at least was spared him, and he was sentenced to be
marooned upon the departure of the fleet. With him
the priest Pero Sanchez de Reina suffered a like punishment.[1] His offence was a grave one, for he was found

---

[1] Herrera speaks of a *clerigo frances* as being the culprit, leaving
it to be inferred that it was Bernardo Calmeta, the chaplain of the
S. Antonio. In the "List of Deaths in the Fleet of Hernando de
Magallanes" it is, however, distinctly mentioned that the offender
was Pero Sanchez de Reina. It is nevertheless worthy of remark that
Calmeta's name is not to be found among those who returned to
Spain, nor among those who perished in the expedition.

guilty of trying to incite the crew to mutiny for a second time, even after the failure of the plot and the justice executed upon its authors. No one would listen to him, and he was soon denounced and made prisoner. Of Antonio de Coca's punishment we hear nothing. We know only that he reached the Ladrone Islands with the fleet and died there.[1]

Magellan's action in the mutiny of Port St. Julian has been made the subject of the severest strictures, more especially by those of the school of fireside criticism. His stratagem of capturing the *Victoria* has been stigmatised as assassination. By one author he is described as "a man of cruel and savage disposition," who "ruthlessly slaughtered his own comrades." But such expressions are as incorrect as they are violent. In times of mutiny, when right is no longer might, and the loyal crew are confronted by overpowering odds, legal measures are occasionally impossible, and fairness worse than a mistake. Mendoza, a mutineer and *ipso facto* worthy of death, only met his punishment—and met it, it should be remembered, at the hands of an alguacil—a few hours before it would otherwise have been inflicted. As a mutineer, moreover, he was well aware of the risks he ran—well aware that, if Magellan could, he would kill him. And finally, we cannot judge sixteenth-century matters by nineteenth-century standards. The taking of a man's life was in those days a small matter. But in expeditions such as these, the

---

[1] Others, among them Andres de San Martin, the cosmographer, are said to have been punished by Magellan, but as we learn this from the evidence of the crew of the *S. Antonio*, which ship deserted the fleet a few months later, and as we know much of the evidence to be untrue, no reliance can be placed upon the assertion. See Navarrete, vol. iv. p. 206.

preservation of discipline was an affair of vital importance. In this case, had the attempt on the *Victoria*
failed, the complete collapse of the work of the armada
must inevitably have followed.

Magellan has also been accused of having acted illegally in the punishment of the mutineers. In the letter
of Maximilian Transylvanus this charge is brought
against him.[1] But though there may be a difference of
opinion as to the justifiability of Mendoza's death, there
can be none whatever upon this question. The "Titulo
de Capitanes," granted by Charles to Magellan upon the
22nd March, 1518, gives the latter full power over the
persons and property of those sailing with him.[2] Correa,
too, is definite upon the point. "The Emperor gave
him power 'of rope and knife' over every person who
went in the armada,"[3] and it is satisfactory to find that
the punishments of Quesada and Cartagena were as
strictly legal as they were well-deserved.

The mutiny was the turning-point of Magellan's
career. Thenceforward, whatever desire to question his
authority may have existed, it remained unexpressed.
The inflexible determination of the man, his strength of
will, his readiness of resource, showed officers and crews
alike that obedience was the best policy. Had they
known what suffering and what peril lay in their path,
it is doubtful whether the resolution and energy of any
single individual would have availed to stop their defection. But Ruy Faleiro had only cast his own horoscope;

---

1 "Erant enim regii quidam ministri, in quos nemo præter Cæsarem
ipsum, ejusve senatum, capitali pœna animadvertere jure potest."

2 *Vide* Navarrete, vol. iv. p. 122.

3 "E lhe deu poder de baraço e cutello em toda' pessoa que fosse
n'armada."—*Correa*, ii. part ii. p. 627.

and so it happened that Magellan sailed southward to the discovery of the strait that bears his name.[1]

[1] It is a singular fact that of the four persons who accompanied the expedition and wrote an account of it, two should have remained absolutely silent upon the subject of the mutiny, and two—the "Genoese pilot" and Pigafetta—have thought it worthy of only the barest mention. The account of the latter is remarkable for its extraordinary inaccuracy. "The Captains *of the other four ships*," he writes, "plotted to kill the captain-general," and he then goes on to say that it was Cartagena who was executed and quartered, while Gaspar Quesada was marooned. It seems incredible that an eyewitness—which he undoubtedly was—should have failed to remember circumstances such as these, and the fact somewhat lessens the value of his book as a credible narrative, although we know that such parts of the diary as were written on the spot, detailing his own experiences, are almost always accurate. Our real knowledge of the affair is due to three documents existing in the Seville archives—an *informacion* drawn up by Magellan at the time, giving the examination of witnesses ; a letter of the Contador Recalde to the Bishop of Burgos, containing the evidence of the deserters of the *S. Antonio* ; and, lastly, an account of the evidence taken in Valladolid, October 18, 1522, concerning certain events of the voyage. The historian Herrera has a tolerably full and correct account of the tragedy, but that of Correa, though nearly as full, is inaccurate in many points, as indeed it is often wont to be.

CHAPTER VII.

THE LAST VOYAGE—II. THE DISCOVERY OF THE STRAIT.

ORDER having once more been established, Magellan kept all hands busily at work during the remainder of his sojourn in Port St. Julian. The vessels were careened and caulked, and such repairs as were found necessary were carried out. The *S. Antonio* especially stood in need of them. The mutineers, in chains, were kept working at the pumps until the carpenters had rendered such work no longer needful. It was not until the day of departure from the bay that they were set at liberty.

Towards the end of April the Captain-general determined to undertake a reconnaissance of the coast in the vicinity. The fear of a more or less prolonged inaction and its effect upon the men most probably led him to this step. The *Santiago*, from her handiness and small draught, was chosen for the work, and her choice was the more indicated from the fact of Serrão being her commander. Few men were so well versed in the art of seamanship and navigation; fewer still were endowed with his experience. He had long used the Eastern seas both as subaltern and captain. From the time of his first command under Rodrigo Rabello in 1506 until his departure on the expedition, he had been constantly in active service. As brother, moreover, of

Magellan's great friend, Francisco Serrão, the Captain-general knew that every trust could be reposed in him. He received instructions therefore to sail along the coast to the southward, examining each bay and inlet. He was not to carry his explorations too far, and if after a certain time nothing worthy of note was met with, he was to retrace his steps and once more rejoin his comrades in Port St. Julian.

It is to Herrera that we are indebted for an account of the voyage. The *Santiago*, working slowly along the coast, arrived on the 3rd May at the mouth of a river of considerable size, nearly sixty miles from the harbour whence she had set out. Serrão named it the Rio de Santa Cruz. The fish were so abundant that he was induced to prolong his stay for six days to lay in a supply. The seals, or sea-wolves, as the sailors termed them, were equally numerous, and of such large size that the Spaniards were astounded. One of them, deprived of the skin, head, and entrails, weighed nearly five hundredweight.[1] Having replenished their stock of provisions, the explorers continued their voyage, but they had barely gone three leagues, when, on the 22nd May, they encountered one of the short but violent storms which at this season render the coast of Patagonia so dangerous. The ship was put under storm canvas, but the rudder having become injured by the heavy seas, she refused to obey her helm, and a sudden squall from the east drove her ashore. Fortunately she took the ground in such a manner that the crew were able to save themselves by dropping from the end of the jib-boom, but they had barely time to escape with their lives. In a

---

[1] The great size of the old males of the fur seals, and their disproportion to the females, is a marked feature of these creatures.

few minutes the ill-fated *Santiago* was in pieces, and
her crew, to the number of thirty-seven men, found
themselves without provisions of any kind, exposed to
the hardships of a most inclement climate, and separated
by seventy miles of pathless wilderness from the succour
of their comrades. The only good fortune attending
them was of a negative kind. But one life was lost—
that of the negro slave of the captain.

For eight days the castaways remained in the neighbourhood of the wreck, hoping possibly to secure some
articles—of food or otherwise—which might prove of
service in the desperate journey that lay before them.
Their hopes were vain. Among the jetsam, however,
were numerous planks, and, mindful of the fact that
between them and safety lay the river they had just discovered—the great Rio de Santa Cruz, a barrier three
miles in width—they started on their march laden with
sufficient of these to enable them to construct a raft
wherewith to cross it. But short as was the distance
they had to traverse, they became so exhausted by
exposure and want of nourishment that they were forced
to abandon the greater part of their load, and did not
arrive at the river until the fourth day.[1] Here at least
they were safe from starvation, for, as they had previously
discovered, its waters abounded in fish. It was resolved
that the main body of the crew should encamp upon the
banks, while two of the strongest of their number should
cross in the little raft they had constructed and endeavour
to make their way to Port St. Julian.

---

[1] *Herrera*, Dec. ii. lib. ix. cap. xiii. It may be wondered why such
toil and hardship were undertaken when a raft might have been built
at the river-side. It is probable, however, that the shipwrecked men
were unprovided with axes, and that there was also insufficient wood
for the purpose.

How these unfortunate men eventually reached their destination, and how severe were their sufferings on the march, we learn from the pages of the Spanish historian already quoted. For eleven days they struggled on, living at one time upon roots and leaves, at another upon such shellfish as they were able to collect upon the shore. At first they attempted to follow the coast-line, as affording them better means of subsistence, but they were soon obliged to relinquish this plan, owing to the marshes that barred their passage and forced them to strike inland. At length the welcome harbour was reached. So altered were they from the hardships they had undergone, that they were recognised with difficulty by their old comrades.

The weather continued so unsettled, that Magellan considered it better to try and reach the shipwrecked party by land, rather than expose another of his vessels to the risk of loss. He accordingly at once despatched a relief party of twenty-four men, laden with wine and biscuit. Like their two comrades, they experienced great hardships from the rigours of the climate and the roughness of the country. No water was to be found on the road, and they were forced to melt the little snow they could discover to supply themselves with drink. On arriving at the river, they found their companions safe, although exhausted by exposure and privation. In parties of two or three—for the little raft could hold no more—the castaways were brought across the river, and the homeward march began. It speaks well for the courage and endurance of the Spaniards that they eventually reached the fleet without the loss of a single man. Good fortune afterwards attended them with regard to the ship's stores and artillery, the greater part of which were saved and picked up by the Captain-general on resuming his voyage to the south.[1]

Upon their return, the crew of the *Santiago* were distributed among the four remaining ships, and Serrão, who had displayed both courage and ability in his conduct of the shipwrecked crew, was rewarded by the command of the *Concepcion*. The ultimate result of the two disasters which had befallen Magellan was greatly to strengthen his hand. In lieu of three disaffected and traitorous captains—Quesada, Cartagena, and Mendoza—the commands were held by Portuguese, in whom he could place complete and absolute reliance. Serrão, as we have seen, took the *Concepcion*, while the *S. Antonio* and *Victoria* were captained by Alvaro de Mesquita and Duarte Barbosa, the former of whom was Magellan's first cousin, the latter his brother-in-law.[2]

The winter was now fairly established, and the cold became more severe. Nor was the weather they experienced such as to tempt to a renewal of their explorations along the coast. But the Captain-general, anxious to learn something of the interior of the country, thought it advisable to despatch a small expedition with that object. Four men only were sent. They were well armed, and were furnished with instructions to penetrate, if possible, to a distance of thirty leagues, to plant a cross, and to put themselves upon a footing of friend-

---

[1] Log-book of the "Genoese Pilot." Medina, vol. ii. p. 401. Correa gives a widely different account of the shipwreck, which, as is the case in many instances, is manifestly incorrect.

[2] Gomara, and indeed Oviedo also, makes Mesquita to be the *nephew* of the Captain-general. "Alvaro de Mesquita queria entrar por el estrecho, diciendo que por alli iba *su tio* Magallanes."—*Gomara*, ch. xcii. p. 85. So, too, does Maximilian Transylvanus—"Una ex his cui ipsius Magellani ex fratre nepos Aluarus Meschita præfuit;" and a few lines farther the words "patruus Magellanus" are used.

ship with any natives they might happen to meet. The nature of the country was, unfortunately, such as to render the expedition a failure. Neither food nor water was to be found. The men were forced to be content with the ascent of a high mountain at some little distance from the coast. Planting a cross upon its summit, and giving to it the name of the Mount of Christ, they retraced their steps, and arrived at the ships, informing Magellan that the country was intraversable and without resources, and appeared to be entirely unpeopled.

It was not long before the latter piece of information at least was proved to be incorrect. The fleet had remained at anchor for weeks in Port St. Julian, and no trace of natives had been seen. One morning, however, the sailors were astonished by the appearance of a man of gigantic stature upon the beach, who sang and danced, pouring sand upon his head in token of amity. Magellan sent a man ashore with instructions to imitate the action of the savage, and, if possible, to make friends with him. This he succeeded in doing, and the new-comer was brought before the admiral. Spaniards and native were equally surprised. The latter marvelled, Gomara tells us, to see such large ships and such little men, and pointing to the sky, seemed to inquire whether they were not gods who had descended from heaven; while the Spaniards, wondering at the great stature of their visitor, concluded that they had come upon a race of giants. "So tall was this man," writes Pigafetta, "that we came up to the level of his waistbelt. He was well enough made, and had a broad face, painted red, with yellow circles round his eyes, and two heart-shaped spots on his cheeks. His hair was short and coloured white, and he was dressed in the skins of an animal

A Patagonian.

cleverly sewn together." The description given of this animal leaves no doubt that it was the guanaco. The skin of the same creature served to make boots for these people, and it was the unwieldy appearance thus given to the feet which led Magellan to apply to the race the name of Patagão.

The man seemed most peaceably disposed, though he did not lay aside his arms—a short, thick bow, and a bundle of cane arrows tipped with black and white stones. Magellan treated him kindly, and ordered that he should be given food. He was shown some of their objects for barter, among others a large steel mirror. So overcome was he on catching sight of himself, says Pigafetta, that he jumped backwards with an unexpectedness and impetuosity which overset four of the men who were standing round him. He was, nevertheless, not unwilling to accept a small mirror as a present, and some beads and bells having been added, he was put ashore under the care of four armed men.

A companion met him upon landing, and confidential relations having been thus established, the Spaniards had no difficulty in persuading the natives to visit their ships. Others, accompanied by their wives, were not long in showing themselves, and eventually several came on board. "The women," we are told, "were loaded by them with all their belongings, as if they were so many beasts of burden. We could not behold them without wonder." They were not so tall as the men, but much fatter, and had breasts half as long as a man's arm. With them "they brought four of those little beasts of which they make their clothing, leading them with a cord like dogs coupled together." The use of these, they said, was to tie up and entice others within range of the arrows of the hunter, who was hidden near. The Spaniards were anxious to secure some of these guanacos, and getting together eighteen of the natives, set half of them to hunt on either side of the entrance of the harbour, but we are not told the result of their endeavours.

Many visits were thus paid by the natives to the fleet, and Pigafetta was enabled to obtain a small vocabulary of their language. One of them, who seemed especially tractable and pleasing, remained with the ships some days. He was taught the Paternoster and Ave Maria, which he pronounced well, but in an exceedingly loud voice, and the priest eventually baptized him with the name of Juan Gigante. The Captain-general gave him a number of presents, with which he was much pleased, and on the following day he returned bringing a guanaco. Magellan, hoping to obtain some more of these animals, directed that further presents should be made him. The man was never seen again, however, and it was suspected that he had been murdered by his companions.

The manners and customs of the Patagonians are described at some length by the supposed Genoese pilot as well as by Pigafetta. The fact that they devoured with great relish the rats which were caught on the ships filled the sailors with astonishment, which was not lessened by perceiving that they did not stop to skin them. Still more astonishing was their power of thrusting arrows down their throats without injury, which was apparently done more as a *tour de force* than for any definite purpose, although Pigafetta regarded it as a species of medical treatment,—" in luogho di purgarsi," as he describes it.[1]

----

[1] Pigafetta and Max. Transylvanus alone mention this story, and Oviedo borrows it from them. It is depicted in De Bry's illustration of Magellan passing the Straits, which is represented in this volume, p. 211.

In spite of Magellan's fixed rule that the fleet should
not be burdened with useless mouths, especially now that
the rations had been reduced, he was so much struck
with the *gigantes*, as they termed them, that he resolved
to bring some of them back with him to Spain as a present to the Emperor. It was some little time before he
was able to put his project into execution, for fifteen
days elapsed before another native was seen. At length,
upon the 28th July, four appeared upon the beach, and
were brought on board the *Trinidad*. Magellan was
anxious to keep the two youngest, but having an idea
that their capture might not be an easy matter, he decided to use strategy rather than force. Loading them
with presents, so that their hands were full, he then
offered them a pair of irons, and, as they were unable
to take them, showed them how they fitted upon the
legs. A couple of strokes of the hammer riveted the
bolts, and the two unlucky savages were prisoners before
they realised their position. When they did so, they
became furious, invoking Setebos,[1] their Great Spirit,
to their aid. Their two companions were conducted
ashore with their arms bound by a party of men who
were instructed to bring the wife of one of the captives,
" who greatly regretted her, as we saw by signs." The
huts of the natives were reached the same day, but as it
was late, the pilot Carvalho, who was in charge of the
party, decided on waiting till the following day. It
happened that on the road one of their charges had
attempted to escape, and in the struggle which ensued
he was wounded in the head. His companions said

---

[1] This name is put into Caliban's mouth by Shakespeare upon two
occasions, *Tempest*, act i. scene 2, and act v. scene 1, and was doubtless borrowed from Pigafetta's narrative.

nothing at the time, but next morning they spoke a few
words to the women, and immediately all took to flight.
At a little distance they halted to exchange shots with
the Spaniards, and in the encounter Diego de Barrasa,
man-at-arms of the *Trinidad*, was struck in the thigh
by an arrow and died immediately.

Magellan attempted to follow the Patagonians, either
with the idea of punishing them, or more probably with
the hope of capturing a woman of the tribe, but he was
unsuccessful, and it seems that—by nature a wandering
people—they disappeared for a time from the neighbourhood. The action of the Spaniards upon this occasion
was, of course, totally unjustifiable according to our
ideas; but it must be remembered that the humani-
tarianism of the present day was at that time not even
in its infancy. A *selvaje* was looked upon as hardly
other than an animal, and giants, such as these were
supposed to be,[1] must have approximated them still
more closely. No doubt the Captain-general regarded
it as his duty to bring such curiosities to his Emperor,
and did not consider his breach of faith as other than a
perfectly justifiable proceeding. The two captives were
placed in different vessels, and we learn from the account
of the Genoese pilot that one arrived in Spain, brought

[1] The actual height and size of the Patagonians remained for a long
time a matter of dispute. An assemblage of very tall people always
causes an over-estimation of their height, and there is no doubt that
Pigafetta's diary gives a *bonâ fide* record of the impression produced
upon the mind of himself and his comrades. Lieutenant Musters, the
greatest authority upon the country, gives the average height of
the men as six feet, while some reach six feet four inches or more.
Their muscular development is very great. Darwin, moreover, in his
Voyage of the Beagle, says, " On an average their height is about six
feet, with some men taller, and only a few shorter. Their height
appears greater than it really is from their large guanaco mantles,
their long flowing hair, and general figure " (chap. xi.).

thither in the *S. Antonio*, when she deserted the rest of
the squadron in the Straits.   According to other accounts,
however, he died before reaching that country.[1]

Weary, no doubt, of the continued inaction, and
anxious to leave a place which must each day have
brought the remembrance of the mutiny to his mind,
Magellan resolved to pass the remainder of the winter
in the Rio de Santa Cruz, which had been discovered by
Serrão in the ill-fated *Santiago*. The ships were now
repaired and refitted, and in good order, and the admiral
hoped to make the passage without encountering one of
the frequent storms which render this coast so dangerous
in winter.   He accordingly gave orders to prepare for
sea.   Before their departure, however, a sentence had to
be carried into effect—that of the marooning of Juan
de Cartagena and his fellow-culprit, Pedro Sanchez de
Reina.[2] For some reason that we do not learn, they
were put on shore nearly a fortnight before the sailing
of the fleet—on Saturday, August 11th. They were provided with " an abundance of bread and wine," Herrera
says;[3] but it must have been a bitter punishment for

[1] Herrera's account of the intercourse of the Spaniards and Patagonians differs widely from the above in certain points. He relates
their first meeting differently, describes the death of Diego de
Barrasa as occurring in a chance *rencontre* with the natives, and
records the despatch of a punitive expedition of twenty men as a
sequel, adding that not one of the enemy was encountered (Dec. ii.
lib. ix. caps. xiii.-xv.). In the letter of Maximilian Transylvanus
there occurs a lengthy description of a visit of seven men of the fleet
to a Patagonian hut some distance inland, followed by an attempt to
capture three of the savages. One only was caught and brought on
board, but his death occurred within a few days. Neither of these
accounts, it should be remembered, are first hand.

[2] In the pay list of the voyage, published by Medina, this name
appears as Pedro Sanchez *de Viena*. Medina, vol. i. p. 193.

[3] *Herrera*, Dec. ii. lib. ix. cap. xiv.

them to watch the departure of their comrades and to
reflect how small was their chance of life—a chance
still further diminished by the altered relations of the
Spaniards with the natives. They were "judged to be
worse off, considering the country in which they were
left, than the others who were drawn and quartered."[1]
Such an opinion seems to have been held many years
later by another culprit, who, curiously enough, in iden-
tically the same locality, found himself confronted by a
like alternative. In June, 1578, when Drake's little
squadron lay at anchor in Port St. Julian, Mr. Thomas
Doughtie was found guilty of a plot against the life of
the admiral. He was offered the choice of death, " or
to be set upon land on the main," or to return to be tried
in England. He chose the first, giving as his reason
that the shame of his return as a traitor would be worse
than death, and that he would not endanger his soul by
consenting to be left among savages and infidels.

On the 24th August, every member of the expedition
having confessed and received the sacrament, the fleet
left the bay.[2] They shaped their course S.W. $\frac{1}{4}$ W., and
two days later arrived off the mouth of the Santa Cruz
river. Their passage was not accomplished without
danger, for the ships were nearly lost in a heavy squall.
"God and the Corpi Santi, however," writes Pigafetta,
"came to our aid," and they reached the shelter of the
river and anchored in safety. The latitude was fixed,
with very tolerable accuracy, at 50°. In this port, of
whose desolate character Darwin has left us a graphic

---

[1] Letter of Recalde. See Navarrete, vol. iv. p. 206.

[2] Before their departure Andres de San Martin took observations to
determine the latitude. The result he obtained was 49° 18' S., which
is wonderfully correct. Herrera, *op. cit.*, Dec. ii. lib. ix. cap. xiv.

account,[1] two months were passed. The time was spent in provisioning the ships with such wood as could be obtained, and with fish, of which there was abundance. On the drying and preserving of a sufficient supply of these their future comfort—perhaps even their future plans—depended, for the stores of the fleet had already begun to reach an alarming stage of diminution. Visits were paid to the coast to the southward, where the wreck of the *Santiago* had taken place, and such articles as had since been washed ashore were recovered.

No occurrence worthy of note befell the navigators during their delay in the river, if we except a supposed eclipse of the sun, recorded by the historian Herrera, but by no single one of those actually present who have left us an account of the voyage. In an age of writing which erred even more in ellipsis than garrulity, this latter circumstance could not, however, be advanced as a conclusive proof of its non-occurrence. "On the 11th October," we are told,"[2] " while in this river, an eclipse of the sun was awaited, which in this meridian should have occurred at eight minutes past ten in the morning. When the sun reached an altitude of $42\frac{1}{2}°$, it appeared to alter in brilliancy, and to change to a sombre colour, as if inflamed of a dull crimson, and this without any cloud intervening between ourselves and the solar body. Not that the body of the sun, either wholly or in part, was obscured, but its clearness appeared as it might in Castile in the months of July and August when they are burning the straw in the surrounding country. This lasted till it reached an altitude of $44\frac{1}{2}°$, when it regained its original brilliancy."

[1] *Voyage of the Beagle*, chap. ix.
[2] *Herrera*, Dec. ii. lib. ix. cap. xiv.

What conclusion to draw from the above passage it is difficult to decide. The haziness of the sun could only have been due to some atmospheric cause. An annular eclipse of the sun certainly did take place October 11th, 1520, but it was not visible upon the coast of Patagonia, the central line crossing the meridian of the Santa Cruz river, more than 30° north of the Equator.[1]

With the advent of October the weather improved, and on the 18th Magellan judged the spring to be sufficiently far advanced for the continuation of his voyage. The fleet was got under way. Feeling sure that he must ere long come upon the object of his search, the admiral ordered the ships to keep along the coast as before. For two days they were baffled by head-winds and bad weather, fighting their way southward inch by inch. At length the wind shifted to the north, and they ran before it on a S.S.W. course for two days more. On the 21st October, 1520, they found themselves in sight of land; "and there," says the pilot Alvo, "we saw an opening like unto a bay." They were off Cabo de las Virgenes, and Magellan had found his long-hoped-for strait at last!

We must pause here for a moment to consider a question of the greatest interest—a question that has never yet been satisfactorily answered. Did Magellan know, as a certain fact, of the existence of the strait? Or was his discovery of it due to a carefully reasoned-out argument based upon the presumed homology of the Cape of Good Hope? Or was it from the blindest of chances, from

---

[1] Oppolzer's *Canon der Finsternisse*, published in the Denkschriften of the Vienna Academy, vol. lii. For this information the writer is indebted to the kindness of Professor G. H. Darwin.

the sort of fortune that guides a caged bird, panting for liberty, to the broken bar of its prison?

In Pigafetta's account of the voyage there occurs a very remarkable passage, so clearly and definitely expressed, that, did it only emanate from a more accurate author, the matter would seem at once and for ever set at rest.   "We all believed," it runs, speaking of the strait, "that it was a *cul-de-sac*; but the captain knew that he had to navigate through a very well-concealed strait, having seen it in a chart preserved in the treasury of the King of Portugal, and made by Martin of Bohemia, a man of great parts."[1]   The matter is also alluded to by Gomara,[2] but he throws doubt upon it, and says that "the chart showed no strait whatever, as far as I could learn;" and his evidence, as that of a contemporary historian, is not without weight.   Herrera, speaking of the offer made by Magellan and Faleiro at the Spanish court, tells us that they proposed to conduct their ships to the Moluccas "by means of a certain strait, at that time not known of by any one,"[3] and, a few lines farther on, gives the story of Martin Behaim's chart, and adds that "from him they obtained much information concerning this strait."   M. Ferdinand Denis, in his *Portugal*, gives us some information as to the *provenance* of this chart.   "On a affirmé," he says, "que le détroit de Magellan avait été clairement indiqué dès le 15me siècle,

---

[1] "Se non fosse stato il sapere del capitano-generale, non si sarebbe passato per quello stretto, perché tutti credevamo che fosse chiuso; ma egli sapea di dover navigare per uno stretto molto nascosto, avendo ciò veduto in una carta serbata nella tesoreria del Re di Portogallo, e fatta da Martino di Boemia, uomo excellentissimo."—Pigafetta, *Primo Viaggio*, Milan edit., p. 36.

[2] *Historia de las Indias*, cap. xci.

[3] "Este seria por cierto estrecho de mar no conocido hasta entonces de ninguna persona."—*Herrera*, Dec. ii. lib. ii. cap. xix.

sur une des deux cartes apportées jadis en Portugal par Don Pedro d'Alfarrobeira, et que l'on conservait pre cieusement jadis dans le couvent d'Alcobaça;" but he offers no opinion as to the truth of the statement. We have yet another of the great historians who discusses the possibilities of Magellan's foreknowledge of his strait —Oviedo, who wrote in 1546, a period which is within measurable distance of the great navigator's voyage. In one passage he speaks with no uncertain voice—"of which strait and voyage none had knowledge or remembrance until the renowned Captain Ferdinand Magellan discovered and showed it to us."[1]   But elsewhere the claims of Martin Behaim are discussed, and he decides that, whether the discovery was due to his suggestion or to the pluck of Magellan, the latter is worthy of all praise, and "more is owing to his capacity than to the science of the Bohemian."

All the foregoing, it will be observed, are the opinions of people writing *after* the event. For the journal of Pigafetta we know to be in many places no journal at all, but to have been written up some time after the occurrence of the various incidents, possibly even not till his arrival in Spain. The question will be asked, Is there any passage of a date anterior to the voyage which would lead us to conclude that the great navigator suspected the existence of an opening from the Atlantic into the Pacific? and it may be answered in the affirmative. Whether that suspicion amounted to actual knowledge it is difficult to say. However, not only have we the record of Herrera as to the examination of Magellan before Charles V.'s ministers, and the exhibition of Pedro Reynel's globe, in which "de industria

---

[1] Oviedo, *op. cit.*, Bk. xx. cap. i.

dexò el estrecho en blanco," but a document is still existing which places the matter beyond a doubt. In the *capitulacion* granted by the King to Magellan and Faleiro on the 22nd March, 1518, the phrase " para buscar *el* estrecho de aquellas mares "—*to go in search of the strait*—is used, and it would seem from the use of the definite article as if some actual known or rumoured strait was intended.

We may now turn to the evidence of various maps and globes. There occurs in the *Tratado* of Antonio Galvão, which was afterwards englished by Richard Hakluyt in 1601, an account of "a most rare and excellent map of the world, which was a great helpe to Don Henry (the Navigator) in his discoueries," and which may possibly have been the starting-point of Magellan's theory of the existence of a Pacifico-Atlantic passage. "In the yeere 1428 it is written that Don Peter, the King of Portugal's eldest sonne, was a great traueller. He went into England, France, Almaine, and from thence into the Holy Land, and to other places ; and came home by Italie, taking Rome and Venice in his way : from whence he brought a map of the world which had all the parts of the world and earth described. The Streight of Magelan was called in it the Dragon's taile." [1]   Galvão, *par parenthèse*, mentions another map, which his friend Francisco de Sousa Tavarez had himself seen, made in 1408, which marked the navigation of the Indies and the Cape of Good Hope. These two are doubtless those alluded to by Ferdinand Denis, and the clear account of them renders them at any rate worthy of mention as a piece of evidence. But they are, after all, but of slight weight in the scale. Of quite another

<hr>

[1] Galvano, Hakluyt Soc., p. 67.

value are two still extant globes, which demand a careful and detailed consideration.

These globes were constructed by Johann Schöner, Professor of Mathematics in Nuremberg, in the years 1515 and 1520. Both are so alike in their outline of South America, that as far as concerns the question under consideration they may be regarded as one.

A glance at the planispheres here reproduced will render a lengthy description unnecessary. Briefly, a Pacifico-Atlantic passage is in them boldly drawn. It is represented in or about latitude 45° S., and in the earlier, or Frankfort, globe a line is traced embracing the coast beyond the strait and enclosing the legend "*Terra ult. incognita*," thus implying—almost without a shadow of doubt—that this strait had been at that date already visited and recognised as a waterway between the two oceans. South of this an indefinite mass of land is figured, to which the name of "*Brasilie regio*" or "*Brasilia Inferior*" is given. Some distance off the eastern mouth of the strait is placed a small group of islands.

What had Schöner in his mind when he gave this strait a place upon his globes? What were his sources of information? Was it fact or conjecture that guided his pencil? These are the questions we have to answer.

Some light is thrown upon them by a work of the cosmographer which was published at the same time as his early globe, and intended to be in great measure illustrative of it.[1] In it he speaks of his "Brasiliæ regio"—that the country was not far from the Cape of Good Hope; that the Portuguese had explored it, and

---

[1] *Luculentissima quædā terræ totius descriptio.* Schöner, Nuremberg, 1515, 4to.

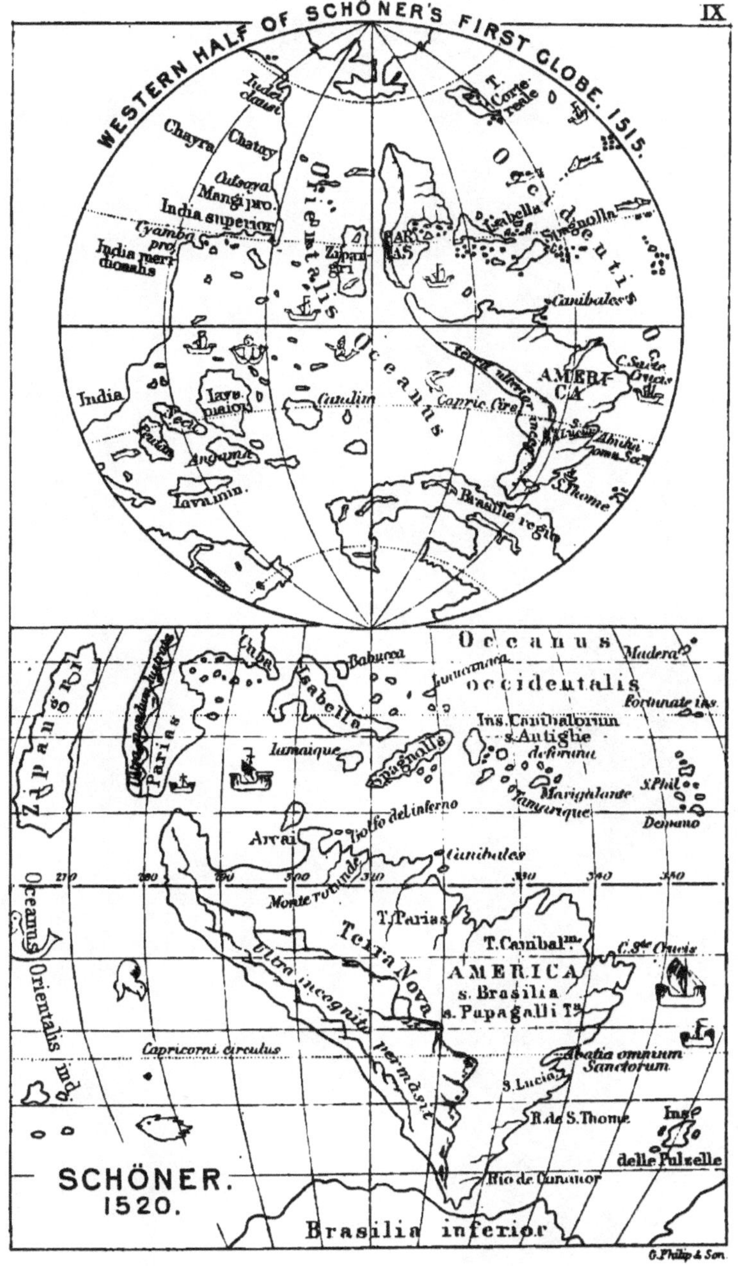

WESTERN HALF OF SCHÖNER'S FIRST GLOBE. 1515.
Indei clausi
Chayra
Chatay
Outsora
Mangi pro.
India superior
Tyamba pro.
India meridionalis
Oceanus Orientalis
Zipan gri
BAR HAS
Isabella
Spagnolla
Oceanus occidentalis
T. Corte reale
Canibales
Oceanus
India
Iava maior
Tecli
Faulu
Angama
Lovnimin
Guulim
Capric. Circl. incogn.
Terra ulterior
AMERICA
C. Savte Crucis
S. Lucia
Abatia omna Sca.
S. Thome
Brasilie regio
Oceanus occidentalis
Zipangri
Ulterius pars Australis
Parias
Cuba
Isabella
Babueca
Iumaique
Spagnolla
Madera
Fortunate ins.
Ins. Canibalorum
s. Antighe de sirma
Marigalante
Tanyurique
S. Phil
Demano
Arrai
Golfo del Inferno
Canibales
Monte rotunde
T. Parias
Terra Nova
Ultra incognita
AMERICA
s. Brasilia
s. Papagalli Tra
T. Cambal
m.
C. Sta Crucis
Oceanus Orientalis Indq.
Capricorni circulus
nermasit
Abatia omnium Sanctorum
S. Lucia
R. de S. Thome
Ins. delle Pulzelle
Rio de Cananor
SCHÖNER. 1520.
Brasilia inferior
270 280 290 300 310 320 340 350
G. Philip & Son.

had discovered a strait going from east to west; that this strait resembled the strait of Gibraltar; and that "Mallaqua" was not far distant therefrom.[1]

All this information was, nevertheless, not gathered at first hand by Schöner. Shortly before he wrote—but how long we do not know, for the title-page bears no date—was published a certain pamphlet in bad German, anonymous, and apparently a confused translation of a Portuguese original—the "*Copia der Newen Zeytung aus Presillg Landt.*" From this he apparently took his description almost word for word, and the question thus shifts itself a point further back into the examination of the *provenance* and authorities of the "*Copia.*"

We do not get very much information from the work itself, but what we do get is very interesting. The captain of the ship, whose voyage it describes, was a "*fast güt frewndt*" of the writer, and the expedition is stated to have been fitted out under the auspices of the Portuguese government by various private gentlemen, *among whom was "Christoffel de Haro."* It is exceedingly probable then that it was either that of Gonzalo Coelho or of Christovão Jacques, and the probability is in favour of the latter. That it was little known

---

[1] Schöner, *op. cit.*, Tract. II. cap. 11, fol. 60 v. "A capite bonæ spei (quod Itali Capo de bona speranza vocitant) parum distat. Circumnavigaverunt itaque Portugalienses eam regionem, et comperierunt illum transitum fere conformem nostræ Europæ (quam nos incolimus) et lateraliter infra orientem et occidentem situm. Ex altero insuper latere etiam terra visa est, et penes caput hujus regionis circa miliaria 60, eo videlicet modo: ac si quis navigaret orientem versus et transitum sive strictum Gibel terræ aut Sibiliæ navigaret, et Barbariam, hoc est Mauretaniam in Aphrica intueretur; ut ostendet Globus noster versus polum antarcticum. Insuper modica est distantia ab hoc Brasiliæ regione ad Mallaquam."

about, and only chronicled *en passant* by the historians, was no doubt owing to the fact that it was a purely commercial venture, in which the obtaining of a good cargo of Brazil-wood and slaves was of greater importance than cosmography.

Dr. Wieser, although admitting that there is strong reason to believe the "Copia" to be the outcome of the voyage of Christovão Jacques, and consequently allowing the strait depicted on Schöner's globes to have been discovered by that explorer, does not admit that it was the strait of Magellan. He dismisses all possibility of such being the case upon the one argument that the "Copia" speaks of it as being in 40° S. The Nuremberg globes and this "Zeytung" can no longer, he says, be adduced in proof of the strait having been discovered before the voyage of Magellan.[1]

A careful consideration of the facts will not necessarily lead every one to the same conclusion as that arrived at by Dr. Wieser. The "Zeytung" is no learned geographical disquisition published by some king's pilot or great cosmographer. It is a very sketchy and mediocre work, written by one who was merely a "*fast güt frewndt*" of the captain, and we cannot therefore place too great dependence upon the accuracy of his "*viertzig grad hoch*." It is easy to see that the exact position of the strait did not interest the author as much as the animals and products of the "Presillg Landt" he describes. Schöner, too, although adopting his text almost word for word, does not accept his latitudes, and the strait is figured in 45° S. Why he should not have placed it yet further to the south it is difficult to say, for if we turn to Ruysch's mappamundi, made in 1507,

<hr>

[1] Wieser, *Magalhâes-Strasse*, Innsbruck, 1881, pp. 41, 47.

we find, written across the lower part of the "Terra Sancte Crucis," a statement to the effect that the Portuguese ships had at that time penetrated as far south as lat. 50°.

The fact that certain islands are figured in Schöner's globes in the neighbourhood of the strait is of some interest.   Whether they are or are not the Falklands it is difficult to say.   In the 1520 globe they bear the text "*Ins. delle Pulzelle*."   That Davis, for whom the honour of the discovery of the Falkland Islands is claimed, should have called them the Virgin's Land, if a coincidence, is at least a curious one.

Perhaps the most important fact in connection with the question of Magellan's foreknowledge of his strait, is that of Christopher de Haro having been the chief person concerned in the fitting out and despatch of the ship whose voyage was the cause of the publication of the "Zeytung."   We must not forget the friendship existing between him and Magellan, nor that he contributed more than a fifth part of the cost of his armada, nor that the great house of which he was one of the leading members, had probably more sources of information at command than any monarch.   Look at the matter how we may, certain broad facts remain :—that both Coelho and Christovão Jacques pushed far south along the shores of South America before Magellan sailed on his great voyage, though how far is unknown ; that a pamphlet, likewise indisputably of an anterior date, describes a Pacifico-Atlantic strait at some length ; and finally, that Schöner considered the information he was possessed of to be sufficiently trustworthy to figure this strait upon his two globes of 1515 and 1520.

Shortly, then, we have three reasons, or groups of

reasons, for supposing that the existence of Magellan's Strait was known prior to the visit of that navigator. Firstly, the passage in Pigafetta deliberately stating that such was the case, and the mention of the fact by various historians; secondly, the use of the phrase "to go in search of the strait" in Charles V.'s *capitulacion* of 1518; and lastly, the evidence of various maps and globes and the "Zeytung aus Presillg Landt." Let us now consider the arguments that can be adduced on the other side of the question.

According to Pigafetta, Magellan derived his information from a chart existing in the King's treasury. We are not told when he saw it. Towards the end of his service with Portugal he was out of favour with the King. He was, indeed, never regarded by him with anything but dislike, and it is therefore improbable that he would be the only person permitted to see it. Gomara, too, says that when Magellan passed into the service of Spain, and his intention of visiting the Moluccas became known, Dom Manoel remained content when he learned that he had promised not to take the route by the Cape, "thinking that he could find no other way nor navigation for the Spices other than that which he (the King) had." Dom Manoel would hardly have felt so reassured had he a chart depicting the straits in his possession, and knew that Magellan had consulted it.

The uncertain, slow, and groping route followed by the fleet is also apparently in favour of a want of definite knowledge on the subject; but it is quite possible that Magellan wished either to assure himself that no more northerly passage had escaped notice, or to make a tolerably complete survey of the coast. Finally, the assertion made by the admiral that he would push on even to lat. 75° S. to find the object of his search shows considerable indefiniteness. And we must not forget that the historians are—save Galvão—one and all silent as to its former discovery.

On the whole, then, the balance of evidence is in favour of a more or less inexact knowledge of the existence of some antarctic break in the vast barrier which America opposed to a western passage. No less indefinite statement can be made with any certainty. It is indeed possible that the wish was father to the thought, and that the explorers of those days, having tried Central and Northern America in vain, and feeling that the land to the south of the Terra Sanctæ Crucis alone offered them a chance, eventually persuaded themselves into a belief in the real existence of the object of their desire. There were reasonable arguments in favour of it also. The fact that the southern part of the continent ever trended to the west, that the vast mass of Africa terminated in a cape, appeared of nó little import to navigators at the beginning of the sixteenth century. An *idée mère* does not take long in growing into a conviction. The shortest route to the enchanted East was the problem which filled the mind of every one. And so they were ready to push their explorations to the farthest limits, that their ships might float on the waters of the Pacific. So absorbing was this idea that it led them to contemplate the most gigantic of projects. If no strait could be found, they would see what human labour would do. They would attempt a task which we, with all the money and resources and engineering skill of the nineteenth century have attempted, only to fail—they would cut a Panama canal. No weightier evidence of the all-absorbing nature

of the work of discovery in those days could be adduced.[1]
Whether Magellan had a previous knowledge of his
strait or not, we can understand how strong was his
determination to do his best to find one.

[1] Gomara, *Hist. General de las Indias*, cap. civ., under the heading
"Concerning the Strait which could be made in order to go more
directly to the Moluccas," discusses the construction of a Panama
canal at considerable length.   The passage is one of great interest.
Four alternative plans are given, and the undertaking is strongly
recommended.   "Sierras son, pero manos ai.   Dadme quien lo quiera
hacer, que hacer se puede : no falta animo, que no faltcrà dinero, i las
Indias, donde se ha de hacer, lo dàn.   Para la Contratacion de la
Especearia, para la riqueza de las Indias, i para un Reino de Castilla
poco es lo posible."   Galvão, at nearly the same date, discusses the
same question (Hakl. Soc. edit., p. 180).

CHAPTER VIII.

THE LAST VOYAGE—III. THE PASSAGE OF THE STRAIT.

THE explorers, we have seen, reached the entrance of the Straits on October 21, 1520. According to Thevet, it was Magellan himself who first descried it.[1] " Ce fut luy qui premier le descouurit sur la minuict, encores que les capitaines des aultres nauires estimassent que c'estoit quelque goulfe, qui n'auoit point d'issuë." It is not improbable that the great desire of his life should lend the leader of the expedition a preternatural keenness of vision, and reward him as it rewarded Columbus.[2] Be that as it may, however, the order was given for the fleet to enter. On their starboard hand they passed a cape, which, since it was St. Ursula's day, they called the Cape of the Eleven Thousand Virgins. The pilot Alvo took the latitude, and found it to be 52° S.[3] The bay within was spacious, and seemed to afford good shelter. The admiral gave orders that Serrão and Mesquita should continue the reconnaissance in the *Concepcion* and *S. Antonio*. Meanwhile the flagship anchored in company with the *Victoria* to await their return, which was not to be deferred for more than five days.[4]

---

[1] A. Thevet, *Les Vrais Pourtraits et Vies des Hommes Illustres*, p. 529.

[2] In the narrative of the anonymous Portuguese published by Ramusio, the strait is called after the *Victoria*, " because the ship *Victoria* was the first that saw it."

[3] Cape Virgins is in lat. 52° 20′ S.

[4] It is probable, assuming Pigafetta's account to be correct, that the vessels anchored in Lomas Bay, upon the south side of the strait.

During the night one of the characteristic storms of these regions broke upon them, lasting until noon upon the following day. It blew, most probably, from the north-east, for they were forced to weigh anchor and make an offing, standing on and off until the weather moderated. The *S. Antonio* and *Concepcion* were in equally bad case. Endeavouring to rejoin the others, they found themselves unable to weather the cape which separated them from the anchorage,[1] and were obliged to put about, seeing nothing but certain destruction before them, for the bay, as they thought it, appeared as such—no opening being visible at its head. As they gave themselves up for lost, they rounded Anegada Point, and the entrance of the "First Narrows" revealed itself. Up these they ran, thankful for their escape, and emerged from them to find themselves in the great bay beyond.[2] They prose-cuted their explorations to the entrance of Broad Reach, and then returned, having rapidly surveyed the neighbouring waters, and assured themselves that the strait led onwards for an immense distance to the south.

Magellan had meanwhile awaited them with more than ordinary anxiety. It was feared that they had been lost in the storm, more especially from the fact that certain "smokes" had been noticed on shore. These they afterwards learnt were caused by fires lit by two men from the missing ships, with the object of revealing their presence, but at the time they were considered to

For he distinctly tells us that the mouth of the "First Narrows" remained unknown to them until discovered by the *S. Antonio* and her consort. This could not have been the case had they anchored in Possession Bay, and they could not well have chosen any other spot. Lomas Bay is also the most natural shelter for a ship—sailing, it must be remembered, upon unknown waters—to select.

[1] Probably the eastern horn of the Great Orange Bank.

[2] St. Philip or Boucant Bay,—the Lago de los Estrechos of Oviedo.

point rather to the conclusion that a shipwreck had
occurred. While the crews
of the two vessels were
speculating upon the fate
of their comrades, the *S.
Antonio* and *Concepcion* suddenly hove in sight, crowd-
ing all sail and gay with
flags. As they approached,
they discharged their large
bombards and shouted for
joy, "upon which," says
Pigafetta, " we united our
shouts to theirs, and thanking God and the Blessed
Virgin Mary, resumed our
journey."

The accounts given by the
two crews were so different
that it is probable that the
vessels separated during
their reconnaissance, and
that one pushed on much in
advance of the other. They
gave it as their opinion
that the inlet led onward
to the Pacific. Not only
had they ascended it for
three days without finding
any sign of its termination,
but the soundings in the

channel were of very great depth, and in many cases they

could get no bottom. The flood, moreover, appeared stronger than the ebb. It was impossible, they said, that the Strait should not be found to continue.[1]

After penetrating three or four miles within the " First Narrows," the admiral signalled the fleet again to anchor, and despatched a boat ashore to survey the country. Most likely the appearance of habitations had attracted his eye, for Herrera tells us that at the distance of a mile inland the men came upon a building containing more than two hundred native graves. On the coast they found a dead whale of gigantic size, together with a great quantity of the bones of these animals, from which they concluded that the storms of that region were both frequent and severe. Passing the Second Narrows, the squadron entered Broad Reach, and anchored on the 28th October off an island at its head.[2]

From the sketchy and confused accounts that have come down to us, it is impossible to reconstruct an exact itinerary of the passage of the Strait, or to present events in any certain chronological order. We are in possession of a few facts which are practically incontestable. We know that the fleet emerged from the straits upon the 28th November ; that on 21st November Magellan issued a general order demanding the opinion of his captains and pilots upon the question of continuing the voyage ; that the *S. Antonio* deserted, and that she deserted almost without doubt in the beginning of November.[3] But

[1] " Porque las corrientes eran maiores que las mengoantes era imposible que aquel braço de mar no pasase mas adelante."—*Herrera*, Dec. ii. lib. ix. cap. xiv.

[2] Alvo's diary. There is every probability that the anchorage at the north of Elizabeth Island, now known as Royal Road, was that chosen by Magellan. Cape S. Severin of Herrera is either Cape St. Vincent or the headland of Gente Grande Bay.

[3] Herrera (Dec. ii. lib. ix. cap. xv.) gives an account of a council

with regard to the chronology of minor events we have to confine ourselves to probabilities. According to Herrera, Magellan took the opinion of his officers at an early period of his passage through the straits. All with one exception were for pushing on. They had provisions for three months still remaining. Fired by the spirit of their chief, it seemed to them a disgrace to return to Spain at this juncture. What had they to show for all the bitter months of hardship through which they had passed? Where were the riches of which they were in search, the islands over which they had been granted seignorial rights? So utterly unknown was the Pacific, so vague the ideas at that time prevalent as to the actual size of the globe they were then circumnavigating for the first time, that there seemed to them no impossibility in the idea that the Spice Islands were already almost within their reach. It were folly at least not to carry on their explorations a little farther now that the summer was before them.

The only voice raised in opposition was that of Estevão Gomes, pilot of the *S. Antonio*. Although a countryman of the admiral, and indeed a kinsman also,[1] he had been for some time upon bad terms with his relative. Pigafetta tells us the hatred he bore him arose from the fact that the despatch of Magellan's expedition did away

held by Magellan with regard to the advisability of the prosecution of the voyage *in which Estevão Gomes, pilot of the S. Antonio, spoke.* But Barros (Dec. iii. lib. v. cap. xix.) gives Magellan's "Order of the Day" *in extenso*, which bears date 21st November. It seems hardly probable that there were two councils upon this subject, or that, if there were, some reference to the fact should not have been made, but it is of course possible. It is also singular that in Magellan's "Order" of 21st November, and Andres de San Martin's reply to it, there should be no allusion to the desertion of the *S. Antonio*.

[1] Barros Arana, *op. cit.*, p. 89.

with hopes he had formed of himself leading a voyage of exploration.[1] Whatever ill-will may have pre-existed was probably increased by the command of the *S. Antonio* having been conferred upon Alvaro de Mesquita instead of himself, the king's pilot. The slight was none the less galling from the fact that his rival was a mere supernumerary borne upon the books of the *Trinidad*, and probably owed his fortune rather to his near relationship to the admiral than to any skill as a navigator or seaman.

The arguments brought forward by Gomes were plausible enough. Now that they had apparently found the strait, he said, it would be better to go back to Spain and return with another armada. For the way that lay before them was no small matter, and, if they encountered any lengthened period either of calms or storms, it was probable that all would perish. Magellan replied as those who knew him probably expected him to reply, albeit unmoved in manner—"*con semblante muy compuesto*"—"that if they had to eat the leather on the ships' yards he would still go on, and discover what he had promised to the Emperor, and that he trusted that God would aid them and give them good fortune." But the opposition of Gomes, whose skill as a pilot was beyond question, must have rendered his position a difficult one. Foreseeing the possibilities of further grumbling, if not mutiny, he issued an order that no one, under pain of death, should discuss the difficulties of the task that lay before them, or the scarcity of provisions with which they were threatened. It is doubtful how far this would have availed had his crews known what misery was in

---

[1] "Molto odiava il Capitano-Generale, il cui progetto fatto alla Corte di Spagna era stato cagione che l'Imperatore non affidasse a lui alcune caravelle per iscoprire nuove terre."—*Pigafetta*, p. 38, ed. cit.

store for them.   For the admiral's words came literally true ; and, broken down with scurvy and privation in their long passage across the Pacific, the men did eat the leather on the yards, and the ships still pressed onward for the Moluccas.

Next day the fleet made sail on a S.S.E. course down Broad Reach, approaching a point on their port hand.[1]   Beyond they came to three channels, of which, according to Herrera, intelligence had been already brought by the *Concepcion* and *S. Antonio*—which two ships had been despatched on a second reconnaissance from Elizabeth Island.   Of these three fjords, " one led in the direction of the Scirocco (S.E.), one to the Libeccio (S.W.) and the third towards the Moluccas."[2] The fleet anchored at some place in the neighbourhood of their mouths, and Magellan ordered the two pilot ships to explore the south-eastern arm.   Meanwhile, in company with the *Victoria*, the flagship followed up the main channel, having left instructions for the future course to be pursued by Mesquita and Serrão.

Rounding Cape Froward, the admiral continued onward for fifteen leagues, when he anchored in a river to which he gave the name of the River of Sardines, from the abundance of those fish they obtained there.   The ships watered and cut wood, which they found so fragrant in burning, that " it afforded them much consolation." Shortly after their arrival in this port they sent on a boat well manned and provisioned to explore the channel further.   In three days it returned with the joyful

[1] Some point between Gente Grande and Useless Bays, possibly Cape Monmouth.

[2] Admiralty and Magdalen Sounds, and Froward Reach of the main channel.

intelligence that they had sighted the cape which terminated the strait, and had seen the open sea beyond.[1] So delighted were the explorers with this happy termination to their anxieties, that salvoes of artillery were discharged, and Magellan and those with him wept for very joy.

Four days or more had now elapsed[2] without sign of the two other vessels, and the admiral accordingly decided to leave the River of Sardines[3] and retrace his steps in search of them. On their way they had leisure to examine the striking scenery by which they were surrounded. On entering the straits, they had found the country desolate and poor, more or less devoid of vegeta-

---

[1] "Dopo tre giorni essi tornarono, e ci riferirono d'aver veduto il capo a cui terminava lo stretto, e quindi il mare ampio, cioè l'oceano." —*Pigafetta*, ed. cit., p. 38.

[2] According to Herrera, a stay of six days was made here, ii. 9, 15.

[3] It is difficult to identify the River of Sardines with any degree of accuracy. From Pigafetta's evidence it would be such a distance from the exit of the straits that the boat journey there and back would take three days. It would not be necessary to proceed beyond Tamar Island to sight Cape Deseado and the open sea, and it is possible to reach Tamar Island from any point in the neighbourhood of Carlos III. Island and return within the time given. Herrera tells us that after leaving the *S. Antonio* at Cape Valentyn, the admiral, *anduvo un dia*—went forward for one day—and then anchored in a river which is evidently the River of Sardines. Alvo says that after rounding Cape Froward they went on about fifteen leagues (*obra de 15 leguas*) and anchored. His journal renders it probable that it lay east of the entrance to Otway Water. A passage farther on in Pigafetta tells us that the River of Sardines was close to the River of Isles, and that the latter had an island opposite to it, upon which Magellan planted a cross as a signal. This island must almost certainly have been one of the Charles Islands, which are full in the fairway of the channel, and admirably suited for the construction of a cairn or signal to attract the notice of any passing ship. Port Gallant and Port S. Miguel, therefore, most probably correspond to the River of Sardines and the River of Isles. In the *Anuario Hidrographico de Chile*, vol. v. p. 393, Andrews Bay is suggested as the River of Sardines.

tion, and consisting of nearly level plains.   Here they were, as Herrera tells us, "in the most beautiful country in the world—the strait a gunshot across," separating high sierras covered with perpetual snow, whose lower slopes were clothed with magnificent trees.[1]   It was not long before they met with Serrão's ship, the *Concepcion*, but she was alone.   Magellan, suspecting perhaps that some accident had happened to the *S. Antonio*, at once hailed and demanded news of her.   Serrão had none to

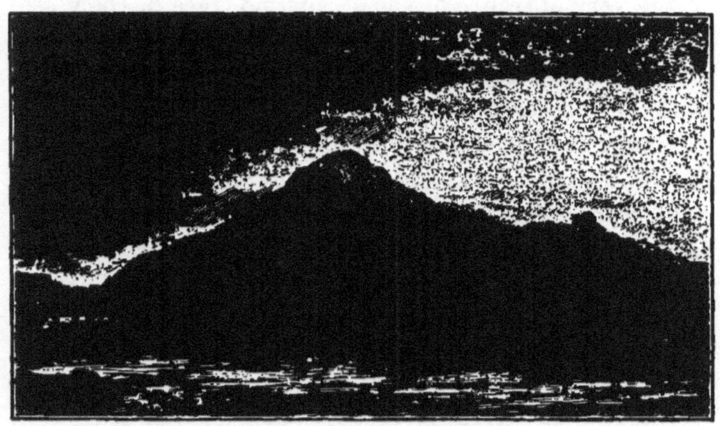

PORT FAMINE, MAGELLAN'S STRAITS.

give.   She had outsailed them almost from the moment of their departure from Cape Valentyn, and they had not seen her since.

[1] The extraordinary suddenness of the change in the scenery of the straits is dwelt upon by Darwin in his *Voyage of the Beagle*, chap. xi. The distance between Port Famine and Cape Gregory in the "Second Narrows" is about sixty miles. "At the former place we have rounded mountains concealed by impervious forests, which are drenched with the rain brought by an endless succession of gales; while at Cape Gregory there is a clear and bright blue sky over the dry and sterile plains."

Upon receiving the news, Magellan at once instituted a search. Admiralty Sound, for the exploration of which the *S. Antonio* had been detailed, was examined to its inmost recesses without result, and the *Victoria* was then despatched northwards with the idea that the missing ship, having misunderstood orders, might return upon her track under the belief that she would meet her consorts at Elizabeth Island. But Broad Reach was found to be deserted, and though the *Victoria* sailed back to the very entrance of the straits, no trace of the vessel was to be seen.

It was scarcely possible that any misunderstanding could have occurred. In the "*Instruccion*" given by the Emperor to Magellan and Faleiro on the 8th May, 1519, the fullest rules were laid down with regard to the course to be pursued upon the accidental separation of a ship from the squadron.[1] One of two things had happened —the *S. Antonio* had either been lost, and lost with all hands, for otherwise their search must have revealed some traces of her, or she had deserted. The men of the *Victoria*, having placed ensigns in two conspicuous positions with letters of instruction buried at their feet, returned to the admiral with the news. He was awaiting them with the other ship in the River of Isles, in close proximity to his former anchorage, the River of Sardines.

The intelligence was a great blow to Magellan, the greater because it occurred at the very moment of his success, and at a time when every ounce of food was of importance in the further prosecution of his journey. Unwilling to realise it, he was anxious to delay some time longer, in the hope that some unforeseen circumstance might have happened, and that at any moment

______

[1] See Navarrete, vol. iv. p. 133, art. ix.

the missing ship might return.   But reflection convinced him of the uselessness of so doing, and he resolved to continue his journey.   Barros tells us that, wishing to know what had occurred, the Captain-general requested the astrologer, Andres de San Martin, to cast the horoscope.   He was informed that the ship had returned to Spain, and that her captain was a prisoner.[1]

There were now but three vessels of the fleet remaining—the *capitana* or flagship, the *Victoria*, and the *Concepcion*.   The desertion of the *S. Antonio* had doubtless caused a new fear in the heart of the leader of the expedition—the fear that her example might be not without its effect, and that even now that he held success in his grasp, it might at any moment be wrested from him.   He was no man of inactivity, masterly or otherwise.   His custom was ever to meet his dangers and difficulties half-way, and disarm them.   And so, rather than permit the thoughts of officers and men to dwell upon the weakened condition of the fleet, and the still more serious loss of provisions,[2] without discussion, he sent an order to each ship that the various authorities should express their opinion upon the advisability of continuing the voyage.

This order, to which allusion has been already made, came into the hands of the historian Barros among various papers of Andres de San Martin.   It was promulgated on the 21st November in the River of Isles.   The astrologer's reply was subjoined, and is the only one remaining to us.   He was of opinion that they should go forward, "so long as they had the full bloom of

---

[1] Barros, Dec. iii. lib. v. cap. ix.   Correa also has this story.

[2] The *S. Antonio* was the largest vessel of the armada, and carried a proportionately large quantity of stores.

summer with them,"[1] and continue their discoveries until mid-January, albeit he did not consider that the straits offered a proper route to the Moluccas. He strongly counselled that the ships should always anchor at night, not only for security's sake, but in order that the crew, toil-worn and weak as they were, should obtain sufficient rest. It is almost incredible that the ships—and sailing ships, it must be remembered—should have attempted such difficult navigation in unknown waters by night. Yet from this we can only conclude that such was the case.

Whether the suggestion was adopted or not, Barros does not inform us, but he gives us the general tenor of Magellan's reply, which was of the usual character. The admiral, it is suggested, only requested the opinions of his officers as a mere matter of courtesy, his intention being to turn back for no one. He gave many reasons for pushing on, adding that God, who had brought them thus far to the discovery of their long-looked-for strait, would in due and fitting time bring them to the ultimate realisation of their desires. Next day, having given a general notification of his opinion, he weighed anchor amid salvoes of artillery, and made his way towards the Pacific.[2]

[1] "Parece que vossa mercê deve ir adiante por ello agora, em quanto temos a frol do verão na mão."—*Barros*, Dec. iii. lib. v. cap. ix.

[2] From passages in the diary of Alvo and the so-called Genoese pilot, Magellan is supposed to have passed on the south side of Carlos III. Island (*Anuar. Hidrogr. de Chile*, vol. v. p. 394, note 41), but there are not sufficient grounds for this supposition. Presuming the fleet to have sailed from Port S. Miguel, it is unlikely that they would have crossed the straits to navigate a much less evident passage. Had they passed on the north side, it is argued, they would have been led off the track into Otway Water. But the entrance to Otway Water is so obviously not the main channel, that it would never have led them to an exploration of its recesses. Moreover, they knew the way from the crew of the boat who had already sighted the Pacific.

MAGELLAN PASSING HIS STRAIT (*from De Bry*).

The constant fires seen upon the southern side of the straits had led Magellan to give to the land the name which it bears to this day, the "Tierra del Fuego." It remained for Schouten and Le Maire, nearly a hundred years later, to prove the truth of his surmise concerning it—that it was no continent, but merely an island or group of islands. "To the left," says the letter of Maximilian, "they thought the land to consist of islands, for on that side they sometimes heard the beating and roaring of the sea, as though upon some farther shore." They must have been nearing the exit. On the evening of the 28th November, 1520,[1] they passed Cape Deseado —"the longed-for cape," as they termed it—and the little armada sailed out upon the hitherto unknown waters of the South Pacific.[2]

Before we leave the strait we must pause for a moment to glance at its nomenclature. Magellan, it has been often said, conferred upon it his own name, but that this was the case we do not learn from any contemporary narrative. Pigafetta figures it as the "Streto Patagonico," and, according to the diary of the anonymous Portuguese, it was called Victoria Strait, since that ship first sighted it, "though some called it the Strait of Magalhães, since our captain was named Fernão de Magalhães." On the arrival of the vessels at the narrow channel beyond Clarence Land the name of Todos os

---

[1] Both Alvo and Pigafetta agree in this date. The anonymous Portuguese gives the 27th as the day, and the Genoese pilot the 26th.

[2] The account given by Herrera of the passage of the straits differs in certain particulars from that here given. The concurring statements of Pigafetta and either of the two pilots have, however, been taken as preferable whenever such concurrence exists. Elsewhere, what is evidently supplemental in Herrera's narrative has been introduced with as strict a regard for chronology as rare-occurring dates render possible.

Santos, or Todolos Sanctos, was conferred upon it—it being All Saints' Day, the 1st November. In 1580 Sarmiento re-christened it the Strait of the Mother of God. But, as may be imagined, the name of its discoverer was too closely associated with it to be put aside, and it has remained, and always will remain, the Strait of Magellan.

We must turn now to the *S. Antonio*, whose base desertion had thrown still further difficulties in the path of the explorers. It appears that, from the moment of

ADMIRALTY SOUND, MAGELLAN'S STRAITS.

separating at Cape Valentyn, the pilot Gomes had determined to put into execution his project of returning to Spain. On the third day, having proved Admiralty Channel to be merely an inlet, the vessel turned northward once more. They did not sight Serrão's ship, the *Concepcion*, which was probably already bound westward up the straits. One author, indeed, tells us that the *S. Antonio* slipped past the entrance of the inlet at night, with the express purpose of avoiding her. Whatever

may have been the case, when the time came to shape
their course for the rendezvous prescribed by the flag-
ship, Estevão Gomes and Geronimo Guerra,[1]—who had
been made *tesorero* of the ship by Magellan himself—
resisted Mesquita's authority, and proposed an immediate
return to Spain. What followed is not clear. The
mutineers, who had laid their plans well, and won over
a large proportion of the crew to their side, declared on
their arrival in Seville that the captain stabbed Gomes,
and that he in turn retaliated by stabbing the captain.
The last at least was true. Mesquita was seized and
placed in irons,[2] and, according to Oviedo, put to the
torture in order that they might obtain from him a
statement to exculpate the mutineers.

Geronimo Guerra was made captain, and with Gomes
as pilot the ship made sail to clear the straits as quickly
as possible. It was proposed at first to return to Port
S. Julian, in order to pick up their two comrades, Cartagena and the priest, who, it will be remembered, had
been left there as a punishment for their share in the
mutiny. But whether it was thought better to proceed
at once to Spain, or whether a visit was actually paid
to the spot without finding their companions, the fact
remains that the *S. Antonio* never brought them back
to their native land.[3] She shaped her course for the

[1] Guerra was a relation of Cristobal de Haro, and had been brought
up by him—"su pariente y criado," Recalde's letter, *Nav.* iv. p. 201.

[2] The date of this occurrence is given in Recalde's letter as the 8th
October—a manifest error, as the fleet did not enter the straits until
the 21st October. The incident must have occurred fully a month later.

[3] Argensola, i. 17, says distinctly that these men did return in the
S. Antonio. But had they done so, we should have had some mention
of the fact in the official letter of Recalde to the Bishop of Burgos.
Moreover, the result of this letter, as we learn from Herrera (iii. 1. 4),
was an order from the Casa de Contratacion to send a ship to rescue

coast of Guinea, where they took water and provisions, the former having already failed from the protracted length of the voyage. From this or other causes the Patagonian they were bringing home fell sick and died. On Wednesday, 6th May, 1521, the vessel arrived at the port of Seville.

Gomes and his comrades had, of course, a well-concocted story to hide their treachery. They complained that the flagship had failed at the rendezvous, and having searched for her in vain they had no alternative but to return to Spain. But they did not confine themselves to excuses. The gravest accusations were brought against Magellan—that he was guilty of great harshness and cruelty, that he sailed at random, and that he lost time and wasted the provisions by endless delays, and that all this was to no good end or profit whatsoever. "Les absents ont toujours tort." Magellan, unable to make a defence, was held for a culprit, and Mesquita—whose loyalty had procured him some stabs from a poignard, the rack, and six months in irons—was thrown into prison as his accomplice. It was in vain that Magellan's father-in-law, Diogo Barbosa, came to his aid,[1] for he remained there until the return of the *Victoria*. The result of the inquiry instituted by the India House, however, was such that Gomes and Guerra, together with two others more especially implicated in the mutiny, were also incarcerated. Beatriz, Magellan's wife, though not actually placed under lock and key, was strictly watched,

them. We hear nothing further of this rescue. It is more than probable that the ship was never despatched, and that the two mutineers expiated their sins with their lives. *Vide* Navarrete, iv. p. lxxxii.

[1] "Diciendo que él debria ser suelto, y los que lo trujeron presos." —*Navarrete*, iv. p. 202.

" in order that she should not escape to Portugal until the facts of the case are better understood." [1]

It is from the letter of the Contador Lopez de Recalde, already alluded to, that we gather most of the details of the *S. Antonio* incident. Two years later, in a memorial presented to Charles V., Diogo Barbosa alludes to the treatment allotted to the various persons concerned in it with a blunt frankness which is unusual even for those days. He complains that the mutineers " were very well received and treated at the expense of Your Highness, while the captain and others who were desirous of serving Your Highness were imprisoned and deprived of all justice." " It is from this," he adds, " that so many bad examples arise—heart-breaking to those who try to do their duty." It must be allowed that his remarks, if not those of a courtier, have at least the merit of being true, and that had Spain treated better those who were at that time only too ready to shed their blood in her service, it would have been not without material effect upon the history of her colonies.

[1] *Vide* Navarrete, iv. p. lxxxiii.

CHAPTER IX.

THE LAST VOYAGE—IV. THE LADRONES AND PHILIPPINE ISLANDS.

THE three remaining ships of the squadron, passing Cape Deseado, directed their course to less inhospitable shores and a warmer climate. Their passage of the strait had cost them thirty-eight days.[1] Although its length was in reality not more than 320 miles, the many incidents that had arisen and the protracted time that they had spent within its limits led them to exaggerate its size, and the distance from mouth to mouth was variously estimated at from 350 to 400 miles.

On reaching the Pacific, the other Patagonian captured in Port St. Julian died. He had been kept on board the flagship, and had apparently reconciled himself in part to his position. To Pigafetta he had become an object of curiosity and interest. " I conversed by signs or as best I could with the Patagonian giant we had on board, making him tell me the names of things in his language, whence I was able to form a vocabulary. When he saw me take the pen in my hand he used to tell me the names of the objects around us, or of some action he

---

[1] Herrera says they were "veynte dias que navegò por aquella estrechura," and Oviedo and Maximilian give the period as twenty-two days. This may possibly mean the actual time occupied in sailing, or perhaps the number of days passed in traversing the narrow part to which the name "Canal de Todos Santos" was more particularly applied.

might imitate. . . . When he felt himself gravely ill of the malady from which he afterwards died, he embraced the Cross and kissed it, and desired to become a Christian. We baptized him, and gave him the name of Paul."

Faring northward to escape the cold, the explorers encountered such favourable weather that the difficulties and privations they had passed through were well-nigh forgotten. The sudden, violent tempests had given place to steady winds which wafted them on their course over the surface of a placid sea, and thankful for their deliverance from their troubles they gave the name of the Pacific to the vast ocean which had afforded them so friendly a reception. "Well was it named the Pacific," Pigafetta writes, "for during this time (three months and twenty days) we met with no storm."[1] At first their course led them along the wild seaboard of western Patagonia. On the 1st December they were some fifty or sixty miles distant from the coast in lat. 48° S., and from that time to the 16th followed a direction which kept them within measurable distance of the land. The abundance of fish astonished the sailors. Pigafetta describes the albacores and bonitos, "which pursue other fish called colondrini.[2] On being followed these spring from the water and fly about a bowshot—so long as their wings are wet—and then regain the sea. Meanwhile their enemies follow their shadow, and arriving at the spot where they fall, seize upon them and devour them—a thing marvellous and agreeable to see."

On the 16th December the general direction of the course of the armada was altered for the first time.

---

[1] Herrera's statement that "anduuieron con gran tormenta hasta los diez y ocho de Deziembre" is not borne out by any of those who sailed with the armada.

[2] The flying-fish :—*Golondrina* (Sp.) = a swallow.

Magellan, thinking he had pushed sufficiently far north-ward, bore away upon a more or less north-westerly track for the lands and islands of which he was in search. Day after day passed, but no land was met with to break the monotony of the apparently endless waste of waters that surrounded them. On the 24th January 1521, after nearly two months' sailing, an islet covered with trees was sighted. On approaching, it was dis-covered to be uninhabited, and, as they could find no bottom with the lead, the course was once more resumed. Its latitude was fixed by the pilot Alvo at 16° 15′ S., and the name of St. Paul's Island was given to it.

Eleven more days of sailing upon a course varying from N.W. to W.N.W., brought them again in sight of land.[1] Small and uninhabited like the first, it afforded them neither water nor fruit. " We found only birds and trees," says Pigafetta, " but we saw there many of the fish called Tiburoni." The island was accordingly called the Isla de los Tiburones, or Shark Island, and " since we found there neither people, nor consolation, nor sustenance of any kind, the name of Desaventu-radas—the Unfortunate Islands—was given to this and St. Paul's Island."[2]

Leaving Shark Island[3] on the 4th February, a steady

[1] Antonio de Brito, in his *resumé* of the voyage sent to the King of Portugal, mentions this island as being 200 leagues from St. Paul's. According to the anonymous Portuguese, the distance separating the two is 800 miles.

[2] Maximilian and Herrera record that the fleet delayed here two days, but we know from Alvo's diary that this could not have been the case.

[3] Meinicke identifies S. Pablo, or St. Paul's Island, with Puka-puka in the Tuamotu Archipelago (lat. 14° 45′ S., long. 138° 48′ W.), and Shark Island, or the Tiburones, with Flint Island in the Manihiki group (lat. 11° 20′ S., long. 151° 48′ W.). Petermann's *Mittheil*, 1869, p. 376. This identification has been accepted by Peschel.

N.W. course was held. The disappointment felt at not
being able to obtain provisions was great, for the condition of the majority of those in the fleet was now
most pitiable. The rations were reduced to the smallest
limits. " Such a dearth of bread and water was there,"
writes Gomara, " that they ate by ounces, and held
their noses as they drank the water for the stench of
it." The Italian historian gives a still more vivid
account of their sufferings. " We ate biscuit, but in
truth it was biscuit no longer, but a powder full of
worms, for the worms had devoured its whole substance,
and in addition it was stinking with the urine of rats.
So great was the want of food that we were forced to
eat the hides with which the main yard was covered to
prevent the chafing against the rigging. These hides,
exposed to the sun and rain and wind, had become so
hard, that we were obliged first to soften them by putting them overboard for four or five days, after which
we put them on the embers and ate them thus. We
had also to make use of sawdust for food, and rats
became such a delicacy that we paid half a ducat apiece
for them." [1]

The result of such privations may be easily imagined.
Scurvy broke out, and broke out in its worst form. The
sufferings of the invalids were aggravated by the lack
of any reserve of suitable food for them, and many died.[2]
Others suffered greatly from pains in the arms and legs.
Few were altogether well, but Pigafetta was one of them.
" I ought to thank God," he says, " for not having

[1] Pigafetta, *Primo Viaggio*, lib. ii.

[2] According to Herrera twenty men perished, but a consultation of
the official " List of deaths " reveals the fact that only seven were recorded between the departure from the straits and the arrival of the
fleet at the Ladrone Islands. *Vide* Medina, i. p. 173.

had the slightest illness during the whole of the period."

Day after day the ships sailed onward—"nihil unquam nisi pontus et undique pontus"—until they reached the Line. Aware from the accounts of his friend Francisco Serrão that the Moluccas did not offer such opportunities for victualling and refitting as he now desired, Magellan thought it best to shape his course further to the north, in the hope, perhaps, of attaining some part of China, with whose wealth and extent he was well acquainted from the accounts of the Chinese traders with whom he had mixed at Malacca. As they progressed upon their voyage, great attention was paid to the navigation. Exact means of estimating their position, it is true, they were without. They were capable of calculating their latitude with tolerable accuracy, although their errors in the estimation of longitude were astounding,[1] and the use of the log was known,[2] as well as the existence both of deviation and variation of the compass. On the latter phenomenon Pigafetta has an interesting passage. Magellan, having ordered a certain course, inquired of the pilots how they had laid it off on the charts. They replied, "as he had ordered it." Upon which he said that "they had laid it off wrong, and that they must apply corrections for the error of the compass (*che conveniva ajutare l'ago calamitato*), which in this part of the world was not attracted with such force as it is in its own quarter—that is, the northern hemisphere."

---

[1] So inaccurate were their methods that Alvo, on arriving at the Philippines, was no less than *fifty-two degrees and fifty-five minutes in error*.

[2] That the log was in use in those days we gather from Pigafetta. "According to the measure we made of the voyage by means of the chain at the poop, we ran sixty or seventy leagues a day."

Columbus upon his first voyage also noted the phenomenon, and endeavoured to explain it.

With its load of human suffering and anxiety, the
armada pressed on for yet another month with a steady
and favourable wind. Their position resembled that
of Columbus before sighting the new world, as day
after day their despairing glances were bent westward
in hopes of land. Then came their reward, and an
end, or at at all events a temporary end, of all their
miseries. On the 6th March land was sighted. A
number of praus came out to meet them, and all
anxiety as to the existence of a population was at
once set at rest. For ninety-eight days they had
sailed over an utterly unknown sea, " a sea so vast that
the human mind can scarcely grasp it," Maximilian
writes in his letter.

The group of islands thus discovered by the fleet was
that now called the Mariannes,[1] or more often, the
Ladrones. To this day, although partially settled by
the Spaniards, they remain as little known, perhaps, as
any part of the accessible world. It is not absolutely
certain which island or islands Magellan first sighted
and visited, but there is not much doubt about the matter.[2] In all probability the high peak of Rota was the
first land to show itself above the horizon. Steering
for this, Guam must have come into view on their
port bow, and discovering it to be the larger of the two,

[1] The islands were thus named in honour of Marianna of Austria,
widow of Philip IV., and Regent of Castile in the minority of
Carlos II.

[2] Maximilian is the only author of any authority who gives indi-
vidual names to these islands. Oviedo and Gomara copy from him.
He calls them Inuagana and Acaca. The former is probably Agana in
Guam, and Acaca or Açaça may perhaps be Sosan in Rota Island.

Magellan altered course to S.W., in order to approach its shores.[1]

Their visit to the islands was a short one. "The inhabitants were a people of little truth," as the Genoese pilot describes them. Hardly had the ships come to an anchor when the natives stole the skiff from under the stern of the admiral's ship, cutting the rope by which she was made fast, and carrying her off with great speed

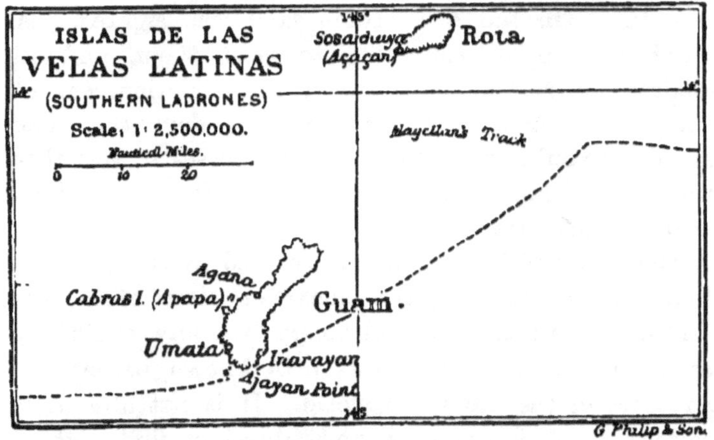

SOUTHERN LADRONE ISLANDS.

and adroitness. They boarded the vessels and robbed the new-comers of everything that they could lay hands on. It was impossible to keep them off. Before long the order had to be given to eject them from the ships, and they found themselves involved in a *mêlée*, which, according to Herrera, became so serious that the Spaniards had to use their artillery, killing numbers of the

---

[1] " Y como fuimos in medio dellas, tiramos al sudueste *y dejamos la una al noroeste.*"—*Diary of Alvo.* This does not at all prove that the ships passed between the two islands, but rather the contrary.

savages.[1] Magellan, much annoyed at the loss of his skiff, weighed anchor and stood on and off during the night lest he should be surprised. In the morning he returned, and landing in person with a force of fifty or sixty men, burnt the village and a number of boats, regained the skiff, and took a quantity of provisions. The natives, who seemed at one time disposed to offer a stout resistance, fled at the first discharge of the arquebuses. No casualties occurred on the side of the Spaniards, but the islanders lost seven or eight men killed. They appear, from Pigafetta's account, to have been quite unacquainted with the use of bows and arrows, for when wounded by one of the latter they would draw it out of their bodies and look at it with great surprise, an incident which aroused the compassion of their antagonists. Their only arms were spears tipped with fish-bone.

In the " *Primo Viaggio* " we are treated to a short description of the manners and customs of the inhabitants of these islands which it is unnecessary to reproduce here. Their praus—stem and stern alike, and fitted with an outrigger—struck with astonishment those who saw this species of boat for the first time. Their speed especially filled them with wonder. As the vessels left the port they were pursued by these craft. So dexterously were they handled that they passed between the ships going at full sail and the boats they towed astern. " They did this so quickly and skilfully," says Pigafetta, " that it was a marvel." It seems still more curious that, considering the relations existing between their visitors and themselves, the people should be quite willing to engage in barter, and that immediately after Magellan had burnt their village, boats should put off laden with

---

[1] This incident is not given by any other narrator.

provisions for that purpose.　Possibly their love of gain overcame every other consideration.　"They are poor, but ingenious, and, above all, thieves," says the Italian historian, "and so for that reason we called these islands the Robber Islands."[1]

Greatly improved in health from the fresh fruit and vegetables they had procured, the explorers left the Ladrones on the morning of the 9th March.　On this day the sole Englishman in the fleet—"Master Andrew of Bristol"—died, the succour having come too late to save his life.　The course was set W. $\frac{1}{4}$ S., and held for seven days.　On the 16th they saw land—the southern point of Samar Island of the Philippines.　Finding the coast beset with shoals, they bore away to the southward and fell in with the conspicuous island then, as now, known by the name of Suluan.　From thence they reached the neighbouring island of Malhou,[2] and anchored for the night.　It appeared to be uninhabited, and next day, being anxious to rest his sick, Magellan ordered tents to be set up on shore and a pig to be killed for them—which animal, no doubt, was obtained during their stay at the Ladrone Islands.　The sight of the fleet attracted the notice of a passing prau, and on Monday, March 18th, the Europeans made acquaintance for the first time with the inhabitants of the Philippine Islands. They were of a very different nature to those of the Ladrone group.　The boat contained some notables from the little island of Suluan, who welcomed the new-comers without fear.　Magellan ordered some caps, looking-

---

[1] We learn from the diary of the Genoese pilot that Magellan gave them the name of Islas de las Velas Latinas, or the Lateen-sail Islands, from the number of craft thus rigged with which they abounded.

[2] Humunu of Pigafetta, who calls their anchorage the "Aquade des bons signes."

glasses, bells, and other trifles to be given to them, and in return was presented with fish and palm-wine. Pigafetta's " figs a foot long, and two cocchi," which he also mentions among the gifts, we have little difficulty in recognising as bananas and coco-nuts. Friendship with the natives was still further cemented by their visiting the ships, and the hopes of the Spaniards were roused by being shown various spices, which must have enabled them for the first time to realise the proximity of the Moluccas.

To the archipelago thus discovered the Captain-general gave the name of St. Lazarus, for he had first sighted the group upon the day sacred to that saint. It was not till long after that the present appellation of the Islas Philippinas was conferred upon them,[1] and meanwhile, curiously enough, they became known to the Portuguese as the Eastern Islands while the Spaniards called them the Islas del Poniente, for, as we have seen, the latter power sailed westward round the world, and the Lusitanians eastward. This circumstance was the cause of yet another oddity. To the first circumnavigators the necessity of altering their day on passing the meridian of 180° was unknown, and so it came about that—the error persisting until quite recent times—Hong-kong and Manila called the same day Monday and Sunday, and it was not until the 31st December, 1844, that the matter was rectified by the omission of that day from the Manilan calendar.

The natives returned to the fleet on the 22nd March as they had promised. They brought an abundance of fruit, coco-nuts, oranges and bananas, and a cock, " to give us to understand that they possessed fowls in their

[1] They were thus called in 1542 after Philip II., son of Charles V.

country." [1] Their chief, who accompanied them, had gold rings in his ears, and bracelets of the same metal, worn by most of them, attracted the covetous eyes of the Spaniards.   With the free supply of vegetable diet the sick improved rapidly.   Each day the admiral went ashore to visit them, and every morning gave them coco-nut milk to drink with his own hands.   It was as good a treatment as could be prescribed by a physician of the present day, and the personal visits of their leader no doubt contributed not a little to their recovery.   After a rest of nine days it was considered that the voyage might be safely resumed, and the order to weigh anchor was accordingly given on the evening of Monday, 25th March. While it was being carried out, an accident happened to Pigafetta which came near to bringing the chevalier and his diary to an abrupt conclusion.   " I was going," he says, " upon the bulwarks to fish, when I put my foot upon a spar wet with rain, and slipping, fell overboard without being perceived by any one. When half drowned, it chanced that my hand touched the sheet of the mainsail which was in the water, and to this I clung and began to shout out until they heard me and came to my aid with the boat, the which help," he reverently adds, " was not due to any merits of my own, but to the protection of that fount of pity, the Virgin Mary." [2]

Leaving Malhou, the fleet struck across to the eastern shores of Leyte, or Seilani, as it was then called, and coasting them arrived on the morning of March 28th at

---

[1] It is probable that this bird was the jungle-fowl (*Gallus bankiva*), which is caught and tamed in large numbers by the natives of the Philippines, and is used to this day for crossing with the domestic fowl.

[2] It was the day of the Annunciation of the Blessed Virgin Mary.

Mazzava or Mazaba, a small island which now appears upon the charts as Limassaua. Here for the first time they exchanged sign language for a more satisfactory means of communication, for Magellan's slave, Enrique of Malacca, found that his Malay was understood. The natives were nevertheless so shy that they would not approach the ship, and the presents that Magellan desired to give them had to be put upon a plank and floated towards them. Two hours afterwards the king came in a large canoe and had a long conversation with the interpreter. Although declining to go on board the *Trinidad*, he permitted some of his men to do so. They received good entertainment at the admiral's hands, and in return the king was desirous of presenting him with a large bar of gold, but Magellan refused, although at the same time thanking him much for his offer.

The next day, which was Good Friday, Enrique was sent on shore to obtain provisions. He returned with the king, who brought dishes of fish and rice to the Captain-general with his own hand. Magellan gave him a Turkish robe of red and yellow and a red cap, and the ceremony of accepting each other upon terms of brotherhood, or *casi-casi*, was gone through.[1] The day was spent in making a prodigal display of the wonders of western civilisation; exhibiting the objects of trade, discharging the artillery, showing the charts and compasses, and describing the events of the voyage. At the admiral's account of the immense size of the Pacific the king was greatly astonished. Equal astonishment was

---

[1] Pigafetta does not give us more details. The ceremony was probably that of "blood brotherhood," consisting in each of the parties tasting the blood of the other, a widespread custom in the Malay Archipelago.

caused by the men in suits of complete armour, who received the cuts and thrusts of their comrades unharmed. At the end of these performances Magellan asked if two of his officers might go ashore with the king to see the things of his country. Permission was given, and the Chevalier Anthony Pigafetta was chosen to be one of them. He has left us a very clear and detailed account of their experiences.

"When we landed," he says, "the king raised his hands to heaven, and then turned towards us. We did the same, and so, indeed, did all the others. The king then took me by the hand, while one of his chiefs took my comrade's, and we were led in this manner under a canopy of canes where there was a *balangai* or canoe, like a galley, on the poop of which we sat, conversing by signs, for we had no interpreter. The king's followers remained standing, armed with swords, daggers, spears, and shields. A dish of pork with a large vessel full of wine was brought, and at each mouthful we drank a cup of wine. If, as rarely happened, any was left in our cups, it was put into another vessel. The king's cup remained always covered, and no one drank from it but he and I. Before drinking he raised his hands to heaven, and then turned to us, and at the moment that he took the cup in his right hand he extended towards me the closed fist of his left, so that at first I thought he was about to strike me. Thus he drank, while I went through the same gestures towards him, seeing that every one did the same towards his companion when drinking. With these ceremonies or signs of friendship we took our dinner, and I was unable to avoid eating meat on Good Friday.

"Before the hour of supper I presented to the king

the many presents I had brought with me.   I enquired the names of numerous objects, and wrote them down. They were struck with astonishment on seeing me write, and on hearing me repeat, in reading, the names they had given me.   Then came supper time.   They brought two large china dishes, the one filled with rice, the other with pork in its gravy.   We ate our supper with the same ceremonies and gestures as before.   We then repaired to the palace of the king, in shape like a sort of hay-loft or rick, covered with banana leaves, and supported on four large beams which raised it from the ground, so that we had to ascend to it by means of ladders.   On our arrival the king made us sit upon a cane mat with our legs crossed like tailors on a bench, and after half an hour a dish of fish was brought, cut in pieces and roasted, another of freshly-gathered ginger, and some wine.   The king's eldest son having entered, he was made to sit next me, and two more dishes were then brought, one of fish with its sauce and the other of rice, to eat with the prince.   My companion, having eaten and drunk too much, became intoxicated.

"For candles they used the gum of a certain tree called *anime*, wrapped up in leaves of the palm or banana. The king now made a sign to us that he desired to retire to rest, and departed, leaving the prince with us, in whose company we slept on cane mats with cushions stuffed with leaves.

"Next morning the king came to seek me, and taking me by the hand led me to the place where we had supped to have breakfast; but the boat which had been sent to take us off having found us, we took our departure at once.   The king was in the best of humours, and kissed our hands on parting, while we kissed his.   There came with us a brother of his, the king of another country, accompanied by three other men. The Captain-general kept them to dinner with him, and made them presents of various objects."

The petty monarch last mentioned, Pigafetta learnt, ruled over the district of Caraca in Mindanao, his jurisdiction extending to the island of Suluan, the land first sighted by the fleet. He was known as the Rajah Calambu,[1] and his brother as the Rajah Siani. His dress as described by the chevalier—the silk cloth on his head, the dagger with a long handle which was all of gold, the chewing of betel, and so on—show that in many ways the costume and customs of that time were no whit different from those of the present day.

The following Sunday, the 31st March, was Easter day. It was the anniversary, too, of the mutiny in Port St. Julian. If Magellan reflected, as he doubtless did, upon the events of that day, it must have been to thank God and his patron saint for the changed aspect of affairs. Then the outlook for him was well-nigh as dark and hopeless as it could be, and he was about to stake his all upon one desperate chance. Now, though disease and desertion had thinned his ranks, he had practically won the game. His great aim had been accomplished, and he had found his straits. The barrier believed to extend from pole to pole to separate the Atlantic from the Pacific had been proved not to exist. And now he had left behind him the perils of

---

[1] Gomara calls him the Rajah Calavar, and says that they made friends with him "sacando sangre de la mano izquierda i tocando con ella el rostro i lengua, que asi se usa en aquellas tierras"—the common ceremony of "blood brotherhood."

that vast ocean which his ships had been the first to
penetrate, and had crossed the meridian of the Spice
Islands. He had discovered an unknown and extensive
archipelago, as rich in gold, apparently, as it was
fertile, and had made friends with some of its kings.
Everything pointed to a happy issue of the voyage and
a continuation of the successes that he had so deservedly
won. No shadow had as yet crossed his path; no
warning of the blow that was so soon to fall.

Good Christian and devout Catholic as he was, therefore, Magellan gave orders that the Easter services
should be celebrated with the utmost ceremonial. The
two kings attended, kissing the cross, and kneeling with
joined hands like their visitors. At the elevation all
the ships fired their broadsides. After mass had been
said, a cross and crown of thorns was brought and presented to the kings, with instructions that it should be
set up on the summit of the highest mountain in the
neighbourhood, that all might see and adore it. This
they expressed themselves most willing to receive, and
the Captain-general then asked if they were at war
with any one, for if such were the case, he would go and
defeat their enemies with his men and ships, and render
them obedient to their authority. "The king answered
that there were, indeed, two islands with which he was
at war, but that it was not then a fitting season to proceed against them, albeit they thanked him for his
offer. The captain replied that, if it pleased God that
he should return, he would bring enough men to conquer all those countries. It was arranged that after
dinner the cross should be planted on the summit of the
mountain, and the festa having been concluded by a
volley from our musketeers who were drawn up in

battalions, the kings and the captain embraced each other, and we returned to the ship."

" After dinner, it being mid-day, we all went ashore in our doublets, and in company with the two kings ascended to the summit of the highest mountain in the neighbourhood, and there planted the cross. The captain then explained the advantages it would bring them. Each one of us adored it, reciting a Paternoster and an Ave, whereupon we descended, crossing the cultivated grounds and going to the *balangai*, where the king caused refreshment to be brought."

Magellan was now anxious to resume his voyage, and inquired which were the best ports for provisions and trade, wishing to turn some of his many articles of barter into gold and spices. He was told that there were three—Ceylon, Zzubu, and Calagan,[1] but that Zzubu was the largest and had the most traffic. "He thanked them and deliberated to go there," says Pigafetta, "for thus his unlucky fate willed that it should be." Upon inquiring for pilots, the king offered to conduct them himself if they would wait for a day or two while he got in his rice harvest, at the same time begging for assistance in the fields. This was readily granted by the Spaniards, "but the kings had eaten and drunk so much the day before that, either because they were intoxicated or because they were ill, they slept the whole day and we could do nothing." By dint of hard work upon the two following days, however, the harvest was got in, and on Thursday, April 4th, the fleet weighed anchor and continued the voyage, after a stay of a week at the island.

[1] Ceylon is another name for the island of Leyte ; Zzubu is Sebu, and Calagan the district of Caraca in Mindanáo.

From Limassaua their course led them north-westward along the shores of Leyte, which they hugged closely to avoid the reefs barring the passage between that island and Bohol. Passing the little island of Canigan (Camigão), they touched at another to which Pigafetta gives the name of Gatigan, a name which it is impossible with any certainty to identify.[1] Here the voyagers were much struck by the Pteropi or "flying foxes"—the huge fruit-eating bats of which so many species inhabit the Malay Archipelago. Pigafetta declares that they were as large as eagles, and describes the capture of one, saying its flesh resembled that of a fowl in taste. The mound-building Megapodes—gallinaceous birds peculiar to the Austro-Malayan sub-region—were also met with and their habits well described. " As large as fowls are certain black birds with a long tail, which lay eggs like (*i.e.* as big as) those of a goose and cover them with sand, and leaving them thus exposed to the sun's heat the chicks are hatched." From Gatigan a westerly course was steered, but, having outsailed the prau of the King of Limassaua, who was piloting them according to his promise, they bore away for the Camotes group, where they awaited him. The good navigation of the Spaniards much astonished him on his rejoining them. At the Captain-general's invitation he went on board the *Trinidad*, and on Sunday the 7th April the fleet entered the port of Sebu.

Before arriving at the town many villages were passed ; evidence that then, as now, the district was one of the richest in the Archipelago. On reaching

---

[1] Presumably this island lies somewhere between Camigão and the Camotes Islands. It is perhaps Jimuquitan or Apit Island.

the anchorage Magellan commanded that the ships
should be dressed, and that simultaneous broadsides
should be fired, " at which," as may be imagined, "the
people were greatly frightened." A messenger was at
once sent ashore with the interpreter, who reassured the
natives by telling them that the artillery had been fired
in honour of the king, and as a sign of peace and
friendship. The king in answer asked the business of
the new-comers, whereupon the interpreter informed
him that his master was an officer of the greatest king
in the world, and that he was on his way to the
Moluccas, but upon hearing of his courtesy and good
fame from the King of Limassaua, he desired to visit
him. The King of Sebu, emboldened by the pacific
attitude of the Spaniards, replied that it was well, but
that he required that every one entering the port should
pay tribute. The interpreter was in no way intimidated. His king, he said, paid tribute to no one, and
if he wished for peace he could have peace, and if he
wished for war he could have war.

It happened that at that moment a Siamese trader
was in the port, a *moro* versed from boyhood in the
affairs of the East. The conquests of the Portuguese
in India and their widespread and increasing influence
were well known to him, and, desirous of saving the
king from the results of a rupture with the Spaniards,
he informed him of the successes of the Europeans in
greater India, and counselled him to make peace. The
King of Limassaua added his influence to the same
end, and eventually the most cordial relations were
established between the Captain-general and the king.
A formal treaty of peace was concluded, the ceremony
of blood brotherhood performed, and an agreement

A SCENE IN SEBU.

entered into whereby the Spaniards were to have the exclusive privilege of trading in the king's dominions.

Magellan, from the very earliest accounts we have of him, appears to have been a man in whom the religious spirit was very largely developed. On the occasion of the conclusion of the treaty—which was arranged on board the flagship by the nephew of the King of Sebu— he alluded at some length to matters of the Christian faith. The statement that when their parents were old they paid no more attention to them, and the command passed to the children, drew from him the rebuke that the Creator expressly imposed upon sons the duty of honouring their father and mother, threatening with eternal punishment those who transgressed this precept. His impassioned address caused many of his auditors to express their desire of becoming Christians, and they begged that he would leave them two of his people to teach them the principles of that religion. Magellan's answer was that of a man singularly free from bigotry. He warned them against adopting Christianity either from fear or from the hope of deriving any temporal advantage from it, and said that he would never harm any one who desired to continue in the belief and observances of his own faith and laws, although he would not conceal the fact that those who became Christians would be more beloved and better treated by his people.

In whatever form his sentences reached the ears of his audience through the medium of the interpreter, the effect produced was all that the Captain-general could desire. The natives at once declared that they desired to become Christians, not from fear, nor from the wish to please their visitors, but of their own free will. They put themselves, they said, in his hands and desired him to treat them as his servants. The captain, with tears in his eyes, embraced the chiefs, and swore by the faith that he had in God, by the fealty that he vowed to his king, and by the habit of Santiago that he wore, that perpetual peace should thenceforward reign between the kings of Spain and Sebu.

Later in the day Pigafetta was despatched with one of the officers to the king, bearing the presents usual on such occasions. These were a robe of yellow and purple violet silk, a red cap of fine material, and some strings of crystal beads, borne upon a silver dish ; together with two gilded glass beakers, which the envoys carried in their hands. They were well received by the king, and his people, standing round, told him of Magellan's speech, and how he exhorted them to embrace the Christian religion. The king asked them to remain to sup with him, but Pigafetta and his comrade made their excuses and returned to the ship. Next day, the 10th April, they again went ashore early. Martin Barreta, who had sailed as a supernumerary of the *Santiago*, had succumbed to the privations endured when crossing the Pacific. A few hours later his comrade, Juan de Aroche, also died. Permission was sought to bury them, and was readily granted. The grave was dug in the open space in the middle of the town, and the funeral conducted with all possible pomp, in order to impress the people. Later the place was consecrated as the Christian cemetery. The Spaniards little guessed how many of their number were destined to leave their bones in Sebu, still less would they have dreamt, had they known it, that none of them should lie at rest within the consecrated area.

Magellan's next object was to commence barter. In

those days this was carried out with some ceremony. A store or large building of some kind was obtained on shore, filled with merchandise, and placed under a strong guard. When all was prepared the shop, for such it really was, was opened, and bartering began. On this occasion the objects were ready for display in two days. The people regarded them with the greatest wonder. For bronze and iron they were ready to exchange gold, giving value to the amount of fifteen ducats for fourteen pounds' weight of iron. For small objects they gave pigs, goats, and rice. The Captain-general gave strict orders that no great desire to obtain gold should be shown, "otherwise," writes the Italian historian, "every sailor would have sold his all for gold, which would for ever have ruined our future trade." It is interesting to note that many appurtenances of civilisation were found existing among the natives. They were possessed of measures of capacity, and knew the use of weights. Their scales were hardly different from those in use at the present day. Formed by a spear-shaft suspended in the middle by a cord, they had on the one arm a basin attached by three strings, and at the other a leaden weight to obtain the equilibrium. "The people live with justice, and good weight and measure," we are told.

The king having expressed his wish to become a Christian, preparations were made for the celebration of his baptism with a becoming amount of ceremonial. In the open space already alluded to in the centre of the town a scaffolding was erected, and decorated with hangings and palm fronds. On Sunday, the 14th April, the rite was performed. Forty men in armour preceded the Captain-general and his officers, before whom the royal standard was borne. On arriving at the place prepared,

Magellan and the king sat in two chairs, one covered
with red and the other with violet velvet, while the
notables sat around on cushions. Before the king was
baptized Magellan instructed him in the meaning of the
ceremony, and told him that if he wished to be a good
Christian he must burn all his idols[1] and worship the
Cross. A large cross was then raised in the market-
place, and the people were told that they must adore it
at morning and at mid-day upon their knees. The
priest then baptized him, together with the prince, his
nephew, the King of Limassaua, and others to the number
of fifty or more. All were clad in white. To the king[2]
the name of Carlos was given, in honour of the emperor;
to his nephew that of Hernando, either out of compliment to Magellan, or to the emperor's brother; while
the King of Limassaua became Juan, and the Moorish
trader, who also appears to have embraced the new faith,
Christopher.

The Spaniards returned to the ships for dinner, after
which the chaplain and many others again went ashore
to baptize the queen. She was led to the place with
forty of her ladies, and while waiting was shown a figure
of the Virgin and Child carved in wood, which she expressed a desire to have,[3] and which, accordingly, was

[1] The idols are described by Pigafetta as being made of wood,
hollowed out behind, with the arms and legs apart, and the feet
turned upwards. They had a rather large face with four very large
teeth, like those of a wild boar, and all of them were painted. They
perhaps resembled the New Guinea *korowaar*, but their size is not
mentioned. The people of Sebu at the present day are nearly all
Christians.

[2] The king's, or rather rajah's, name, for he was of the latter rank,
was Humabon or Hamabar, according to Gomara.

[3] Both Pigafetta, who gave her the figure, and Herrera mention
this circumstance (Dec. iii. lib. i. cap. iii.). It is curious that years

presented to her by Pigafetta. She took the name of
Joanna, after the unhappy mother of Charles V., while
the wife of the Rajah of Limassaua was baptized as
Isabella. The example thus set by their rulers was
followed immediately by the lower classes, and on that
day no fewer than 800 persons were received into the
Church. The news soon spread, and the people arrived
in hundreds, until in eight days all the inhabitants of
Sebu were baptized, and some belonging to other
neighbouring islands. Maximilian Transylvanus records
that the number was 2200, but it very possibly exceeded
this considerably.

It seems probable, from Pigafetta's account, that the
authority of this King or Rajah of Sebu was not so fully
recognised by the surrounding chiefs and kinglets as it
should have been. Magellan, now that he had concluded
an alliance with him, was, of course, anxious to strengthen
his position as much as possible. With this object in
view he summoned a meeting of his two brothers and
various chiefs who had exhibited a tendency to disobedience, and informed them that if they did not render a
proper homage to their sovereign he should order them
to be put to death, and their property to be confiscated.
Such a notice his auditors were not in a position to gain-
say, and they promised to obey. One of them, however,
seems to have repented afterwards, and having again
refused to submit to his authority, a punitive expedition
was sent against him, which plundered and burnt his
village, and erected a cross over the smoking ashes.

afterwards, in 1565, when Miguel Lopez de Legaspe arrived at Sebu,
he discovered this figure, which was regarded as an idol. The crosses
set up by Magellan were also in existence, and in consequence the
later missionaries gave to the place the name of the City of Jesus. —
Colin, *Labor Evangelica,* lib. i. cap. xix.

"Had they been Moors," writes Pigafetta, "we should have set up a column as a sign of their hardness of heart, for the Moors are more difficult of conversion than are the Gentiles."[1]

For these services, and in token of affection, the king presented Magellan with a pair of large gold earrings, two bracelets, and two anklets, set with precious stones. Spaniards and natives were now upon the best of terms, but the Captain-general, finding that the idols were not burnt, as he had ordered, and that offerings of meat were still made to them, reproved his converts severely for their breach of faith. They excused themselves by saying that they were preserved to restore to health a sick man, brother of the prince,[2] "the most valiant and wisest man on the island," who lay so ill that for four days he had not spoken. Filled with zeal for his religion, Magellan said that if the king had true faith in our Lord, and burnt all the idols, and caused the sick man to be baptized, he would at once recover, and so sure was he of this, he added, that if it were not so he would cheerfully consent to forfeit his head. The king agreed, and a procession was accordingly arranged with the greatest pomp and show that lay in the Spaniards' power. Formed in the great square by the cross, it proceeded to the house of the sick man, who was found unable either to speak or move. He was baptized, and the Captain-general asked him how he felt. The "faith cure" was not long in taking effect, for the patient answered immediately that by God's grace he was tolerably well.

---

[1] It seems probable that this village was one of the King of Mactan, although we are not actually told so.

[2] Maximilian calls him a grandson of the king.

"This great miracle was done under our very eyes," says the pious old historian. On the fifth day the man rose from his bed, burnt an idol that he had in his house, and proceeding to the sea-shore, where were several temples in which it was the custom to eat the meat offered to the idols, caused them to be destroyed. The natives tore them down, shouting "Castille, Castille," and declared that if God gave them life they would burn as many idols as they could find, even if they were in the house of the king himself. The influence and prestige of the Spaniards had now reached such a point that it seemed impossible that anything should ever occasion its downfall. Yet, as we shall see, it was to last for a few days only, and to be annihilated with a rapidity and completeness even more astonishing than that of its establishment.

CHAPTER X.

THE LAST VOYAGE—V. BATTLE OF MACTAN AND DEATH OF MAGELLAN.

It is probable that Bulaya—the village burnt by order of the Captain-general, on the occasion of the chastisement inflicted on the rebel chiefs—was situated on the little island of Mactan or Matan, whose rajah, Silapulapu, had rendered an unwilling obedience to the authority of the Sebu potentate. He could not understand, he said, why he should do homage to one whom he had been accustomed for so long to command. The action taken by the Spaniards had not rendered his attitude in any way more submissive. While he was meditating upon some method of revenge, one of his chiefs, by name Zula, sent a small present to the admiral, together with a secret message to the effect that if he did not give a more suitable offering it was through no fault of his own but rather from fear of the rajah, adding that if Magellan would help him with a boat and a few of his men, he would undertake to subdue his chief and hand over the island to the Spaniards.

Upon receipt of the message, Magellan at once resolved to take the affair in hand. Although at first opposed to the enterprise, the King of Sebu was anxious to assist him when he saw that he was determined upon going. João Serrão, the captain's staunch adherent and right-hand man, the old and tried warrior of a hundred fights, was altogether against it. Not only was nothing to be gained by it, he argued, but they had already lost a number of men, and it would be unwise to leave the vessels as unprotected as they would be obliged to leave them, for the expedition needed a considerable force. But it was in vain that he protested. Filled with religious enthusiasm at his successes in Sebu, Magellan desired to push them still farther, until the whole archipelago should recognise the authority of Spain and be received into the bosom of the Catholic Church. He was one, moreover, to brook no opposition from an individual whom he regarded as a rebel rather than an enemy. Action with him followed close upon resolve. Nothing, apparently, could ever make him reconsider a determination, and if he took counsel it was for form's sake only. And so Serrão's wiser words of caution were put aside, and the expedition was prepared. At the last moment his officers besought him not to go in person. But he would not have been Magellan had he listened to them. Good shepherd as he was, writes Pigafetta, he refused to desert his flock.[1]

At midnight on Friday, 26th April, all was ready, and the expedition left Sebu. The Spaniards numbered sixty men all told. The Rajah of Sebu, the prince, a number of the chiefs, and a force of about a thousand men accompanied them in a fleet of twenty or thirty war-canoes. The Europeans had three boats only. The little island of Mactan is close to Sebu, forming in fact its harbour, and the spot chosen for landing was probably

---

[1] "Noi molto lo pregammo acciò non venisse a questa impresa in persona, ma egli como buon pastore non vollo abbandonare il suo gregge."—Pigafetta, *op. cit.*, p. 97.

not more than four or five miles distant from the fleet. It was reached three hours before daylight. No attempt was made to surprise and carry the town. The captain desired to try persuasion before force. Few men, probably, loved the din of battle more dearly than did he, or joined with more readiness in a desperate undertaking. But here the affair seemed mere child's-play, and he probably did not think it possible that any number of naked savages could be a match for the sixty armour-clad Europeans he brought against them. And so, with characteristic straightforwardness, he sent the Moorish trader to Silapulapu, informing him that if he would submit and pay the tribute, no harm should be done to him, but if not, " he would learn how our lances wounded."

The answer returned was defiant enough, that " if the Spaniards had lances so also had they, albeit only reeds and stakes hardened by fire; that they were ready for them, but they besought them that they would not attack before morning, as they expected reinforcements at daylight."

This message, the most transparent of ruses, was of course recognised by Magellan as such. Warned, no doubt, by their previous encounter, the natives had ditched and staked the town and had dug pitfalls. A night attack would have been all in their favour, but they did not succeed in deceiving their enemies. The King of Sebu also counselled waiting for daylight. When it arrived, he begged the Captain-general to be allowed to lead the assault. With his thousand men and a few Spaniards to aid and inspire them, he declared the victory to be certain. Magellan, it is needless to say, would not hear of it. He ordered his friend and ally to remain in the canoes with his men.   He begged that they would look on, and note how his men could fight.[1]

Owing to the coral reef surrounding Mactan, the boats from the fleet were unable to approach the shore. So far off, indeed, had they to remain that it was necessary to wade for a "distance of two good crossbow shots" before the attacking party set foot upon the beach.   Of the sixty men, the Captain-general and forty-eight landed.   The other eleven remained with the boats to guard them, and to serve the bombards.[2]

As they stepped ashore, the dawn of the 27th April 1521 broke over the island.   It was Saturday, a day specially chosen by the admiral, as he had a great veneration for it.[3]   Alas! for his choice!   Alas! for the spectacle of prowess that he had charged his Sebu allies to watch![4]   Of valour, indeed, there was enough and to spare, but it availed nothing against the blunder he had made of under-estimating the strength of his opponents.   From the moment of landing it became evident that a determined resistance would be made. Numbers of natives—varying, according to different accounts, from fifteen hundred to six thousand—surrounded them.   Pigafetta, who was himself of the attacking party, records that they were divided roughly

---

[1] Herrera, Dec. iii. lib. i. cap. iv.   *Vide* letter of Maximilian.

[2] Gomara (cap. xciii. p. 87) and Maximilian state that Magellan took forty men only.   Herrera (Dec. iii. lib. i, cap. 4) says that fifty-five landed.   But Pigafetta's account, here given, must be preferred.   It is that of a participator in the engagement, and is evidently written with care and accuracy.

[3] "Giorno dal Capitano stesso prescelto, perché v'aveva una particolare divozione."—Pigafetta, *op. cit.*, p. 100.

[4] "Subuthicis uero ostendit, se non eos ad pugnandum, sed ad suorum fortitudinem et in bello robur spectandum adduxisse."— *Letter of Maximilian.*

into three bodies, of which one opposed their advance, while the others assailed them in flank. The captain accordingly marshalled his men in two companies, as affording a better means of defence. It is probable that the ground greatly favoured the natives. It is not now, and probably was not then, the custom in the Philippines to build the houses of a village in very close proximity to each other, and the trees and gardens by which they are generally surrounded, together with the thick bush which covers the uncultivated ground, afforded the best of cover to the islanders. Close fighting was impossible, and hence, while the Spaniards were hardly able to fire a shot with any certainty, they were exposed to a continuous and galling fire of spears and arrows. Showers of stones were also thrown, and though the men were well protected about the body by their corslets, it was not long before some of the missiles began to tell upon their limbs. It seems that but few arquebusiers were of the party. Such as there were kept up a desultory fire with the crossbow men for some time, but to little effect, and the natives, seeing the comparative harmlessness of the European weapons, grew emboldened. Magellan, realising that the ammunition was being wasted, shouted to his men to reserve their fire, but his orders were disregarded in the confusion of the *mêlée*.

The attacking party were now getting so hard pressed that the Captain-general directed a small detachment to advance and set fire to a group of houses not far distant. The plan was not attended with the success that he had desired. So infuriated were the islanders at the destruction of their property—for, the wind having aided the Spaniards, twenty or thirty of the houses

were soon in flames—that they returned to the attack
with redoubled energy, and, cutting off some of the
incendiary party, succeeded in killing two of them.
From this moment the issue of the day was practically
decided. Magellan, whose right leg had been pierced
by an arrow, saw that a further advance was impossible,
and gave orders to retreat. In vain, however, did he
command that the movement should be executed slowly
and in order. Had his orders been carried out, the
result of the battle might have been different. But to
the Spaniards, spoilt by facile victories, a reverse was
attended with unknown terrors, and the greater part of
them fled immediately in wild disorder. Six or eight
only were left to support their gallant commander in a
steady retreat to the beach, surrounded by swarms of
savages who poured in a heavy fire of arrows and spears
upon the courageous little band. So heavy was it, says
Pigafetta, who stayed by his beloved captain to the
last, that we could hardly offer any resistance. Then
the water's edge was gained, but no aid could be
obtained from the boats. Their distance from the fight
was so great that it was useless to bring the bombards
into action, and friend so mixed with foe that even had
they been within range it would have been impossible.
And so, fighting hand to hand, and step by step retreat-
ing, the coral reef was traversed, until they were distant
a bowshot from the shore, and the water reached their
knees.

Then the end came. The natives, confident in their
numbers, and caring little for the weapons of the Europeans, pressed them still harder. Twice the captain lost
his helmet, and a little later he received a spear wound
in the right arm. The islanders recognised his rank,

and directed their attacks especially against him ; and finding the bodies of their antagonists invulnerable, they endeavoured to wound them in the legs or face. The length of their spears being greater than that of the Spanish lances, gave them still further advantages. But, in spite of this, the resistance of Magellan and his men was determined and obstinate to a degree. The King of Sebu, recognising the gravity of their situation, had landed some of his men to draw off the attack, but it was too late. The rest must be told in Pigafetta's own words.

"Thus we fought for an hour or more, until at length an Indian succeeded in wounding the captain in the face with a bamboo spear. He, being desperate, plunged his lance into the Indian's breast, leaving it there. But wishing to use his sword he could only draw it half way from the sheath, on account of a spear wound he had received in the right arm. Seeing this the enemy all rushed at him, and one of them with a long *terzado*, like a large scimitar, gave him a heavy blow upon the left leg which caused him to fall forward on his face. Then the Indians threw themselves upon him with iron-pointed bamboo spears and scimitars, and every weapon they had, and ran him through—our mirror, our light, our comforter, our true guide—until they killed him.

"While the Indians were closely pressing him he several times turned round towards us to see if we were all in safety, as if his obstinate resistance had no other object than to give time for the retreat of his men. We who fought with him to the last, and were covered with wounds, when we saw him fall, made for the boats, which were then on the point of pushing off. . . . There perished with him eight of our men [1] and four of the Christian Indians. We had, besides, many wounded, among whom I must count myself. The enemy lost only fifteen men.

" He died, but I trust that your Illustrious Highness [2] will not permit his memory to be lost, the more so since I see born again in you the good qualities of so great a captain, one of his leading virtues being his constancy in the worst misfortune. At sea he endured hunger better than we. Greatly learned in nautical charts, he knew more of the true art of navigation than any other person, in sure proof whereof is the wisdom and intrepidity with which—no example having been afforded him—he attempted, and almost completed, the circumnavigation of the globe." [3]

So died Magellan, his life wasted in a miserable skirmish with savages. The manner of his death has been related by various historians, the most trustworthy of whom differ in no essential point. The account of Pigafetta, who fought by his side, is doubtless correct, but in a desperate struggle such as that in which the great navigator perished, it is not astonishing that the minor

[1] According to the official list of deaths seven died, but one succumbed later to his wounds.

[2] Pigafetta's book, it must be remembered, was dedicated to Villiers de l'Isle Adam, Grand Master of Rhodes.

[3] Pigafetta, *op. cit.*, pp. 99 *et seq.* The last paragraph runs as follows in the original :—" Egli mori ; ma spero che Vossignoria Illustrissima non lascerà che se ne perda la memoria, tanto più che veggo in lei rinate le virtù d'un sì gran Capitano, poiché una delle principali virtù sue fu la constanza nella più avversa fortuna. Egli in mezzo al mare seppe tollerar la fame più di noi. Intelligentissimo di Carte nautiche, sapea più d'ogni altro la vera arte del navigare ; del che è una sicura prova l'aver saputo col suo ingegno, e col suo ardire, senza che nessuno gliene avesse dato l'esempio, tentare il giro del Globo terracqueo che quasi avea compiuto."

details of the onlookers' stories should vary. Thevet states that he was killed by an arrow,[1] which is partly borne out by Nicholas of Naples, a sailor of the *Victoria*, in his examination as a witness in support of Jaime Barbosa's claim to Magellan's estate in the year 1540. " I was by his side and saw him killed by arrows and a lance-wound which pierced his throat."[2] Whether he met his death by spear or arrow, however, matters little. He fell as we should expect him to fall, fighting bravely, and up to the last moment of his life thinking of others rather than himself.

When the King of Sebu heard the news he burst into tears. With the victory in their power they had deliberately thrown away every chance, and had suffered a most disastrous defeat. Silently, and with bitter sorrow at their hearts, the Spaniards decided to return, and the little flotilla recrossed the bay to Sebu. Their anguish was the more poignant since the body of their commander remained in the enemies' hands. The same evening a special messenger was sent to Silapulapu demanding it, and offering to give whatever merchandise he desired upon its return. It was in vain that he pleaded. The rajah's reply was that for nothing in the world would they give back the captain's body, for they desired to preserve it always as a monument of their triumph. It was in vain, too, that Barbosa, the brother-in-law of Magellan, made renewed offers. The victors

---

[1] " A matan fallut venir au combat, où ce vaillant Capitaine Magellan fut tué d'vn coup de flesche qu'vn Matanois lui tira au visage."— Thevet, *Vrais Povrtraits et Vies des Hommes Illvstres*, Paris, 1584, p. 529.

[2] " Este testigo estaba á la sazon junto con él á su lado, é lo vido matar de saetadas ó una lanzada que le dieron por la garganta."— Medina, *op. cit.*, vol. ii. p. 311. Also see Navarrete, iv. p. 286 *et seq.*

were inflexible, and the bones of the brave old warrior
and explorer rest to this day in Mactan.

We do not know with any certainty where he fell,
but the Spanish have attempted to identify the village
upon which the attack was made, and a tasteless monument has been erected to his memory on the spot.
Under the copious rains and exuberant vegetation of

MONUMENT TO MAGELLAN IN MACTAN.

such a climate it seems to have suffered not a little.   A
little longer and the place thereof, perhaps, shall know
it no more.   But Magellan needs no monument.   His
name is written for ever, not only on his straits,[1] but

[1] " For ever sacred to the Hero's fame,
These foaming straits shall bear his deathless name."
—*Mickle's Lusiad*, bk. x., p. 275.

upon the heavens, whose face, as astronomer and navigator, he had scanned so often, in fair weather and foul, in every quarter of the globe.[1]

From the history of the last voyage of Magellan alone a fair idea might be gathered of the great commander's character, even had we known nothing previously about him. Its leading features do not alter. As he was in his youth in India— cool in danger, unselfish, and possessed of a determination almost without parallel—so he remained to the end, until he fell in the little island of Mactan, before the cane spears of a horde of naked savages. On the very occasion of his death he exhibited these qualities in a most striking manner. The details of the engagement which we are possessed of show that his actions were distinguished as much by coolness as by bravery. To his unselfishness, without a shadow of doubt, he owed his death. "His obstinate resistance had no other aim than to give time for the retreat of his men," Pigafetta tells us. Yet the expedition was undertaken in defiance of the advice of his officers and the entreaty of his friends. His fate was the outcome of an excess of self-reliance, of too blind a confidence in his own unaided judgment.

By birth, education, and life, Magellan was a gentleman—nay, more, an aristocrat, and *aristocrate au bout des ongles.* Of noble family, reared at court, and a Queen's page, he passed into the Indian service under the first Viceroy, with the flower of Spain for his comrades. With such a chief and fellow-officers, and at such

---

[1] The honour of having first made known the Magellanic Clouds cannot be ascribed to the navigator. In 1515 Peter Martyr mentions them in his *De Rebus Oceanis et Orbe Novo,* and they were apparently known to the Arabs five hundred years earlier. *Vide* Humboldt's *Kosmos,* Sabine, 2nd ed., vol. ii. p. 289.

a period, the best qualities of his nature could not but become developed. Later, as we have seen, he served under Albuquerque. The fact that he was in India with the two ablest Viceroys, and that his long service was at the most exciting part of that country's history, had doubtless not a little influence upon his character. Magellan was a born leader of men from sheer force of character and strength of will. But there was more than mere energy in him. That he was a man of considerable intelligence there is no doubt from the evidence of other writers besides Pigafetta, and entirely apart from the question of whether he was or was not previously aware of the existence of the straits of which he went in search. But the most charming trait in his character is the carelessness of self which reveals itself so often in the history of his life, the readiness to sacrifice himself on all occasions for others. How he died we have just seen. But we must not forget his action on the occasion of the wreck on the Padua bank, when he volunteered to remain with the sailors; or the aid which, at imminent risk of his life, he afforded Serrão at the attempted massacre of the Portuguese at Malacca. With his own hands he tended his sick crew in the Philippines, after having shared on equal terms with them the privations of their voyage across the Pacific. With mutineers and traitors, in fact with all who rebelled against authority, even if only mere shirkers or grumblers, he was no doubt a hard master; but to those who served him faithfully and did their duty he ever remained a staunch friend. Moreover, he bears a name of untarnished honour. There is no single story against him, nothing to hide or to slur over; no single act of cruelty even in that age of cruelties.

R

A question of no little interest yet remains for consideration—the question of what rank ought to be assigned to Magellan as a navigator and explorer. In the history of geographical discovery there are two great successes, and two only, so much do they surpass all others—the discovery of America, and the first circumnavigation of the globe. Columbus and Magellan are the only possible competitors for the supremacy. Were the vote of the majority taken, it would without a shadow of doubt be recorded in favour of the former. We can see easily enough that it could not well be otherwise. Fortified by the dangerous possession of a little knowledge, the mass would grant the palm to him who first brought the vast continent of America to the ken of Europeans. It is difficult to free the mind from the influence of the well-known couplet over the grave of Columbus :—

" A Castilla y a Leon
Nuevo mundo dió Colon."

But, without detracting in any way from the ample honour which is his just due, an unbiassed comparison of his great voyage with that of Magellan leaves the latter navigator with the verdict in his favour on almost every point. If it be claimed for Columbus that he crossed an ocean of vast size whose western half was unknown to the inhabitants of the old world, it is equally incontrovertible that Magellan traversed a far vaster sea, upon whose waters no European ship had ever floated. When Columbus started on his voyage, his work lay immediately before him. Magellan did not arrive at the Pacific until more than a year after he weighed anchor from S. Lucar de Barrameda, for months of which he had undergone great and continued hardships. While

the great Genoese made land on the thirty-sixth day
after leaving the Canaries, the little armada of Magellan
struggled for no less than three months and eighteen
days across the unknown waste of the Pacific.   Little
wonder that they said it was more vast than the imagi-
nation of man could conceive ! As an explorer then, the
merits of Magellan must be ranked as superior to those
of the discoverer of the New World. The long-foreseen
mutiny, the ceaseless tempests and cold of Patagonia,
the famine that stared him in the face, failed to daunt
him, and he carried out an expedition infinitely more
lengthy and difficult in the face of incomparably greater
hardships.

It is more difficult to adjudicate upon the respective
merits of the two great discoverers as navigators.
Columbus was an acute observer, and though his deduc-
tions were by no means always correct, they evince considerable ingenuity and reasoning power. We know that
he was a maker of charts and maps before he started
upon his great voyage, and that he was in communication with the leading cosmographers of the day. Nevertheless he can hardly be called one of them. Girava
indeed, writing in 1556, speaks of him as " a great sailor,
but a poor cosmographer." [1]   Whether his judgment is
correct or not we cannot well decide at this our present
date. Columbus's discovery of America is surrounded
with such a halo of glory that we are blinded by its bril-
liance, and forget that it was, after all, but an accident.
For he died, as we know, in the belief that he had
reached Asia ; ignorant of the fact that a yet vaster
ocean than that he had already traversed lay between
him and the object of his desire. It was a magnificent

____

[1] Luciano Cordeiro, *De la découverte de l'Amerique*, p. 24.

mistake doubtless—a mistake which in its results was worth a hundred accurate reasonings—but it was a mistake nevertheless.

Magellan we know to have been a cosmographer and navigator of exceptional skill. He is mentioned constantly as such during the period of his service in the East. Returning to Portugal, he applied himself heart and soul to his favourite science, his chief study being to establish some trustworthy method for obtaining longitude. His long acquaintance with Ruy Faleiro, who appears to have been one of the ablest astronomers of the day, perfected him in his science so far as it then went, and he left Seville with a reputation hardly inferior to that of his instructor. It is probable that Pigafetta's *Treatise of Navigation* was the outcome of Magellan's teaching. The successful way in which the latter conducted his ships upon his last great voyage speaks highly of his skill.[1] Neither as geographer nor astronomer can he be ranked beneath Columbus, and Lord Stanley's dictum that he is " undoubtedly the greatest of ancient and modern navigators," is an opinion which a careful investigation obliges us to accept.[2]

Few details have been handed down to us concerning the personal appearance of Magellan. We know, as has already been stated, that he was rather below than above the ordinary height, and that the wounds he received in

---

[1] It is asserted by one of Magellan's detractors that he reached the Philippines by mistake, intending to proceed to the Moluccas, but being ignorant of their position. Not only was he perfectly well acquainted with their situation, as is evidenced by the letter written by him to Charles V. immediately before starting on his voyage (Navarrete, iv. p. 189), but we are especially told by the Genoese pilot that Magellan kept to the north on purpose, knowing that it was impossible to refit and obtain proper provisions in the Moluccas.

[2] *First Voyage*, p. lviii.

Africa had made him slightly lame, but our knowledge
is practically limited to these facts. M. Ferdinand Denis,
in his *Portugal*, gives an engraving of a portrait of the
navigator, stated by him to exist in the Louvre. It is
not now to be found in that collection. Sr. Vargas y
Ponce, in his *Relacion del Ultimo Viage al Estrecho de
Magallanes*, gives a beautifully-engraved portrait, executed by Selma, from a painting then (1788) in the
possession of Don Felipe Vallejo of Toledo.[1] This
painting was a copy of another existing in the gallery
of the Duke of Florence, and ascribed, probably erroneously, to Titian.[2]

The Versailles collection contains a striking portrait,[3]
copied by Larivière from a reputed original now existing
in the Château de Beauregard, near Blois. It represents
a man of singularly refined and intelligent features and
of no little personal beauty, which is rendered not less
attractive from a certain shade of melancholy in the
expression. It is this portrait, never previously en-
graved, which has been chosen for the frontispiece of
this volume.

[1] This plate was afterwards used by Navarrete in his *Coleccion de
Viages*, vol. iv., and a reproduction was made later for Lord Stanley's
First Voyage, published by the Hakluyt Society.

[2] Vargas y Ponce, *op. cit.*, preface, p. xiii.

[3] No. 3091 in the Soulié Catalogue.

CHAPTER XI.

*THE LAST VOYAGE—VI. ARRIVAL AT THE
MOLUCCAS AND RETURN TO SPAIN.*

Upon the arrival in Sebu of the survivors of the
Mactan disaster, one of the first duties performed was
the election of a successor to the post of captain-
general. A dual command—a not unusual custom in
those days—was resolved upon, and the choice of the
electors fell upon Duarte Barbosa and João Serrão.
Both were navigators of no ordinary merit, who had
seen long service under Almeida and Albuquerque in
India, and both were Portuguese by birth.

At the time of the conversion of the Sebu people, it
will be remembered, a large store had been opened in
the town, and much bartering had been carried on. We
do not know whether the Spaniards had any definite
reason to suspect treachery, but if such was the case
they took the best measures to induce it, for one of their
first acts was to transport this merchandise again to
the ships. A more ill-advised step could hardly have
been conceived. Their defeat at Mactan had seriously
damaged their prestige in the eyes of the islanders, and
it behoved them to make as light of it as possible. The
withdrawal of the goods from their store was tantamount to a confession of weakness—was courting attack,
in short.

The disaster came soon enough, whether the distrust exhibited by the Spaniards was or was not a factor in it. What actually tempted the King of Sebu to the base act of treachery of which he was guilty seems uncertain. By some historians it is said that the chiefs who had made difficulties in submitting to his authority united to form a common cause, and sent to inform him that if he did not assist them in exterminating the Spaniards and seizing their ships, they would kill him and lay waste his country.[1]   Others declare the treachery to have originated in the fleet itself—a story related so circumstantially that it is impossible not to give some credence to it.   Magellan's slave, Enrique of Malacca, the interpreter to the expedition, had been wounded slightly in the Mactan affair, and remained obstinately in his bunk, "*atendiendo á su salud,*" and declining to move.   As his injury was very trivial and his services were greatly needed, Barbosa rated him soundly, telling him that though Magellan was dead he was still a slave and the property of Donna Beatriz, that disobedience was not for dogs such as he, and that he would get a sound beating if he did not do what he was told with readiness and alacrity.   The man obeyed and showed no resentment at the time, but he nursed his revenge and resolved to betray the Spaniards at the first opportunity.   Going in secret to the King of Sebu, he told him that his masters had decided to attack the town and carry him away captive on their ships, but that if he would follow his advice he might turn the tables upon them, and soon become owner of all their belongings.[2]   Improbable as the story was, its acceptation no

---

[1] *Barros*, Dec. iii., lib. v., cap. x. ; *Herrera*, Dec. iii., lib. i., cap. ix.

[2] Maximilian and Gomara, cap. xcii. p. 87, give the same story,

doubt fell in with the king's desires, and he resolved at once upon a plan for the massacre of his former friends and the seizure of their vessels.

It had been previously settled that an offering of jewels should be made by the native monarch to the King of Spain in recognition of his authority and protection. All having been arranged, a message was sent to the commanders to intimate that the present was ready, and that they were desirous of offering it in due form. They therefore begged their presence, and that of every one who could be spared from the fleet, at a feast. Barbosa accepted without hesitation—Serrão had misgivings. But the arguments or banter of his friend gained the day, and he agreed to go.

On the morning of Wednesday, May 1st, the two captains rowed ashore in company with twenty-seven others.[1] Fortunately for Pigafetta, a wound which he had received in the face on the occasion of the Mactan affair prevented his joining the party, which included many people of importance. The cosmographer, Andres de San Martin, the *escribanos* Sancho de Heredia and Leon de Espeleta, and the priest, Pedro de Valderrama, were of it. With them, too, was one Luiz Affonso de Goes, a Portuguese, supernumerary of the *Trinidad*,[2]

as does Pigafetta in his *Primo Viaggio*, and Sebastian del Cano in the evidence given by him before the Alcalde Leguizamo in October 1522, with the exception that they make Serrão, not Barbosa, rate Enrique.

[1] According to Pigafetta only twenty-four were with them, but the above number must be correct, for two turned back, and twenty-seven appear in the list of killed.

[2] In the official death-roll, under the date of April 27th, the day of the Mactan tragedy, we find the name of Cristóbal Rabello, who is described as captain of the *Victoria*. Under the date of May 1st occurs the entry of Luis Alfonso de Lois, (*sic*) who is given a like description. Yet we know that Duarte Barbosa had been appointed

João Carvalho, the pilot, and Espinosa, the alguacil. The king awaited them upon the beach, surrounded by numbers of his people, to escort them to the place where the feast had been prepared. But treachery was in the air, and others beside Serrão had an instinctive feeling of some approaching disaster. Espinosa and Carvalho, seeing Valderrama led away alone in a suspicious manner, resolved instantly to turn back. Their caution saved them, but they alone of all the party escaped with their lives. Hardly had they got back to the ships and related their story when a great disturbance was heard on shore. The natives had gradually surrounded their guests, and on a given signal had fallen upon them with spear and kris. Hopelessly outnumbered, the Spaniards fought to the end, selling their lives as dearly as they could. Carvalho, who was now in command, and had apparently hove short his cables in anticipation of the disaster, weighed immediately, and approaching the shore poured broadsides into the village. At the same moment a group of natives came down to the water's edge dragging with them João

captain of that ship after the mutiny. How can these apparently conflicting statements be reconciled ?

A possible explanation is afforded by a few stray words in the bulky pay-list of the armada, under the name of Duarte Barbosa. They state that the captain-general placed Barbosa under arrest in Sta. Lucia Bay because he went away with the natives. He was guilty of a like offence in Sebu, being away three days from his ship, although the admiral sent a message to him to bid him return. He may, perhaps, have been deprived of his command in consequence and succeeded by Rabello, while after the engagement at Mactan he would take command of Magellan's ship, while de Goes captained the *Victoria*. It is far more probable that the entries are wrong, and that Barbosa never lost his command. He at least drew pay as captain all this time, and the promotion neither of Rabello nor de Goes is mentioned in the pay-list. *Vide* Medina, vol. i. p. 190.

Serrão, bound, and bleeding from many wounds. They were desirous of bartering his life for cannon and merchandise.[1] Serrão shouted to his friends the terrible story of his comrades' death, and implored Carvalho to cease firing, or he too would be murdered, and then, turning to his captors, said that if they took him to the ships they would receive whatever they demanded. This they refused to do, fearful of retaliation on the part of the Spaniards. Serrão was a fellow-countryman of Carvalho, and was, moreover, his *compadre*, his boon companion. It seemed hardly necessary to appeal to him for succour in such an hour, but seeing that no steps were being taken to despatch a boat to his assistance, Serrão implored that this might be done before it was too late. No boat, however, was sent. He did not know—he could not believe—that his friend intended, in cold blood, with a depth of cowardice and treachery beyond parallel, to leave him to be murdered. But so it was. As the ships slowly made sail and stood out to sea his friend's baseness dawned upon him. In the name of their friendship he again and again begged and implored his help. Then, seeing that it was in vain, he solemnly cursed him, praying God that at the last great day He would require Carvalho to render an account of his actions in this affair.[2]

As the vessels left, their crews, watching, saw the savages turn upon their captive. A little later and loud cries came from the midst of the crowd, portending his

---

[1] "Pedian por él dos bombardos, y dos bares de cobre, y algunas bretañas ó telas de lienzo."—*Letter of de Brito to the King of Portugal*, Navarrete, iv. 309.

[2] It appears from the account of Pignfetta that it was a far viler sin than cowardice of which Carvalho was guilty—that he refused to rescue Serrão in order to get the command.

death. At the same time another party were seen tearing down the cross that had been erected near the church.[1] Rapid and complete as had been the conversion of the natives, their recantation was no less so.

With grief and despair in their hearts the members of the now much-weakened expedition resumed their voyage. Not only were they greatly reduced in numbers, but the comrades they had lost were the strongest of the party. Many also were men of importance in the command or navigation of the ships. On mustering all hands it was found that only 115 remained of the original 270 or more who left Seville.[2] The *Concepcion*, too, was leaky and unserviceable, and so, rather than run the risk of being undermanned and of losing her cargo, they resolved to burn her, after transhipping the best of her stores into the other vessels. This was accordingly done off the island of Bohol, and, while Espinosa was made captain of the *Victoria*, Carvalho was confirmed in his command as captain-general, a post which he did not very long retain.

The course was now shaped to the southward for the Moluccas,[3] and coasting the western promontory of the great island of Mindanão, where they touched and made friends with the natives, they bore away for Borneo,

---

[1] Argensola, lib. i. p. 19.

[2] The account of the Genoese pilot states the number to have been 108 men, that of Barros 180. The latter number is evidently incorrect. The *S. Antonio* left Seville with nearly seventy men on board, and since she received her share of the *Santiago's* crew, it is probable that she did not desert with much fewer than eighty men. The list of deaths up to this time numbered seventy-two. This would leave about 120 men.

[3] Burney, in his *Discoveries*, p. 71, argues that Magellan did not know the latitude of the Moluccas, and in another passage supports his argument by a passage from Pigafetta:—"In quest' isola,

having on their way undoubtedly received intelligence of the city now known as Brunei. Their track took them to the island of Cagayan Sulu. Pigafetta speaks of the very large trees in it,[1] and records that its few inhabitants were Moors banished from Borneo, who regarded the new-comers as gods. Provisions were now running very short, and their first object being to obtain them, they enquired for Palawan, where they heard that rice was procurable. They were directed northward again, and after running twenty-five leagues hit off its southern end, and coasted it for a considerable distance to the north-east. So reduced were they that but eight days' provisions remained, and they had had for some time under consideration the project of establishing themselves in some island and supporting life as best they could upon the fish and vegetables it might chance to afford them. Such a rash step was fortunately unnecessary. Palawan was found to be a promised land, abounding in pigs, goats, poultry, and fruits, and—more important still—in rice. They placed themselves upon a footing of blood-brotherhood with the chief in whose district they had landed, and after a few days' stay left on the 21st June[2] for Borneo. They had been astonished to find in the port a negro named Bastião, who spoke Portuguese tolerably well, having acquired it in the

prima che perdessimo il nostro capitano-generale, ebbimo noticia di Malucco." It is hardly necessary again to refer to Magellan's own letter to Charles V., giving their exact position (Navarrete, iv. p. 189), or to explain that the quoted passage merely records the fact that those islands were not unknown to the inhabitants of the Philippines.

[1] These large trees seem to have disappeared, possibly as a result of subsequent volcanic eruptions. None of remarkable size, at least, were seen by the author in his visits to this island in the *Marchesa* in 1883 and 1884.

[2] The MS. of S. Bento da Saude has "21st day of July."

Moluccas, where he had become a Christian. With some difficulty they prevailed upon him to act as pilot, but when the time came for their departure he was nowhere to be found. The Spaniards did not permit themselves to be discouraged. Finding a ship about to enter the harbour they took her, and compelled three Moors whom they found aboard, and who said that they were pilots, to conduct them to Brunei.

Passing between the islands of Balábac and Banguey, the *Trinidad* and *Victoria* hugged the Bornean coast, and sighting " an exceedingly great mountain, to which they gave the name of St. Paul "—the present Kina Balu—anchored at some islands near the mainland.[1] The Bornean coast is beset with shoals and sandbanks, necessitating the utmost care in navigation, and the ships crept cautiously along, anchoring at night near the mouth of the Brunei river. Here they landed their pilots, together with a representative from the fleet, leaving them to make their way by land to the city to prepare the Sultan for their arrival, while the ships, having watched the course taken by some junks, were enabled to pick up the very difficult channel by which it is approached, and navigate it successfully for some distance. Next day praus arrived with presents from the Sultan, and piloted them to the usual berth, which appears to have been three or four leagues from the city—not as now, in its very heart.

Pigafetta describes Brunei very much as it is in the present day,[2] a vast collection of houses built entirely on

---

[1] The Mantanani Islands of the present charts.

[2] His account betokens a long-existent civilisation, even in those days. Chinese money, it is interesting to note, was alone in circulation.

piles in the water.   Its situation, in a lake-like expansion of the river, is singularly picturesque and quite unique in character.   It must, however, have been of larger size then than now, for the Italian narrator speaks of the " 25,000 fires or families " of which it was composed.   At the present time there cannot even be that number of inhabitants.   The palace of the Sultan was then built on shore.   Its great halls hung with silk brocades, its rooms full of courtiers, and the elaborate ceremonial observed, are now things of the past, and the Sultan lives, like his subjects, in a pile-built dwelling, which, in point of decoration and even repair, is but little superior to the surrounding dwellings.   The elephants with their magnificent trappings, which bore the Spanish officers to the Sultan's residence, have been for decades past unknown as domestic animals, and it is even suggested that the wild ones, which are only to be found in the north-east portion of the island, are the descendants of those escaped from captivity.   But for centuries past the daily market—one of the most curious sights of the Eastern world—has been carried on at high tide, and will be, probably, so long as the city endures.   The dense pack of canoes, the enormous-hatted women occupying them, the incessant movement of the little craft, and the strident cries with which business is conducted, together form a scene which is not less likely to impress the traveller of to-day than the Chevalier Antonio Pigafetta of three centuries and a half ago.

Although the people of Brunei had treated those of the fleet with apparent good-will, it seems that the latter, after trading for three or four weeks, were not without suspicions of treachery.   Their experience at Sebu

THE CITY OF BRUNEI.

had made them thoroughly mistrustful.   They had, too, definite cause for alarm, for five of their number, having been sent on shore to obtain wax with which to caulk the vessels, were detained by the Sultan.   At the same time some large junks came to anchor in close proximity to the *Trinidad* and *Victoria*, and between them and the bar. Next morning the watch were alarmed at seeing two hundred praus or more advancing upon them from the city, divided into three squadrons.   The two ships at once got under weigh, and making straight for the junks, opened fire upon them without further ceremony, capturing one and driving others ashore.   The result of the action intimidated their smaller antagonists, and the praus returned.   Next morning, the 30th July, the Spaniards sighted a large junk, which they attacked and captured without difficulty.   Their prize was commanded by a son of the King of Luzon himself, captain-general of the Sultan of Borneo.   He was returning from a punitive expedition to the south part of the island, of which some districts appear at that time to have been desirous of Javanese rather than Bornean rule.

With these hostages Carvalho doubtless hoped to get back the men who had been detained by the Sultan, Sripada.   One of them was his own son by a Brazilian woman.   The other two, for two had already got back to the ships, were ordinary seamen—two Greeks of Corfu and of Naples.[1]   It is probable that they were deserters, or had perished in some street quarrel, for they were not returned.   Carvalho, who was apparently a man of bad character, had meanwhile permitted the

---

[1] The death-roll of the expedition makes two others to have been left behind in Borneo, one of whom was the escribano of the *Trinidad*.

Luzon prince to escape, having secretly received from him a very large ransom, which he appropriated to his own use. The others, to the number of fourteen or sixteen, were kept prisoners on board, and with them three women of great beauty who had been found in the junk. They were destined as a present to the Queen, writes Pigafetta, but Carvalho kept them for himself.

Retracing their course, the *Trinidad* and her consort sailed north-east along the Bornean coast in search of a port in which to careen and repair before continuing the voyage to the Moluccas. Passing Cape Sampanmangio, the flagship took the ground and remained for some hours, but was eventually got off without injury. Shortly after, a harbour was found which seemed suitable for their purposes. It was in an islet off Banguey or Balambangan islands, so far as can be made out from the indefinite records left us.[1] A stay of no less than six weeks was made here. The ships were beached, thoroughly overhauled and caulked. Each man worked according to the best of his knowledge and ability, but in the face of many difficulties. The greatest labour had to be gone through in obtaining wood for their work, the ground being covered with briars and thorns, and the men without shoes to protect their feet.

On the 27th September the explorers once more resumed their voyage. During their stay in Port St. Mary—as they named the harbour—they lost the bombardier of the *Victoria*, who died from the wounds he had received in the engagement at Mactan. Either on leaving the port, or at an earlier period—as we prefer to follow Herrera or the Genoese pilot—Carvalho was

---

[1] According to Herrera, this port was on the Bornean coast, while Pigafetta speaks of it as being in Palawan.

deprived of his command. His conduct had for a long time proved his incapacity for the position.. Gonzalo Gomez de Espinosa, the alguacil, was appointed commander-in-chief, and Juan Sebastian del Cano took the post of captain of the *Victoria*. His conduct on the occasion of the mutiny in Port St. Julian had been deserving of great blame, but the ranks had been greatly thinned by the desertion of the *S. Antonio* and the disasters in the Philippines, and with his known ability as a navigator, the choice could not well have fallen upon any other. Making an easterly course for the island of Cagayan Sulu, the vessels fell in with a junk, which they engaged and captured. It had on board the Governor or Rajah of Palawan, with whom they had previously been on terms of friendship. Under Magellan such acts of semi-piracy would not have been encouraged, but it was characteristic of the new command that every strange ship should be looked upon as fair game. As a ransom they demanded four hundred measures of rice, twenty pigs, as many goats, and a hundred and fifty fowls, to be paid within eight days. This figured as a tribute to the King of Spain,[1] and on receiving it—the 7th October—they returned the rajah some of his krisses and arquebuses, and, having added a few presents, permitted him his freedom.

Rounding Cagayan Sulu, the vessels sighted the island of Sulu, and would have visited it but for a head wind which compelled them to bear away for the southwest point of Mindanão. This they coasted, and, passing between it and Basilan, sailed for some distance up the Gulf of Mindanão. Here they fell in with a large prau, which, following their usual custom, they

---

[1] Document No. xxvii. of Navarrete, vol. iv. p. 296.

captured, after a desperate resistance in which seven of her crew were killed. For the first time the nearness of their goal was revealed to them, for they found that the captain had actually been in the house of Francisco Serrão in Ternate. The end of their troubles was approaching, and the riches of the Spice Islands—the

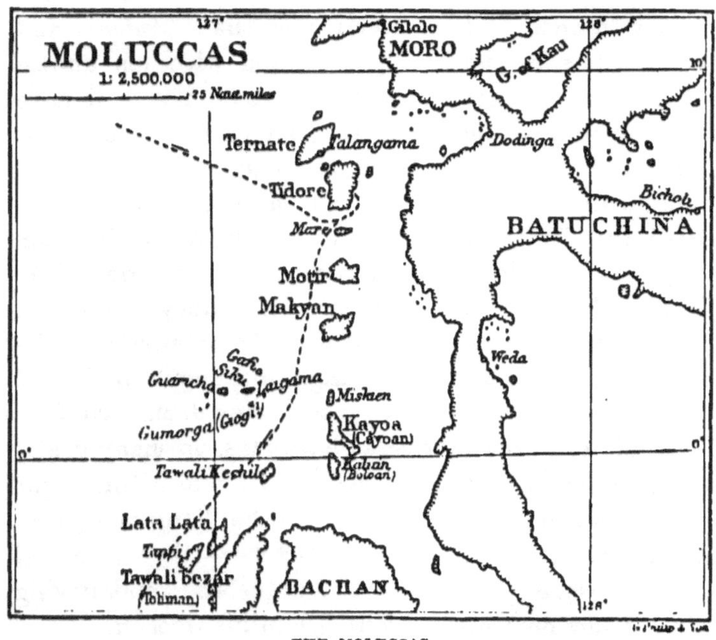

THE MOLUCCAS.

long-sought Eldorado of the old world—were about to become a reality.

Upon the details of the course of the two ships after leaving Mindanão it is not necessary to dwell. They steered southward, passing the Sanghir and Talaut islands, and, sighting the northern extremity of Celebes, altered course to the south-east. On Wednesday, the

6th November, they passed between Mean and Zoar—now known as Tifore and Mayo islands, and a little later the high peaks of Ternate and Tidor appeared to their delighted gaze. How overjoyed the half-starved and toil-worn mariners must have been we can imagine. "The pilot who had remained with us," says Pigafetta, "told us that they were the Moluccas, for the which we thanked God, and to comfort us we discharged all our artillery. Nor ought it to cause astonishment that we were so rejoiced, since we had passed twenty-seven months, less two days, always in search of these Moluccas, wandering hither and thither for that purpose among innumerable islands."

On the afternoon of Friday, November 8th, 1521, the *Trinidad* and *Victoria* rounded the southern point of Tidor, and anchored in twenty fathoms, close to the shore of that island, discharging their broadsides as a salute to the king.[1] Next day he came on board in state. An astrologer and prophet, Almanzor—as he was named—declared that he had divined the arrival of the strangers.[2] He met them with the warmest welcome. "After such long tossing upon the seas, and so many dangers," he said, "come and enjoy the pleasures of the land, and refresh your bodies, and do not think but that you have arrived at the kingdom of your own

[1] Francisco Serrão, on the occasion of the first discovery of the Moluccas in 1511, found that the Malays had been established for over forty years upon the islands. He had settled, it will be remembered, at Ternate, the sultan of which island was not on friendly terms with the monarch of Tidor, and for this reason the Portuguese became paramount in the former island, while the Spaniards identified themselves chiefly with Tidor.

[2] Argensola gives a similar story with regard to the King of Ternate, Boleyfe or Abuteis, when first visited by Serrão and his Portuguese.

sovereign." Whether he regarded the Spaniards in the light of future allies who would help him against his enemies does not appear, but this explanation of the warmth of his reception seems the most probable. He doubtless dreaded the aid that the Portuguese were able to afford the people of Ternate if they so desired. The Spaniards, anxious to make treaties with him and without delay to load their ships with the coveted spices, encouraged his friendship to the utmost of their power, and loaded him and those of his suite with presents. So much did they give him, indeed, that they were requested after a time to cease their gifts, for " he had nothing worthy to send to our king as a present, unless, now that he recognised him as his sovereign, he should send himself." In spite of his humility of speech Almanzor was of kingly presence and bearing. Servants carrying golden vessels for water, betel, and other necessaries stood always in attendance, and his son bore a sceptre before him. Under no conditions would he bow or even incline his head, so that in entering the cabin of the flagship he was obliged to do so by the opening from the upper deck, so as not to stoop, which he would have been obliged to do had he entered by the door from the waist of the ship.

On the 10th November, Carvalho and others went ashore, and after a long conversation with the king a treaty appears to have been signed,[1] by which he acknowledged the sovereignty of Spain. He asked for the royal standard and the emperor's signature, and seeing the eagerness of the Spaniards to commence the lading of their ships, informed them that though he had not in Tidor a sufficiency of cloves ready, he would himself go

---

[1] Navarrete, vol. iv. p. 296.

TIDOR VOLCANO, SEEN FROM TERNATE.

to the island of Batchian, where he trusted he should find enough.

Although Magellan was no longer with them, it may be imagined that the Spaniards lost no time in making inquiries for Francisco Serrão, his great friend and relation, of whom they must have heard so much. He was dead. The manner of his death was more or less shrouded in mystery, but they learnt that it had taken place seven or eight months previously, almost indeed at the same time as that of their great commander. He had been captain-general of the King of Ternate when that monarch was at war with the Sultan of Tidor, and having succeeded in beating the latter in various engagements, he compelled him to give his daughter in marriage to the King of Ternate, and to send him many sons of the chiefs of Tidor as hostages. The King of Tidor never forgave him, and Serrão having visited that island some years later to trade in cloves, the king caused him to be poisoned.[1]

On Monday, November 11th, one of the sons of the King of Ternate came to visit the ships, having with him the Javanese widow of Serrão and her two little children. Aware of his hostility to their host, Espinosa and his officers were uncertain how to act, but Almanzor sent them a message to do as they thought fit. They accordingly had their interview with him in their boat, and presented him with various gifts. In his prau was a certain Indian named Manoel, servant of one Pedro Affonso de Lorosa, a Portuguese who had formerly

---

[1] According to others, he was poisoned by a Malay woman who acted under Portuguese orders, while Argensola states that Don Tristão de Meneses despatched him back to India, being afraid of his acquiring too much power, and that he died on board ship on his way to Goa. Argensola, i. pp. 8, 17.

resided in Banda, but after Serrão's death had settled in Ternate. From this man the Spaniards learnt that although enemies of the Sultan of Tidor, the Ternate chiefs were at heart in favour of Spain. On hearing this they wrote to Lorosa, telling him to visit the fleet without fear.

The prices for barter were agreed upon, and a house arranged for the accommodation of the merchandise on the following day. It is interesting to note the estimate of the respective values of articles in those days. The standard measure of cloves was the *bahar* of 406 lbs. This could be obtained for ten ells of red cloth, fifteen of yellow, fifteen hatchets, thirty-five glass goblets, seventeen catties of cinnabar or quicksilver, twenty-six ells of common linen, a hundred and fifty knives, fifty scissors, forty caps, ten Guzerat cloths, or a hundred-weight of bronze. The Brunei gongs were as much esteemed then as now, and for every three of them— doubtless the spoil of some of their prizes—they were able to purchase two *bahars*. All these prices nevertheless were prospective, for as yet no cloves or spices of any kind were to be obtained. The Sultan sent one of his sons to the island of Motir, and announced his intention of visiting Batchian in person in order to see what could be done. The Spaniards, anxious to please him in every way, gave him the three women and the men they had captured in the Prince of Luzon's junk, and killed all the pigs they had on board, which had always been a source of great annoyance to him as a Mohammedan.

On the evening of the 14th November the Portuguese Lorosa arrived in a prau, and they were enabled for the first time to obtain news from civilised lips of what had passed in the Moluccas.   He had come with Serrão in the first expedition of 1511, and was well acquainted with native politics.   He told them that Don Tristão de Meneses, whose large ship had left for Banda only a few months before, had brought news of the departure of Magellan's armada from Seville, and had informed them that the King of Portugal had sent ships both to the Cape of Good Hope and to the Rio de la Plata to intercept it, and that, learning later that Magellan had passed westward, he wrote to the Viceroy of India, Diogo Lopez de Sequeira, to despatch a fleet of six vessels to the Moluccas against him.   This Sequeira was unable to do, owing to renewed difficulties with the Arabs in the Red Sea, and a galleon which he had sent later under the command of Francisco Faria had been unable to reach its destination.   The trade of Portugal in the islands must have been considerably developed, even at this date, for Lorosa informed his hearers that a great number of junks went yearly from Malacca to Banda to purchase nutmegs, returning by way of Ternate to complete their cargo with cloves.

Two days later the Moorish king of Gilolo, an ally of Almanzor, visited them, and was given a quantity of presents.   Great numbers of the natives of Ternate also came, their boats laden with cloves, desirous of commencing trade.   But Espinosa, who did not wish to offend the Sultan, thought it best not to begin to sell the merchandise until his return from Batchian.   This took place on the night of November 24th, amid great rejoicings.   The Sultan's prau passed between the *Trinidad* and *Victoria* with drums beating, while the Spanish ships fired their broadsides in his honour.   The Captain-general was informed that for four days there would be a continuous supply of cloves.   The Sultan was punctual to his promise, and next day they began the lading of the ships.   " As they were the first cloves we took aboard, and as they were also the chief object of our voyage, we discharged many bombards for joy." [1]

On the following day the Sultan informed them that it was the custom, when the first loads of cloves were embarked on a vessel, that he should give a feast to the crews and merchants, and he begged them, therefore, to attend an entertainment he proposed to give at which the King of Batchian would also be present.   Espinosa and his men, however, who had not forgotten the Sebu incident, instantly suspected treachery, and refused. Their suspicions were, nevertheless, unfounded, for, though they learnt afterwards, on trustworthy authority, that certain of the chiefs had counselled their assassination, they also learnt that the Sultan had indignantly rejected so base a suggestion.   His loyalty to Spain and admiration of the Spaniards were doubtless sincere enough.   Nor was he the only person to express a desire to become a vassal of the emperor.   Many of those in authority in the neighbouring islands were also ready to place themselves under Charles's protection.   On 16th November a treaty was signed with the King of Gilolo, on the 19th of the same month with the Rajah of Makian, and on the 16th or 17th December with the King of Batchian and various notables of the island of Ternate.[2]   The King of Batchian sent a slave and two bahars of cloves as a present to the emperor.   He was desirous of presenting ten bahars, but so heavily laden

---

[1] Pigafetta, *op. cit.*, p. 148.

[2] Documents collected by Muñoz. *Vide* Navarrete, vol. iv. p. 297.

were the ships, Pigafetta tells us, that Espinosa was afraid of taking more.

Among his presents was one which greatly pleased and astonished the Europeans—some skins of the bird of Paradise. The mention made of them by Maximilian Transylvanus in his letter to the Cardinal of Salzburg is perhaps the first record that we have of the existence of these birds, although it is hard to believe that the Portuguese, who had at this time been for ten years upon the islands, were not perfectly well acquainted with them. The natives of New Guinea seem, from Pigafetta's account, to have prepared the skins in precisely the same manner as that in use at the present day. To the Malay traders, judging from Maximilian's letter, they were apparently .common objects. "The Mohammedans, who travelled to those parts for commercial purposes, told them (the Kings of Marmin) that this bird was born in Paradise, and that Paradise was the abode of the souls of those who had died, wherefore these princes embraced the religion of Mohammed, because it promised wonderful things about this abode of souls." The fact that the skins were prepared with the feet cut off doubtless caused the fable—given us by Maximilian and copied by a hundred authors —that they passed an entirely aerial existence, never alighting upon the ground nor upon any tree that grew upon it. Sometimes, report ran, they were seen to fall dead from the sky,[1] and for these reasons, and from

---

[1] Pigafetta, *op. cit.*, p. 156, calls the birds *uccelli morti*, which seems, to those acquainted with the Moluccas, to point to the existence of a regular trade in the skins even in those days, for the trade name at the present day is *burong mati*,—words of precisely similar meaning. The Italian tells us that they were also called *bolondinata*, a misprint for *bolon divata* or *diuata*, which Oviedo corrects. This is only a form of *burong dcwata*, *i.c.*, the birds of the gods.

their beauty, the skins were much valued, and they were supposed to render their wearers safe and invincible in battle.

If there had been an insufficient supply of cloves at the time of the arrival of the fleet, there was certainly no lack of them as the weeks wore on, and the time for sailing approached. The Sultan issued a proclamation that all who had them might sell, after which, says Pigafetta, "*comperammo garofani a furia*," "we bought them like mad." The prices in consequence went down very much. For four yards of ribbon a bahar was obtainable, and at length, each man wishing to have his share in the cargo, and having no more merchandise to barter, gave one his mantle, and another his coat, and another his shirt or other garments to obtain them.

On Monday, 16th December, they bent new sails to the ships, each adorned with the Cross of St. James of Galicia, and with the motto, "This is the Device of our Good Fortune." Eighty barrels of water were put on board each vessel, and the preparations for departure pushed forward. Their wood they had arranged to obtain at the little island of Mareh, whither the king had sent a hundred men to cut it. Anxious to be provided with the best sources of information concerning the Moluccas and their trade, they offered Lorosa, the Portuguese, a high salary, and succeeded in persuading him to accompany them to Europe. He embarked at the risk of his life, for a Ternate chieftain—a friend of the Portuguese—attempted to seize him, with the intention of delivering him to the commandant of Malacca. Lorosa escaped upon this occasion, but an unlucky fate having thrown him a few months later into the power of his countrymen, he paid for his desertion with his head.

The time had now arrived for the departure of the *Trinidad* and her consort. The Sultan of Tidor was inconsolable. He was as an unweaned child, he said, whom its mother was about to leave, and he was the more disconsolate since he had got to like not only the Spaniards but so many of the products of their country. He besought of them that they would not fail to return as quickly as possible, and meanwhile begged that he might be left some artillery in order that he should be the better able to defend his country. He was accordingly presented with some arquebuses that had been taken in the prizes captured off the Bornean coast, besides some swivel guns and four barrels of powder.

On Wednesday, December 18th, all was ready. Much as the weary and wave-tossed explorers longed for rest and the pleasant land of Castile, they were heartily sorry to leave the Moluccas, where they had obtained so warm a welcome and so valuable a cargo. No one could bid adieu to so beautiful a country without regret. The charm of existence there, once tasted, can never be forgotten. " What need is there of many words ? " says Maximilian.[1] " Everything there is humble and of no value, save peace, ease, and spices. The best and noblest of these, and the greatest possible good, namely, peace, seemed to have been driven by men's wickedness from our world to theirs." Alas ! it did not long remain there. For half a century or more from the time of which he spoke, the most atrocious acts of cruelty and treachery daily wrote the annals of the islands in blood.

[1] " Quid multa ? Omnia apud hos humilia ac sordida præter pacem, otium et aromata."

The Sultans and Rajahs of Tidor, Gilolo, and Batchian, together with a son of the King of Ternate, came to bid farewell to their visitors, and to accompany them as far as the island of Mareh. The *Victoria* was first aweigh, and standing out a little waited for the flagship, which was in difficulties with her anchor. While engaged over this, a leak of the most alarming kind was suddenly discovered; "the water rushed in with as much force as if it came through a pipe," but nowhere could they discover its exact situation. Learning what had occurred, del Cano returned and took up his former anchorage. The men were kept day and night at the pumps, but in vain, and the leak gained on them. Such divers as were available were employed, but to no purpose, and the Sultan sent to a distant part of the island for three other men who were possessed of special skill. These dived with their long hair loose, so that the inrush of the water should act upon it, and thus indicate the leak; but although they remained more than an hour in the water, they were unable to find it.

The condition of the *Trinidad* was evidently serious, and a meeting was held to decide upon their course of action. Eventually it was settled that the *Victoria* should take advantage of the east monsoon, and sail for Spain without delay, while the flagship should discharge cargo, undergo a thorough refit, and start at the change of the monsoon for Panama. This decision arrived at, the captain of the *Victoria*, fearing that she also might spring a leak on account of the heavy cargo and the long voyage before them, thought it better to lighten her of some of her cloves. This was done, and some of the crew were put ashore, preferring to remain in the Moluccas, since they feared the ship could not last out

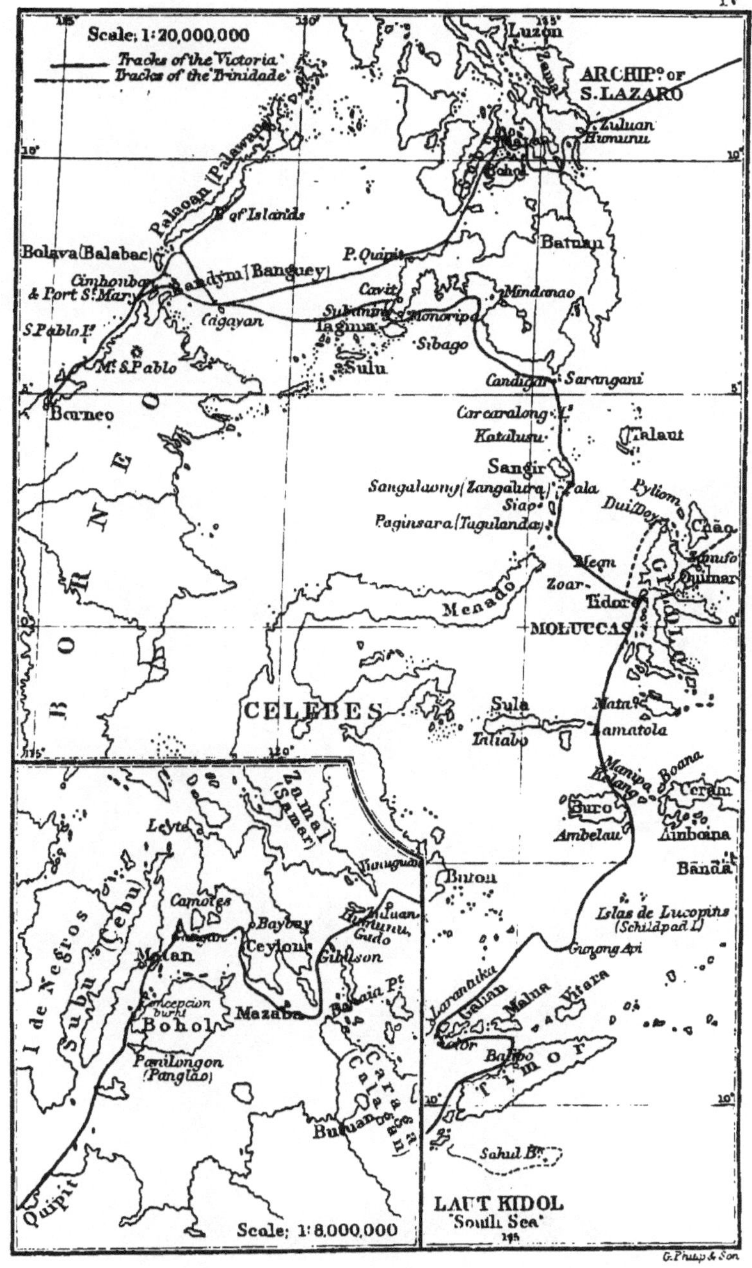
Scale: 1:20,000,000
Tracks of the 'Victoria'
Tracks of the 'Trinidade'
Luzon
ARCHIP.º OF S. LAZARO
Zuluan
Homonu
Matan
Bohol
Palaoan (Palawan)
I.º of Islands
Bolava (Balabac)
Batuan
P. Quipit
Cimbonban
Bandjin (Banguey)
Cavit
Mindanao
& Port S.t Mary
Cagayan
Subanin
Monoripa
S. Pablo I.º
Taguma
Sibago
M.t S. Pablo
Sulu
Candigar
Sarangani
Barneo
Carcaralong I.º
Talaut
Katalusu
BORNEO
Sangir
Pala
Pyliom
Sangalaong (Zangalura)
Siap
Dui Doya
Chão
Paginsara (Tagulanda)
Mesi
Zonufo
Quimar
Megu
GILOLO
Menado
Zoar
Tidore
MOLUCCAS
CELEBES
Sula
Mata?
Inhabo
Lamatola
Manipa
Boana
Kilang
Ceram
Buro
Ambelau
Ainboina
Banda
Buton
Islas de Lucopins
(Schildpad I.)
Zamal (Samar)
Gunong Api
Leyte
Vanuguan
Camotes
H. Juan
Baybay
Homonu,
I de Negros
Gudo
Subu (Cebu)
Ceylon
Gibilson
Larantuka
Galian
Malua
Vitara
Matan
Concepcion
Batuia Pt
burnt
Mazaba
Alor
Bohol
Baypo
Timor
Panilongon
(Panglao)
Caragan
LAUT KIDOL
Quipit
'South Sea'
Sahul B.k
Buluan
Scale: 1:8,000,000
G. Philip & Son

the voyage. Those that were to remain behind busied themselves in writing letters to their friends and relations in Spain, and on Saturday the 21st December, at midday, del Cano started on his voyage. The ships took leave of one another by a mutual discharge of bombards, while, amid tears and embraces, the friends of many months' mutual hardships bade adieu. The greater number were destined never to see each other again.

Gonzalo Gomez de Espinosa, with fifty-three men, remained with the flagship. The crew of the *Victoria* consisted of sixty men all told, of which forty-seven were Europeans and the rest natives. A hundred and one souls only were thus left of the two hundred and eighty who had originally sailed.

Touching at Mare, and taking on board the wood that had been cut for them, the *Victoria* shaped a S.W. course, which took her to the west of the Batchian group. Anchoring at one of the Xulla islands on their way, they reached Buru on Friday, the 27th December, and obtained fresh provisions. On New Year's eve they were off the Lucopin or Schildpad Islands, and sighting the great island barrier which stretches from Timor to Sumatra on the 8th January 1522, passed through it in a storm so severe that all vowed a pilgrimage to N. S. de la Guia.[1] The ship was allowed to run before the gale on an easterly course, coasting the southern side of the chain, and eventually the island of Mallua— now Ombay—was reached in safety.

Here they spent fifteen days. The ship stood in need of caulking, and the crew were kept at work at it.

---

[1] What passage was chosen by the *Victoria* is uncertain, but there is no doubt that it was either Flores Strait or Boleng Strait, from details in Pigafetta and Alvo's log-book.

Ombay is to this day almost unknown, and the description given by the *Victoria's* people of its inhabitants is probably true even now. They seem to have been of Papuan origin, judging from Pigafetta's account of their " hair raised high up by means of cane combs with long teeth," and also by the beard being encased in reed tubes, " a thing," he adds, " which seemed to us most ridiculous."

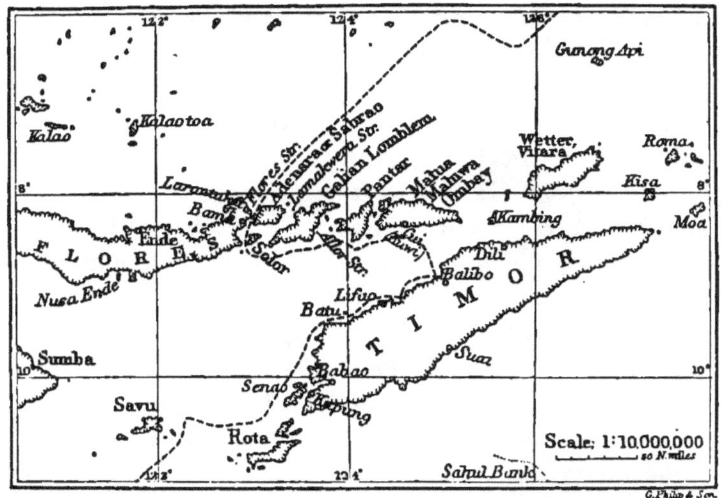

TIMOR AND FLORES.

On Saturday, January 25th, del Cano sailed from Ombay, and having run some twenty miles to the S.S.E., arrived at the large island of Timor. The Portuguese at that time had no settlements upon it as they have now, and indeed had never even visited it, but it was renowned throughout the archipelago for its trade in sandalwood and wax, and at the time of the Spaniards' visit a Luzon junk was trading in the port at which they touched.   Having some difficulty in getting provisions, the captain ordered one of the chiefs who had visited the vessel to be detained until he ransomed himself with live stock, but on receiving this del Cano gave him an equivalent value in articles of barter and sent him away satisfied.   The *Victoria* then continued her voyage, coasting the north-western side of the island until its terminal cape was reached.   On the 13th of February she was put on a S.S.W. course across the Indian Ocean for the Cape of Good Hope.[1]

Day after day that course was held, except indeed when necessity compelled them, as it too often did, to strike all sail for purposes of repair.   On the 14th March they kept a point or two more to the west, and four days later, while taking their mid-day observations, land was sighted ahead.   An attempt was made to fetch it and anchor, but they were unable to do so, and they accordingly lay to until the following day.   No landing, however, was effected, and the ship bore away to the north.   The island was that now known as Amsterdam Island.

---

[1] Gomera, cap. xcviii. p. 91, records the visit of the *Victoria* to Ende or Flores Island, which would tend to prove that she passed through Flores Strait.   His account also speaks of a mutiny at Timor. "Huvo alli un motin, i brega, en que murieron hartos de la nao;" and Oviedo (xx. cap. ii.) has also a passage which seems to bear this out— "Y algunos fueron descabeçados en la isla de Timor por sus delictos." Both, probably, borrowed from Pigafetta's words, "chi fuggi nell'isola di Timor, e alcuni pur vi furono condannati a morte pe' loro delitti" (p. 183).   But the official death-list does not make any mention of such executions, while, on the other hand, it records the deaths of fifteen men on the high seas and the desertion of two others.   Pigafetta tells us that the ship left Tidor with a complement of forty-seven, and we know that she reached the Cape Verdes with thirty-one—a number that exactly tallies, presuming that Pigafetta did not count himself. We are therefore forced to reject the story of the mutiny.

Their long voyage had already begun to tell both on ship and men. On the 3rd April they were again compelled to strike all sail and busy themselves with the repairing of the ship. What these repairs were we are not told, but they were probably connected with the state of her hull, for she was then leaking considerably. The crew, after such long service within the tropics, felt the cold greatly. The meat had all become unfit for food. Their lack of salt had not permitted them properly to cure it, and hence all hands were reduced to a diet of rice, and rice only. Upon such rations there is little wonder that sickness broke out. So enfeebled were the crew that it was debated whether they should not make for Mozambique, where the Portuguese had been long established. "But the greater number of us valued honour more than life itself," says Pigafetta, "and so we resolved at all hazards to attempt the return to Spain."

From the 7th to the 16th April the *Victoria* held her course between the fortieth and forty-first parallels of latitude. South of this she did not sail, and with a strong wind and heavy sea she bore to the north on the following day. For nearly a month they pressed on, until on the 8th May they sighted the high land of South Africa, and anchored on the following day. They were at fault both in latitude and longitude, for they had imagined themselves to have passed the meridian of the Cape. Running along the south coast they arrived off the mouth of the Rio del Infante, or Keiskamma river, on the 11th. They were not destined to pass the dreaded Cape without accident, for in heavy weather on the 16th May they carried away their foretopmast and sprung their fore-yard. Two days later they passed Cape

Agulhas.[1] Again they had to stop for repairs, and again they struggled on. Scurvy and starvation had reduced them to the greatest misery and distress. Nearly one-third of their own number had died, and nine of the thirteen natives. Pigafetta was almost the sole person in health. " We noticed a curious thing in throwing the bodies overboard," he says; " the Christians remained with the face turned up to heaven—the Indians with the face downwards."

The Line was crossed on June 8th, and on the 1st July a meeting was held to decide whether they should or should not touch at the Cape Verdes. The conclusion was foregone, for dire necessity had rendered it impossible for them to proceed further. They arrived on Wednesday, July 9th, at Santiago, and anchored in the port. Knowing that they ran great risk of being seized, instructions were given to those who went ashore to conceal who they were, and to pretend that they came from America, giving out that the other two ships of their squadron had preceded them to Spain, but that they had been delayed by the loss of their foretopmast on the Line. We learn from Alvo's diary that they were well received and supplied with provisions by the Portuguese. On the night of Sunday, 13th July, they put to sea, the weather being threatening and the port unsafe. In the morning they returned and lay on and off while they sent a boat for rice. One trip was made, but she did not again return. They waited until next day in vain, and then stood in towards the port, when a boat came

---

[1] Correa, ii. pt. ii. p. 634, says that the *Victoria* met and spoke the ship of Pero Coresma, then on her way to India, off the Cape. The incident is mentioned by him alone, and is probably one of his many inaccuracies.

.alongside and ordered them to surrender. The secret had leaked out, either by the bragging of one of the crew at a wineshop, or, as Maximilian tells us, by an attempt made by a sailor to sell some of his cloves.[1] In his answer, del Cano temporised, and asked for the return of his boat and men; but seeing some caravels preparing to get under weigh, they crowded all sail and escaped, leaving their comrades in the hands of the Portuguese.

They had now but eighteen Europeans and four natives left on board—scarce enough to work the ship; for, although improved in health and strength by the fresh provisions, and cheered by the prospect of their rapidly-approaching return, the greater number of them were upon the sick-list. Their sufferings were not to endure much longer. Soon the welcome shore of Spain hove in sight. It proved to be Cape S. Vincent, and keeping away to the east and south the *Victoria* arrived off San Lucar de Barrameda on Saturday the 6th September. On Monday the 8th—three years all but twelve days from the date of their final departure from Spain—they anchored near the mole of Seville. The First Circumnavigation of the Globe was accomplished, and a voyage brought to a conclusion which was, and is, without parallel in its history of determination and suffering, disaster and success. With what delight must they not have discharged their salvoes of artillery, and recounted their adventures to the crowds who flocked to welcome them. Yet, amid their joy, the vows that they had promised so often in the hour of danger were not forgotten. On the day following their arrival all

---

[1] This latter statement is borne out by the evidence of Alvo and Bustamante. *Vide* Navarrete, vol. iv. pp. 292, 294.

such as were able to walk went in procession, barefoot and carrying tapers, to the shrines of S. Maria de la Victoria and S. Maria de Antigua, and offered their heartfelt thanks for their safe return.

Before the advent of the *Victoria* it was not realised that circumnavigation of the globe implied the loss or gain of a day, according to the east or west direction of the voyage. The Spaniards were accordingly much astonished, on reaching civilisation, to find themselves out in their calculations. The fact is given to us by Ramusio in his introduction to Maximilian's letter, and Eden,[1] in the quaint language of his day, also comments upon it :—" And amonge other notable thynges . . . wrytten as touchynge that vyage, this is one, that the Spanyardes hauyng sayled abowt three yeares and one moneth, and the most of them notynge the dayes, day by day (as is the maner of all them that sayle by the ocean), they founde when they were returned to Spayne that they had loste one daye. So that at theyr arryuall at the porte of Siuile, beinge the seuenth daye of September, was by theyr accompt but the sixth day. And where as Don Peter Martyr declared the strange effecte of this thynge to a certeyne excellente man, who, for his singular lernynge, was greately aduanced to honoure in his common welthe and made Themperour's ambassadoure, this worthy gentelman, who was also a greate Philosopher and Astronomer, answerd that it coulde not otherwyse chaunce unto them, hauynge sayled three yeares continually, euer folowynge the soonne towarde the West."

The thirteen men left at the Cape Verde Islands were released and sent on to Lisbon very shortly afterwards

---

[1] *Decades of the Newe Worlde*, Lond. 1555, ff. 214, 215.

in a homeward-bound ship from Calicut, and the united crew were received by the emperor at court.[1] Of the Indians, all except one were sent back to the Moluccas in Loyasa's expedition in 1525. That one unwittingly owed his detention to his over-shrewdness. "On arriving in Spain," says Oviedo,[2] "the first thing he did was to inquire how many reals went to a ducat, and how many maravedis to a real. And going to the *vendas* and grocers' shops, he was wont to buy a maravedi's-worth of pepper, informing himself on all points concerning the value of spices in our country; and so sharp was he about it that the authorities feared his knowledge, and hence he himself brought it about that he never returned to his native land." The after-history of that intrepid and amusing traveller, the Chevalier Antonio Pigafetta, shall be related in his own words:—"Then, leaving Seville, I repaired to Valladolid, where I presented to His Sacred Majesty Don Carlos neither gold nor silver, but other things far more precious in the eyes of so great a sovereign. For I brought to him among other things a book written with my own hands, giving an account of all the events which had happened from day to day in our voyage. Thence I set out as best I could, and went to Portugal, where I related to King John the things which I had seen. Returning by way of Spain, I came to France, where I presented some things from the other hemisphere to the Regent-mother of the most Christian King Don Francis. Then I turned my face towards Italy, where I gave myself and what slight services I could render to the renowned and most

---

[1] Herrera, Dec. iii. lib. iv. cap. iv.
[2] Oviedo, xx. cap. iv.

illustrious Signor, Philip de Villers Lisleadam, the most worthy Grand Master of Rhodes."[1]

The ultimate fate of the *Victoria* we learn from Oviedo. After making one voyage in safety to the West Indies, she was again despatched to Cuba. But though she reached her destination she never returned. Caught in some Atlantic gale, her timbers, rotten from age and tropic seas, must have proved unequal to the strain. Such at least we may conjecture, for neither of her, nor of those that sailed in her, were any tidings ever heard.

[1] Pigafetta, *op. cit.*, p. 183.

CHAPTER XII

THE LAST VOYAGE—VII. FATE OF THE "TRINIDAD."

To complete the history of Magellan's voyage, we must return to the *Trinidad.* Her condition was such as to necessitate the discharge of all her cargo, and a thorough examination of her timbers. She was accordingly dismantled. Her artillery, cargo, spars, and fittings were sent ashore, and placed under guard in the store which the Sultan of Tidor had allowed them to erect, and the vessel having been careened the work of her repair was at once commenced. While engaged upon it Espinosa received a visit from the King of Gilolo, who begged for cannon or firearms to aid him in subduing some rebels with whom he was fighting. A small number of Spaniards were sent to his assistance, and before they returned the Indians had worked so well under the direction of the captain that the ship was ready for sea.

It was decided to leave certain goods and articles of barter upon the island, as much that a centre of Spanish influence might be established as that trade should continue until the arrival of the next armada. Luis del Molino was therefore selected as officer in charge, Juan de Campos acted as clerk and treasurer, and Alonso de Cota, Diego Arias, and Master Pedro—one of the Flemish bombardiers—formed the remainder of the garrison.   Carvalho, the deposed captain-general, had died on the 14th February.

On the 6th April, 1522, the *Trinidad* sailed upon her long voyage to Panama—a destination she was fated never to attain.   She was manned by a crew of fifty-four men, all told, and took a cargo of a thousand quintals, or nearly fifty tons, of cloves.   The course resolved on led them northwards, coasting the west shores of Gilolo until its terminal cape was reached.   Rounding it they came in sight of Chão or Porquenampello and Pyliom—two islands now known as Morti and Rau—and passed between them and the mainland of Gilolo on a southerly course.   Their object was to make "Quimar,"[1] a district under the authority of the Sultan of Tidor, where fresh provisions were awaiting them.   After a stay of eight or nine days they again made sail on the 20th April,[2] and, steering eastward, ran out into the open sea, when they set an E. $\frac{1}{4}$ N. course.   Head winds, however, compelled them to alter it, and they ran to the N.E. and N.N.E. until, on the 3rd May,[3] two small islands were sighted.   To these—which were in all probability Warwick and Warren Hastings Islands—they gave the name of the islands of St. Anthony.   The ship was now navigated for the Ladrones, one of the northern islands of which—conjecturally Agrigan—was visited, and a native taken on

[1] Quimar and its port Zanufo, Camafo, or Camarfyn (which are doubtless synonymous), have been variously identified with Morotai or Morti, and the N.E. arm of Gilolo.   The port at which they called is more probably Komo, on the northern peninsula of that island, a conjecture further borne out by the Paris MS., which says that on leaving it they "steered seventeen leagues eastward, and came out of the channel of the island of Batechina (Gilolo) and the island Chão."

[2] The 25th April, according to the Paris MS.

[3] May 6th, Paris MS.

board. It is difficult to explain why, on leaving this group, a persistent north-easterly course should have been held, but so it was. They met, as might well be imagined, with constant head winds. Espinosa was probably more fitted for an alguazil than a captain.[1] The latitude of 43° N. was finally reached, but long before this they had begun to run short of provisions. Eventually they were reduced to rice, and rice only. Ill-provided with clothes and accustomed for so long to a tropical climate, they were unable to endure the cold. Disease found them a facile prey. To crown their misfortunes, they encountered a severe storm which lasted for five days and caused them the loss of their mainmast, besides considerable injury to their poop and forecastle. Under these circumstances it was found impossible to proceed, and Espinosa resolved to return by way of the Ladrones to Tidor. His effort to regain the island he first visited was unsuccessful, and he brought up off Saipan, or Pamo,[2] as it was then called. Here the native he had picked up on his outward voyage ran away, together with three of the sailors,[3] who were fearful of the epidemic which was at that time so rapidly reducing the crew in numbers. The return from the Ladrones to Gilolo was effected in six weeks, and they

---

[1] We are not informed who undertook the navigation of the ship. It was probably Juan Bautista Punzero, to whom de Brito declares the arrival of the fleet at the Moluccas to have been due, or possibly the Genoese Leon Pancaldo or Pancado—certainly not Espinosa, who was a person of no education and could not even write his own name.

[2] Otherwise Mao. *Vide* Navarrete, iv. p. 100.

[3] Oviedo, lib. xx., cap. xvi., tells us how, more than three years later, the ships of Loyasa came across one of these men, Gonzalo de Vigo, in Tinian. His two companions had been killed by the natives. This deserter was of much use to them, and he was taken on to the Moluccas.

anchored off Dui, an island near its northern point. Further than that it was impossible for them to proceed. Three-fifths of their number were dead, and the rest were so disabled by scurvy and other disorders that they could no longer navigate the ship.

Meanwhile a considerable change had taken place in the aspect of affairs at Tidor. On the 13th May, little more than a month after their departure, a fleet of seven Portuguese vessels, manned by over three hundred men, and under the command of Antonio de Brito, sailed into Ternate roads. His visit had, perhaps, been partly induced by finding in Banda—the port whence he came —one of the five Spaniards left behind in Tidor by Espinosa, who had doubtless gone thither for the sake of trade. De Brito's first step, as appears by his own letter to the King of Portugal,[1] was to demand the surrender of the store-house and its contents, together with the men in charge. They had no course open to them other than to yield to such a force. Possession was at once taken of the building, and the stores appropriated —the captain-general demanding of the Sultan what right he had to admit the Castilians when the Portuguese had been so long established in the islands.

Espinosa had not been long at his anchorage before the news of the arrival and doings of the Portuguese was brought to him. He resolved, nevertheless, to give himself up to de Brito, so deplorable was his condition. Spain was, moreover, upon good terms with Portugal, and he hoped for fair treatment. He therefore sent a letter by Bartholomew Sanchez, clerk of the *Trinidad*, to the Portuguese captain-general, begging succour. No answer arriving, Espinosa weighed anchor

---

[1] Navarrete, iv. p. 305.

and struggled on for a few miles to the port of Bena-
conora, where he was at length met by a caravel and
other small craft with Simon d'Abreu, Duarte de
Resende, Don Garcia Enriques, and twenty armed
Portuguese. They gave the captain a letter from de
Brito,[1] and at once took possession of the ship, seizing
all the papers and log-books which could be found, as
well as her astrolabes and ·quadrants. She was then
brought in and anchored off Ternate, and her cargo
discharged. It was the last voyage she was destined
to make. During her unlading a heavy squall caught
her, and she went ashore and broke up. Forty bahars
of cloves were lost in her, but her timbers and fittings
were saved, and served in the construction of the fortress the Portuguese were then erecting in Ternate, and
in the repair of their ships.

It was in vain that Espinosa protested against the
action taken by the Portuguese. They replied that he
had done his duty to his sovereign, and that they should
do the same to theirs. He asked that they would at
least give him a certificate of the items of the ship's
cargo, in order that he might render an account of it
to the emperor, but he was told that if he wished an
account rendered he should render it himself from the
yard-arm of his vessel. He was called upon to deliver
the royal standard, but this he declined to do, saying,
that since he was in their power they could of course
seize it, but that he was unable, as an officer of the
emperor, to surrender it.

When the *Trinidad* was brought to her last anchorage
she had on board but nineteen survivors of the fifty-four

---

[1] For this letter, which is dated 21st October, 1522, see Navarrete,
iv. p. 295.

men who had sailed in her but six months previously. Pedro Affonso de Lorosa — the Portuguese who had deserted from Don Tristão de Meneses — was also with them.　His fate did not remain long in doubt, for he was executed shortly after his arrival.　Of the five men left in Tidor in charge of the stores one had died, three were prisoners of the Portuguese, and Luis del Molino was at large among the islanders.　On receiving a message from Espinosa he came in and gave himself up. From these men the others learnt what had taken place in their absence.　The Portuguese had levelled the factory and storehouse to the ground, seizing all the rigging and fitting of the ships, together with the cloves and other spices that had been collected.　Espinosa and his men were able to realise what was before them. Could they have seen the letter written by Antonio de Brito upon the subject to his royal master, their fears would scarcely have been alleviated.　" So far as concerns the master, clerk, and pilot "—it runs—" I am writing to the captain-general that it would be more to your Highness' service to order their heads to be struck off than to send them there (*i.e.*, to India).　I kept them in the Moluccas, because it is a most unhealthy country, in order that they might die there, not liking to order their heads to be cut off, since I did not know whether your Highness would be pleased or not.　I am writing to Jorge de Albuquerque to detain them in Malacca, which, however, is a very healthy climate." [1]

With this laudable desire for their speedy decease in the heart of their captor, it may be imagined that the outlook of the Spaniards was not of a very promising

[1] De Brito's letter to the King of Portugal, *vide* Navarrete, iv. p. 311.

nature. The sick were, however, sent to a temporary hospital.[1] The remainder went to the fortress upon Ternate, which the Portuguese were at that time engaged in building. There they were set to work upon it—Espinosa himself being ordered to labour with the others, an order that he declined to obey. It is negatively to the credit of de Brito that he thought it best not to press the matter. But they were subjected to many indignities, being openly and grossly abused before the natives in order that the authority and repute of the emperor might be as far as possible belittled.

In this manner the twenty-three prisoners were detained in Ternate until the end of February 1523, when, with the exception of two carpenters whom de Brito needed, they started on their homeward voyage—a voyage destined to be protracted from months into years, and to end at last with the safe return of but four of their number. Terrible as had been the mortality on board the *Victoria*, it was as nothing compared with that of the *Trinidad*.

The men were first taken to Banda. Four of them who left Ternate together never reached the island, and of the junk in which they sailed no tidings were ever heard. The others were detained in Banda four months and then despatched by way of Java, at whose ports they touched, to Malacca, where they came into the hands of Jorge d'Albuquerque, who was at that time Governor. More delays took place here. We have seen how de Brito gave actual instructions for their detention, lamenting, nevertheless, the healthiness of the

---

[1] Great mortality prevailed at first in the Moluccas, as we learn from de Brito's letter. Within two months of his arrival he had lost fifty of his men, and only fifty remained in health.

climate. It was, however, sufficiently malarious or insanitary to bring four of the unhappy wanderers to the grave. Anton Moreno, a negro slave of Espinosa, was appropriated by Albuquerque's sister, and it was not until five months had passed away that the voyage of the survivors was resumed.

From Malacca the prisoners, for such they still were, were sent to Cochim. They appear to have embarked in two or more ships. The junk in which Bartholomew Sanchez, Luis del Molino, and Alonso de Cota sailed was never more heard of, and when the others reached their destination the annual homeward-bound fleet had sailed. Despairing of ever getting back to their native land, two of their number, Leon Pancaldo and Juan Bautista Poncero,[1] ran away and concealed themselves on board the *Santa Catalina*, each ignorant of the other's presence. This ship was bound for Portugal, but on arriving at Mozambique the two stowaways were put ashore, with the intention of returning them to Cochim. Both men, however, succeeded in disappointing their captors, for Juan Bautista died, and Leon Pancaldo, hiding himself just as Diogo de Mello's ship started for Cochim, managed to ship on board a homeward-bound vessel commanded by Francisco Pereira. Upon his arrival at Lisbon he was thrown into prison, but was eventually set free by order of the king.

Meanwhile the others remained behind at Cochim. Vasco da Gama, then viceroy, had remained deaf to their entreaties for release. On Christmas Eve, 1524, he died, and was succeeded by Don Enrique de Meneses, who, more compassionate than his predecessor, consented

---

[1] This man, who originally sailed as maestre of the *Trinidad*, is described in various lists as Punzerol and Ponce de Leon.

at length to their departure. But their numbers had sadly decreased. Four, as we have seen, had died during their detention in Malacca, and three more had fallen victims to their hardships in Cochim. Juan Rodriguez of Seville had escaped in the ship of Andres de Sousa, which was bound for Lisbon. There remained but three men, Gonzalo Gomez de Espinosa, the captain; Gines de Mafra, seaman of the *Trinidad*; and Master Hans or Aires, bombardier of the *Victoria*.[1] Nor were their troubles over upon landing in the Peninsula, for they were thrown into the common prison, where, overcome by his previous sufferings and the treatment to which he was subjected, Master Hans died. Espinosa and Gines de Mafra remained incarcerated for seven long months, when the former was released. Mafra, having in his box some log-books and nautical works or notes written by Andres de San Martin, was supposed to be a pilot, and was detained longer. On proving his rank and condition he was permitted his liberty a month later; but the books were seized, and afterwards, as far as can be learnt, came into the hands of João de Barros the historian.[2]

Four men, and four men only, thus remained alive out of the fifty-four who sailed in the *Trinidad* from Ternate—Espinosa, Mafra, Pancaldo, and Juan Rodriguez of Seville. Espinosa was well received by his sovereign,

---

[1] There is a discrepancy in the various documents concerning this third individual. According to some, it was Morales the surgeon who returned with Espinosa and died in the Lisbon prison, while the bombardier Aires came back in the *Victoria*, and was one of those who went to court to be presented to Charles V.

[2] Barros, Dec. iii. lib. v. cap. x. p. 656. In this passage he speaks of having got papers and books from Duarte de Resende, who "took them from the astrologer Andres de San Martin," besides those he obtained from Espinosa.

who rewarded him, and—if we may credit a passage in Oviedo—granted him a patent of nobility and a life-pension of 300 ducats.[1] But so mean were the officials of the India House that they actually docked him of his pay during the time that he was a captive in the hands of the Portuguese, alleging as a reason that it was incontestable that while in that condition he was no longer in the service of Spain ! On the 14th January, 1528, Espinosa instituted a plaint to recover this money. A long *procés* was the result, but whether he gained his cause or not is not recorded.[2]

The fame of Magellan's voyage resounded through the length and breadth of the Peninsula, and reached all parts of Europe. Charles V., who had just arrived from Germany, on learning of the arrival of the *Victoria* wrote at once from Valladolid to Sebastian del Cano, instructing him to appear at court with two of the best-instructed of his crew—"los mas cuerdos y de mejor razon." The whole number, as we have seen, were ultimately presented. Charles. was generous to del Cano beyond his deserts. He was granted an annual pension of 500 ducats, and a coat-of-arms commemorating the services he had rendered to Spain.[3] Fortune befriended him indeed. The little we know of him in Magellan's voyage—for until his appointment after the wholesale massacre at Sebu he was comparatively an obscure personage—is far from being in his favour. He

---

[1] Oviedo, bk. xx. cap. iv. The king, he says, " le hizo merçedes y le conçedió un privillegio de muy nobles armas."

[2] *Vide* Medina, vol. ii. p. 180.

[3] *Arms*, or ; two cinnamon sticks in saltire proper, three nutmegs and twelve cloves ; on a chief gules a castle, or. *Crest*, a globe bearing the motto, " Primus circumdedisti me." *Supporters*, two Malay kings, crowned, holding in the exterior hand a spice branch, proper.

took an active part in the mutiny at Port St. Julian, and gave evidence at Valladolid upon certain events of the voyage which was so biassed, and in some cases so untrue, that he forfeits much of his claim to our admira-

COAT-OF-ARMS AND AUTOGRAPH OF DEL CANO.

tion. As Vergara says,[1] "Elcano did not always remember the loyalty due to Magellan and his memory." Neither can he be given any very great credit for his

[1] *Anuario Hydrogr. de Chile*, vol. v. p. 396.

navigation, for it must not be forgotten that when he took the command the hitherto unknown Pacific had been crossed, and the ship was far beyond the longitude of the Moluccas, and distant from them only six hundred miles. Antonio de Brito, moreover, in his letter to the King of Portugal, tells us that after the death of Magellan, Juan Bautista Poncero was the chief navigator. But to del Cano fell the good fortune of bringing home the *Victoria*, and, as her captain, the honours accorded upon the occasion of such a great event naturally fell to his share.

It may be imagined that the arrival of the *Victoria* was a matter of no little joy to Alvaro de Mesquita, the unhappy captain of the *S. Antonio*. It will be remembered how the mutineers of that vessel, deserting their captain - general in his

STATUE OF DEL CANO, GUIPUZCOA.

hour of need, overpowered their commander and brought him, wounded and in irons, to Seville. Although their story was but half-believed, Mesquita was still kept incarcerated, as was the manner of those times. Now, set at liberty, he was rewarded in common with his former friends and comrades, upon whom pensions and various distinctions were conferred. For some reason, perhaps the length of time that had elapsed since the occurrence, a corresponding punishment does not seem to have overtaken the mutineers.

The papers in the Seville archives give us full details of the spices brought back in the *Victoria*. The bulk of the cargo consisted of cloves, and of these, exclusive of the *quintalades* or free freight permitted alike to officers and men, there were 520 quintals, or about twenty-six tons of our weight. The value of this was estimated at 7,888,684 maravedis—in other words, £4536—and in addition there was a certain quantity of cinnamon, mace, nutmeg, and sandalwood which raised the value nearly £600 more. On the whole, despite the frightful losses both of ships and cargo during the voyage of the armada, the venture had been successful. Deducting the value of the *Victoria* and her fittings, and of the articles of barter aboard her, from the original cost of the entire expedition, the value of the spices was found to exceed the latter by some £200.

We have done now with the great expedition of Magellan, and with the return of "that unique, that most famous ship, the *Victoria*," as Oviedo calls her. "The track she followed," he exclaims, "is the most wonderful thing and the greatest novelty that has ever been seen from the time God created the first man and ordered the world unto our own day. Neither has anything more notable in navigation ever been heard or described since the voyage of the patriarch Noah."[1] The extravagant terms of admiration, the flowery

----

[1] Oviedo, bk. xx. cap. iv.

periods, the elaborate metaphors characteristic of the period in which they lived, were lavishly used by the historians who chronicled the voyage. The keynote was struck by Maximilian Transylvanus in his Salzburg letter:—"Digniores profecto nautæ quæ æterna memoria celebrentur quam qui cum Iasone ad Colchidem navigarunt Argonautæ," and the theme has been introduced by every one who has written upon the subject, from Argensola and Gomara to Camoens. The latter, indeed, seems to have borrowed the idea of a famous verse in the Lusiad from Oviedo, and turns Magellan's praise into Gama's.[1]   But all this praise and glory came too late for Magellan's family, as they did for the immortal commander. His wife was dead and his only child was dead, and he himself lay at rest in a little islet in the far Pacific.

[1] Cessem do sabio Grego, e do Troiano
   As navegaçoẽs grandes que fizeram
   Calle-se de Alexandro e de Trajano
   A fama das victorias que tiveram
   Que eu canto o peito illustre Lusitano
   A quem Neptuno, e Marte obedeceram.
   Cesse tudo o que a Musa antigua canta
   Que outro valor mais alto se alevanta.
                                   —*Canto* i. 3.

APPENDIX.

APPENDIX I.—GENEALOGY OF THE FAMILY OF MAGALHAES.

Gil de Magalhães.

Three sons. — Ruy Pais de Magalhães. — Gil or Ruy or Pedro de M. = Alda de Mesquita [1] (d. of Mart. Gonzalvez Pimenta and Iñez de Mesquita).

A daughter (*m.* —— de Sousa).

Payo Rodriquez de M. = Felipa Pereira. (a sea-captain who served in Guinea). — Lorenzo de M.[2]

J. da Sylva Telles = Thereza. — Ginebra = Pero Cão. — Isabel. — FERNÃO (*b.* circa. 1480, *d.* April 27, 1521). = Beatriz Barbosa (d. March 1522). — Diego de Sousa.

Luiz da Sylva Telles.

Francisco da Sylva Telles.[3]

Antonio da Sylva de Magalhães de Faria.

Gonzalo Alvares Moveira da Sylva.

Rodrigo [4] (*b.* Feb. 1519, *d.* Sept. 1521).

THE BARBOSA FAMILY.

Diogo Barbosa = Maria Caldera. (Comendador of the Order of Santiago).

Duarte, *d.* May 1, 1521 (accompanied Magellan on his voyage). — Isabel = Alonso Ortiz, Caballero de Sevilla. — Jaime.[5] — Beatriz = Fernão de Magalhães. — Gaspar de Viernes, = Guiomar. Caballero de Sevilla.

Rodrigo.

[1] Alvaro de Mesquita, who went with Magellan on his final voyage, was a son of Alda de Mesquita's brother.

[2] Claimed the property of Magellan in a *procès* dated February 5, 1567.　　　[3] Author of the will quoted on p. 23.

[4] The birth of a second child has been erroneously recorded by some authors. But "Doña Beatriz mal parió del 2ndo preñado que tuvo." *V.* Medina, vol. ii. p. 383.

[5] In an *Auto fiscal,* June 19, 1540, Jaime claims the property of Magellan for himself and his sisters Isabel and Guiomar.

II.

MAGELLAN'S WILLS.

THE first will of Magellan was discovered in Lisbon in 1855 by a descendant of the great navigator. It was executed at Belem on 17th December, 1504, on the eve of his departure with Almeida's expedition, before the notary Domingo Martins. It is in many ways more interesting than his final will. While the latter is written in Spanish and in the stilted legal phraseology which proclaims it the work of the notary-public, that executed at Belem bears evidences of being more or less the product of his own pen, and is in his native tongue. The most important clauses run as follows :—

"I desire that, if I die abroad, or in this Armada in the which I am now proceeding for India in the service of my Sovereign, the Most High and Mighty King, Dom Manoel, whom may God preserve, that my funeral may be that accorded to an ordinary seaman, giving to the chaplain of the ship my clothes and arms to say three requiem masses."

"I appoint as my sole heirs my sister Donna Thereza de Magalhães, her husband, João da Silva Telles, and their son, my nephew, Luiz Telles da Silva, their successors and heirs, with the understanding that the aforesaid my brother-in-law shall quarter his arms with those of the family of Magalhães, which are those of my ancestors, and among the most distinguished, best, and oldest in the kingdom; founding, as I hereby found, in the male line—or in the female in default thereof—descendants of the aforesaid my sister Donna Thereza de Magalhães, and her husband, my brother-in-law, and their son, Luiz Telles da Silva, a bequest of twelve masses yearly to be said at the altar of the Lord Jesus in the Church of S. Salvador in Sabrosa in connection with my property, the quinta de Souta, in the aforesaid parish of Sabrosa, that it may be a legacy *in perpetuo*, and that it may remain for ever as a memorial of our family, which it will be the duty of our successors to re-establish, should it through any chance or misfortune fall into desuetude, without increase or diminution in the number of the masses, or other alteration.

"And everything that I thus ordain I desire may be carried out justly, and remain without alteration henceforth and for ever, should I die without legitimate offspring; but should I have such, I desire that he may succeed to all my estate, together with the same obligation of the entailed bequest, that it remain established as such, and not in any other form; in order that the barony may increase, and that it may not be deprived of the little property I own, the which I cannot better, or in any other manner bequeath."[1]

Magellan's Last Will.

In the name of the Most High and Mighty God our Lord, who is without beginning and reigns without end, and of the most favoured Glorious Virgin, Our Lady, Holy Mary, His blessed Mother, whom all we Christians own as Queen and Advocate in all our actions; to their honour and service, and that of all the Saints of the courts of Heaven. Amen.

Know all ye by these presents, that I, Hernando de Magallanes, Comendador, His Majesty's Captain-general of the Armada bound for the Spice Islands, husband of Doña Beatriz Barbosa, and inhabitant of this most noble and most loyal city of Seville, in the precinct of Santa

[1] De Barros Arana, *Fernão de Magalhães.* Trad. de F. de M. Villas-Boas. Lisboa, 1881, p. 177.

Maria, being well and in good health, and possessed of such my ordinary senses and judgment as God our Lord has, of His mercy and will, thought fit and right to endow me ; believing firmly and truly in the Holy Trinity, the Father, Son, and Holy Ghost—three persons and one only true God, as every faithful Christian holds and believes, and ought to hold and believe, and being in fear of death, which is a natural thing from which no man can escape ; being willing and desirous of placing my soul in the surest and most certain path that I can discern for its salvation, to commit and bring it unto the mercy and forgiveness of God our Lord, that He, who made and created it, may have compassion and pity upon it, and redeem and save it, and bring it to His glory and His heavenly kingdom.

Whereas I am about to proceed in the King's service in the said Armada, by these presents I make known and declare that I make and ordain this my Will, and these my bequests, as well of my goods as of my body and soul, for the salvation of my soul and the satisfaction of my heirs.   Firstly, the debts owed by me and to me owing : they are such as will be found written in my book of accounts, the which I confirm and approve and acknowledge as correct.   The following are the legacies bequeathed by me :—

Firstly, I commend my soul to God our Lord, who made and created it, and redeemed me with His precious blood, and I ask and beseech of the ever-glorious Virgin Mary, Our Lady, His blessed Mother, that, with all the Saints of the heavenly kingdom, she may be my intercessor and supplicant before her precious Son for my soul, that He may pardon my sins and shortcomings, and receive me to share His glory in the kingdom of heaven.   And when this my present life shall end for the life eternal, I desire that if I die in this city of Seville my body may be buried in the Monastery of Santa Maria de la Vitoria in Triana—ward and precinct of this city of Seville—in the grave set apart for me; And if I die in this said voyage, I desire that my body may be buried in a church dedicated to Our Lady, in the nearest spot to that at which death seize me and I die; And I bequeath to the expenses of the chapel of the Sagrario of the Holy Church of Seville, in grateful remembrance of the Holy Sacraments which from the said church I have received, and hope to receive, if it be the will of God our Lord, one thousand maravedis; And I bequeath to the Holy Crusade a real of silver; And I bequeath to the Orders of the Holy Trinity and Santa Maria de la Merced of this city of Seville, in aid of the redemption of such faithful Christians as may be captives in the country of the Moors, the enemies of our holy Catholic faith, to each Order a real of silver; And I bequeath to the Infirmary of San Lazaro without the city, as alms, that they may pray to God our Lord for my soul, another real of silver; And I bequeath to the hospital de Las Bubas of this city of Seville, to gain its intercession, another real of silver; And I bequeath to the Casa de San Sebastian in Tablada, to gain its intercession, another real of silver; And I bequeath to the Holy Church of Faith in Seville another real of silver, to gain its intercession; And I desire that upon the said day of my burial thirty masses may be said over my body—two *cantadas* and twenty-eight *rezadas*, and that they shall offer for me the offering of bread and wine and candles that my executors desire; And I desire that in the said monastery of Santa Maria de la Vitoria a thirty-day mass [1] may be said for my soul, and that the accustomed alms may be given therefor; And I desire that upon the said day of my burial three poor men may

---

[1] Treintanario de misas cerrado.

be clothed—such as I have indicated to my executors—
and that to each may be given a cloak of grey stuff, a
cap, a shirt, and a pair of shoes, that they may pray to
God for my soul; And I also desire that upon the said
day of my burial food may be given to the said three
paupers, and to twelve others, that they may pray to
God for my soul; And I desire that upon the said day
of my burial a gold ducat may be given as alms for the
souls in purgatory.   And I confess—to speak the truth
before God and the world and to possess my soul in
safety—that I received and obtained in dowry and marriage with the said Doña Beatriz Barbosa, my wife, six
hundred thousand maravedis, of the which I made
acknowledgment before Bernal Gonzalez de Vallecillo,
notary-public of Seville; and I desire that before everything the said Doña Beatriz Barbosa, my wife, may be
paid and put in possession of the said six hundred
thousand maravedis, her dowry, together with the arras
that I gave her.

And forasmuch as I am proceeding in the King's
service in the said Armada, and since of all the gain
and profit which with the help of God our Lord may
result therefrom (save and excepting the first charges of
the King), the share allotted to me is one-fifth of the
whole, in addition to that which I may acquire from the
merchandise which I take with me in the said Armada—
of all this which I may acquire from the said Armada I
desire to set aside one-tenth part, touching which, by
this my will and testament, I desire and order, and it is
my wish, that the said tenth may be expended and distributed in the manner following :—

Firstly, I desire and order, and it is my wish, that
one-third of the said tenth part may be given to the said
monastery of N. S. Santa Maria de la Vitoria in Triana,
for the construction of the chapel of the said monastery,

and that the monks of the said monastery may henceforth for ever engage to pray to God for my soul.

Furthermore, I desire, and it is my wish, that the remaining two-thirds of the said tenth part shall be divided into three equal parts, of which one part shall be given to the monastery of N. S. Santa Maria de Monserrat, in the city of Barcelona; another to the monastery of San Francisco in the town of Aranda de Duero, for the benefit of the said monastery; and the third to the monastery of S. Domingo de las Dueñas, in the city of Oporto, in Portugal, for such things as may be most necessary for the said monastery; and this bequest I make that they may pray God for my soul.

Furthermore, I will and desire, and it is my wish, that of the half of the rest of my estate of the said Armada belonging unto me, together with that of the other estate of which I am possessed in this said city of Seville, one-fifth part may be set aside to fulfil the necessities of my soul, and that my executors out of this said fifth part may fulfil these necessities of this my will and testament, and whatever more may seem fitting unto them for the repose of my soul and conscience.

I desire, moreover, that there may be paid to Cristobal Robelo, my page, the sum of thirty thousand maravedis from my estate, the which I bequeath unto him for the services he has rendered unto me, and that he may pray God for my soul.

And by this my present will and testament, I declare and ordain as free and quit of every obligation of captivity, subjection, and slavery, my captured slave Enrique, mulatto, native of the city of Malacca, of the age of twenty-six years more or less, that from the day of my death thenceforward for ever the said Enrique may be free and manumitted, and quit, exempt, and relieved of every obligation of slavery and subjection, that he may act as he desires and thinks fit; and I desire that of my estate there may be given to the said Enrique the sum of ten thousand maravedis in money for his support; and this manumission I grant because he is a Christian, and that he may pray to God for my soul.

And whereas His Majesty the King has granted unto me, my sons, and my heirs in tail male the governorship of certain lands and islands that I may discover with the said Armada, according to the terms contained in the *Capitulacion* made with His Majesty, together with the title of Adelantado of the said lands and islands discovered, and also the twentieth part of their produce, and other benefits contained in the said *Capitulacion;* by these presents, and by this my will and testament, I declare and name for this *mayorazgo*—in order that, upon my decease, he may succeed to the above—Rodrigo de Magallanes, my legitimate son, and the legitimate son of the said Doña Beatriz Barbosa, my wife, and thereafter unto any legitimate son that God may grant him; and should he have no legitimate sons born in wedlock to have and inherit the above *mayorazgo*, I desire and command that the other legitimate son or daughter whom God may give me may inherit,[1] and so successively from father to son; And if by chance a daughter should hold the *mayorazgo*, in such a case I desire that the son whom God may give her to inherit the said *mayorazgo*, shall take the name of Magallaes [*sic*], and bear my arms without quartering them with any others; And, should he fail to take the name of Magallaes and to bear my arms, in such case I desire and order, and it is my wish, that a son or nephew or nearer relation of my lineage may inherit the said *mayorazgo*, and that he may live in Castile, and bear my name and arms; And if—which may God forbid—the said Rodrigo de Magallaes my son should die

---

[1] Doña Beatriz was at that time *enceinte.*

without leaving sons or daughters born in wedlock, and that I should beget no other sons nor daughters to succeed to the *mayorazgo*, I desire and order, and it is my wish, that Diego de Sosa, my brother, who is now living with His Serene Majesty the King of Portugal, may inherit the above, and come and live in this kingdom of Castile, and marry in it, and that he adopt the name of Magallaes, and bear the arms of Magallaes, as I bear them—the arms of Magallaes and Sosa; And if the said Diego de Sosa, my brother, have neither sons nor daughters born in holy wedlock to inherit the aforesaid *mayorazgo*, I desire and order, and it is my wish, that Isabel de Magallaes, my sister, may inherit the said *mayorazgo*, provided that she call herself Magallaes, and bear my arms, and come to reside and marry in this kingdom of Castile.

And furthermore, I desire and order, and it is my will, that if the said Diego de Sosa, my brother, or the said Isabel de Magallaes, my sister, succeed to the aforesaid *mayorazgo*, they shall be obliged to assist the said Doña Beatriz Barbosa, my wife, with the fourth part of all that the said my *mayorazgo* produces, fairly and justly, and without let or hindrance soever; And I desire that the Comendador Diego de Barbosa, my father-in-law, may undertake the charge of the person, goods, and *mayorazgo* of the said Rodrigo de Magallaes, my son, and of the child or children with whom the said Doña Beatriz Barbosa, my wife, is now pregnant, until they reach the age of eighteen years, and that during this period the said Comendador Diego Barbosa may receive and collect all the produce and rents which the said estate and *mayorazgo* may produce, and give and deliver to the said Doña Beatriz Barbosa, my wife, his daughter, the fourth part of all that may therefrom result, until such time as my sons aforesaid be of the age stated; the said my wife, Doña Beatriz Barbosa, living widowed and chastely; And if she should marry, I desire that there may be given and paid to her the sum of two thousand Spanish doubloons, over and above her dowry and arras, and the half of the accumulations thereon.[1]

Furthermore, I desire, and it is my will, that the said Comendador Diego Barbosa may take and receive, as his own property, one fourth part; and that he may expend the remainder in the maintenance and education of my sons; And likewise, I desire and order, and it is my wish, that if the said Diego de Sosa, my brother, or the said Isabel de Magallaes, my sister, inherit the aforesaid my *mayorazgo*, that above and beyond that which I have desired may be given each year to the said Doña Beatriz Barbosa, my wife, they shall be obliged to give each year to the said Comendador Diego Barbosa, for the remainder of his life, two hundred ducats of gold, to be paid from the estate of the said *mayorazgo*.

Furthermore, I desire that, if the said Comendador Diego Barbosa collect the aforesaid my estate, he may give of it to the said Isabel de Magallaes, my sister, for her marriage, such as seems fitting to the said Comendador Diego Barbosa.

Furthermore I desire that of the fifty thousand maravedis that I have for my life and that of the said Doña Beatriz Barbosa, my wife, from the Casa de Contratacion of the Indies in this city of Seville, the said Doña Beatriz, my wife, may give to the said Isabel de Magallaes, my sister, the sum of five thousand maravedis per annum until the arrival of my estate resulting from this my present voyage, when the said Comendador Diego Barbosa can give her that which I have arranged and desired in this my will that he should give her for her marriage.

---

[1] Allendo su doto ó arras do lo que ba do haber do su mitad do multiplicado.

And this my will and testament having been fulfilled and discharged, together with the bequests and clauses therein contained, relating to the aforesaid my possessions, whether fixtures, movables, or live-stock, in compliance with that herewith prescribed and expressed, I desire that all and everything of the said possessions which may remain over and above may be had and inherited by the said Rodrigo de Magallaes, my legitimote son by the said Doña Beatriz, my wife, and by the child or children of which the said Doña Beatriz is now pregnant, being born and living the period that the law requires, whom—the said Rodrigo de Magallaes, my son, and the child or children of which the said my wife is pregnant—I appoint and establish as my legal residuary legatees, equally the one with the other; And if, which may God forbid, the said my son, or child borne by my wife, die before attaining the proper age for the succession, I desire that the said Doña Beatriz Barbosa, my wife, may inherit the said my estate, save and excepting that of the *mayorazgo*, and I appoint and establish her as my residuary legatee.

And for the discharge and quitment of this my will and testament, and of the bequests and clauses concerning the said my estate therein contained, in compliance with that herewith prescribed and expressed, I hereby appoint as my executors for the payment and distribution of the said my estate, without hurt to them or theirs, Doctor Sancho de Matienzo, Canon of Seville, and the said Comendador Diego Barbosa, my father-in-law; And I bequeath to the said Doctor Sancho de Matienzo for the burden thus laid upon him in the fulfilment and discharge of this my will the sum of thirty gold ducats and two pesos.[1]

. . . .

---

[1] Here follows the customary conclusion in legal terms.

Done in Seville, in the King's Customs of this city of Seville, Wednesday, the twenty-fourth day of the month of August, in the year of the birth of our Saviour Jesus Christ one thousand five hundred and nineteen. And I, the said Comendador Hernando de Magallaes, sign and confirm it with my name in the register, in the presence of the witnesses Diego Martinez de Medina, Juan Rodriguez de Medina, and Alfonso Fernandez, notaries of Seville.

III.

PERSONNEL OF MAGELLAN'S ARMADA.

FROM various causes—the haste in the despatch of the ships, combined with the difficulty in obtaining hands; the shipping of some of the crew in the Canaries; and, perhaps, the purposed omission of certain names owing to the ships having become more largely manned by Portuguese than would have seemed desirable to the authorities—it is impossible to arrive at the exact number of persons who sailed with Magellan upon his final voyage. From the official lists, and from the casual occurrence of names in the numerous and lengthy *autos fiscales* connected with the expedition, we gather that at least 268 individuals embarked. The actual names of such a number are given. It is more than probable that there were others who were neither entered in the ships' books nor the subject of casual mention, and it may be affirmed with tolerable certainty that between 270 and 280 persons manned the five ships which formed the squadron.

The flagship is known to have carried a crew of 62 men, the *S. Antonio* 57, the *Concepcion* 44, the *Victoria*

45, the *Santiago* 31.   Of the other 29 who are mentioned
by name, we do not know the ships.   After the loss of
the *Santiago*, her crew was distributed among the other
vessels, and it may be concluded that when the *S.
Antonio* deserted in the Straits of Magellan, she did not
carry away with her less than seventy men.   Practically,
then, the heroes of the voyage—that wondrous voyage
which, with amusing hyperbole, Oviedo and others have
compared to those of Jason and Ulysses—were as nearly
as possible 200 in number.   How many returned we
have already seen.   Thirty-one of the *Victoria's* crew
reached home, and months—nay, years—later, four of
those who had sailed in the *Trinidad*.   The remaining
hundred and sixty or seventy men had perished !

An examination of the ship's books shows that each
vessel carried a captain and one or more pilots—who
were without exception Portuguese — a *maestre* and
contramaestre—who would correspond to the mates of a
merchant vessel—a purser, steward, carpenter, barber,
caulker, and cooper.   Two classes of sailors were borne
—the *marineros*, or A.B.'s, and the *grumetes*, or ordinary
seamen.   Of the former the flagship carried 14, and 10
grumetes ; the other vessels a few less.   Upon each ship
were three gunners or *lombarderos.*   All these men were
foreigners, generally French, but sometimes Germans or
Flemings.   The master-gunner of the flagship was a
certain Maestre Andrew, of Bristol, the only Englishman in the expedition.[1]   Three or four chaplains seem
to have accompanied the fleet, but only one surgeon, the

---

[1] Master Andrew had married a certain Ana Estrada of Seville,
and had also, apparently, changed his religion, for we find that the
sum of 4014 maravedis was paid in his name after his decease to
the Brotherhood of Nuestra Señora de la Vitoria.   The amount of
his pay is given in one of the documents of the Seville archives : it
was at the rate of £12, 18s. 9d. per annum.

Bachelor Morales, whose duties must indeed have been arduous. Various pages and body-servants of the officers completed the lists of the ships' crews. The young men of good family, who took part in the expedition from love of adventure or desire for advancement in military service, shipped as *sobresa'ientes* or supernumeraries. In this class came Duarte Barbosa, Magellan's brother-in-law, and Alvaro de Mesquita, his cousin.

A glance at the list of the officers and crews of the five ships reveals a great number of Portuguese names. On the 17th June, 1519, Charles V. sent a special order to Magellan and Ruy Faleiro that no one of that nationality should accompany the expedition except four or five for the service of each of them. Later, hearing several of the *grumetes* are Portuguese, he writes that they must be dismissed. But there was a great dearth of men, no matter of what nationality. The expedition was cried throughout Seville, and advertised at the street corners and on the quays, but the pay offered was so scanty that it was found impossible to obtain hands. Crimping was not permitted. Several of Magellan's officers were accordingly sent to other ports to endeavour to get the necessary complement, and Charles's regulations as to the admission of Portuguese had ultimately to be relaxed. In a later Cedula permission is given for the enrolment of twenty-four, twelve to be nominated by the Emperor, and twelve by Magellan. We find, however, that thirty-seven at least sailed on the voyage, and as some of these entered themselves as of Seville or some other Spanish port, it is probable that even this number is not inclusive and final. The numerous nationalities represented have already been commented upon. After the Portuguese came the Genoese and Italians in point of numbers. Of these there were thirty or more. The French numbered nineteen. There were besides Flemings, Germans,

Sicilians, Corfiotes, Malays, Negroes, Moors, Madeirans, and natives of the Azores and Canary Islands. Despite the fleet sailing from Seville, only seventeen men are entered as of that city. The Biscayans, as was always the case on such expeditions, were largely represented.

IV.

STORES AND EQUIPMENT OF MAGELLAN'S FLEET.

FROM various documents existing in the Seville archives we gather extraordinarily precise details, not only as regards the articles supplied to the Armada, but also as to their price and their exact distribution among the different ships. This information is of much interest, showing as it does what stores were at that period considered necessary. It also throws light upon various events connected with the preparation of the fleet of which we should otherwise have remained in ignorance.

Ships, Fittings, &c.

			Maravedis.[1]
The *Concepcion*, with rigging and boat . . .			228,750
The *Victoria*, do. do. . . .			300,000
The *S. Antonio*, do. do. . . .			330,000
The *Trinidad*, do. do. . . .			270,000
The *Santiago*, do. do. . . .			187,000
Bringing ships from Cadiz to Seville, and expenses of Juan de Aranda in going to Cadiz . .			24,188
Workmen careening ships, &c.			13,482
Carpenters for repairing ships . . .			104,244
Caulkers for caulking ships			129,539

[1] 1000 maravedis may be reckoned at 11s. 6d.

	Maravedis.
Sawyers for sawing planks, &c., for ships . .	6,790
Wood for beams and planking, &c. . . .	175,098
Nails used in repair of ships, together with the supply for the voyage	142,532½
Oakum do. do.	31,670
Pitch, tar, and resin do. do.	72,267½
Grease do. do.	53,852
173 pieces of canvas for sails, &c.	149,076
Twine for sewing the above, with needles and awls, and money paid for making . . .	32,825
Masts, yards, and spare spars	37,437
Skiff purchased for the *Trinidad*	3,937½
Pumps, bolts, and nails	15,475
Oars and sweeps	6,563
Leather bags, hose, and leathers for the pumps .	9,364
Pulleys and blocks	1,285½
3 timbers for knees	3,687½
8 large blocks	4,204
Standing and other rigging, and rigging ditto .	34,672½
3 large pitch ladles	511
13 lighters of ballast for the ships	1,962
32 yards of coarse canvas for making sacks for the ballasting	807
Pay of workmen and sailors during the preparations for the voyage	438,335½
Thirteen anchors	42,042
8 saws, large and small	1,008
Bits and braces, large and small . . .	1,762
6 pickaxes to dig the ditch to careen the ships .	663
76 hides to make pitch-brushes to pay the ships .	2,495
Fuel used in pitching the ships	4,277
Pilots for bringing ships from S. Lucar to Seville .	1,054½
221 quintals of cables and hawsers and 1000 arrobas of hemp to make the rigging and cordage, which, together with cost of manufacture (38,972 ms.) and money paid for sedge and esparto-grass rope (14,066 ms.), make .	324,170½
80 flags, and the painting of them, with a royal standard made of taffety	25,029

Maravedis.

Cost of the " bergantym "	49,504
Expenses of Duarte Barbosa in Bilbao when he went to buy the articles for the ships, together with those of Anton Semeño	84,144

Artillery, Munitions, Arms, &c.

58 culverins, 7 falconets, 3 large bombards, and 3 " pasamuros," all from Bilbao . . .	160,135
50 quintals of gunpowder from Fuenterrabia and freight	109,028
165 lbs. of powder for proving the artillery in Bilbao	5,477
Shot and cannon-balls of iron and stone . .	6,633
6 moulds for making cannon-balls . . .	3,850
221 arrobas 7 lbs. of lead for bullets, save 84 arrobas used as plates for leading the seams of the ships	39,890
Paid for mounting the artillery	3,276
Wages of the *lombarderos*	8,790
100 corselets with armlets, shoulder-plates, and helmets, and 100 breastplates with throat-pieces and helmets from Bilbao	110,910
60 crossbows with 360 dozen arrows from Bilbao .	33,495
50 arquebuses from Biscay	10,500
Coat of mail and two complete suits of armour for the Captain-General from Bilbao . . .	6,375
200 shields from Bilbao	6,800
6 sword-blades for the Captain from Bilbao . .	680
95 dozen of darts, 10 dozen javelins, 1000 lances, 200 pikes, 6 boarding-pikes, &c., from Bilbao	44,185
120 skeins of wire for the cross-bows, &c. . .	2,499
Cleaning the arms, 6 lbs. of emery, leathers, tacks, buckles, &c.	3,553
50 flasks and prickers for the arquebuses, and 150 yards of fuses	5,611

Stores, &c.

Biscuit, 363,480 maravedis, *i.e.*, 2138 quintals 3 lbs., at 170 maravedis per quintal, hire of sacks, portage, &c.; total	372,510

	Maravedis.
Wine, 508 butts from Jerez, 511,347 ms. and costs thereon ; total	590,000
50 cwts. beans ; 90 cwts. chick-peas ; 2 cwts. lentils	23,037
47 quintals 3 arrobas of olive-oil	58,425
200 barrels anchovies, 238 dozen large dried fish	62,879
57 quintals 12 lbs. dried pork	43,908
7 cows for the voyage (14,000 ms.), 3 pigs (1180 ms.), and meat for workmen ; total	17,740
984 cheeses, weighing 112 arrobas	26,434
417 pipes, 253 butts, 45 barrels for the wine and water (230,170 ms.), staves, oil-vessels, barrels for the cheeses, jars for vinegar, &c.; total	393,623
21 arrobas 9 lbs. of sugar, at 720 ms. per arroba	15,451
200 arrobas vinegar	3,655
250 strings of garlic and 100 ditto onions	2,198
18 quintals of raisins, &c.	5,997
16 quarter casks of figs	1,130
12 cwts. of almonds in their shells	2,922
54 arrobas 2 lbs. of honey	8,980
2 quintals of currants	750
3 jars of capers	1,554
Salt	1,768
3 quintals 22 lbs. of rice	1,575
1 cwt. of mustard	380
Preserved quince	5,779
Medicines, unguents, salves, and distilled waters	13,027
5 pipes of flour	5,927

Hardware and Store-Room Articles.

	Maravedis.
Copper kitchen utensils : 6 large cauldrons, weighing 280 lbs. (6165 ms.), 5 large pots, weighing 132 lbs. (3700 ms.), 2 baking ovens, weighing 171 lbs. (7695 ms.), 1 pot weighing 27 lbs. (1215 ms.), and large vessel for pitch, weighing 55 lbs. (2200 ms.) &c. ; total	21,515
10 large knives	884
42 wooden pint measures for the rations	516
8 arrobas of candles, and grease for 42 arrobas more, &c.	3,440

	Maravedis.
89 lanterns	1,430
9½ lbs. ornamented wax candles for the consecration of the ships	495
40 cartloads of wood	8,860
40 yards of coarse canvas for table-cloths	1,280
14 large wooden trenchers	476
Chain for large cauldron	158
12 bellows	256
22½ lbs. beeswax for waxing thread and for the crossbows	1,530
12 large knives (*calabozos*) for the steward's room	768
5 large iron ladles	204
100 mess-bowls, 200 porringers, 100 choppers, 66 wooden platters, 12 mortars, 62 trenchers, all from Bilbao	5,834
20 lights for the lamps	240
12 funnels	330
5 hammers	125
18 extra trenchers	995
Brass pestle and mortar for the dispensary	653
35 padlocks, given to the stewards	3,622
Irons, handcuffs, and chains, &c.	3,091
20 lbs. of steel for the pikes, &c.	240
An arroba of stamped iron weights	297
50 spades and pickaxes	2,400
20 bars of iron	1,600
56 iron pikes and hammers and 2 large iron mallets	2,531
2 great ship's lanterns	1,200
8 pair of pincers	360
Boathooks, awls, &c.	1,224
50 quintals 20 lbs. of iron in small bars	24,938
Mats and baskets for the entire fleet	10,639
Fishing gear : 2 seines (*chinchorros*), (costing 8500 ms.), 6 chain hooks (125 ms.), floats for the seines (425 ms.), fishing-lines and cords (8663 ms.), harpoons and fish-spears from Biscay (8715 ms.), 10,500 fish-hooks (3826 ms.); total	30.254
Forge, bellows, anvil, and fittings from Biscay	9,147

	Maravedis.
15 blank account-books, 5 wherein to keep the accounts of the fleet, and 10 for the officials to keep current accounts	1,211
Stevedores' wages for lading the ships . . .	2,635
2 grindstones, and a hone for the two barbers .	2,125
5 drums and 20 tambourines, given to the people of the fleet to serve for their pastime . .	2,895
The furniture (*el ornamento*) and all the necessary appliances for the chaplain to say Mass . .	16,513
3700 ms. paid the pilots for bringing the ships from Seville to S. Lucar, and 1985 from S. Lucar over the bar to the sea . . .	5,685
Paid Rodrigo de Garay for his work . . .	11,250
Paid Juan de la Cueva do. do. . . .	7,500
Carriage of quicksilver, vermilion, and other articles	12,014
Paid courier who came from Portugal and returned to the Court	5,625
Paid for posts and couriers to and from the Court	45,000
Paid to the Caravel, and for rations for the messenger sent with letters to the Canary Islands	6,750
Paid to Luis de Mendoza to purchase various necessaries in the Canary Islands . . .	15,000

Charts and Nautical Instruments.

Paid Nuño Garcia to buy parchments for the charts	1,125
1 dozen skins of parchment given to the above .	900
Another dozen do. do. .	864
7 charts constructed by the orders of Ruy Falero .	13,125
11 charts made by Nuño Garcia by the orders of Fernando Magallanes	11,250
6 charts caused to be made by Ruy Falero, and one sent to the King	13,500
6 wooden quadrants made by Ruy Falero . .	1,121
1 wooden astrolabe made by the said Ruy Falero .	750
1 planisphere ordered to be made by the Captain Magallanes for the King	4,500
Paid to the said Magallanes for 6 metal astrolabes with rulers	4,500

	Maravedis.
Paid to the same for 15 compass needles　.　.	4,080
Paid to same for 15 wooden quadrants, bronze-fitted	1,875
Gilt compass in a box, sent to the King with chart mentioned above　.　.　.　.　.　.	476
Leather case for the planisphere　.　.　.　.	340
12 hour-glasses bought by the Captain　.　.　.	612
2 compass needles that the Captain has　.　.　.	750
6 pairs of compasses　.　.　.　.　.　.	600
Paid to Nuño Garcia for 2 compass needles　.　.	750
Paid for the correction of an injured compass needle　.　.　.　.　.　.　.　.	136
4 large boxes for four compasses, which Ruy Falero had made　.　.　.　.　.　.　.	884
16 compass needles and six hour-glasses, sent by Bernaldino del Castillo from Cadiz　.　.	6,094

Articles of Trade and Barter.

20 quintals of quicksilver.

30　　do.　　vermilion.

100　　do.　　alum.

30 pieces valuable coloured cloth at 4000 ms. per piece.

20 lbs. of saffron.

3 pieces "veintenes,"[1] silver, red, and yellow.

1 piece Valencia stuff.

10 quintals of ivory.

2 pieces of coloured velvets.

200 common red caps.

200 coloured kerchiefs.

10,000 fish-hooks.

1000 maravedis-worth of combs.

200 quintals of lump copper.

2000 brass bracelets.

2000 copper　do.

10,000 bundles of yellow *matamundo* (?).

200 small brass basins of two sorts.

2 dozen large basins.

20,000 small bells of three kinds.

---

[1] Pieces of cloth containing 2000 threads to the warp.

400 dozens of German knives of the commonest kind.
40 pieces of coloured buckram.
50 dozen scissors.
900 small looking-glasses, and 100 larger size.
100 quintals of lead.
500 lbs. of crystals, which are diamonds of all colours.

Total, 1,679,769.

We learn from the same document that four months' pay was given in advance, and that the number of persons receiving it was 237. Either some of those who accompanied the expedition did not receive pay—as, for example, the *sobresalientes*, many of whom were doubtless young men of good family—or some forty or more persons must have joined the fleet on the eve of its departure, which we have reason to believe was the case.

Another document informs us how the various stores and provisions were distributed among the five vessels of the squadron. A proportionate division of the latter was made according to the ship's burthen. The flagship took two cows, the other vessels one each. One surgeon alone being carried, all the medicines went with him on the *Trinidad*. The two *ornamentos* with robes and all necessaries for Mass were carried on the flagship and the *S. Antonio*.

V.

THE FIRST CIRCUMNAVIGATORS OF THE GLOBE.

From Pigafetta's journal we learn that thirty-one men of the *Victoria* eventually returned home. Herrera also (Dec. III. lib. iv. cap. 4) gives the names of thirty-one as going to Court to relate their adventures to the Emperor.

Thirteen of these had been seized by the Portuguese in the Cape Verde Islands, but they were released shortly afterwards and sent at once to Seville.

Herrera's list has been copied by numerous writers, even by those of late date, such as Lord Stanley of Alderley and De Barros Arana, without any attempt, apparently, to verify it. It is nevertheless very erroneous, as a careful consideration of the documents relating to the expedition shows. The following lists have been corrected as far as is possible.

Returned to Seville in the " Victoria."

1. Miguel de Rodas, *contramaestre* of the *Victoria*.
2. Miguel Sanchez, of Rodas, *marinero*[1] of the *Victoria*.
3. Martin de Isaurraga, of Bermeo, *grumete*[1] of the *Concepcion*.
4. Nicholas the Greek, of Naples, *marinero* of the *Victoria*.
5. Juan Rodriguez,[2] of Seville, *marinero* of the *Trinidad*.
6. Vasco Gomez Gallego,[3] Portuguese, *grumete* of the *Trinidad*.
7. Martin de Judicibus, of Genoa, superintendent of the *Concepcion*.
8. Juan de Santandres, of Cueto, *grumete* of the *Trinidad*.
9. Hernando de Bustamante, of Merida or Alcantara, barber, of the *Concepcion*.
10. Antonio Pigafetta, of Vicenza.
11. Francisco Rodriguez, of Seville, a Portuguese, *marinero* of the *Concepcion*.
12. Antonio Ros or Rodriguez, of Huelva, *marinero* of the *Trinidad*.
13. Diego Gallego, of Bayonne, *marinero* of the *Victoria*.

[1] *Marinero* and *grumete* corresponded more or less with our A.B. and ordinary seaman.

[2] Three men of this name sailed on the voyage. The other two were borne as *marineros* on the *Concepcion*. One died on the voyage; the other, nicknamed "el Sordo," was one of the four survivors of the *Trinidad*.

[3] Not Vasco Gallego, pilot of the *Victoria*, who died February 28, 1521.

14. Juan de Arratia (or de Sahelices), of Bilbao, *grumete* of the *Victoria*.
15. Juan de Acurio, of Bermeo, *contramaestre* of the *Concepcion*.
16. Juan de Gubileta,[1] of Baracaldo, page, of the *Victoria*.
17. Francisco Albo,[2] of Axio, *contramaestre* of the *Trinidad*.
·18. Juan Sebastian del Cano, of Guetaria, master of the *Concepcion*.

Seized by the Portuguese in the Cape Verdes.

1. Maestre Pedro.[3] from Tenerife, of the *Santiago*.
2. Richard,[4] from Normandy, carpenter of the *Santiago*.
3. Pedro Gasco, of Bordeaux, *marinero* of the *Santiago*.
4. Alfonso Domingo, *marinero* of the *Santiago*.
5. Simon de Burgos, Portuguese, servant of the Captain, Luis de Mendoza, *Victoria*.
6. Juan Martin, of Aguilar de Campo,   do.   do.
7. Roldan de Argote, of Bruges, bombardier of the *Concepcion*.
8. Martin Mendez, of Seville, accountant of the *Victoria*.
9. Gomez Hernandez, of Huelva, *marinero* of the *Concepcion*.
10. Ocacio Alonso, of Bollullos, *marinero* of the *Santiago*.
11. Pedro de Tolosa, of Tolosa in Guipuzcoa, *grumete* of the *Victoria*.
12. Felipe de Rodas, of Rodas, *marinero* of the *Victoria*.
13. Juan de Apega.[5]

Among the first circumnavigators must likewise be included the four sole survivors of the ill-fated *Trinidad*,

---

[1] Or Zúvileta or Zubieta.

[2] Or Alvaro or Calvo, the pilot who has left us the log-book record of the voyage.

[3] Maestre Pedro, who is probably identical with Herrera's Pedro de Indarchi, was shipped in Tenerife on 1st October 1519.

[4] Variously called Ricarte, Rigarte, Ripart, Ruxar, or Ruger Carpintete.   His birth-place is given as Bruz (?) or Ebras (?).

[5] This man, mentioned by Herrera, is probably identical with Juan Ortiz de Gopega of Bilbao, steward of the *S. Antonio*.

Herrera gives the following names in his list as being among the survivors:—Lorenzo de Iruna, Juan de Ortega, Diego Garcia, Pedro de Valpuesta, and Martin de Magallanes.   All these men, however,

although they did not return to Spain until long after.
They were :—

1. Gonzalo Gomez de Espinosa, alguacil of the fleet.
2. Gines de Mafra, of Jerez, *marinero*.
3. Leon Pancado (or Pancaldo), of Saona near Genoa, *marinero*.
4. Juan Rodriguez (el Sordo), of Seville, *marinero*, formerly of
   the *Concepcion*.

Finally, the name of Hans Vargue ("Maestre Ance")
should perhaps be placed in the roll of honour. This
man—a German—was master-gunner of the *Concepcion*,
and was afterwards borne on the *Trinidad*. He reached
Lisbon with Espinosa and Gines de Mafra, and being
thrown into prison with them immediately on his arrival,
perished there.

died on the voyage, and their deaths are recorded in the official list.
It is a curious circumstance that they should all without exception
have died near the termination of the voyage. Lorenzo de Iruna
succumbed as the *Victoria* was rounding the Cape, while Martin
Magellan, the last of the five, died on the 26th June 1522, almost
within sight of the Cape Verde Islands.

GEORGE PHILIP AND SON, LONDON AND LIVERPOOL.

MAPS

ILLUSTRATIVE OF THE PROGRESS OF DISCOVERY IN THE NEW WORLD.

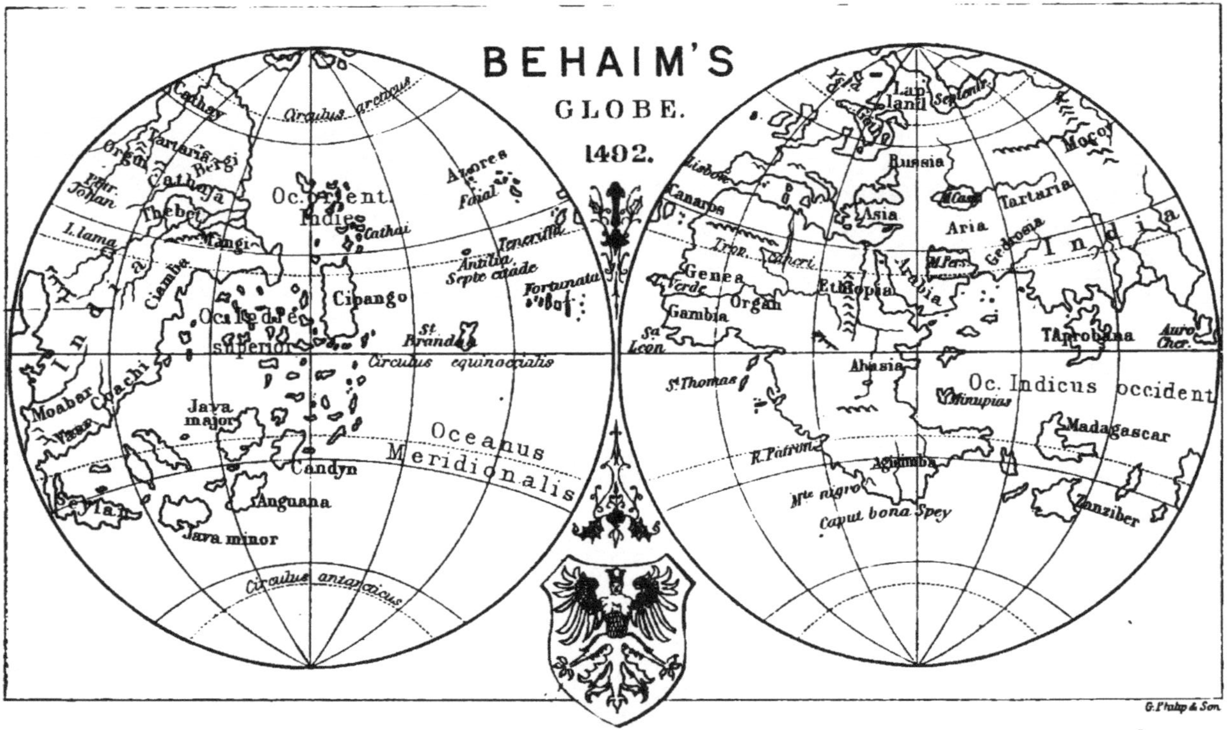

BEHAIM'S
GLOBE.
1492.
Cathay
Circulus arcticus
Orgču Tartaria Bergi
Pstr. Johan
Cathaja
Thebet
Azores
Fdial
Oc. orient.
Indies
I. lama
Mangi
Cathai
Ciambi
Teneriffa
Antilia
Septe citade
Cipango
Fortunata
Oc. IIde dée
superior
St.
Brandā
India
Circulus equinocialis
Moaber
Cruchi
Java
major
Vasa
Oceanus
Meridionalis
Candyn
Anguana
Sexla
Java minor
Circulus antarcticus
Lisboe
Canarea
Y-g-
Lap
lanii Septentr
Gau
Russia
Asia
Moco
Mass
Tartaria
Aria
Gedrosia
Tror.
Caheri
M.Pers
India
India
Genea
Verde
Organ
Ethiopia
Gambia
Sa
Leon
Ahasia
TAprobana
Auro
Cher.
St.Thomas
Oc. Indicus occident
Afinupias
Madagascar
R.Patrum
Agumba
Mte nigro
Caput bona Spey
Zanziber
G. Philip & Son.

C. delmar ysiano
Gronland
Scocia
Bosaventura
Hibernia
Anglia
Obrassile
Rio delos galeatos
EUROPA
Açores
Parima
Babuca
Somento
Faial
Lisboa
Lacco del lodro
Mamana
Isabella
Tamiabnaca
Cuba
Spagnolla
Boriquem
Mil virgines
Galapo
Madera
Lamuigua
I. de forana
Ferro
Canaria
Marigalana
Riqua
I. Gigant
Todos Santos
C. Verde
GOBOA
Brasil
Arcay
C. del inferno
Y. de la rapossa
Y. de los canibales
Bucoia
C. de cecado
Rio de fonsoa
C. de los Perlos
Ponta de las guleras
St. Liona
Rio grande
Golfo fremoso
C. Palmas
Terra nova
Canibales
S. Roche
S. Maria de gratias
Terra Sanctae Crucis
Sancta Gruris
S. Mich!
I. Tebas
Serra de S. Maria de gratia
H. S. Francisco
M. fregoso
Porto real
Abatin om. Sant.
Rio de S. Augustino
HYDROGRAPHIA
sive
CHARTA MARITIMA
PORTUGALENSIUM.
c.1504.
R. Brasil
M. Pasqual
P. Segoro
S. Lucu
Serra do S. Thome
Pagus S. Pauli
Rio da refens
First published in 1513
Iordan
R. de S. Ant?
R. de Cananer
P. de S. Sebastian
P. de S. Vincente
BRAZIL
G. Philip & Son.

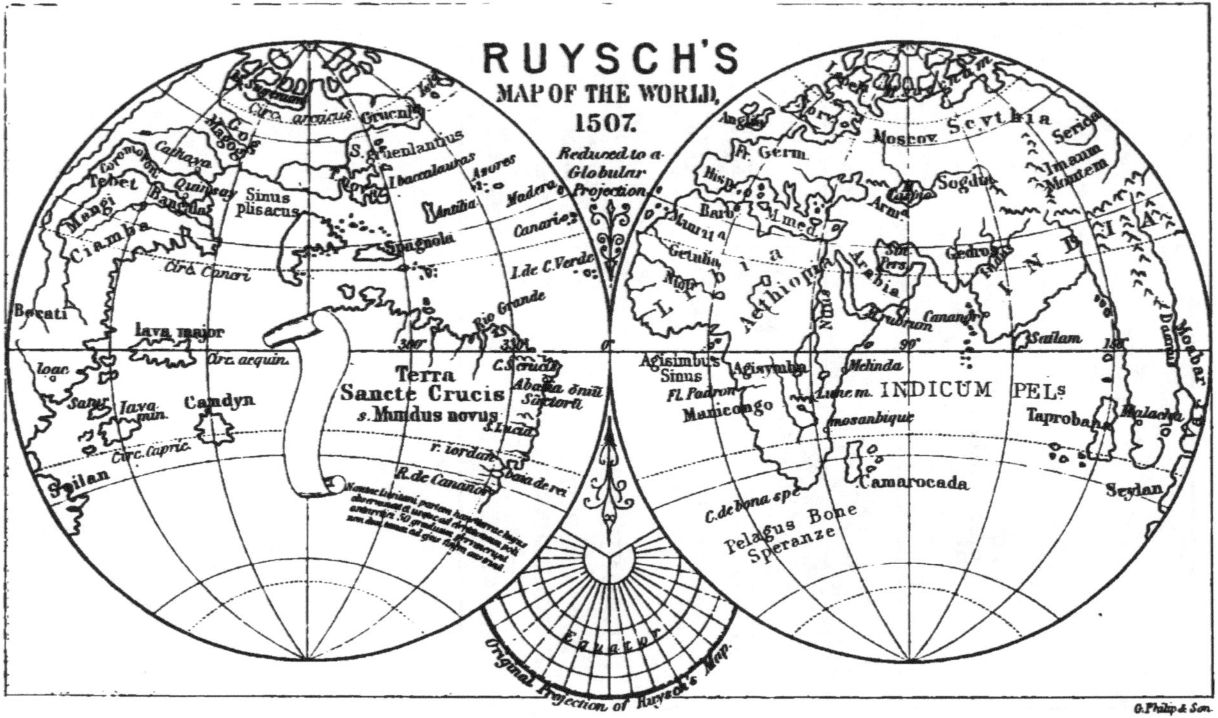
RUYSCH'S
MAP OF THE WORLD,
1507.
Reduced to a Globular Projection
Original Projection of Ruysch's Map.
Equator
Terra
Sancte Crucis
s. Mundus novus
INDICUM PELs
Pelagus Bone Speranze
Cathaya
Tebet
Mangi
Ciamba
Sinus plisacus
Iava major
Iava min.
Candyn
Seilan
Circ. arcticus
Circ. Canc.
Circ. acquin.
Circ. Capric.
S. Groenlantius
Antilia
Spagnola
Madera
Canaries
I. de C. Verde
Rio Grande
r. iordan
R. de Cananor
baia de rei
Fr. Germ.
Hisp.
Barb.
Mauri a
Getulia
Aethiopia
Arabia
Moscov
Scythia
Sogdia
Imaum Montem
Sailam
Melinda
Manicongo
mosanbique
Camarocada
Taprobana
Malacha
Seylan
C. de bona spe
Agisimbus Sinus
Fl. Padron
Seri
Anglia
Norv.
Gedrosia
Canangor
Moabar
G. Philip & Son.

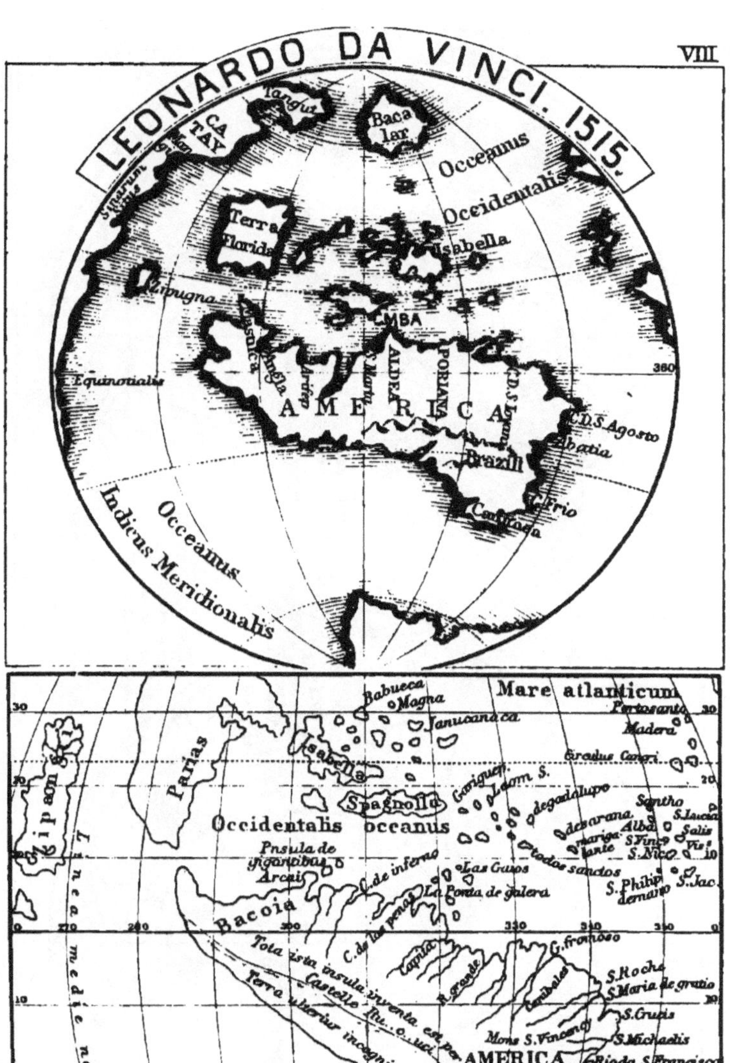
VIII
LEONARDO DA VINCI. 1515.
CA TAY
Tangut
Bacalar
Occeanus
Occidentalis
Terra Florida
Isabella
Tarpugna
CIMBA
Jamaica
Andem
S. Marta
ALDEA
POBIANA
C.D.S.Iane
AMERICA
C.D.S.Agosto
Abatia
Equinotialis
Brazill
C.frio
Cananea
Occeanus Indicus Meridionalis
Mare atlanticum
Babueca Magna
Portosanto
Januoanaca
Madera
Parias
Isabella
Ercules Canri
Spagnolla
Goriguei
J. dom S.
degadalupo
Santro
desarana
Alba
S.Lucia
Occidentalis occeanus
mariga
Solis
Pnsula de gigantibus
ante
S.Vince
Arcai
C.de inferno
todos sanctos
S.Nico
Las Gusos
S. Philip
S.Jac.
Bacoia
La Porta de galera
demaro
C.de las penas
Tota ista insula inventa en per
Capia
G.fronoso
Castelle su...o...uci
R.Grande
S.Roche
Terra ulterius incognita
Embolo
S.Maria de gratio
S.Crucis
Mons S.Vincen
S.Michaelis
AMERICA
Rioda S.Francisco
Tropicus capricornus
S.Lucia
Abatia om Sandos
Portoseguro
"HAUSLAB"
Insulae delle Pulcelle
Rio de reens
GLOBE
c.15.
R.Jordan
Rio Cananor

SCHÖNER'S
GLOBE.
1523.
From a
Facsimile in
H. Stevens' Johann
Schöner. London 1888.
Linea divisionis Castellanorũ e Portugalliĩ
Mangi
Cathay
Arctic Circule
Baccalaos
Schani popit: U. Sinaru
Sinus mag.
Sina
Tropic Cancr.
La Florida
Cuba
Cohol
Iucana
Espanola
Gasith
Moluccæ
Mare
Siloli
Anthio
Darienus
Antiglia
Senotormus
Insule Infortunate
C. S. Crucis
Terra firma non minus continens
Brisilica terra
C. S. Mariæ
Crete
Pha. S. Iuliani
Muthil
Badan
Paris
EUROPA
Tartaria
ASIA
Mongal
Hispa
Barbaria
India
Ciambe
Iabva int.
Alexa
Arabia
AFFRICA
Senega
C. Viride
Melli
Meroe
Aden
Goa
Iabva
Calecute
Irgo
Ginnia
C. de pabnis
Cameroos
Malacca
S. Thome
Mani Congo
Melinde
Quiloa
Samatra oli Taprobana
Angrodas aldus
S. Lorẽo
Iava
Hoc itinere reversi sunt
navigabone minus egressi sunt
C. bonespei
Cabo Godanige
Sandales
Antarctic Circule

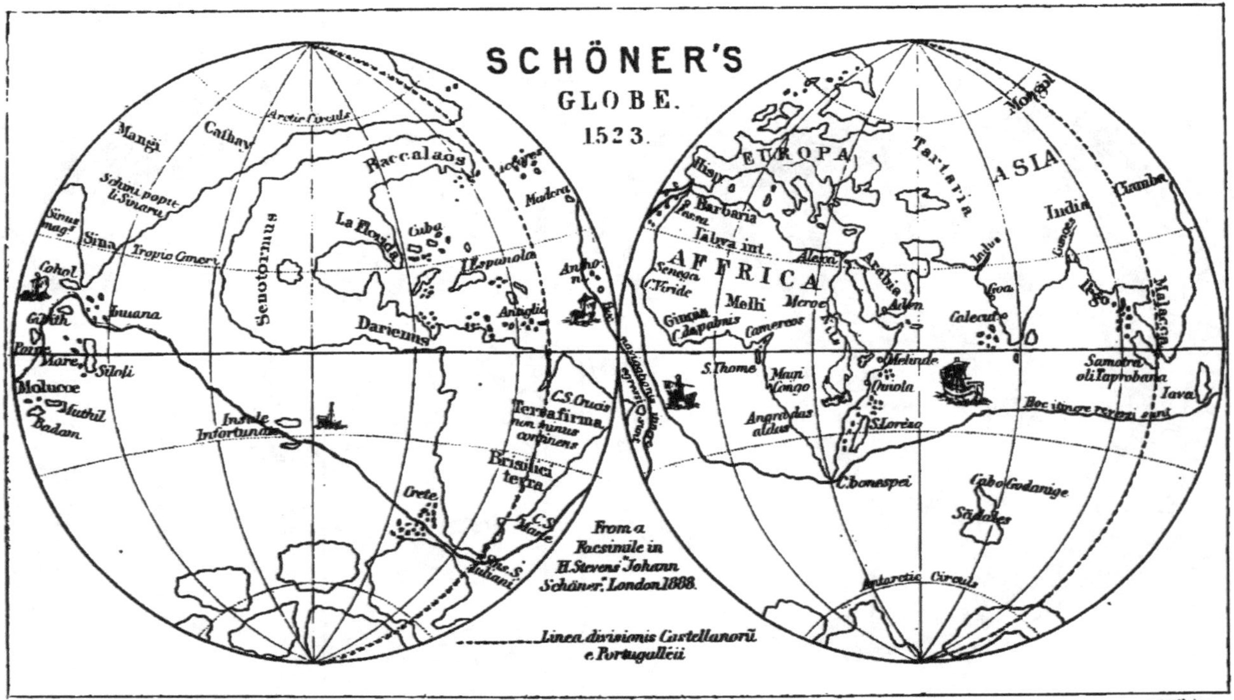